Praise for Patricia Davids and her novels

"A sweet tale with well-drawn characters and a few unexpected turns."
—*RT Book Reviews* on *Their Pretend Amish Courtship*

"Davids' deep understanding of Amish culture is evident in the compassionate characters and beautiful descriptions."
—*RT Book Reviews* on *A Home for Hannah*

"Descriptive setting and characters."
—*RT Book Reviews* on *Plain Admirer*

Praise for Jan Drexler and her novels

"Drexler has delivered a pleasing read with touches of romance, suspense, drama and faith."
—*RT Book Reviews* on *A Home for His Family*

"The interaction between family members serves to entertain."
—*RT Book Reviews* on *A Mother for His Children*

"An interesting blend of gangsters and Plain folk"
—*RT Book Reviews* on *The Prodigal Son Returns*

After thirty-five years as a nurse, **Patricia Davids** hung up her stethoscope to become a full-time writer. She enjoys spending her free time visiting her grandchildren, doing some long-overdue yard work and traveling to research her story locations. She resides in Wichita, Kansas. Pat always enjoys hearing from her readers. You can visit her online at patriciadavids.com.

Jan Drexler enjoys living in the Black Hills of South Dakota with her husband of more than thirty years and their four adult children. Intrigued by history and stories from an early age, she loves delving into the world of "what if?" with her characters. If she isn't at her computer giving life to imaginary people, she's probably hiking in the Hills or the Badlands, enjoying the spectacular scenery.

PATRICIA DAVIDS

*Their Pretend
Amish Courtship*

&

JAN DREXLER

An Amish Courtship

HARLEQUIN® LOVE INSPIRED®

 LOVE INSPIRED BOOKS

Recycling programs for this product may not exist in your area.

ISBN-13: 978-1-335-99475-2

Their Pretend Amish Courtship and An Amish Courtship

Copyright © 2018 by Harlequin Books S.A.

The publisher acknowledges the copyright holders of the individual works as follows:

Their Pretend Amish Courtship
Copyright © 2017 by Patricia MacDonald

An Amish Courtship
Copyright © 2017 by Jan Drexler

CONTENTS

THEIR PRETEND
AMISH COURTSHIP

Patricia Davids

This book is lovingly dedicated to my father, Clarence Stroda. He taught me a lot about making my way in the world and keeping God in my life. Thanks, Dad.

And God hath set some in the church,
first apostles, secondarily prophets,
thirdly teachers, after that miracles,
then gifts of healings, helps, governments,
diversities of tongues.
—*1 Corinthians* 12:28

Chapter One

"You are going and I don't want to hear another word about it, Fannie. Nor from you, Betsy. Do you hear me?"

When Fannie's mother shook a wooden spoon at one or both of her daughters, the conversation was over.

"Ja, Mamm." Betsy beat a quick retreat out of the kitchen.

Fannie glared after her. The little coward. Without her sister's help, Fannie had no chance of changing her mother's mind. Seated at the table in her family's kitchen, Fannie crossed her arms on the red-checkered tablecloth and laid her head on her forearms. *"Ja, Mamm,* I hear you."

There had to be a way. There just had to be.

"Now you are being sensible." Belinda Erb turned back to the stove and continued stirring the strawberry jam she was getting ready to can. "I will write to my *mamm* and *daed* tomorrow. They insist on sending the money for your bus ticket. I expect you'll be able to leave the middle of next week. It will be a relief to know one of us is helping *Daed* look after *Mamm* while she recovers from her broken ankle."

"A week! That isn't much time to get ready to go to Florida." How was she going to come up with a plan to keep from going in a week?

"Nonsense. It's plenty of time. You have two work dresses and a good Sunday dress. What else do you need?"

Fannie sat up and touched her head covering. "I need another *kapp* or two."

Her mother turned around with a scowl on her face. "What happened to the last one I made you?"

"I lost it."

"When you were out riding like some wild child, no doubt. It's time you gave up your childish ways. Anna Bowman and I were just talking about this yesterday. We have been too lenient with our youngest *kinder*, and we are living to rue the day. She is putting her foot down with Noah, and I am doing the same with you. When you come back from Pinecraft at Thanksgiving, you will end your *rumspringa* and make your decision to be Amish or not."

Fannie had heard about Anna's plans to see Noah settled and she felt sorry for him, but she had her own problems.

Her mother turned back to the stove. "I have given up on seeing you wed, though it breaks my heart to say so."

Here came the lecture about becoming an old maid. She wasn't twenty-two yet, but she had been hearing this message since she turned nineteen. That was how old her mother had been when she married. Why did everyone believe the only thing a woman wanted was a husband? "Betsy isn't married and she is two years older than I am."

"Betsy is betrothed to Hiram. They will marry next fall."

Fannie sat up straight. "When did this happen?"

Why hadn't her sister mentioned it? Betsy and Hiram had been walking out together for ages. Fannie thought Hiram would never get up the courage to propose.

"Hiram came to tell your father and me last night."

"Then why does Betsy want to go to Florida?"

Fannie's mother took her time before answering. "She

loves her grandparents and wishes to spend time with them while she can. As you should."

After pulling the jam off the stove, Fannie's mother came and sat beside her at the table. "Why are you so dead set against going?"

Fannie knew her mother wouldn't approve of the promise she'd made. "I have made plans with my riding club for this summer."

"Your horses and your club won't take care of you when you are old. *Mamm* writes that there are plenty of young people in Pinecraft during the fall and winter. You may want to stay longer."

"Young people but no horses."

"Enough about horses!" Fannie's mother rose to her feet. "You have chores to finish and I must get these jars of jam done. It's a wedding gift for Timothy Bowman and his bride. Timothy's mother told me they plan to leave on their wedding trip after the school frolic."

Fannie clamped her lips together. Her mother wanted to change the subject. It wouldn't do any good to argue; Fannie knew she'd only be wasting her breath. She left the room and found her sister gathering clothes off the line in the backyard. Fannie joined her, pulling down stiff wind-dried pants and dresses. "*Mamm* said you went and got engaged to Hiram."

"It was time. I'm not getting any younger."

"That's a poor reason to marry."

"It's reason enough for us. We are content with each other. You are blessed to have this opportunity." Betsy clutched a pillowcase to her chest. "I have always dreamed of seeing the ocean. I can't imagine how big it must be. Hiram has no desire to see the sea."

"Doesn't he have a desire to please you?" That, in a nutshell, was what was wrong with getting married.

"It would be an expense we couldn't afford. Perhaps someday."

"I would gladly send you in my place, but I don't imagine Hiram would be happy about…that…" Fannie's words trailed away as an idea took shape in her mind. "That's it. I need a Hiram."

"What are you babbling about now?"

It was so simple. "Betsy, would you go to Florida if I couldn't? What if *Mamm* decided you should go instead of me? Would Hiram understand?"

"He knows we must honor our elders. I would gladly take your place, but *Mamm* has her mind made up."

"If she knew I was being courted, she would bend over backward to keep me here. She is desperate to see me wed."

"She's desperate to see you interested in any young man instead of your horses. Who is courting you? Why didn't you tell me about him?"

"I have to go." Fannie shoved the clothes in her arms at her sister. There was only one fellow who might help her.

"Noah, where are you? I need to speak to you."

Working near the back of his father's barn, Noah Bowman dropped the hoof of his buggy horse, Willy, took the last nail out of his mouth and stood upright to stare over his horse's back. Fannie Erb, his neighbor's youngest daughter, came hurrying down the wide center aisle, checking each stall as she passed. Her white *kapp* hung off the back of her head, dangling by a single bobby pin. Her curly red hair was still in a bun, but it was windblown and lopsided. No doubt it would be completely undone before she got home. Fannie was always in a rush.

"What's up, *karotte oben*?" He picked up his horse's

hoof again, positioned it between his knees and drove in the last nail of the new shoe.

Fannie stopped outside the stall gate and fisted her hands on her hips. "You know I hate being called a carrottop."

"Sorry." Noah grinned as he caught the glare she leveled at him.

He wasn't sorry a bit. He liked the way her unusual violet eyes darkened and flashed when she was annoyed. Annoying Fannie had been one of his favorite pastimes when they were schoolchildren.

She lived on the farm across the road where her family raised and trained Standardbred buggy horses. Noah had known her from the cradle, as their parents were good friends and often visited back and forth. Fannie had grown from the gangly girl he liked to tease at school into a comely woman, but her temper hadn't cooled.

Framed in a rectangle of light cast by the early-morning sun shining through the open top of a Dutch door, dust motes danced around Fannie's head like fireflies drawn to the fire in her hair. The summer sun had expanded the freckles on her upturned nose and given her skin a healthy glow, but Fannie didn't tan the way most women did. Her skin always looked cool and creamy. As usual, she was wearing blue jeans and riding boots under her plain green dress and black apron.

He preferred wearing *Englisch* jeans himself. He liked having hip pockets to keep his cell phone in, something his homemade Amish pants didn't have. His parents tolerated his use of a phone because he was still in his *rumspringa*. He knew Fannie used a cell phone, too. She had a solar-powered charger and allowed other Amish youth to use it if they didn't have access to electricity.

"What do you need, Fannie? Did your hot temper spark

a fire and you want me to put it out?" He chuckled at his own wit. He and his four brothers were volunteer members of the local fire department. Patting Willy's sleek black neck, Noah reached to untie the horse's halter.

"This isn't a joke, Noah. I need to get engaged, and quickly. Will you help me?"

He spun around to stare at her in shocked disbelief. A marriage proposal was the last thing he'd expected from Fannie. "You had better explain that remark."

"*Mamm* and *Daed* are sending me to live with my grandparents in Pinecraft, Florida, until Thanksgiving. I can't go. I've told my folks that, but they insist. Having a steady beau is the only way to get them to send Betsy instead."

At least Fannie wasn't suffering from some unrequited love for him. He should have been relieved, but he was mildly annoyed instead.

He opened the bottom half of the Dutch door leading to the corral and let his horse out. Willy quickly trotted to where Fannie's Haflinger mare stood on the other side of the fence. The black gelding put his head over the top rail to sniff noses with the golden-chestnut beauty.

Noah began picking up his tools. "I hear Florida is nice."

Fannie grabbed the top of the gate. "Are you serious? My grandparents get around on three-wheeled bicycles down there. They don't have horses. Can you imagine staying in a place with no horses?"

He couldn't, but he didn't think much of her crazy idea, either. "I'm not going to get hitched to you because you don't want to go to Florida."

Indignation sparked in her eyes. "What's wrong with getting hitched to me? I'd make you a *goot* wife."

She stepped back as he opened the stall gate. "Fannie,

you would knock me on the head with a skillet the first chance you got. You have a bad temper."

"Oh!" She stomped her foot, and then sighed heavily. "I do have a temper, but I wouldn't do you physical harm."

"Small consolation considering how sharp your tongue is. Ouch! Ow!" He jumped away from several imaginary jabs.

Her eyes narrowed. "Stop teasing. I don't want to actually marry you, *dummkopf.* I said *engaged*, not *married*, but I guess it doesn't have to be that serious. Walking out with me might do. If not, we can get engaged later. Anyway, we will call it off long before the *banns* are announced and go our merry ways."

He didn't like being called a dumbhead, but he overlooked her comment to point out the biggest flaw in her plan. "You and I have never acted like a loving couple. Your parents would smell a rat."

"Maybe, but maybe not. *Mamm* has been telling me for ages that it's time I started looking around for a husband."

He closed the stall gate and latched it. "Better go farther afield for that search. The boys around here all know you too well."

She wasn't the kind of woman he'd marry. He might enjoy teasing that quick temper, but he wouldn't want to live with it.

Her defiant expression crumpled. She hurried to keep up with him as he went outside. "Don't be mean, Noah. I need help. I can't go to Florida. My *daed* has two mares due to foal this month."

"They will foal without you, and your father can certainly handle it."

She walked to her mare standing patiently beside the corral. "Trinket will miss me. I can't go months without seeing her."

Fannie loved horses, he knew that, but he sensed she

wasn't telling him the whole story behind this scheme. "Trinket will survive without you. What's the real reason you don't want to go?"

She sighed heavily and folded her arms tightly across her chest. "You may have heard I took a job working for Connie Stroud on her horse farm."

"*Mamm* mentioned it." His mother kept up on all the local news. How she was able to learn so much about the community without the use of a forbidden telephone was a mystery to him.

"Connie raises and trains Haflingers. Trinket was one of her foals. Connie's father passed away two years ago and she is having a hard time making a go of the place. She gives riding lessons and boards horses, but she needs to sell more of her Haflingers for a better price than she can get around here if she is going to make ends meet."

"If she can't sell a horse without you in the state, she's a poor businesswoman."

He walked over to two more horses tied to the fence. One was his niece Hannah's black pony, Hank. The other was Ginger, a bay mare that belonged to his mother. Speaking softly to Hank, Noah ran his hand down the pony's neck and lifted his front foot. He found the shoe was loose and too worn to save. He checked the pony's back foot, expecting to find it in the same condition.

Fannie walked over to Hank and began to rub him behind his ears. The pony closed his eyes in bliss and leaned into her fingers. "I'm deeply beholden to Connie. I need to help her save her stable."

Noah glanced at Fannie's face and was surprised by the determination in her eyes. Fannie might be hotheaded and stubbornly independent, but she was clearly loyal to this friend. "How does pretending to be engaged help her?"

"It keeps me here. Not a lot of people know what amazing horses Haflingers are. I came up with the great idea of an equine drill team using Connie's Haflingers plus my Trinket. We are going to give exhibitions at some of the county fairs and then at the Ohio State Equine Expo. I have seven Amish girls from my riding club who have already joined us."

"Your parents are permitting this?" It was an unusual undertaking for an Amish woman.

She looked away from him. "We haven't been told we can't do it. You know how crazy the *Englisch* are for anything Amish. If we can generate some interest, show what Connie's horses can do, I know it will help her sell more of them. Besides, everyone in the group is depending on me to teach them—and the horses—the routines. Our first show is in a week."

Fannie had a way with horses that was unique. He'd always admired that about her. "I'm sure your parents will come around if you make them see how much you want to stay."

"*Mamm* won't. She has her mind made up. She says Betsy is more help to her than I am because I'm always out in the barn. Betsy likes to cook, sew, mend and clean, while I don't. I'll die down there if I have to give up my horse." Fannie sniffled and wiped her eyes with the back of her hand.

Noah put Hank's hoof down to stare at Fannie. He considered putting his arm around her shoulders to comfort her, but thought better of it. "Would it help if I talked to your folks?"

"*Nee*, it won't do any good. *Mamm* will know I put you up to it."

"I'm sorry, Fannie, but don't you think your idea is a bit dishonest?"

She shook her head. "If you ask to court me today, *actu-*

ally ask me, then it won't be a lie. I can tell *Mamm* we are walking out with a straight face and a clear conscience."

"I don't see how, when you concocted the whole thing."

"You have to help me, Noah. I don't know what else to do. Betsy would *love* to spend a few months with our grandparents and see the ocean. You don't have to tell anyone you are dating me. All you have to do is take me home after the singing on Sunday and I'll do the rest. Please?"

Why did she have to sound so desperate?

Fannie wasn't making enough headway in swaying Noah. She took a deep breath and pulled out her last tool of persuasion. "What are your plans for this summer?"

He looked suspicious at her abrupt change of topic. "We are putting up hay this week. We'll start cultivating the corn after that if the rain holds off."

"I didn't mean farmwork. Are you playing ball again this summer?" She flicked the brim of the blue ball cap he wore instead of the traditional Amish straw hat. Once he chose baptism, he would have to give up his worldly dress.

He ducked away from her hand. "I'm in the league again with the fellas from the fire department. I'm their pitcher. If we keep winning like we have been, we have a shot at getting into the state invitational tournament."

She twined her fingers in Hank's mane. "You must practice a lot."

"Twice a week with games every Saturday. In fact, we have a makeup game tonight with the Berlin team, as we were rained out last weekend."

"You wouldn't mind missing a few of your practices or even a game for a family picnic or party, would you?"

"What are you getting at, Fannie?"

"I'm not the only one you'll be helping if you go out

with me. Your mother has been shopping around for a wife for you. Did you know that?"

His expression hardened. "You're *narrisch*. Up until this minute I was starting to feel sorry for you."

She almost wavered, but she couldn't let Connie down. "I'm not crazy. With all your brothers married, you are the last chick in the nest."

"So?"

"So she's worried that you are still running around instead of settling down. She has asked a number of her friends to invite their nieces and granddaughters to visit this summer with the express notion of finding *you* a wife among them. They'll be here for picnics and dinners and singings all summer long, so you can size them up."

"*Mamm* wouldn't do that." Amish parents rarely meddled in their children's courtships.

"Well, she has."

"My mother isn't the meddling sort. At least, not very often."

Fannie shrugged. "Mothers are funny that way. They don't believe we can be happy unless we are married, when you and I both know we are perfectly happy being single. Are you ready to spend the summer dodging a string of desperate-to-be-wed maidens?"

"*Nee*, and that includes you and your far-fetched scheme. No one will believe I'm dating you of my own free will."

She felt the heat rush to her face. "You kissed me once."

He arched one eyebrow. "As I remember, you weren't happy about it."

"I was embarrassed that your brother Luke saw us. I regretted my behavior afterward, and I have told you I was sorry."

"Not half as sorry as I was," he snapped back. "That glass of punch you poured on me was cold."

She *was* sorry that evening ended so badly. It had been a nice kiss. Her first.

She and Noah had slipped outside for a breath of fresh air near the end of a Christmas cookie exchange at his parents' house the winter before last. She had been curious to find out what it would be like to be kissed by him. Things had been going well in his mother's garden until Luke came by. When Noah tried for a second kiss after his brother walked away, she had been so flustered that she upended a glass of cold strawberry punch in his lap.

"That was ages ago. Are you going to berate me again or are you going to help me?" Fannie demanded.

He leaned over the pony's back, his expression dead serious. "Find some other gullible fellow."

Her temper flared and she didn't try to quell it. "Oh! You're just plain mean. See if I ever help you out of a jam. You were my last hope, Noah Bowman. If I wasn't Amish I might actually hate you for this, but I have to say I forgive you. Have fun meeting all your prospective brides this summer." She spun on her heel and mounted her horse.

"If I'm your last hope, Fannie Erb, that says more about you than it does about me," he called out as she turned Trinket around.

She nudged her mare into a gallop and blinked back tears. She didn't want him to see how deeply disappointed she was.

Now what was she going to do?

Chapter Two

Noah regretted his parting comment as he watched Fannie ride away. She didn't have many friends. She was more at ease around horses than people. Her reputation as a hothead was to blame but he knew there wasn't any real harm in her. Her last bobby pin came loose as she rode off. Her *kapp* fluttered to the ground in the driveway.

Willy raised his head and neighed loudly. He clearly wanted the pretty, golden-chestnut mare with the blond mane to come back.

"Don't be taken in by good looks, Willy. A sweet disposition lasts far longer than a pretty face. I don't care what Fannie says—*Mamm* isn't in a hurry to see me wed."

He walked out and picked up Fannie's *kapp*. At the sound of a wagon approaching, he stuffed it into his back pocket. His cousins Paul and Mark Bowman drove in from the hayfield with a load of bales stacked shoulder high on a trailer pulled by Noah's father's gray Percheron draft horses. The *chug-chug* sound of the gas-powered bailer could be heard in the distance where Noah's father was pulling it with a four-horse hitch. Noah's brothers Samuel and Timothy were hooking the bales from the back of the machine and stacking them on a second trailer.

"Who was that?" Mark asked.

"Fannie Erb." Noah watched her set her horse at the stone wall bordering her family's lane. Trinket sailed over it easily.

"She rides well," Paul said with a touch of admiration in his voice.

"She does," Noah admitted.

"What did she want?" Mark asked.

Noah shook his head at the absurdness of her idea. "She's looking for a beau. Are you interested?"

Mark shook his head. "*Nee*, I'm not. I have a girlfriend back home."

His brother Paul nudged him with an elbow. "A man can go to an auction without buying a horse. It doesn't hurt to look and see what's out there."

Mark and Paul had come from Bird-In-Hand, Pennsylvania, to stay with Noah's family and apprentice with Noah's father in the family's woodworking business. The shop was closed for a few days until the Bowmans had their hay in, and Noah was glad for the extra help.

Mark scowled at his brother. "A man who doesn't need a horse but goes to the auction anyway is wasting a day *Gott* has given him. You know what they say about idle hands."

"I won't suffer from idle hands today—today—today. I'll have the blisters—blisters—blisters to prove it," Paul called out in a singsong voice. The fast-talking young man was learning to become an auctioneer.

Mark maneuvered the hay wagon next to the front of the barn. The wide hayloft door was open above them, with a bale elevator positioned in the center of it. Noah pulled the cord on the elevator's gas-powered engine. It sprang to life, and the conveyer belt began to move upward. Noah glanced toward the house and saw his brother Joshua jogging toward them. Noah sat on the belt and rode up to the hayloft. Joshua came up the same way and the two men waited for the bales their cousins unloaded.

After stacking the first thirty-five bales deep in the recesses of the hayloft, Noah and Joshua moved to the open loft door to wait for the next trailer load to come in from the field.

Joshua fanned his face with his straw hat and then mopped his sweaty brow with his handkerchief. "It's going to be another hot one."

The interior of the barn loft would be roasting by late afternoon, even with the doors open. Noah pulled off his ball cap and reached into his back pocket for his handkerchief, but pulled out Fannie's *kapp* instead.

The silly goose. Did she really think he would agree to court her at a moment's notice? Only she could come up with such a far-fetched scheme. He tucked her *kapp* back in his pocket and wiped his face with his sleeve, determined to stop thinking about her.

He leaned out of the loft to see how close the second wagon was to being full. "Looks like I'll have time to finish putting a new horseshoe on Hank before they get here. We have some pony-size shoes, don't we?"

Joshua nodded. "On the wall in the tack room. I had John Miller make a full set for Hank right after I brought him home."

"Goot."

"I can take care of him later," Joshua offered.

"Checking the horses' feet is my job. I only have Hank and Ginger left."

"What does Ginger need?"

"I noticed she was limping out in the pasture. I haven't had a chance to see why."

"I can take care of her. I know you want to have your work done before you head to your ball game."

"Danki, bruder."

"You can return the favor some other time. I'm looking forward to your game next weekend. It should be a *goot* one. Walter Osborn can knock the hide off a baseball when he connects."

Walter was an English neighbor and volunteer fire fighter. Part of his job was to gather the Amish volunteers in the area and deliver them to the fire station when the call went out. He was also a good friend of Noah's.

"Walter is the best catcher in the league and our power hitter. If we can get into the state tournament, he'll have a chance at being scouted by the pros. Those men don't come to these backwater places. Walter deserves a chance to show what he's got."

Joshua settled his hat on his head. "Are you hoping to be scouted by a pro team?"

"Where'd you get that idea?" Noah avoided looking at his brother. He'd never told anyone about his dream.

"*Mamm* and *Daed* were talking about it the other day. Your coach has been telling everyone you have a gift. It's easy to see how much you love the game, but you'll have to stop playing soon. You will be twenty-two this fall. Your *rumspringa* can't go on forever."

Noah gave the answer he always gave. "I intend to enjoy a few more years of my running-around time before I take my vows. I'm in no rush."

Giving up his English clothes, his cell phone and the other worldly things he could enjoy now would be easy. But could he give up the game? That would be tough. He loved playing ball. Out on the pitcher's mound, with the pressure mounting, he felt alive.

He suspected that Fannie felt much the same way about her horses. She would hate giving up her riding but she would have to one day. Riding a horse astride was considered worldly and only tolerated before baptism. A rush of sympathy for her surprised him.

He pushed thoughts of Fannie and her problems to the back of his mind as he climbed down the ladder in the barn's interior and headed to the tack room. He needed to concentrate on winning the game tonight. It would bring him one step closer to his goal.

To find out if he was good enough to play professional ball.

If he was good enough, he believed it would be a sign from God to go out into the world and use his gift. If he didn't have the level of talent that his coach thought he did, that would be a sign, too. A sign that God wanted him to remain in his Amish community. Either choice would be hard but he had faith that God would show him the right path.

He was finishing Hank's shoeing when he heard the sound of a buggy coming up the lane. His mother and his sister-in-law Rebecca pulled to a stop beside him in Rebecca's buggy.

His mother graced him with a happy smile from the driver's seat. "We have just heard the nicest news."

"What would that be?" He opened the corral gate and turned Hank in with the other horses. The second hay wagon was on its way.

"The bishop's wife told me two of her nieces have arrived to spend a month visiting them. I have invited them to supper this evening," his mother said quickly.

"And I received a letter telling me my cousins from Indiana are coming to visit." Rebecca smiled at the baby in her arms. "I'll certainly be glad to have a pair of mother's helpers with me for a few months. This little fellow and his brother wear me out."

"So, both your cousins are girls?" he asked trying not to appear uneasy. Had Fannie been right?

His mother exchanged a coy glance with Rebecca. "They are, and all the young women are near your age. I'm sure you'll enjoy getting to know them. Maybe one will catch your eye. I might even talk your father into hosting a few picnics and singings this summer. Won't that be *wunderbar*?"

"Sounds like fun, but you know I'll be gone a lot this summer, and I have a ball game this evening."

His mother frowned. "It won't hurt you to miss one of your silly games. I insist you join us for supper and meet the bishop's nieces."

"The team is depending on me. I can't cancel now. It's important to them."

A stern expression settled over his mother's face. "And this is more important. Noah Bowman, we need to have a talk."

His heart sank when his mother stepped out of the buggy. She rarely took the lead in family matters. Normally his father took him aside for a talk after some indiscretion. Rebecca drove the buggy on to the house, leaving them alone.

His mother folded her arms over her chest. "Your father and I have spoken about this and prayed about it, and we have come to a decision. My *sohn*, you are our youngest. Your father and I have been lenient with you, letting you dress fancy and not plain, letting you travel with your team and keep your cell phone, but you are old enough to put away these childish things as all your brothers have done. It's time you gave serious thought to finding a wife."

He leaned close trying to cajole her with his smile. He didn't want her to worry about a decision he couldn't make yet, so he told her what he thought she wanted to hear.

"You don't have to worry about me, *Mamm*. I plan to join the church in due time. If that is *Gott*'s will."

"You give lip service to this most solemn matter, but nothing in your actions gives me cause to believe your words."

He took a step back. She was dead serious. If his parents forbade his ball playing, he would have to do as they asked or leave home. He wasn't ready to make that choice.

The odds of getting picked up by a major-league team were a thousand to one against him, but he needed to know if he was good enough. Why had God given him this talent, if not to use it?

What could he say that would change his mother's mind?

He shoved his hands into his hip pockets and rocked back on his heels. His fingers touched Fannie's *kapp*. Would she still agree to a courtship or had he burned that bridge with his taunting?

Swallowing hard, he pulled the *kapp* from his pocket and wound the ribbons around his fingers. "I didn't want to say anything, but I have plans to see someone before my game tonight."

His mother glanced from his face to the head covering in his hand. "Who?"

"Fannie. Fannie Erb."

His mother's eyes brightened as she smiled widely. She took his face between her hands and kissed his cheek. "Oh, you sweet boy. You don't know how happy I am to hear this. The daughter of my dearest friend. Why didn't you tell me?"

"I thought I had a plan to stay, but it fell through." Fannie and Connie had finished exercising two of Connie's horses and were brushing them down before returning them to their stalls.

"What plan was that?"

"I asked Noah Bowman to pretend to court me and he turned me down." Fannie patted Goldenrod's sleek neck and ran her fingers through the mare's cream-colored mane. She hated to admit her failure to her friend.

Connie swept a lock of shoulder-length blond hair away from her face and gave Fannie a sympathetic smile. "Thanks for trying. Don't worry so. The team will carry on without you."

"Will they?"

The girls were all younger than Fannie was. They didn't believe in the project the way she did. They weren't beholden to Connie the way she was. If Connie had to sell her property, Fannie would lose more than a friend. She'd lose the job she loved. Riding and training horses was more than a childish pastime. It was what Fannie wanted to do for the rest of her life.

Fannie's Amish upbringing put her squarely at odds with her dream. Although some unmarried Amish women ran their own businesses, it wasn't common. Some worked for English employers but only until they chose to be baptized. Most worked in their family's businesses. Her parents and the bishop wouldn't approve of her riding once she was baptized, she was sure of that. Unless she chose to give up her Amish faith, it was unlikely she could follow her dream.

Could she leave behind all she had been raised to believe in? She wasn't ready to make that decision. Not yet.

"I think the team will do fine," Connie said, but she didn't sound sure.

Fannie pushed her uncertainty aside to concentrate on her friend. "I wanted to do this for you. I owe you so much."

Connie continued to brush her horse. "You have to get over thinking I did something special, Fannie. I didn't."

"You kept me from making the biggest mistake of my life. That was something special."

"It was your love of horses that led you to make the right decision. I only wish those other young people had made the same choice."

"So do I." Fannie cringed inwardly as she thought about the night that had ended so tragically less than two months after her seventeenth birthday.

"Have you settled on the number of patterns the girls will perform?" Connie clearly wanted to change the subject, and Fannie let her.

"Not yet, but I will before I leave. Have you had any inquiries from the ad you ran on the Horse and Tack website?"

"Lowball bids, nothing serious. Maybe I'm just a poor marketer. These horses should sell themselves. If I had the money, I'd have a professional video made. That might do the trick."

"My father says the *Englisch* want an angle, a story. A good horse for sale isn't enough. It has to be an Amish-raised and Amish-trained horse. That's okay for him, but it doesn't help you."

"I can always say raised near the Amish and trained as the Amish would, but that lacks punch even if it is accurate."

Fannie shook her head and realized her *kapp* was missing. *Mamm* would be upset with her for losing another one. She pulled a white handkerchief from her pocket. She always carried two for just this reason. She folded it into a triangle and tied it at the nape of her neck.

A woman should cover her head when she prayed, and Fannie was in serious need of prayers. She couldn't believe it was part of God's plan for her to abandon her friend and to leave her beloved horses behind. "It amazes me how the *Englisch* think anything Amish must be better. We are the same as everyone else."

"You're right. There are good, hardworking people everywhere. If only hard work were enough to keep this place going. I'm glad my father isn't here to see how I've run it into the ground."

"You took care of your father as well as any daughter could. It wasn't possible to grow the business while he was so ill. You had a mountain of your father's medical bills to pay and you have done that. You will get this place back to the way it was and even better."

Fannie followed Connie's gaze as she glanced around the farm. Only four of the twelve stalls in the long, narrow barn were being used by boarders. The barn was beginning to show signs of wear and tear. The red paint was faded and peeling in places. Cobwebs hung from the rafters. A soggy spot at the end of the alley showed where the roof leaked, but all the Haflinger horses in the paddock and pasture were well cared for, with shining coats that gleamed golden brown in the sunshine. Connie took excellent care of her animals.

Attached to the barn was an indoor riding area where Connie's nine-year-old daughter, Zoe, was practicing her trick-riding moves on her Haflinger mare. Connie had once crisscrossed the United States performing at rodeos and equestrian events as a trick rider herself. She paused in her work to watch her daughter.

"I have got to make a go here, Fannie. I have to leave my daughter something besides tarnished belt buckles, fading ribbons and debts. I don't want to sell any of this land. My father made me promise that I wouldn't and I want to honor his wishes. After I'm gone, Zoe will be free to sell or stay. That will be my gift to her. A woman should be able to choose her own path in life."

"I couldn't agree with you more."

Connie shot her a puzzled glance. "Strange words coming from an Amish lass. I thought an Amish woman's goal in life was to be a wife and a mother."

"It is for most of the women, but I can't imagine being so tied down. I certainly don't want to marry and give some oaf the right to boss me around." To give up riding horses was like asking her to give up part of her soul.

"Does that mean you are thinking about leaving the Amish? I know some young people do, but won't you be shunned if you decide to leave?"

"My church believes each person must make that choice. If I leave before I am baptized into the faith, I won't be punished, but I know my parents won't allow me to continue staying at home. If I do decide not to be baptized, I was hoping I could work for you full-time and get my own place someday."

"If your plan with the drill team works out, I sure would consider taking you on full-time. I've never seen anyone as good with horses as you are. But don't give up on the idea of marriage. I can't see you settling for an oaf. It will take a special fellow to get harnessed to you, but I think he exists and I can't wait to meet him."

"I don't think he exists and I'm sure not going to waste my time looking for him."

"If I'd had that attitude before I met Zack, I wouldn't have Zoe now. It was a fair trade. Look at that girl go. She is fearless." Maternal pride glowed on her face as she watched her daughter circling the arena on her horse.

"She's really getting good," Fannie said. Trick riding was something she had always wanted to try.

"Better than I was at her age. I shouldn't encourage her, but I can't help it. The girl is like a sponge. She soaks in everything I tell her. I guess I'm one of those mothers who relive their glory days through their kids."

"Do you miss it?"

Connie paused in her work. "Sometimes I do, but that life is behind me along with my failed marriage to Zoe's father. Dad's illness was the excuse I used to come home, but that wasn't the whole truth. I missed staying in one place. Zack was the one with a restless spirit. Besides, I didn't want Zoe to grow up in a camper, always headed down the road to the next rodeo. I wanted her to have a home—a real home—and Dad gave us that."

She cupped her hands around her mouth. "Point your toes down, Zoe. Keep those legs straight and arch your back more."

"Like this?" Zoe shouted.

"That's better. That's a pretty good hippodrome stand."

Zoe grinned and waved one hand in acknowledgment as she stood atop the back of a gently loping golden horse with a wide white blaze down its face.

"Zoe is going to miss you," Connie said, turning back to Fannie.

"Don't give up on me yet. I may still find a way to stay." Fannie had no idea what that would be, but she wouldn't stop trying.

Connie put down her brush and motioned toward a pitchfork leaning against the wall. "Good. Until then, you still have work to do. I don't pay you much, but I expect you to earn it."

Fannie laughed as she picked up the fork. "I would exercise your horses for free, but cleaning stalls will still cost you."

Connie untied the lead ropes of both horses. "I'll put these two away. You start on stall five and work your way down. George should be here soon. That man is always late. I wish I hadn't hired him."

George was another part-time stable hand at the farm. Connie insisted she couldn't afford full-time help, but in

Fannie's eyes, George wasn't worth even part-time wages. He spent most of his time flirting with the girls in Fannie's riding group—or any woman who came to the farm.

Connie motioned toward her daughter. "I'll be back after I help Zoe with her technique. She's getting flat-footed again and that's dangerous, even on Misty."

Fannie set to work in the stall Connie had indicated, but her mind wasn't on the tasks before her. She still had to find a way to convince her parents that Betsy was the one they needed to send to Florida. No amount of pleading by her and her sister had changed their mother's mind so far. Their father might be persuaded, but their mother was adamant.

If only Noah had agreed to her plan. She wanted to be angry with him, but she couldn't. He was right. Her idea bordered on being dishonest, even if it was for a good cause. She didn't want to be courted by anyone, but having Noah reject her outright was humiliating. She wasn't that ugly, was she? There had been a time when she liked him—a lot. She tossed a forkful of straw into the wheelbarrow at her side.

She had liked being kissed by him, too. A lot. Jabbing the fork into the pile of dirty straw, she tried to forget about that night. She was the *dummkopf* for dumping her drink on him. He sure wouldn't try that again.

"Fannie, can I talk to you?"

She shrieked and spun around at the sound of Noah's voice, sending her forkful of dirty straw flying in his direction.

Chapter Three

Noah stared at the debris clinging to his navy blue ball-uniform pants and white socks. "Remind me to make sure you have empty hands before I speak to you in the future."

He looked up to see Fannie's shocked expression change to a guarded one. "Why are you here? Was there some insult you forgot to offer?"

"My first instinct is to say I'm saving one for another day, but I'm actually here to apologize and to hear you out."

Her eyes narrowed. "Are you saying you'll help me?"

He brushed down the front of his pants. Was he really going to go through with this? "Are you going to keep throwing things at me?"

"That was an accident."

"Accidents seem to happen around you often." At least, it seemed that way to him, as he'd been on the receiving end of them more than once.

She folded her arms over her chest. "I thought you were going to apologize."

Time to get on with it. "Fannie, please accept my apology for calling you crazy."

"All right. I forgive you."

"*Danki.* Now it's your turn."

She thrust out her chin. "For what?"

"For calling me a *dummkopf*."

"Lots of Amish folks have nicknames. That's mine for you."

He threw his hands in the air. "What am I even doing here?"

She reached out and caught hold of his arm. "I'm sorry. Please forgive me for calling you names. Will you help me?"

"I think a courtship—a pretend courtship—could be in my best interest as well as yours."

She squealed. "Noah, I could hug you right now."

He held out both hands. "Drop the pitchfork first."

She laughed softly, a bright, happy sound he discovered he liked. Leaning the implement against the wall, she turned back to him. "What made you change your mind?"

"You were right about *Mamm*'s plans for my summer. How did you know?"

"Rebecca, Mary and Lillian were talking about it at the quilting bee last week."

That the three of his sisters-in-law were in on it didn't surprise him. Wedded bliss was catching in his family. He started picking the loose straw from his socks. "What were you doing at the quilting bee?"

"Quilting. We were making a wedding gift for my cousin. Caring for horses isn't all I know how to do." She offered him a handkerchief from her pocket.

He used it to wipe his hands. "I didn't mean it that way."

"I can cook, clean, sew and manage a house. I just prefer taking care of horses."

"I don't blame you. *Mamm* made all her sons learn to cook, in case we had to take care of ourselves again. I learned, but I never liked it. Actually, Timothy is a good cook. Samuel, Joshua and I can get by, but Luke can't boil water."

He was stalling, trying to decide if he was making the right decision. Going out with Fannie wouldn't be that bad, would it? He liked horses almost as much as she did. That would give them something to talk about. How would she feel about his playing ball all summer? She said she wasn't ready to settle down, and he believed her, but what if she changed her mind after going out with him? He didn't mind teasing her, but he didn't want to hurt her feelings if she fell for him.

She tipped her head to the side. "When did you and your brothers have to take care of yourselves?"

He realized she didn't know the story. He launched into it with relief. Anything to delay the moment.

"When I was two, my mother became very ill. So ill that my father feared for her life. The way she tells it, there was a terrible blizzard. Rather than risk taking all of us out in the storm, *Daed* left Samuel in charge, bundled my mother in all the quilts we could spare and set out for the doctor's office in town. The doctor was able to get mother to the hospital, but the storm was so bad that *Daed* couldn't get back. Samuel took care of us and all the farm animals for three days until the blizzard let up. All we had to eat for those three days was bread soaked in milk with honey, because Samuel didn't know how to cook anything."

"How old was he?"

"If I was two, he would have been ten."

"By the time I was ten I could cook almost anything—fried chicken, baked ham."

"How is your bread?"

She folded her arms over her chest. "I make *goot* bread."

"And your cakes?"

"Light as a feather angel food, or do you prefer dense, gooey shoofly pie?"

"Shoofly, hands down. What about your egg noodles?"

"They could be better but they won't choke you. Why all the questions about my cooking?"

He took a deep breath. "My *daed* always said a man should never date a woman he wouldn't marry. I'll never marry a bad cook, so I won't date one."

She clasped her hands together. "So you *are* going to walk out with me?"

He rubbed his damp palms on his pants. "I want you to know that I'll be playing ball a lot this summer. You might miss some parties and such because I won't be able to take you."

"That's okay. I'm not much of a party person. Besides, I'll be busy with my equestrian team. But we will have to see each other often enough to convince my parents we are dating."

"Okay. I guess I'm in."

She jumped at him and gave him a quick hug before he could stop her. Then she flew out of the stall calling back, "I have to tell Connie."

What had he gotten himself into? Would a summer of being paraded before unknown and hopeful women be worse than a summer of Fannie?

It would, because his parents would make sure he stopped playing ball. He couldn't let that happen. His friends were depending on him and he needed to know if he was good enough to become a professional player. God would decide, but Noah knew he'd have to do the work.

Fannie rushed back into the stall a few seconds later. "*Danki*, Noah. You have no idea how much this means to me."

"We are helping each other. I think."

Moving to stand in front of him, she gazed into his eyes. "If you truly feel this is wrong, Noah, you shouldn't do it. I'll find another way."

"It isn't exactly honest, but we aren't hurting anyone. I've walked out with a few girls and it never led to marriage. There's no reason I can't take you home from church a few times or to a party to see if we would suit."

She drew back. "We won't. I'm sure of it. You are not the man I want to marry."

"*Goot* to know. I was worried."

"Don't be. By the end of August, I'll be ready to take Betsy's place in Florida if she wants to come home. You're right, we aren't hurting anyone. Betsy wants to go in my place. She is much better at caring for the elderly than I am, and our grandparents deserve the best."

"I see your point there."

"Do you? Connie does need my help, too. You can see that for yourself. This place will soon be on its last legs."

"That's no lie," George Milton said from the doorway. A handsome man with dark hair and dark eyes, George was an English fellow a couple of years younger than Noah. Noah knew him only slightly.

"This is a private conversation, George." Fannie leveled a sour look at him.

"Excuse me!" He rolled his eyes and walked on.

"You don't care for him?" Noah asked. He didn't, either.

"He is sloppy in his work. As I was saying, I'll enjoy riding on the drill team enormously, I won't lie about that, but I can and will be as much help to my mother as Betsy would be. Plus, I can still help my father with his horses. I'm willing to work hard and see that no one suffers because of this decision."

Noah's conscience pricked him. Fannie's reasons for this pretend courtship were more selfless than his. He simply wanted to keep playing ball.

Her face brightened. "I won't make demands on your

time, Noah. If you happen to like one of the women coming to visit, I'll step aside and give you free rein."

He managed a half smile. "A fella isn't likely to get such a generous offer from a normal girlfriend."

She slapped his shoulder. "Well, you are a fortunate fellow, Noah Bowman. I'm not an ordinary girlfriend."

With a toss of her pretty head that reminded him of her spirited mare, Fannie walked out of the stall with a sassy stride that drew his attention to her trim figure. Among the earthy and familiar smells of the stable, he caught a whiff of something flowery.

Nope, there was nothing ordinary about Fannie.

Realizing he'd forgotten to give her the *kapp* she had dropped, he pulled it from his pocket and lifted it to his nose. A scent that reminded him of his mother's flower garden in summer clung to the fabric. Since Amish women didn't use perfume, he knew the smell must be from the shampoo Fannie used.

Flowery and sweet. Not what he expected from a girl who spent most of her time with horses.

He walked out into the arena and saw her with a half-dozen other Amish girls. They were saddling Connie's horses. All of the girls eyed him intently as Fannie left them to speak to him. "The rest of my team is here. Do you want to watch us practice?"

"Another time. Walter is waiting outside to drive us to our game in Berlin. Do they all know about us?" He jerked his head toward the girls.

"Only Connie knows."

He squared his shoulders and held out Fannie's *kapp*. "That's a relief. I guess I should get this over with. Fannie, may I take you home after church tomorrow?"

She glanced over her shoulder and then leaned close.

"If you have to grit your teeth to ask me out, Noah, no one will believe we like each other."

His mouth fell open. He snapped it shut and glared at her. "That is exactly what I said. *Ja* or *nee*, Fannie. Can I take you home after church or not? I don't have all day."

Her sweet smile didn't reach her eyes. "As much as I would like to refuse your kind offer, I won't. I will almost be happy to go out with you."

He crossed his arms over his chest. "And I will be sincerely happy when this charade is over."

She took a step closer and whispered, "Not nearly as happy as I will be."

"You ungrateful minx. Enjoy your time in Florida." He turned away.

She caught his arm before he had taken a single step. "I'm sorry, Noah. Really. Please don't go away mad. I will do better."

"I must be *ab en kopp*, off in the head. Otherwise, why would I be here?"

She looked over her shoulder and then turned to him with resignation written across her face. "You're right. No one will believe we are a couple. I'm not as pretty as the girls you've gone out with in the past. I'm much too horsey for most men to look my way. I don't know how to act around a fella who shows some interest, so I act as if I don't care. You've been a friend to me in the past and I hope that we can be friends again in the future. I'm sorry I put you in an awkward situation."

If she had been a motherless kitten, she couldn't have looked more forlorn. It was too bad he had a soft spot for kittens. He looked toward the group of young women watching them and sighed heavily. "Fannie, we might not be friends after this, but your teammates are gonna believe we're a couple."

Calling himself every kind of fool, he took her by the shoulders, pulled her close and kissed her cheek. Then he beat a hasty retreat before she had time to react.

Fannie pressed a hand to her tingling face. Had Noah wanted to kiss her, or had he done it purely for effect?

For the effect, the sensible part of her insisted. The less sensible part of her wondered if he liked her—just a little. She stared at the door where he'd disappeared until the sound of giggling and a wolf whistle penetrated the fog in her mind.

She turned to face her teammates, ignoring George's leering stare from across the arena. "We have a lot of work to do and only a short time to do it. Mount up. Zoe, start the music."

Connie came over and handed Fannie Trinket's reins as the strains of "She'll Be Coming 'Round the Mountain" blared from a speaker on the arena railing. The group had decided on the song because the rolling cadence of the music matched the gait of their horses.

Connie held on to Trinket's reins as she gazed at Fannie's face. "Just remember that people who play with fire often get burned."

"I'm not going to get burned," Fannie said quietly, praying that was true. "I know the difference between real and pretend."

"For your sake, I hope so."

Every time Fannie looked up from her hymnal on Sunday morning, she caught sight of Noah's reflection in the mirror on the wall behind the bishop and preachers at the front of the room, and she started thinking about Noah's kiss all over again.

The service was being held at the home of John Miller,

the local blacksmith. The widower lived with his mother on a small farm a mile from Fannie's home. Like many Amish homes, the walls of the downstairs could be opened up to accommodate members of the congregation during services that were held every other Sunday. Wooden benches had been placed in two rows where women sat on one side while the men sat on the other.

She should be minding the words of the bishop's preaching, but all Fannie could think about was riding home with Noah that evening. After the singing that would be held for the youth following supper. After dark.

Would he kiss her again?

She gave herself a mental shake. The whole idea was ridiculous. How could she pretend to be interested in Noah when she wasn't? The longer she thought about it, and she'd spent most of the night thinking about it, the less she wanted to go through with it. The only answer was to call the whole thing off.

She couldn't silence the talk among the girls who'd seen him kiss her, but it would die down and none of them were likely to spread the story if Noah didn't come around again. George would forget about it soon enough, and he knew very few Amish folk.

Calling it off was the right decision. She would tell Noah as soon as she had the chance.

She glanced at the mirror again. She could see a half dozen of the young unmarried men and boys in the reflection. They were all seated at the back of the room nearest the door. They would be the first to leave when the three-hour service was over. Several of them drew frowns from the ministers by their restlessness as the end approached. Fannie couldn't blame them. The backless wooden benches were hard. She focused again on the heavy black songbook in her hands. She had been desperate, and her spur-of-the-moment plan had been foolish. There had to be a better way. If only she could think of one.

"Why is Noah Bowman watching you?" Betsy whispered in her ear.

Fannie glanced up and met Noah's eyes in the mirror. He nodded slightly to acknowledge her. A rush of heat filled her cheeks and she looked down quickly. "I have no idea."

"*Shveshtah*, you're blushing." Betsy smirked, causing several nearby worshippers to look their way.

Fannie shot her sister a fierce stare and Betsy turned her attention back to the bishop. Fannie glanced in the mirror again.

Unlike yesterday, Noah was dressed plain in black pants and a black coat over a pale blue shirt. He was indistinguishable from the other Amish men around him except for the shorter haircut he wore. He wasn't the most handsome one of the Bowman brothers. Luke was the best looking while Samuel was the most hardworking, but Noah was nice looking in his own way. She liked his eyes the best. Her sister called them forget-me-not blue. Fannie liked the way they sparkled when he smiled. And he was almost always smiling.

Except when he was around her.

Not that she smiled that much around him, either. Ever since that evening in his mother's garden, they seemed to rub each other the wrong way. Fannie couldn't put her finger on the reason.

People around her began singing and Fannie joined in, knowing it was the final hymn of the service. Normally the preaching seemed long, but not today. Today it ended all too quickly. When she walked outside, Noah was waiting for her off to the side of the house with his straw hat in his hands. She clutched her fingers together and walked toward him.

"You look like a martyr heading to your own execution. Try smiling." He nodded to someone behind her.

Fannie swallowed the comment that sprang to her lips and smiled instead. "Is this better?"

"Vennich."

"A little is better than nothing." She looked over her shoulder and saw his mother smiling warmly at them. Anna winked at her and waved before snagging Fannie's mother by the arm, and the two of them walked away with their heads close together.

Fannie kept her grin in place with difficulty as she turned back to Noah. "You didn't tell your mother we were going out, did you?"

He gave her a sheepish look and shrugged. "I kind of did."

Fannie pointed to their mothers as they stood talking to each other. "She's going to tell my mother, and I haven't mentioned it to her."

"Mamm put me on the spot."

"In what way?"

He grabbed Fannie's arm and led her around the side of the building. "She said I had to end my *rumspringa* and look for a wife this summer. She meant it, so I told her I was already seeing you. This is what you wanted, isn't it? This was your idea."

Why hadn't she thought this through before rushing over to see Noah? "I was thinking my mother was the only one who needed to believe we were going out. I didn't consider how your mother would feel about it."

"She's thrilled. Very, very thrilled."

Fannie closed her eyes and cringed. "Of course she is. She and my mother are the best of friends. How are we going to break it to them that we aren't getting married?"

"Whoa. Slow down, Fannie. Don't get ahead of yourself. We haven't had a date yet. Let's stick to the plan at least until the second week of August."

That was the weekend of the Horse Expo, but he didn't know that. "Why then?"

"The state invitational baseball tournament is being held that weekend."

She took a step away from him. "Wait a minute. You told your mother we were going out so you could keep playing baseball this summer?"

"Don't take that tone with me. I have my reasons for agreeing to this just like you had your reasons for coming up with this idea."

And to think she had been wondering if he liked her even a little. "It'll never work. I'm sorry I ever suggested it."

"Don't be hasty. I'm willing to give it a try, unless you have your heart set on leaving for Florida next week."

She folded her arms across her middle. How could she tell Connie she'd changed her mind after assuring her friend she would help her? She couldn't. "It looks like you and I are stuck with each other for the summer. Very well. What are your plans for our first date?"

"We do what normal people do. We'll stay for the singing tonight and I'll take you home afterward."

"Don't expect an invitation to come in and visit, the way normal couples do."

"If I get home too early, my parents are going to think we didn't hit it off."

"So drive around for an hour or two."

"I'm not wearing out a good horse just to make you happy."

"You wouldn't know a good horse if you tripped over one."

"How can you, of all people, say that?"

She opened her mouth to reply, but his brother Joshua came around the corner of the building. "Here you are. It's our turn to go in and eat, Noah."

"*Danki*, I'm coming."

Joshua smiled at Fannie. "Would you care to join Mary and Hannah when they go in? I know they would enjoy visiting with you."

"*Danki*, Joshua, but I have to find my sister."

"We are getting up a game of horseshoes after lunch. Noah and I will take on you and your sister, won't we, *bruder*?" Joshua seemed intent on getting her together with the rest of Noah's family. Had Noah's mother told them all that she and Noah were dating?

She forced a bright smile for Noah. "I'd love the chance to beat Noah at any game of his choosing."

Joshua laughed. "Well, don't pick baseball. Did he tell you he pitched a no-hitter yesterday? Against the league champions from last year. Everyone at the fire station thinks this year's trophy will look awesome on our wall. The boy has an amazing arm."

Fannie was surprised when Joshua winked at her, too. "I'm glad he's finally showing some sense in his personal life."

She wanted to sink into the ground.

Joshua left when he heard the sound of his wife's voice calling him, but Noah lingered.

Fannie's temper cooled rapidly. "I'm sorry."

"Don't worry about it. We seem to be trapped by our little deception. Do we tell them now or let them down gradually?"

"Gradually, I guess. We started this so we might as well finish it. The next time I have a brilliant idea, don't listen to me."

"I won't."

She stared at her feet for a long moment. "A no-hitter. Wow, that's quite an accomplishment."

"It was due more to great fielding by the team than my pitching. *Gott* smiled on us."

She was glad to hear him giving credit to others and to God. The awkward silence grew between them. Finally, she said, "I do need to find my sister."

"Sure. See you later at the horseshoe pit."

"Okay."

"Don't think I'll take it easy on you," he said as he walked away.

"The thought never crossed my mind, but you'd better not."

A small grin curved his lips. There was a distinct twinkle in his eyes. "You won't knock me in the head with a horseshoe, will you?"

"I have already promised to stop throwing things at you."

"*Goot.* I'll hold you to that." His grin turned to a wide smile just before he rounded the corner.

Fannie leaned back against the wall of the house as a funny feeling settled in the center of her stomach. He sure was an attractive fellow when he smiled.

She shook her head at her own foolishness. "I'm not going to fall for him. This was definitely my worst idea yet."

It would be difficult to guard her emotions if she had to spend much time in his company. If he was being nice to her, she wasn't sure she could do it.

Chapter Four

"I'm glad that's over with." Noah held out his hand to help Fannie into his open buggy after the singing that evening.

"So am I." Fannie ignored his hand and climbed in by herself. "Did you see everyone staring at me when I first came in? I almost turned and ran."

"Now that you mention it, I can't think of the last time I saw you at a young people's gathering."

"They're a waste of time if you aren't shopping for a potential spouse."

"Not everyone is looking to marry. A lot of us just want to have fun."

"The boys are there for fun. The girls are all looking for someone to marry. I noticed plenty of them eyeing you. Especially the bishop's visiting nieces. In the future, could you at least act as if you are interested in me?"

"Maybe I'm not that good of an actor," he snapped.

"Work on it or this will be pointless." She scooted as far away from him as she could get without falling out the other side of his buggy.

She was right to rebuke him. He had neglected her, but a group of his friends had wanted to talk baseball. He got caught up in the conversation until it was almost time to go home. That's when he noticed Fannie sitting beside her sister and her sister's beau, and recalled why she was there. He'd spent the last half hour sitting beside Fannie but mostly talking to Hiram as Fannie fumed. He knew the buggy ride home was going to be a rough one.

Deciding he should smooth the troubled waters with a compliment or two, he climbed in beside her. "I noticed during the singing tonight that *Gott* has given you a fine voice."

"*Danki.* You have a pleasant voice, too." She stared straight ahead with her arms clasped tight across her middle. Was she nervous? It wasn't as if it was a real date.

"You don't have to hang off the side. I don't bite."

"I do," she quipped, but she relented and inched a little closer.

"Do you want to drive?" He offered her the reins.

She looked at him then. "Why?"

"I'm just asking. I know you're almost as good a driver as I am."

She sat up straight and planted her hands on her hips. "*Almost* as good?"

He flinched at her offended tone. That had been the wrong choice of words. So much for smoother waters. "Do you want to drive or not?"

"All right." She accepted the reins and neatly turned Willy to head out of John Miller's yard. It was after ten o'clock, and the other couples and singles were already gone.

Noah propped his feet on the dash rail and crossed his hands behind his head. "Willy has a tendency to drift to the left."

"I see that." She corrected the horse's line and stopped him at the highway, where John Miller's lane intersected it at the top of a steep hill. When she was sure the way was clear, she eased Willy out onto the blacktop.

At the bottom of the hill, a hundred yards away, the road ended in a T. Beyond the roadway the tree-lined river slipped silently through the farmland. Fannie turned Willy onto the road that skirted the riverbank. Breaks in the trees occasionally gave Noah a glimpse of moonlight rippling on the water's surface.

He studied Fannie's face as she sat beside him. A soft wind fluttered the ribbons of her *kapp* and tugged at the curls she tried so hard to confine. She held the reins with confidence, as he knew she would. He'd seen her helping her father train horses to pull buggies since she was knee-high. "Nice night for a drive."

"I reckon. Driving at night makes me nervous."

So the unflappable Fannie had a weakness. "Why?"

"I'm always afraid a car will come up behind me too fast and run into me."

"It happens. We can't know when *Gott* will test our faith with such a trial. Do you want me to take over?"

"*Nee.* I must overcome this fear."

He worried about the tremor in her voice. She really was scared—but determined. "What do you think of Willy?" he asked, to take her mind off her apprehension.

"He's a sweet goer. Nice smooth gait. A high stepper but not absurdly high. He has a soft mouth and responds to a light touch on the reins. He's a *goot gaul.*"

"And you said I wouldn't know a good horse if I tripped over one."

She sent him a sidelong glance, but seemed to consider her words for a change. "Sometimes my mouth says things before my brain can stop it. Forgive me."

An olive branch? He gladly accepted it. "You are forgiven. I've been known to speak rashly, too."

"Sadly, that seems to be all we have in common."

"We both like horses."

A hint of a smile lifted one corner of her mouth. "There is that."

"I'm sure we'll find other things we can agree on by the end of the month. I'll try if you will."

"I reckon there's no harm in trying. At least you aren't as boring as Hiram. I don't know how my sister stands him."

"It might be uncharitable of me, but I have to agree. He is a boring fellow. If you don't love pigs, there's no point in striking up a conversation with him."

She giggled and Noah relaxed. The drive wasn't so bad after that. It wasn't long before the fence that marked her lane came into view up ahead. She turned Willy neatly into her driveway and pulled him to a stop in front of her house. The building was dark except for a dim light glowing in the kitchen window.

She handed Noah the reins. "Would you like to come in?"

"I thought you weren't going to ask me in."

"Another one of my mouth-before-brain moments."

It was an accepted custom for an Amish girl to invite her date in for a visit, even though her parents would be in bed. The young man and woman were expected to be on their best behavior. They would talk or play board games until very late as they got to know each other.

"I don't see Hiram's buggy. Do you think he's gone home already? I know he left with your sister."

"He never stays long."

Noah shrugged. "He's an odd duck. Sure, I'd like to come in."

"Really?" The look of shock on her face was priceless.

He hopped down, secured Willy and turned to help Fannie out of the buggy, but she was already standing on the ground. "You don't have to come in, Noah. We can pretend you did."

"I think we've done enough pretending for a while, don't you?"

"I reckon you're right."

She led the way inside and closed the door quietly behind him. "I made some cinnamon-raisin biscuits this morning. Would you like one?"

"Sounds *goot*."

"Do you want to sit in the living room or here in the kitchen?" She had her hands clenched tightly together.

"The normal place for a couple to visit is in the living room, but I like the kitchen better. It's cozy." He took a seat at the table.

She seemed to relax. "I agree. No point in trying for a normal courtship at this point."

Moving to the cupboard, she removed two plates and placed two biscuits on his and one on hers. She sat down at the table and pushed his plate toward him. He wasn't hungry, but he pulled off a small piece and ate it. The raisins were plump but the dough was tough.

"How is it?" she asked.

"It won't choke me."

She scowled and opened her mouth but he forestalled her. "Brain first, mouth second, Fannie."

Her scowl faded and she blushed. "They aren't my best."

"They're far better than anything I could make. I imagine cooking is like playing ball. It takes a lot of practice to get good enough to make it look easy."

"Do you practice your pitching at home?"

"Some. I have to pester my brothers or my cousins to catch for me. They don't always have time."

"Have you always liked playing ball?"

"Are you kidding? What boy doesn't? Don't you remember all the recesses we spent playing softball at school?"

"I remember staying in to write I'm sorry for something

or other on the blackboard a hundred times. I was always in trouble. I wasn't any good at hitting the ball so I wasn't picked for a team very often."

"I used to get you in trouble a lot. I thought it was funny to see you get angry. Your face got so red. I'm sorry about that."

She shrugged. "We were kids."

"Still. It wasn't kind of me."

They talked about school for a while, sharing memories and funny stories from their childhood days. It surprised Noah that she recalled so many of his exploits. The Bowman boys were known for their adventuresome natures, but he wasn't the wildest one.

"Luke was the worst of us," Noah admitted. His brother had left the Amish and gotten into trouble with the English law over drugs, bringing shame to the family.

Fannie's eyes filled with sympathy. "No one would know it now. He's changed for the better."

"*Gott* and Emma changed his heart." Luke had become a devout member of the faithful, much to his family's joy.

"Does your brother Timothy like teaching school? It's unusual for a man to become a teacher." She nibbled on the edge of her biscuit.

"He loves it, especially since his wife, Lillian, teaches there, as well. You heard the school is holding a frolic, didn't you? The school board has decided to add a wing to the building for the upper classes that Timothy teaches. They are pouring the new foundation next week."

"We heard about it. *Mamm* and *Daed* have said they will help."

"That's great. The more hands we have, the easier the work will be."

She sighed heavily. "It's odd to think about our school changing as much as it has."

"You haven't said you forgive me for teasing you the way I did back then."

"I forgive you." She looked at him from under lowered brows. "Just don't do it again."

He chuckled. "If you don't throw stuff at me, I won't call you carrottop, copperhead, fire-eater or ginger nut ever again."

"Aw, thanks for nothing. Ginger nut? No one ever called me a ginger nut."

"Did I miss that one when we were young?"

She plucked a raisin from her biscuit and tossed it toward him. He caught it in his open mouth and she giggled.

He sat up straighter. "I say you can't do that again."

"And I say I'm not going to spend time sweeping the kitchen floor after my failures. Besides, I think it's time you went home."

He checked the clock on the wall, surprised to see how late it was. "I reckon you're right. Our team has a game next Saturday. Would you care to come and watch?"

"I can't. We have our first competition at the Wayne's County Fairgrounds that day. That's if I'm not on my way to Florida. You can come watch us practice at Connie's place on Tuesdays and Thursdays at six."

"Are you sure I won't be bored?"

"I doubt it. You appreciate good horses the same way I do."

"I'm thinking not as much as you do. Our team, the Fire Eaters, practice on Wednesdays and Fridays at five o'clock over behind the fire station. You're welcome to come watch us."

She wrinkled her nose and shook her head. "Talk about boring."

"Do I sense disdain for the sport I love?"

"I think it's silly to see grown men acting like little

boys throwing a ball at each other and trying to hit it with a stick."

He scowled at her. "Is it sillier than a bunch of girls riding their horses in circles?"

She rose and folded her arms across her middle. "I think it is."

He pressed his lips together and settled his straw hat on his head. "I don't have a comeback for that. It is time I went home."

"Don't worry. I'm sure you'll think of the perfect thing to say before you get across the road."

"Now you imply my wit is slow." He shook his head, moved to the door and jerked it open. "What have I done to deserve this?"

"I won't begin the litany of your sins, Noah Bowman. It would take me the rest of the night to list them." Her face was expressionless as she slammed the door behind him.

Noah felt like banging his head on it. Ten minutes ago he'd been enjoying himself and thinking Fannie had certainly grown into an interesting woman. In the blink of an eye she was back to insulting him like a schoolgirl.

He walked to his buggy and untied Willy from the hitching rail in front of her house. "This is proof the whole thing is a bad idea, but now I'm stuck with it."

He'd do well to think of this courtship as a business deal, one that got them what they both wanted, but it was sure going to be a painful summer.

"Anna Bowman tells me you and Noah have been seeing each other. Is this so?" Fannie's mother asked, once they were alone the next morning.

Fannie swept the breakfast crumbs from the table and tossed them in the trash before answering. "We've been out together."

"I thought it was odd that you wanted to stay for the singing yesterday. Did he bring you home last night?"

"If you must know, he did."

"Well? How is it going?"

"Better than I expected."

That was the truth. Fannie couldn't believe how much she had enjoyed sitting alone with him in the kitchen and just talking. It was as if they had both put aside the masks they wore in daily life. Until she insulted him. When would she learn to think before she spoke?

"So?" her mother prompted.

"So, what?"

"Child, you will drive me insane yet. Did he ask you out again?"

"Sort of. He invited me to come to his ball game on Saturday, but I'll be leaving so it doesn't matter."

"Of course it matters. I had no idea you and Noah were seeing each other. You should have said something sooner. Anna and I dreamed of seeing you two wed when you were still in diapers."

Fannie rolled her eyes. "We aren't getting married, *Mamm*. We've only started walking out together."

"But it was a nice date, *ja*?"

"*Ja*, it was nice, but he knows I'm leaving. I'm going to need new shoes before I head to Florida. Do you think we could go shopping tomorrow?" Fannie glanced at her mother from the corner of her eye. Was she wavering?

"Your sister has new shoes."

"Betsy doesn't wear the same size I do."

"I thought you wanted to stay here and ride horses with your friends."

"I do. It's important to me, but I realize you won't change your mind." Fannie wiped at a stubborn spot of dried jelly on the table. "If Noah is still unattached next year, maybe he'll ask me out again. Of course, his mother has invited a number of young women to visit them this summer, so I can't hold out a lot of hope."

Fannie's mother cupped one hand around her chin and tapped her lips with one finger. "Your sister is in the garden picking string beans. Ask her to come in."

"Okay." Fannie concealed a smile as she went out the door. Maybe, just maybe, her idea was going to bear fruit, after all.

At the garden gate, she called to Betsy. "*Mamm* wants to see you."

"What for?"

"I think she wants to ask you about going to Florida."

Betsy dashed to the gate carrying a blue plastic bucket half-full of beans. "Really? That would be *wunderbar*."

Fannie didn't want to hold out false hope. "She hasn't said for sure."

"I'll do my best to convince her." Betsy shoved her bucket into Fannie's hands and scampered through the gate. "You might as well get used to doing my chores. There's eight rows left to pick."

Fannie stared at the large garden loaded with produce that needed to be canned soon. Any free time she wanted would have to come after her work was done. She was going to have a busy summer. Opening the gate, she crossed to the beans and started picking where her sister had left off.

Entering the kitchen fifteen minutes later with a full pail, Fannie found her mother washing glass pint jars in the sink. The pressure cooker sat on the stove waiting to be loaded. Fannie fairly itched to hear her mother's decision, but instead of asking, she transferred a portion of her beans into a large bowl, rinsed them, sat down and began snapping them into equal lengths after discarding the stems.

Betsy came up from the cellar with a cardboard box full

of dusty jars. She grinned at Fannie and nodded. She put the box on the counter beside her mother. Instead of jumping for joy, Fannie kept snapping beans, but she couldn't hide her grin.

Her mother placed the last jar in soapy water to soak and turned around. After drying her hands on her apron, she smoothed her dress. "I must speak with your *daed.*"

Fannie knew her father had the ultimate say in family matters, but he seldom went against his wife's wishes. As soon as her mother went out, Betsy flew to her sister and pulled her to her feet. She hugged Fannie and swung her around. "I'm going to see the ocean!"

"I'm glad you're happy about it."

"*Happy* is a poor word for this feeling." Holding Fannie at arm's length, Betsy stared at her with wide eyes. "How did you manage to change her mind?"

"Noah Bowman asked to walk out with me."

"I wondered who took you home from the singing. Noah Bowman? I never would have guessed. And that's all it took for *Mamm* to change her mind?"

"You know how desperate she is to see me wed."

"I do. Believe me, I do. I'm sure she thinks this is your last chance."

Fannie leaned back and frowned. "I wouldn't call it my last chance. I'm not even twenty-two."

"I've never seen anyone as determined to become an old maid as you are. You haven't had a date in years."

"Only because I wasn't willing to give up my free time. I'll date when I'm ready."

"Sure, if you say so. I don't care what the reason is. I'm going to Florida." Betsy threw her hands in the air and spun out of the room.

Fannie went out to gather more beans. Her mother was in the kitchen when she returned. She motioned for Fannie to join her at the table. "Sit for a moment. I have something to tell you."

Fannie took a seat and tried to keep her face blank.

Her mother steepled her fingers. "Your father and I have talked it over, and we believe Betsy should go to stay with my parents."

"She'll be happy to hear that, but what about Hiram?"

"They are betrothed now. That will not change if she is gone for a few months. I would feel terrible if I ruined your chances with Noah by sending you away."

Fannie tried hard to conceal her elation. "Is it still okay that I ride with the girls at Connie's place?"

"As long as your riding doesn't interfere with other things."

"It won't. I'll be as much help to you as I can, I promise."

"I was thinking of the time you might spend in Noah Bowman's company."

"He lives across the road. We'll see each other often enough."

"Men need prompting when it comes to courting, Fannie. You must make a good impression on him and show him you'll make a *goot* wife. Anna and I will arrange for the two of you to get together a few times a week."

Fannie shook her head. "*Mamm,* I'm not going to throw myself at Noah."

"I'm not asking you to do that. We're simply going to nudge him in the right direction. Your father says the boy has baseball practice at the fire station on Wednesday evening. You should go, and you should take all the men something sweet to eat."

"There are plenty of chores waiting for me. I don't have time to sit and watch Noah throw a ball."

Her mother scowled at her. "Most young women are

thrilled at the idea of spending a little extra time with their beau. Are you saying you have already decided the two of you won't suit? If that's the case, there's no reason you can't go to Florida as we first decided."

"I'm not saying we won't suit," Fannie said quickly. "We've only gone out once. It's too soon to tell if we are meant for each other or not. Only *Gott* knows the one who will become my helpmate for life."

"This is true. Only *Gott* can bring forth the bounty of my garden out of the dirt, but I still have to pull the weeds and water the seedlings. A courtship is no different. You must do your part."

"I will, but you and Anna shouldn't interfere. Too much water can drown the seedlings."

Fannie's mother looked as if she wanted to argue, but to Fannie's surprise, she leaned back in her chair and said, "We will leave the courting to you *kinder*, but you must put some effort into the relationship. Anna will tell Noah the same. Going to watch him play ball is a start."

"We are hardly children, *Mamm*."

Her mother chuckled and cupped her hands around Fannie's face. "Both Anna and I are delighted that you two have found each other after all these years living right across the road from each other. Nothing could make us happier than seeing you and Noah wed. Just think, someday Anna and I could be sharing grandbabies."

Fannie swallowed hard against the sudden tightness in her throat. How were she and Noah going to get out of this mess without hurting both their mothers?

Chapter Five

"*Mamm*, I don't think this is a good idea."

From inside their buggy, Fannie looked over the vehicles in the parking lot beside the fire station late on Wednesday afternoon. There were six buggies parked along the edge of the gravel lot. The rest were pickups, a motorcycle, several scooters, a few bicycles and two SUVs. Several dozen spectators, Amish and English men and women, sat in the bleachers behind the backstop. Four young Amish boys sat in the grass along the third baseline. If she walked out to talk to Noah, the whole community would be speculating about their relationship before the next church meeting.

Fannie's mother made a shooing motion with her hand. "All men like to eat. Have faith in your mother. I snagged your father, didn't I? It was no easy task, but it was my cooking that did the trick. Now, go speak to Noah. I expect you home before dark."

Fannie got out of the buggy with a large hamper over her arm. Noah stood on the pitcher's mound facing a batter. He hadn't seen her yet. He leaned forward with the ball behind his back. He adjusted the brim of his ball cap, nodded once, checked the runners on second and third base and then threw a lightning-fast pitch. The umpire called a strike.

The ball field was a recent addition to the fire station grounds. The previous fall more than a dozen fires had been started in their community. Many Amish thought English teenagers were setting the blazes and distrust of the English ran high. When they learned the arsonist was an Amish person, the son of the school board president, everyone was shocked. In gratitude for the firemen's hard work, and to ease a few consciences, the men of the community improved a field behind the station from a cow pasture to a well-maintained ball diamond.

Fannie walked to the edge of the backstop. "Excuse me. May I speak with you?"

The umpire, the man she assumed was their coach, called a halt to the practice. He took off his face mask and she recognized Eric Swanson, the captain of the local fire department. "Is there something I can do for you, miss?"

"I have some snacks that I thought your players might enjoy."

He glanced at his watch. "That's real kind. We have about thirty minutes of practicing left. If you would like to leave them here, that would be fine."

Fannie was tempted to leave the hamper and scamper back to the buggy, but one look at her mother's face convinced her she needed to remain where she was. "Might I have a word with Noah first?"

The man frowned, but motioned for Noah to come in. "Take five, guys."

Noah trotted over to where she stood. "Fannie, what are you doing here? What's wrong?"

"Nothing's wrong. You invited me." She felt like a complete fool as the rest of the team and spectators stared at them.

Noah didn't look happy. "You didn't exactly express an interest in my invitation at the time."

"*Mamm* has changed my mind for me." Fannie looked over her shoulder in time to see her mother turn the buggy around and head toward home.

Noah shook his head. "I don't understand."

She lowered her voice to a whisper hoping they wouldn't be overheard. "I'm here to impress you with my baking skills and show you I'm interested in all that you do. According to my mother, I have to put more effort into impressing you. Please act impressed instead of annoyed."

He frowned. "This is the reason you interrupted our practice?"

She glanced around at the people staring at them. "What did you imagine I would do when you invited me?"

"I don't know. Sit quietly on the sideline and watch."

"In other words, be meek and silent as a good Amish woman should."

"I don't know why I thought you could manage that."

"Noah, can this wait until later?" his coach asked.

"Sure," Noah said loudly before turning back to Fannie. "Thanks for coming, but I have to finish practicing."

He wasn't overjoyed to see her, but she'd expected as much. Pretending to enjoy someone's company was much harder than she thought it would be. "*Mamm* left me here, so you will have to take me home afterward."

"I can't. I have plans. Captain Swanson surprised us all with tickets to the Cleveland Indians game tonight and we'll barely make it if we leave here right after practice. I don't have time to take you home."

"What am I supposed to do?" she asked with a quick frown.

"It isn't that far for you to walk."

"Walk home alone?"

"Why don't you ask one of the other Amish guys to take you? I'm sure someone will. Ask the bishop's son, Rob Beachy, he's here. His cousin Simon plays shortstop for us."

It wasn't a long walk. Less than two miles but that wasn't the problem. "Arriving home alone will surely convince my mother you are growing fonder of me by the hour. Letting the bishop's son take me home will convince her you are head over heels in love with me," Fannie said through gritted teeth, not holding back her sarcasm.

Noah's face hardened with displeasure as he leaned close. "I'm not going to miss a Cleveland game for the sake of a courtship that's not real."

"I don't imagine you'd miss that for a real courtship. Woe to the woman you pick to be your wife, Noah Bowman, that's all I can say. Enjoy the food. I hope it chokes you." She shoved the hamper into his hands and marched away. She wasn't about to sit and watch him practice his silly game.

Noah wanted to call Fannie back but thought better of it. There wasn't any point in trying to talk to her when she was upset. She could be the most stubborn, irritating and frustrating woman he'd ever met. It took her all of ten seconds to have him seeing red.

No, it wasn't all her fault. He'd spent an hour today listening to his mother sing Fannie's praises and offering him advice on courting her. He'd been ready to confess everything, except he knew what was at stake for both himself and Fannie. The deception didn't sit well with him, but he shouldn't have taken his sour mood out on her. She might have suggested the idea, but he was the one who jumped on the wagon when it looked like his plans for the summer were in jeopardy.

Eric Swanson came up beside him. "Noah, I don't normally make a point of getting involved in my player's personal lives, but may I give you some advice?"

"I reckon you will, no matter what I say." Eric was Noah's friend as well has his coach and captain of the fire department. He respected Eric opinion.

"I played for two years in the minors."

"For the Red Sox farm team. I know."

"In all that time, I rarely saw a pitcher with the kind of speed and control you have. I've been talking to people I know about you. Don't let something or someone distract you now, when we are so close to getting you in front of major-league scouts."

Noah shook his head. "I won't."

Fannie wouldn't become a distraction if he kept his head in the game.

"I'll see that he stays with the program," Walter said, joining them as he tossed the ball in the air and caught it.

Eric nodded once. "Good. Let's win the next four games and get this team to the state invitational. I understand you must have conflicted feelings, Noah. I'm not pressing you to make a decision you aren't ready to make. Just keep an open mind and give the team your all."

"I will." Noah smacked his fist into his glove.

"All right. Play ball," Eric yelled.

Walter smiled at Noah as he handed him the ball. "I respect your religious beliefs, too, and I understand if you choose to stay here, but I don't want to spend my life in Bowmans Crossing growing corn and milking cows with my dad. I never got to college, my folks didn't have the money for it, so I couldn't play college ball and get noticed that way. This could be my only shot at the pros. I'm not getting any younger, so keep your head in the game and not on a girl."

"It's not serious."

"I'm glad to hear that. Maybe a scout will pick both of us up for the same team. Wouldn't that be a hoot? You and me, pitching and catching in the major leagues. We'd put Bowmans Crossing on the map."

Noah walked back to the mound. He wasn't sure he wanted a life outside the Amish, but what if Eric was right? What if he *was* good enough? Didn't he deserve a chance to find out?

If he failed, he would know for certain it was because God wanted him here.

Noah left the blacksmith's shop on Thursday afternoon a little before six. He had come to consult with John Miller about a crack in Ginger's back hoof that his brother Joshua had discovered. John promised he would be over the next day to fit her with a special shoe to protect her foot from further injury. Noah had left her in a box stall to limit her movements until then.

At the bottom of the hill, Noah saw a young Amish girl cantering along the river's edge and wondered if she was headed to Connie Stroud's place. Today was the day Fannie told him that her group was practicing.

He hesitated as he wrestled with his conscience. He hadn't come this way with the intention of going on to Connie's farm, but he knew he should. He and Fannie had not parted on the best of terms the day before. She'd made an effort to come see him play ball. The least he could do in return was to watch the drill team that meant so much to her. It was a small olive branch but it was worth a try. The way things were going between them now, no one was going to believe they were courting seriously. He just hoped Fannie didn't run him off as soon as he poked his head into the barn.

Willy resisted slightly when Noah turned him away from home, but he was soon trotting along nicely. The rhythmic clatter of Willy's hooves on the pavement and the gentle creak and jingle of his harness were familiar sounds Noah had heard all his life. He could hear the birds in the trees along the river and the sound of the wind sighing through the branches. It was soothing to his troubled heart.

When a car roared around him and sped away, he spared a moment to pity the driver who was missing so much of God's beauty along this winding country road.

He turned into Connie's lane a mile and a half farther down the highway. White board fences lined both sides of the drive. On one side, golden Haflinger mares grazed peacefully while their frisky foals raced to the fence to gaze at Noah and whinny at the unfamiliar horse.

Half a dozen horses of assorted colors were tied to the hitching rail beside the barn. He tied Willy up beside them and walked into the riding arena.

Eight girls, including Fannie, were already mounted on matching Haflingers. Music blared from a speaker on the railing as the group cantered down the center of the arena by twos. At the far end, they split apart and circled back to their starting point, keeping close to the railing. He stood quietly and watched them work as they repeated the maneuver. He knew all of the girls except for two. They must belong to another church group.

"What do you think of them?"

He turned to see Connie had come in behind him. She moved up to the rail and leaned on it as he was doing. "The spacing between them needs to be tightened. Other than that, they make a pretty sight."

"Haflingers are so much more than pretty ponies. That's what I want people to see."

"If anyone can prove that point, Fannie can."

"She is throwing her heart into this. I would like to see her succeed for her own sake and not just for the sake of my farm."

The riders came halfway down the railings and turned in to form two circles in the center of the ring, all while maintaining the same speed. One of the horses sped up and bumped into the horse in front of it. Fannie immediately called a halt to the exercise. Noah could hear her talking softly to the inattentive rider. She didn't look or sound upset. It surprised him a little when she patted the girl's arm and said something to make her smile.

The group all walked back to where Connie was standing. There were several unhappy faces on the young riders.

"These things are going to happen," Fannie said. "No one should be upset. Better that they happen in practice and not during a show."

"Have they had a good warm-up?" Noah asked, noting how restless some of the horses were acting.

He couldn't tell if Fannie was happy to see him or not.

"We were late getting started so we went straight into our routine," she said.

"Giving them a warm-up will help both your horses and your riders settle in."

"He's right," Connie said. "Most of the horses have been in their stalls all day and they are eager to stretch their legs."

Fannie got off her mare. "All right, take them around a few times and let them work off some steam."

"Take them outside into the south paddock where there is more room to run," Connie suggested.

"Be back in ten minutes," Fannie said.

The riders happily complied and they were soon out the doors and galloping across the green field, except for one.

Susan Yoder had been stopped by George, who was lounging against the side of the barn with a broom in his hand.

"George, I need your help moving a stock tank," Connie called across the way.

"I can help you," Noah offered.

"Thanks, but I'd rather get George away from Susan. She's only fifteen and he's almost twenty. I'll be back when the girls come in." She walked away, leaving Fannie and Noah alone.

"Doesn't Trinket need a warm-up?" Noah stroked the mare's nose.

"We had a good gallop on the way over. What are you doing here?"

"You invited me, remember?"

"Barely, but I didn't expect you to interfere with our practice."

"What did you imagine I would be doing when you invited me? Ah, wait. Let me guess. I'm to sit quietly on the sideline and watch. Is it all right to say I'm sorry for that remark? I had my own mouth-before-brain moment. Does it sound familiar?"

She almost smiled. "Maybe. So, why did you come today?"

"Because it's what I would do if I was your boyfriend. Was your mother upset that I didn't take you home last night, or did you get in undetected?"

"She and *Daed* were still up when I got home. *Mamm* was disappointed, but when I told them you had tickets to a Cleveland Indians game, *Daed* said he completely understood. He said he had gone to a game once and has always wanted to go again."

"He should go to the spring training camp. I know several Amish families who time their vacations to do just that. The atmosphere then is not as rowdy as their regular-season games. It's much more suited to a family outing."

"I'll tell him. Did they win?"

"They did. It was an awesome game. It made the long drive there and back worthwhile."

"I'm glad that you got to go, then." She sounded as if she meant it.

"*Danki*. And I haven't thanked you for the brownies and cookies you brought us. Everyone on the team appreciated them, including me."

She peeked at him from beneath lowered lashes. "They didn't choke you?"

He chuckled. "Not a bit. They must have been one of your better efforts."

"They were."

At least she hadn't ordered him off the property. He relaxed and sought to draw her out. "I've seen a few horse drill teams before. Tell me what you are planning for your riders."

"We have covered the basic patterns. Straight line abreast, where horses and riders travel side by side. Then the nose-to-tail exercise, which lines the team up front to back."

"Along the rail?"

"It can be done along the rail, but we are working on a serpentine pattern around the arena. After that move, we line up. Everyone rides single file down the centerline, and when they reach the end of the arena, the first rider and horse turn left. The second rider and horse turn right, and so on. When our two lines meet at the centerline again, riders and their horses pair up and continue riding."

"Sounds complicated."

"It's easier to understand when you see us in action. I'm hoping to add some advanced maneuvers after our first show on Saturday."

"What would that be?"

"A ninety-degree turn. We will ride single file along

the rail and then riders turn their horses to the center of
the arena at the same time. We go from riding nose to
tail to riding abreast. When we reach the other side of the
arena, we turn in the opposite direction so we are riding
nose to tail again."

"A neat move, if you can pull it off."

"We can. We will."

"I like your confidence. There must be other moves."

"We haven't started practicing them yet, but once we
have the basics down we'll add a mini sweep."

"Explain that."

"We ride along the rail of the arena in an oblique pattern. Someone looking at it from the side would see each
horse's nose is in line with the knee of the rider in front
of it. What you saw us trying a while ago is called a pinwheel."

"I've seen that done."

"Susan and I hold our horses side by side in the center of the arena, facing opposite directions. We're called
the pivots. The other girls line up alongside us, facing the
same direction as the pivot rider. Then the whole formation rotates around us while we circle our horses in place."

"So, everyone has to ride a little faster than the rider to
her inside in order to keep the line straight."

"That's right. It sounds simple but it's pretty hard."

"I look forward to seeing you pull it off." He liked the
eager light in her eyes and the way they sparkled when
she was talking about her plans. It used to be that he had
to make her mad to enjoy the sparks in those lovely eyes,
but watching them shine with eagerness was every bit as
satisfying.

Fannie blushed at what she sensed was a compliment
from Noah. He seemed genuinely interested in what she

was doing. If they could find some common ground it would make it easier to keep up their pretend courtship. "The girls have been practicing very hard. We meet for two hours twice a week. Sylvia Knepp rides for almost an hour to get here."

"That is dedication. I think you mentioned they are all a part of your riding club."

"They are. Before this project we met a few times a month for trail rides and such. Sometimes we would set up jumps for fun. We've shared tips on how to teach our horses tricks." She put her arms around Trinket's neck. "We love horses."

"I can tell."

"Like you love baseball?" He must, if he was willing to date her just to keep playing.

He smiled and shook his head. "I don't think the two compare. Horses can love you back."

It was a good answer, and that smile of his warmed her inside. When he was being nice, she didn't have to pretend to like him.

"Have your parents changed their minds about sending you to Florida?"

"Betsy leaves next Monday unless *Mamm* sees that you and I don't suit."

"Then this fake courtship wasn't such an outlandish idea, after all. If we can keep it up, we'll both have what we want."

The warmth in her chest died away. It was all makebelieve. She was foolish to start liking him and wishing he'd smile at her more often. "I can keep it up if you can."

He looked away. "I reckon I will have to."

The riders returned from their warm-up and lined up beside Fannie. She needed to concentrate on these girls, not her infatuation with Noah. She gestured toward the young riders. "I want you to meet my team."

She started from left to right. "Susan Yoder is riding Carmen. Rose King is riding Goldenrod. Karen Ebersol has Freckles."

"She has white dots on her face and chest," Karen explained, patting the mare's neck.

"Does she have a short temper to match?" Noah cast a sly glance at Fannie.

Fannie ignored him.

"Oh, *nee*," Karen assured him. "She is as sweet as the day is long."

The next girl leaned forward, the only one with dark hair in the group of blue-eyed blondes. "I'm Sylvia Knepp and this is Maybelle. My father works in your family's furniture shop."

"I know him well. He's our master carver. My brother Samuel says he listens to the wood better than anyone he has ever met."

"What does that mean?" the girl beside Sylvia asked.

"This is Pamela Lantz," Fannie told Noah. "She is riding Comet."

He nodded to Pamela. "My brother says a skilled woodcarver must understand what the wood wants to become. He must listen to it. There is no point in trying to carve a ram's head on a piece that is better suited to the grace of a willow tree. The wood won't cooperate. *Gott* places gifts in all people and all things. We must respect that."

"Our gift is understanding horses," the girl on the end said. The last two riders were twins. He couldn't tell them apart, but he made a guess as to who they were.

"My brother Timothy speaks often of Abbie and Laura Lapp, the new girls in his class and how well they do in school, but which of you is Abbie?"

The one on the end held up her hand. "I'm Abbie, and I'm the oldest by ten minutes."

"By six minutes," Laura said with a scowl. "I'm better at math."

Noah noticed Fannie trying not to laugh at their sibling rivalry. "They are riding Copper and Morning Mist."

"Misty for short." Abbie patted her mount's neck.

"All of the horses except Trinket belong to Connie. She picked the ones with the closest coat colors for the most impressive effect."

"What do you call yourselves?" he asked.

"We didn't want a fancy or prideful name, so we are The Amish Girls," Susan told him with a grin.

He chuckled. "Very appropriate."

Fannie made a little shooing motion with her hands. "We have dawdled enough. Time to work on our pinwheels and on our double circles. Zoe, can you start the music?"

"I'll get it," George called from near the back door. He crossed to the speaker system, fumbled for a minute, and then stepped to the side as a rap song blared forth. The lyrics were disgusting. Sylvia covered her ears. Fannie and the other girls stared at George in shock.

"Turn that off!" Noah yelled.

George started laughing. "It's a harmless little joke. It's funny."

Noah strode to the machine and pulled the plug, silencing the music. "No, it isn't."

George had plugged his phone in to the speakers instead of the MP3 player.

Connie came rushing in. "If you would like to keep this job, George, you'd better start showing more respect to our guests."

"It was a joke, Connie. Don't get bent out of shape."

She unplugged his phone and tossed it to him. "You have work to do."

He slipped his phone in his hip pocket and ambled off.

Connie turned to Noah and Fannie. "I am so sorry. I'll make sure nothing like this happens again."

Fannie wished she could believe that, but George didn't seem to care if their performance benefited Connie. He wasn't putting any effort into saving the stable. He was just out to amuse himself. Maybe he wasn't worried about finding another job, but Fannie knew if Stroud Stables went under, her dream of continuing to work with horses would go under with it.

She couldn't let that happen.

Chapter Six

"We have been invited to visit the Erb family today."

Noah wasn't surprised by his mother's announcement at breakfast on Sunday. It was the off Sunday, a day without church services. Visiting family and friends was a normal way to spend the day, but he knew this wasn't a normal invitation. His mother and Fannie's mother were determined to provide their children with every opportunity to be together. When he and Fannie called off their courtship, he feared both mothers were going to be deeply disappointed.

Noah knew better than to try and get out of going, and he realized he didn't want to miss the outing. He wanted to find out how Fannie's first riding event had turned out. He was even looking forward to telling her about his game.

The morning progressed like any other, but not as fast as he would have liked. The milking had been done before breakfast by Noah, his father, Mark and Paul. The horses, cattle and pigs were fed after breakfast by Samuel and Joshua. The guinea hens, chickens and ducks were let out of their coops to forage and their eggs were gathered by Noah's mother and Rebecca. Joshua's wife, Mary, and Timothy's wife, Lillian, soon joined the other women in preparing a lunch to take along while Hannah and her dog, Bella, entertained the babies on a quilt on the dining room floor.

Noah checked on Ginger's hoof and washed both the family's buggies before harnessing the horses and hitching them up. It was almost noon before Luke and his wife, Emma, arrived. Once they did, the family made the short drive over to the Erb farm in three buggies.

Fannie's father was standing in front of the house. "Welcome, neighbors. We have set the picnic tables down by the creek. You know the way, Isaac," he said as he waved them through.

"Jump on the back, Ernest, unless your wife wants you to start jogging."

Ernest laughed and patted his ample belly. "She'd better not complain of my size, 'cause it's her good cooking that's done this to me."

Noah opened the door and moved Hannah to his lap to make room for Ernest. It was a tight fit but no one minded. Fannie's father soon had them all laughing at his jovial stories and jokes.

The buggy jolted over the rough pasture track for a quarter of a mile before Isaac pulled to a stop beneath the wide-spreading branches of a group of old river birch trees. A shallow creek flowed across a natural stone shelf formation before tumbling off the edge in a miniature waterfall barely a foot high. There were already two buggies parked in the shade.

Noah set Hannah on the ground and she raced away to join Fannie, Betsy and two other young women who were wading in the water with their dresses hiked above their knees. He could pick out the sound of Fannie's laughter from the others and he smiled. It was good to see her having fun.

He and his brothers carried the ice chests and hampers

to the picnic tables set up under the trees. The bishop and his wife were sitting on lawn chairs beside the creek below the falls. They had their fishing poles in the water. Noah's father and Ernest strolled over to join them.

Noah's mother took the hamper from his hand and turned to his cousins. "You boys run along and enjoy yourselves. The two girls with Fannie and Betsy are the bishop's nieces, Margret and Helen Stolfus. I'm sure Fannie will introduce you."

"We met them at the singing last week." Mark had his gaze fixed in their direction, prompting Noah to wonder which young woman had caught his fancy. Noah and his cousins walked casually to the water's edge.

"Is the water cold?" Noah asked when Fannie caught sight of him.

"*Nee*, it's *wunderbar*." She waded toward him with an ornery grin on her face. She bent low and scooped a handful of water, sending it spraying in an arch toward him. Knowing Fannie, he had quickly moved behind his cousins. Mark and Paul were splattered across their shirtfronts.

Margret and Helen chided her for her mischievous behavior, but Fannie didn't look chastised as she grinned at him.

Noah's cousins took off their shoes and rolled up their pants legs. They were soon exploring the creek with the young women. Paul began his auctioneer call, to the amusement of everyone, as he sold them fish swimming in the stream left and right. Noah sat on the grassy bank and watched. Fannie came over and sat beside him, keeping her bare toes in the water.

"Do either of them catch your fancy?" she asked.

He pretended to look the young women over carefully. "It's hard to tell at first glance. What about you? Mark and Paul are both single, although Mark has a girlfriend back home."

"They seem like nice fellows, but I'm not looking for a man to marry."

"Yet. You aren't looking for a man to marry yet." He'd never noticed what pretty feet she had, small and neat, with dainty toes pink from the cold water. Several tiny fish were investigating them, as well.

"I might wed someday, but I see no point in rushing into something that's lifelong. Do you see the minnows nibbling on my toes? That tickles." She pulled her feet out of the water and tucked them under her hem.

"Fannie, on Sunday night, just before you shut the door in my face, you said something I can't stop thinking about."

"Did I?"

"You said if you had to list my sins, it would take all night. Have I somehow offended you greatly? If I have, I'm truly sorry."

"You were never as bad as some of the boys who teased me. You and I got along so well when we were little, but when we went to school, you stopped being my friend and I didn't have any others."

"Is that why you were always so angry?"

"I come by my bad temper naturally but it has nothing to do with the color of my hair."

"So you say. I'm dying to know how your first drill team competition went yesterday."

She smiled brightly. "Are you?"

"I asked, didn't I?"

She half turned toward him. "You should have seen us. The horses were awesome. Abbie had some trouble keeping Misty in step during the pinwheel, but otherwise the girls did a great job. We took second place."

"Second out of two entries?" he asked to goad her.

"Second out of six entries." She bowed her head slightly, not rising to his baiting.

"Impressive."

"What about you? Did you win your game?"

"It was close, but we pulled it out. Walter hit a homer that brought in the two winning runs."

"I'm glad you won."

"Are you?" He leaned forward to swirl his fingers in the water.

"I said so, didn't I?"

"You also said the water was *wunderbar*." He flicked a few drops at her face.

She giggled and wiped her cheek on her sleeve. "'*Wunderbar* refreshing' is what I meant."

"I thought so." He leaned back on his hands as he grinned at her. Fannie was good company when she wasn't hurling insults at him. How long would it last?

Fannie glanced away from Noah's smiling face. If only he wasn't so good-looking and sweet. When he smiled at her, she wanted to smile back and bask in his warmth. She kept her eyes focused on the tiny fish darting back and forth in the clear water, in case something of what she was feeling showed in her face. The last thing she needed was to start caring for Noah beyond their friendship.

Wouldn't that be a just reward for concocting their fake courtship? To fall for the fellow who wouldn't be able to get rid of her fast enough come August.

Sitting here enjoying his company wasn't solving anything. She got to her feet. "I should help get the meal on. I see the bishop has reeled in his line. I think that means he's ready to eat."

"Looks to me like he's coming our way." Noah rose to his feet beside Fannie as the bishop approached.

"Good afternoon, Brother Noah, Sister Fannie. The Lord has given us a fine day to enjoy our fellowship."

"Indeed He has," Noah agreed.

"Noah, I would speak with Fannie alone for a few moments, if you don't mind."

Her heart dropped to her knees. Had he somehow learned of their agreement?

"Of course," Noah said, and cleared his throat. He walked away, but glanced back once, his eyes filled with concern.

Fannie gripped her fingers together. "What did you wish to speak to me about, Bishop Beachy?"

"I understand you have formed a riding group with some of the younger girls in our congregation and you are their leader."

"That's true."

"I watched your performance at the fairgrounds yesterday. I wasn't happy to hear the *Englisch* music being played, or to see you girls putting yourselves into the public eye in such a bold way, but as none of you are baptized members of our faith, I won't object to that."

Something in his voice told her he wasn't finished. "But you are objecting to something."

"I'm told you practice at the home of an *Englisch* woman."

At least this wasn't about her courtship. "We do. Connie Stroud is her name. She is allowing the girls to ride her Haflinger horses."

"I have already spoken to your father about this, because I was hoping that he would be able to help, but he says he cannot. Several parents have come to me with concerns."

"What kind of concerns?"

"They feel their daughters are not being adequately

supervised. They believe having the girls exposed to *Englisch* ways and music is not good for them."

"What are you saying?"

"Someone other than you must be the group leader. You are young and unmarried. Unless you can find an Amish adult, preferably a married man, to oversee this group, these parents are going to remove their children from it."

She couldn't believe this. "But we have worked so hard."

"Fannie, you can't ask our parents to send their *kinder* to a place that makes them uncomfortable. I won't change my mind about this. It is in the best interest of all our members to know our children are looked after properly."

When he walked away, Fannie sat down on the creek bank and put her head in her hands. Who could she ask? Who would be willing to devote so much time to their project if her own father couldn't?

Noah waited until the bishop was out of earshot before he approached Fannie again. She looked pale and shaken. How much trouble were they in?

He took her hand and pulled her gently in the direction of a thick stand of willows where they would be out of sight. A large fallen log lay in a clump of grass a few feet from the water's edge. Noah led Fannie to it and sat down.

"What did the bishop have to say?"

"That I may have to disband my riding group."

"So this wasn't about us? You and me? That's a relief."

"*Nee*, it isn't about you at all." She jerked her hand from his. "It's about me letting my friends down."

"Don't get angry. Tell me what he said."

"Some of the parents have complained that the girls aren't being properly chaperoned at Connie's place."

"That's ridiculous." The moment he uttered the words he recalled the way George had pressed his attentions on

Susan and played such ugly music. He shouldn't have been surprised that there were objections. "What are you going to do?"

"Whatever I have to do. I've come too far to give up now. I can't let Connie down."

"The bishop didn't say you had to stop, only that you and the girls needed a chaperone."

"Preferably a married man."

"Then that's what you will do. I'm sure someone will help."

"Maybe."

"Don't give up before you have tried to find someone. Have faith. If you don't mind me asking, why are you so beholden to Connie? What has she done to earn such loyalty? Besides selling you that pretty mare."

Fannie stared at the creek without answering him. He waited quietly, hoping she would trust him enough to share what was clearly a deeply personal story.

She tossed a piece of bark from the log into the creek and watched it swirl away. "A couple of months after my seventeenth birthday, I went to stay with my cousin over by Walnut Grove. Maddy and I were the same age and as close as sisters. We got along so well because we were so much alike."

"She had the same red hair and hot temper?"

Fannie smiled sadly. "Exactly. We could quarrel one minute like a pair of spitting cats and be laughing and hugging the next."

"She sounds like a *wunderbar goot* friend."

"She was." Fannie closed her eyes.

"Was?" he prompted, guessing the answer.

"She died."

"I'm sorry." The Amish didn't often speak of the dead so he didn't press for more details.

"It was *Gott*'s will. Maddy was determined to try everything during her *rumspringa*." Fannie grew quiet and pensive, staring into the water.

"By *everything*, I take it you mean things you didn't want to try. Drinking? Drugs?" She nodded yes to each.

He stripped the leaves from a willow branch and let them fall into the water. "*Rumspringa* can be a difficult time for some. My brother Luke got into drugs during his running-around time. It took prison and the mercy of *Gott* to bring him to his senses, but not until my family had suffered greatly. My mother said it was *Gott*'s test of our faith in Him."

"I remember how upset your mother was. I can't count the number of times I saw her crying in my mother's arms."

He looked at Fannie in surprise. "I didn't realize that. She always seemed so strong to me. So unwavering in her faith."

"My father says strength isn't about standing up to adversity with faith as a shield. It's about being brought painfully low but rising again, each and every time, with renewed faith in *Gott*'s plan for our eternal salvation. Our reward is not on this Earth."

"Wise words."

She nodded. "Maddy had a boyfriend. An Amish fellow from a neighboring town who often borrowed a car. At night, Albert would stop at the end of the lane and honk his horn, the signal for us to slip out and go riding around. We went to dances and movies. Sometimes we didn't come home until dawn."

"That's not unusual. I've come in at first light myself, once in a while. You still haven't told me how Connie fits in all this."

"The county fair was on and I wanted to go. Maddy thought it would be a dull time, but she went with me because her boyfriend was busy. Connie was at the fair showing several of her stallions. My father had purchased Trinket for me a few months earlier, so Connie and I already knew each other. She invited us to stop by the horse barn that evening and have supper with her and Zoe in their camper. When we arrived, we could hear loud music from a party going on at the other end of the barn. Connie was busy cooking, but I noticed one of her horses was kicking at his belly."

"Not a good sign for any horse. Colic?"

Fannie nodded. "Maddy wandered down to the party as Connie and I took a closer look at the horse. Maddy came back all excited and said we had to go. Security was making the noisemakers leave. She knew the kids at the party and they were taking a van to another friend's house. I knew Connie would be busy treating her horse, so I started to go with Maddy. Connie stopped me. She said the young men in the group had been drinking heavily all evening and it wasn't safe to go with them. Maddy went anyway."

"You didn't?"

"I almost did, but Connie said her horse needed to be walked and she didn't want to leave Zoe alone in the camper at night, so I stayed. Maddy and her friends were all killed that night when the drunk driver tried to beat a train at the crossing. I would have died, too, if Connie hadn't stopped me."

"*Gott* was great and merciful to place her there, but you chose to stay and help someone in need."

"That's what Connie says."

"I understand now why you feel you must repay her kindness." He hesitated a moment, but decided to share his story, too.

"Walter is the catcher on our team. He dreams of playing major-league ball. And he works toward that goal every chance he gets. The night we were fighting a barn fire over at Silas Mast's place, I got into a tight spot. My coat somehow got hooked and I couldn't get loose. A burning beam was about to come down where I was standing. I couldn't get out of the way. Walter saw what was happening. He pulled his gloves off to free my coat just as the beam fell. He knocked it aside with his bare hands. His dreams of a ball career could have ended then and there. Thankfully, his burns were only minor."

"Is that why you're determined to get your team into the state tournament?"

"It's a big part of my reason. He's an excellent player and he deserves to be seen by the pro scouts that will be at the state invitational. And I like to play ball, too. It will be a win-win if we get there." He decided not to share his own desire to pitch in front of pro ball scouts. For some reason, it didn't seem to be the right time.

"I pray you succeed in helping Walter."

"As I pray you succeed in helping Connie."

"And I'm not sure how I'm going to do that if we have to give up our drill team."

"Surely one of the parents will take over. The girls know how important this is to you."

"This is the busiest time of year for our families. I'm not sure any of them will think they have the time to spare. I am almost ashamed to ask. Connie isn't one of us."

"Can't you practice somewhere besides her farm?"

"If I can't find someone to lead us, I'm not sure what the point will be. I doubt the parents who went to the bishop will allow their girls to travel to other fairs and shows with only Connie and me to chaperone them. I simply have to find someone."

"You will," he said to encourage her. "I have faith in you."

"I hope it isn't misplaced."

"Look on the bright side. The bishop didn't take us to task for faking our courtship."

A fleeting smile brightened her face for a moment. "True, but if he had seen the look of panic in your eyes, the cat would have been out of the bag for sure."

He swiped his hand across his brow. "I felt like a five-year-old getting caught with my hand in the cookie jar."

She laughed out loud. "I imagine you got caught doing something sly almost as much as I did."

"That's the bare truth. Hey, do you remember the time your mother caught us throwing tomatoes against the back of your house?"

"You were throwing them. I was watching."

"You threw some. Fess up."

"Nary a one against the house. I simply fetched them from the garden and handed them to you."

"If I remember correctly, you started throwing them at me. What made you so mad?"

"You said I couldn't hit the house because I threw like a girl. I wanted you to take that back, so I showed you exactly how hard I could throw."

He laughed. "We had some good times in our younger days."

"We did." She smiled and looked down, a pretty blush making pink patches on her cheeks.

When they weren't squabbling, Noah was surprised at how easy it was to talk to Fannie. Her story about her cousin moved him deeply. He understood how strong the bonds of friendship could be, even with an outsider. A week ago he wouldn't have believed it was possible, but he had come to like Fannie a lot. Did she feel the same?

"Sometimes I forget I'm not really courting you."

He held his breath, waiting for her response.

She rose to her feet but she wouldn't look at him. "I always remember it isn't real. Don't worry. Before the end of the summer you will be free again."

He reached for her hand. "Fannie—"

She brushed at the backside of her skirt and started walking. "We should get back to the others. It's getting late. We want our folks to think we slipped away for some time together, but we don't want them to come looking for us."

He had his answer. Fannie wasn't willing to turn their game into the real thing. He should accept that.

But he didn't want to.

Keep walking. Don't look back. Don't ask him if he is being serious. I know he is only kidding. He'll turn it into a joke and I'll start crying.

It was only because her emotions were already raw from recounting a painful time in her life. She wouldn't cry because she liked him far more than she should.

As she came out of the trees, Fannie saw the families were gathered at the tables, waiting for the bishop to lead them in a blessing. A wave of heat crept up her face when she realized everyone was looking her way.

She took a deep breath and kept moving. Were her parents convinced that she and Noah were serious about each other? Convinced enough to take Betsy to the bus station tomorrow? She prayed they were, but realized it might have all been for nothing if she couldn't convince someone to become the team's chaperone.

She took a seat beside her sister at the end of one table. "What's wrong?" Betsy asked.

"Nothing."

"Did you and Noah have your first fight?"

"We've had more than one already."

Betsy folded her hands together. "Don't tell *Mamm* until after I leave tomorrow, please."

"I won't. It's the bishop who has dampened my mood."

"What's he done?"

"He told me I have to give up my drill team if I can't find an adult to chaperone us. Can you think of anyone who might do it?"

"*Daed* might."

"The bishop already asked him and he said no."

"Maybe Timothy Bowman would. There isn't any school over the summer. He likes helping kids."

Fannie looked down the table toward the newlyweds. "*Nee*, for I heard *Mamm* say they'll be leaving on their wedding trip after the school frolic."

"Okay, I'm out of ideas. Maybe it's for the best. It will give you more time to spend with Noah."

That was exactly what she didn't need. It was becoming more difficult to hide how much she liked him. It was easier to pretend she didn't and that she didn't care what he thought of her.

Betsy leaned in close. "Is he a good kisser? I've always suspected he would be."

"That's none of your business."

"Not good, then. Too bad. Maybe he'll get better with practice. Hiram has improved with my coaching."

"Betsy, stop talking and eat your lunch before I pour a glass of this lemonade over your head."

Betsy giggled. "What would your beau think of such poor behavior?"

Fannie glanced down the table and saw Noah watching her. "He'd be glad it wasn't his head."

Chapter Seven

"**Y**ou haven't said how things are going between you and Fannie. Someone told me the two of you aren't getting along." Noah's mother tried to sound casually interested, but he knew better. She was dying to know every detail of what had taken place while he and Fannie had been out of sight at the picnic the day before. She glanced briefly in his direction and then resumed making sandwiches at the kitchen counter.

"Who said such a thing?" he asked.

"Someone. Is that true?"

"You shouldn't listen to gossip." He took the plate she handed him. It held a thick turkey sandwich and pickle spears. He was on his way to relieve his brother Samuel on the cultivator. The forecast promised rain and they were only half-done weeding the cornfields.

"It wasn't gossip. I'm just curious about the two of you."

"You haven't been curious about the other girls I've dated in the past."

"They haven't been the daughter of my dear friend. I was curious about them, I just didn't show it."

"Fannie and I are getting to know each other. It's too

soon to tell if we'll make a *goot* match. She's got a short temper—that's one drawback in her character."

His mother turned back to the counter to prepare sandwiches for the rest of the men who would be in soon. "That's just her young age. Her father has spoiled her and let her run wild too much. She will mature into a fine, demure woman, I'm sure of it."

"Fannie and I are the same age, but you may be right. We're too young to think about settling down. I think I should call it off with her."

"I didn't say that, and it's past time you settled down. Your father and I have agreed you can continue with your ball playing this summer as Fannie and her family don't seem to mind, but your *rumspringa* has gone on long enough."

Of course he couldn't get out of this so easily.

"What makes you believe Fannie will make me a good wife? Because you and her mother are best friends?"

She turned to smile at him. "Because you and Fannie have been friends for ages. Even as babies you played well together."

"I don't remember being friends with her. I remember squabbles and her kicking my shin a time or two."

"You teased each other mercilessly as *kinder*, that's true, but a boy doesn't tease a girl he dislikes."

"And a man doesn't court a girl because he's seeking a friend. He courts her because he's searching for a woman to fall in love with."

"To be in *lieb* is a wonderful, romantic thing, but love changes over time. Friendship, true friendship, endures. I love your father, but he is my best friend first."

She turned back to the stove. "Besides, I see the way you and Fannie watch each other. Your eyes are always seeking her."

He was surprised to realize she was right. He was always looking for Fannie these days. Was she out riding? Was she shopping at his mother's store or working with her father's horses? Was she avoiding him? "She is an unusual person. I'm never sure what she'll do next."

"Her mother tells me she has settled down and is helping with the household chores much more readily that she used to. I would say that is a *goot* sign."

"Don't read too much into that, *Mamm*."

"If you say so. Your brother Luke tells me you have been trying to find a chaperone for Fannie's riding club."

"Without any success. I hope she has found someone. She has her heart set on preforming at the Horse Expo next month to help her friend showcase her Haflinger horses. I never asked, but how do you feel about Fannie's project?"

"The girls are not baptized. It isn't a very modest undertaking, but I have no objection to it. Children should have fun while they can. Adulthood comes all too quickly and childish things must be put aside."

"I'm glad you don't object."

"What does Fannie think of your ball playing?"

"She doesn't understand the game so she doesn't have an opinion one way or the other. She knows it's important to me, just as I know her riding is important to her."

"She will soon find other things that are more important, like having children and making a home for her family."

He tried to picture Fannie in a domestic role, but he couldn't see it. That opinion he kept to himself. His mother wanted to believe they were made for each other and he didn't want to shatter her hopes. At least not yet.

Shame rose in his chest as he realized he would have to one day—but not today.

"Have you heard when Timothy and Lillian are leaving on their wedding trip?" he asked, to change the subject.

"They have decided to postpone it until the spring."

"Any reason?"

"Timothy says they want to spend more time with her family and he knows your father could use his help in the furniture shop this summer, since you haven't been available."

He pushed back his chair and swallowed the last bite of his sandwich. "Which is another way of telling me I'm slacking on my work. I'll do better. I don't have to see Fannie as much as I have been."

"That was not my meaning and you know it."

He laughed and kissed her cheek. "If Fannie were more like you, I'd marry her in a heartbeat."

She gently pushed him away. "Get out of here and stop trying to flatter me. If she is the one *Gott* has chosen for you, I pity her."

On the following Thursday, Noah drove his buggy to Connie's farm hoping that Fannie had been able to find someone to supervise her group. She was alone in the riding arena, taking a Haflinger gelding over a set of low jumps set up along the perimeter. When she cleared the last jump, she turned toward Noah and rode over.

He reached over the railing to pat the horse's neck. "I don't see the others, so I take it you haven't had any success in finding a chaperone."

"I haven't. Everyone I have talked to is either busy or they don't approve of what we are doing. What harm is there in demonstrating our riding skills?" She sounded so dejected. It wasn't like Fannie to admit defeat.

"I imagine some people see it as prideful."

"It isn't about us. It's about the horses."

"It's about Connie's horses and she is an outsider. Distrust of outsiders runs deep for many Amish. I'm sure some people believe she is exploiting their children for her own gain."

She scowled at him. "Whose side are you on?"

"I'm on your side, but I can see both sides. I would do it if the bishop agreed."

Her face brightened. "You would?"

"Unfortunately, he said it wouldn't be proper, as I'm a single fellow."

"I'm grateful that you asked. What's the use? I might as well see if Connie can get some of her money back for the entry fees she had to pay. I feel like such a failure."

"You can't take the whole blame upon yourself. Perhaps this is *Gott*'s will for Connie."

"I know, but it makes me angry."

"Does being angry at *Gott* help?"

She had the grace to look ashamed. "*Nee*, it does not."

"Then don't let bitterness into your heart. It's hard to weed out when it takes hold."

"I was so sure I could do this."

"Did you get your sister off to Florida?"

"We did, and I miss her already. Which is funny because we were always fighting."

"It was the same with me when my brothers moved out. Now that I don't have to share a room with anyone, it's lonely at times. Timothy and I became a lot closer when it was just the two of us."

"Where are he and Lillian going for their wedding trip?"

"They were going to stay with her folks in Wisconsin, but they have decided to postpone the trip until the spring."

He suddenly straightened. "Have you asked Timothy and Lillian if they would chaperone your group?"

"*Nee*, I didn't think they would be here."

"They're the perfect couple to do this. They're married and respected teachers. No one could object to their supervision."

"Let's go ask them."

"Now?"

"Have you got something better to do?"

"I don't, but aren't you supposed to be exercising Connie's horses?"

"I have one more to ride after I'm done with Benny, but why don't I saddle the other one for you and we'll exercise them by riding to Timothy's place. Connie won't mind if we can secure a chaperone."

Noah had ridden astride many times as a boy, but it had been a while. "I wish Timothy hadn't given up his cell phone. It would have been so much easier to call him. Which horse is it?"

"Joker. He's in stall number six. Do you think Timothy might agree? I'm afraid to hope."

"Never be afraid to hope. First Corinthians, chapter thirteen—'and now abideth faith, hope, charity, these three…'"

"'But the greatest of these is charity,'" she finished, and he smiled.

Fannie found herself smiling back at Noah. He was willing to help her and her team. He genuinely seemed to care about her efforts to help Connie. If he had been trying to endear himself to her, he couldn't have gone about it in a better way. It felt wonderful to have his support.

Ten minutes later, they were cantering along the edge of the river toward the covered bridge at Bowmans Crossing. Timothy and Lillian lived on the other side of the ridge, beyond the river. Both horses were eager to run, but Noah held his mount beside Fannie's mare.

They passed by his house before they reached the bridge. His mother was in her garden. She raised a hand and called a cheerful greeting. Fannie waved back.

"It makes me feel rotten," Noah said under his breath.

"What does?"

"*Mamm* is so happy we are dating. I'm sure going to hate to tell her we've broken up when the time comes."

"I know what you mean. My mother is happy about us, too."

Fannie slowed her mount to a walk as they entered the covered bridge, alert for oncoming traffic. Cars sometimes sped through without slowing. Once they were on the other side, Fannie urged her horse to a faster pace, eager to find out if Timothy would become their manager. The road curved around the hillside where the school was located and then zigzagged back and forth up a steep ridge through the dense woods.

At the top of the ridge, Fannie pulled her horse to a stop. "Let's rest them a minute. I love this spot."

A natural clearing off to one side of the road presented a breathtaking view through a break in the trees. The farmland spread out below was a colorful patchwork of fields and woodlands laid out like a giant crazy quilt. The clearing also provided a secluded spot for young couples, Amish and English, looking to be alone.

She glanced at Noah. Had he come here with any of the girls he'd dated before? She couldn't bring herself to ask.

He swung out of the saddle, and walked back and forth. "My legs aren't used to straddling a horse. I should have driven my buggy and tied these horses on behind. It would have been the same amount of exercise for them."

"Take a hot bath tonight, that will help any sore muscles. Connie likes her mature horses to be ridden three or four times a week. It helps them behave well for her riding classes. If someone comes looking to buy a horse, she can let them ride with confidence, knowing the horse won't buck or balk."

"Makes sense, but that's a lot of horseback riding each week. How many does she have?"

"Forty, but only twenty-five of them are for sale."

"Forty? That's a lot of hay and oats as well as saddle blisters. I can see why she needs to broaden her market."

"The breed is gaining in popularity. We just need to show more people what they can do."

"I admit I've always thought of them as little draft horses."

"That's what they were bred for in Europe. They came from the mountainous areas of Austria and northern Italy. A stallion known as 249 Folie was born in 1874. He is considered the foundation sire. Modern Haflingers can trace their lineage back to Folie through one of seven bloodlines."

"You really are taken with the breed, aren't you?"

"Because they try hard to do whatever we ask of them."

He mounted Joker again. "Let's hope Timothy can save The Amish Girls team." He groaned as he swung up into the saddle. "I haven't ridden astride in ages. I'm rusty."

"You ride well."

"The horse has a smooth gait."

"It's a breed characteristic. They are gentle and willing to please. They make wonderful pets for children."

"Will your father be raising them instead of Standardbreds anytime soon?" he asked with a grin.

She laughed. "I doubt it. He loves a high stepper as much as you do."

"I like it when you laugh."

She blushed. "It's not like it's a rare thing."

"Rare enough. You worry too much."

"I know that to worry is to doubt *Gott*'s mercy and love, but I can't help it. Don't you worry that you will lose a game or not be invited to the state tournament?"

"I play my best, and if it is *Gott*'s will that we lose, I accept that."

"When I lose I think it's because I didn't try hard enough."

"You'll be more content if you learn to let go of your fear of failure."

"I'm not afraid of failing."

"Aren't you?"

Maybe she was afraid of failing, but she was more afraid of disappointing her friend. She glanced at him from the corner of her eye. "Why did you come with me today?"

"Why did you ask me?"

"Timothy is your brother."

"Lillian is your friend. You didn't need me to come along. Maybe you like my company," he suggested.

"You can be fun sometimes. When you are being nice."

"A compliment from *karotte oben*. Things really have changed."

"I'm perfectly willing to scold you if you feel you need it."

"*Nee*, I prefer you this way."

"What way is that?"

"Not throwing things at me or kicking my shins."

She tipped her head. "Some of those were accidents, some you deserved. What are you going to do when baseball season is over?" she asked to change the subject.

"I'm not sure." He grew somber. "A lot depends on if we make it into the tournament."

"How so?"

He hesitated for a long moment. "My coach, the guys on my team, they tell me I'm really good. Good enough to play professional ball."

She couldn't have been more surprised if he'd said he

wanted to fly airplanes. "Are you considering that? I confess I never imagined you living a worldly life. You seem so happy among us."

"*Gott* has given me a mighty gift. If I'm to use it to honor Him, I don't see how I can accomplish that here."

"'Neither do men light a candle and put it under a bushel, but on a candlestick, and it giveth light unto all that are in the house.' Matthew 5:15." She understood his dilemma.

"Exactly. I'm not like Luke was when he left. He hated all things Amish, hated the restrictions and rules. I see their purpose. I love my family and they would be disappointed if I left, but perhaps that is *Gott*'s plan for me. I will know by the end of the tournament."

"How?"

"If I get an offer from a professional scout, then I will know my place is elsewhere."

"Does your family know this?"

"I'm not ready to tell them."

"No wonder you agreed to my proposal. I had no idea how important playing ball is to you."

He chuckled. "Who would have thought that you and your Haflingers would ride to my rescue? The Lord moves in mysterious ways. Let's go see if Timothy can ride to the rescue of The Amish Girls."

They headed down the winding road on the far side of the ridge. Fannie had plenty of time to think about the confidence Noah had shared with her.

It had never entered her mind that he would leave the community. The thought of just how much she would miss him was sobering. And all the more reason to keep a tight rein on her feelings for him.

It didn't take them long to reach Timothy's home. They found the newlyweds together in the garden.

"Noah, this is a surprise." Timothy stopped working and leaned on his hoe.

"A pleasant one," Lillian said, rising to her feet with her apron full of new potatoes. "Come inside. I have a fresh pot of coffee on the stove."

"Have you bought yourself a new pony?" Timothy asked, taking the reins as Noah stepped down.

"Just exercising this one for a friend. You own a Haflinger, don't you, Lillian?" Noah asked.

"I do. Goldie is a wonderful cart horse. What can we do for the two of you?"

Fannie followed Lillian into the house. "I have something to ask you and your husband."

"Let's sit. I'll get the coffee." Lillian dumped her load of potatoes in the sink and washed her hands before getting out mugs.

When everyone had a cup, Fannie glanced from Lillian to Timothy. "My riding club has been preparing a drill team program at Connie Stroud's horse farm."

"Noah has told us the bishop won't let you continue there," Lillian said.

"Not unless we can find someone to chaperone us. I was wondering if you might take on the task, Timothy?"

"Me? I don't know anything about equine drill teams."

Noah leaned forward. "You don't have to. Fannie can manage the team. What she needs is someone respectable to make sure the girls are not unduly influenced by their *Englisch* surroundings."

"Have there been undue influences?" Timothy asked.

"No," Fannie said quickly.

"Yes," Noah said a second later.

Fannie took a deep breath and nodded. "Some of the girls were made uncomfortable by the attention of Connie's hired man and his music."

"Then the bishop was wise in his decision," Lillian said softly.

"Connie has said it won't happen again," Fannie stressed.

"She may mean well, but few *Englisch* understand our ways well enough to judge what is acceptable and what isn't." Timothy took a sip of his coffee.

"How much time would this involve?" Lillian asked.

"Four hours a week and travel to several local shows before we go to the Horse Expo next month."

Timothy scratched the new beard darkening his cheeks. "That's a big commitment, Fannie."

"I know it is." She folded her hands on the table and waited. If God wanted her plan to continue, He would move Timothy to accept. Noah had told her to have faith and she was trying.

"I'll help all I can," Noah said. "I can take care of chores here for you, if need be."

Lillian took a sip of her coffee and put her cup down. "I would be interested in watching the girls from our school perform."

Timothy nodded slowly. "I reckon it might be considered an educational opportunity for them. Horses supply our transportation and help us till our fields. Everyone should have an understanding of how to train and handle them."

"The girls learn cooperation, not just between horse and rider, but between each other. It takes practice and commitment. To do it well takes a team effort." Noah glanced at Fannie, and she smiled her thanks.

"Kind of like baseball," Timothy said.

"Kind of," Fannie agreed.

"If it is educational and does not conflict with our teach-

ings, I believe it to be a worthwhile project." Timothy sat
back and winked at his wife.

"Then you'll do it?" Fannie pressed her palms together.

"*Ja*, we will do it." He reached for his wife's hand across
the table.

"In fact, we were hoping to be asked," Lillian said with
a smile. "I belonged to a riding club when I was a girl. I
made some lifelong friends and wonderful memories."

"I must speak to the bishop first, but I'm sure he won't
object. When do we start?" Timothy looked to Fannie.

"Tuesday at six o'clock in Connie Stroud's riding arena."

Timothy nodded. "We will see you there."

Noah stood and held out his hand. "*Danki, bruder.* You
have made a whole gaggle of girls happy."

"*Ja, danki*, Timothy. This is *wunderbar.* I can't wait
to tell everyone." Fannie jumped to her feet, too, almost
knocking over her mug in her haste. Lillian caught it before the contents spilled into Noah's lap.

Feeling foolish, but still excited, Fannie left the house.
Outside, she spun in a circle and threw her arms around
Noah. "I'm so happy!"

He slipped his arms around her waist. "I'm happy that
you're happy."

"Are you?" She stared into his eyes, amazed at the way
they darkened.

"I said so, didn't I?" Slowly, he bent his head toward
her, and she knew he was going to kiss her.

Chapter Eight

Noah waited, expecting Fannie to turn away from him, but she didn't. He should stop, but he wanted to taste her sweet lips, feel them pressed against his. The strength of those desires shook him to his core. Unsure of her reaction, he lifted her chin with his hand. "I would like to kiss you, Fannie."

"Then why are you talking?" She closed her eyes.

Because he was a fool and because he didn't want to take advantage of her innocence. She was excited that her drill team could continue. He was only her pretend beau. She deserved a real one. Someone who was sure of his place in her life. God had not yet shown Noah if he belonged in the Amish world or the outside world. Until that changed, he didn't have the right to kiss her. "I don't think this is the time or place."

She stepped back, a hurt expression filling her eyes. "Let me know when you think the right time might be and I'll see if I'm busy or not."

Sweeping around him, she headed to her horse.

"Fannie, let me explain."

She didn't slow down. Mounting her horse, she slipped

Joker's reins loose and took off at a gallop with both horses, leaving Noah behind.

He heard the door of Timothy's house open and his brother came out. "I couldn't help noticing Fannie looked out of sorts just now. Is something amiss between you?"

"She drives me *narrisch*." This whole masquerade was insane. It was tying him up in knots. Did she like him or not? One minute he was sure she did. The next minute she was furious with him and he didn't understand why.

"My wife can drive me crazy, too. *Gott* designed women that way. It keeps us men humble."

"The moment something isn't going right, Fannie's temper takes over and she flies off the handle instead of listening to reason."

"Noah, I've seen you gentle a skittish filly that no one could handle. It took time and effort, but you never gave up. Now Ginger is the sweetest horse on the farm and the one *Daed* trusts to take *Mamm* where she needs to go. You must put some of that effort into understanding Fannie."

"Horses are different than people."

"Are they? Don't we respond to patience and kindness? Don't we want someone to understand our fears, to reward us when we have done well? The biggest mistake you can make in a relationship is to guess at what the other person is feeling. You have to ask and you have to listen. Honesty is the only way two people can live their lives together in harmony."

Honesty was something sorely lacking in his relationship with Fannie. "I'll have a talk with her when she cools down."

"*Goot.* Can I give you a lift home?"

"Can you take me to the Stroud farm? Willy is there."

"Sure. If we hurry, maybe we can reach the farm before Fannie leaves."

"No need to rush. I think it's going to be a while before her temper cools."

"What did you say to her?"

"The same thing I always seem to say to her. The wrong thing."

"I thought Noah's team has a home game at the fire station today. Aren't you going to go watch him?" Fannie's mother asked on Saturday afternoon, as she washed a strainer full of fresh beets from the garden.

Not if I can avoid it.

"I want to finish my chores. Are there more clothespins? I need some to hang out this last load of laundry." Fannie put the heavy hamper full of damp dresses and pants on the kitchen table.

"There are some in a package on the shelf above the washer."

"I just missed seeing them. *Danki.*"

"I can hang those out. Go watch Noah's game. I'm sure his whole family will be there. All the men say he's a *wunderbar* pitcher, as good as the *Englisch* professional players."

"I've heard that." She wasn't in any hurry to face Noah. First he'd said he wanted to kiss her, and then he said it wasn't the right time. Her eagerness for his kiss had to be what changed his mind. He'd been repulsed by her lack of modesty.

She had certainly made a fool of herself. Standing with her eyes closed waiting for his kiss like a dope. He must have been laughing at her the whole time. In spite of telling herself not to fall for him, she had anyway.

"I'm sure Noah is modest about his talent, as any *goot* Amish man should be."

Noah had his finer points. Fannie had to admit that.

"When he pitched a no-hitter, he said it was because his team did a great job fielding the ball and kept the other team from getting on base."

"I'm glad to hear that. Go to his game. I can hang out the laundry when I'm done with this."

"He'll play for nine innings, there's no rush. I'll hang these and wash the kitchen floor and then I'll go. I promised you I'd be more help around the house and I meant it."

"I admit I'm surprised at how much help you have been, child. Your father says you aren't neglecting your barn chores, either."

Fannie picked up the hamper. "Taking care of the horses isn't a chore in my book, but I don't think I realized how hard you and Betsy work."

Glancing over her shoulder, her mother smiled. "Taking care of my home and my family is not a chore in my eyes. It's a privilege to serve the Lord thus, for these are His greatest gifts to me."

"I never looked at it that way." Fannie always hated being inside when a beautiful day outdoors begged her to take one of the horses for a gallop across the fields. She assumed her mother had given up such pleasures for the drudgery of being a wife because it was expected. Was she truly happy in her role?

The front door opened and Fannie's father rushed in. "Fannie, Willow has gone into labor. I knew you'd want to be with her until she gives birth."

Fannie's pulse surged. She had been with Willow's mother when she was born and had helped raise the beautiful Standardbred mare. This was Willow's first foal, and Fannie was hoping for a filly that would stay on the farm and become a broodmare instead of being sold.

As quickly as Fannie's elation rose, it settled again. She

had too much to do to spend the day in the barn. "Let me know what she has, *Daed*."

A small frown creased his brow. "All right. I will come get you when her time is close."

"She is going to watch Noah play ball," her mother explained.

His frown vanished. "*Ach*, I reckon I knew the day would come when horses would take a backseat to a boyfriend. Came sooner than I was expecting."

"Not for me, it didn't," her mother said, scrubbing away at the beets.

"It's as it should be, I reckon," he said with a wink for Fannie. "But I will miss our times together working the horses."

"I'll still be here. Noah and I don't seem to be getting along that well."

"Oh?" Her mother turned around. "Is this why you are dragging your feet to watch him play?"

"Had a quarrel, did you?" Her father's sympathy was almost more than she could bear.

"Something like that."

"Don't be afraid to admit when you are wrong," her mother said.

Tears pricked the back of Fannie's eyes. "Why do you assume I'm the one in the wrong?"

Her mother came and put an arm around her. "Because I know what a temper you have. If the two of you won't suit, so be it. But don't throw away a chance at happiness when two simple words are all that is needed. Saying *I'm sorry* heals many hurts. If you wait because you think the other person must say it first, the wound grows out of proportion to the injury. Forgiveness heals the forgiver as well as the forgiven. Do you want to tell us what happened?"

Fannie shook her head. How could she admit she was

upset because Noah hadn't kissed her? He had offered to explain, but she had been too humiliated to listen to him.

"Seek him out and tell him what is troubling you. You won't feel better until you do."

Maybe her mother was right. Fannie nodded. "I'll speak to Noah after his game tonight."

Fannie hefted the laundry basket and went outside. Having made the decision to listen to Noah's explanation didn't make her any more eager to face him.

Noah considered the sign for a low inside pitch Walter was giving him. He nodded. It was a good call for the left-handed batter. Winding up, he checked the runner on first and threw with all his might. The batter swung, but the ball smacked into Walter's glove untouched for a third strike. The runner on first made a dash for second base, but Walter fired a beeline throw to their shortstop, Simon. He tagged the runner out ending the fourth inning. The hometown crowd cheered loudly.

Noah jogged off the mound and checked the lawn chairs and quilts along the baselines on his way to the dugout. There was no sign of Fannie among the Amish men and women enjoying the game. He tried not to let his disappointment show. Clearly, she was still angry with him.

"Noah, you're up," Eric said, nodding toward the batter's box.

After selecting his favorite bat from the group hanging on the fence, Noah took several practice swings and stepped up to the plate. A second later, pagers began going off around the field. Noah, along with the other firefighters present, tossed their equipment to anyone close and ran toward the fire station building, where the large double doors were going up as the siren overhead began to sound. Noah didn't give the game another thought.

"We have a structure fire reported at 2391 Raintree Road," Eric explained, as the men began pulling their fire gear over their ball uniforms.

Noah knew the address. It was an Amish home about five miles away. He prayed the family was safe.

"At least I don't have to go pick anyone up," Walter said, pulling on his coat. "Our crew is already here."

John Miller, Joshua and Timothy rushed in. As married men, they no longer played for the team, but they always came to home games to cheer on their fellow firefighters.

As soon as everyone was geared up they climbed into the smaller truck with Walter behind the wheel. They pulled out behind the main engine and followed it out to the highway. When they turned the corner, Noah caught a glimpse of Fannie standing beside her cart in the parking lot. She raised a hand and waved.

He waved, too, and sat back with a sense of profound relief. She had come to see him play, after all. He couldn't believe how happy that made him. When he could, he would find a chance to explain himself. If she would listen.

Fannie yawned. It was well after midnight as she sat on a bale of hay in the barn watching Willow's new colt struggle to his feet. She jumped and pressed a hand to her heart when Noah sat down beside her. "You startled me."

"Sorry. I was trying not to disturb them." He nodded to the new mother and baby.

"How did you know I was out here?"

"I saw the light on, but thought it must be your father out here. So I threw some pebbles against your window. I picked the wrong one. Your father opened it and told me where you were."

"You really threw pebbles against my window? Why?"

"That's how a fellow gets a girl to sneak out late with him, isn't it?"

It was true. Most Amish couples courted in secret after the parents had gone to bed, but she wished he had come over because he wanted to see her, not because it would make their false courtship more believable. "My folks will not doubt we are serious now."

"I thought as much, after your *daed* opened the window. Fannie, I came to apologize to you."

"That's not necessary. I'm the one who stormed off in a fit of temper."

"I think I gave you just cause. Can we talk about it?"

She stared at her feet. "Is there anything to say? I thought you were going to kiss me and you didn't. My lack of modesty repulsed you."

He lifted her chin with one finger, making her look at him. "Is that what you think? Nothing could be farther from the truth. I wanted to kiss you, Fannie."

"So, why didn't you?"

He clasped his hands together in his lap. "It didn't seem right. We are only pretending to court. The man who kisses you should be a man who genuinely deserves that honor."

"You kissed me once before."

"I was young and impatient then. I wasn't thinking about the right thing to do."

"Did you…did you like kissing me?" She couldn't believe she'd found the courage to ask him that.

"Very much. I like you Fannie. I do. You drive me nuts, but I like you. If you want to call this courtship off, I understand. You don't have to worry about going to Florida and you have your chaperone now."

"If we break up, won't your parents expect you to end your *rumspringa*?"

"I can deal with that, if they do."

"This was my idea. I will hold up my end of the bargain."

"Are you sure?"

"I am. And I'm sorry I rode off and left you yesterday. That was childish of me."

"Actually, as stiff as I am from my one-way ride, I'm not sure I would have been able to walk if I had ridden back with you. Can we start over and be friends, Fannie?" He covered her hand with his.

The warmth of his touch spread through her body. "We can't start over," she said, "but we can be friends from now on out."

"*Goot.* I'd like that. Have you named this young fellow?" He nodded toward the foal.

He still held her hand. She didn't pull away. His touch was comforting. "Not yet. I'm waiting to see what kind of personality he has, first."

"I'd call him Wobbles. Look at those long legs. He has no idea how to make them work."

She grinned. "*Wobbles* wouldn't be a very good name if you were trying to sell him as a buggy horse."

"You're right. *Fancy Stepper* would be a better name." He let go of her and rubbed his hand over his face.

She gazed at him in the lantern light. "You look tired. Was it a bad fire?"

He nodded. "It was a shed, not the house, thank the Lord, but it took us a long time to put it out. The farmer had his winter store of firewood in it, and it was really close to his barn. It took all we had to keep it from spreading."

"That's a shame. I hope no one was hurt."

"One of the neighbors that arrived before we did suffered some smoke inhalation and minor burns trying to toss out as much wood as he could. He and the farmer saved maybe a quarter of it."

"What was the cause? Was it arson?" Her community had been devastated by a series of arson fires the previous fall. If not for the generosity of outsiders and English friends like Connie, many of those affected would have been ruined, as none of the Amish carried insurance. Having it was seen as doubting God's protection and mercy.

"It wasn't arson. One of the sons went to fetch his mother more wood for the cookstove. He accidentally knocked over his kerosene lamp."

She glanced at the lantern glowing above their heads. "That's why *Daed* only allows battery-operated lamps out here."

"Same with my folks. I'm sure the family's church will bring them enough wood to get through the winter and more. I know I'll be taking some over."

"That is one of the best things about being Amish— knowing no matter what tragedy befalls us, the community will rally around us and lighten our burden."

"That's true of the Amish, but also true of many *Englisch* folks. Besides our fire crews, all of the opposing team members followed us to the scene to help fight the fire tonight. They aren't even from around here."

"My dad says people are born good. Any evil that grows in them is because they weren't shown the ways of goodness as they grew up."

He nodded. "That's why being a parent is such a great responsibility."

She glanced at him out of the corner of her eye. "Do you hope to be a parent someday?"

"Sure. I see how it has changed my brothers. I see how happy and content they are. Maybe *fulfilled* is the word I'm looking for."

"You don't think they resent giving up their freedoms, even a little?"

He shook his head. "If they do, I've never seen a sign of it."

She kept her eyes on the young colt nosing his mother for a meal. Somehow it was easier to talk to Noah in the quiet stable with the darkness held at bay by a single lantern. "Do you think your sisters-in-law are content, too?"

"I've never given it much thought. I don't see why not. *Gott* has given them what most women seek. A man who loves them. Children to be loved in turn and a home where they can be happy together as a family. Wouldn't you be content with that?"

Would she? "I'm not sure."

"Why do you say that?"

"My *aenti*, my mother's youngest sister, is only five years older than I am. We were close until she fell head over heels in love and married at eighteen. They moved away to Illinois to live with his family. We still exchange letters all the time."

Fannie looked at Noah. "She isn't happy in her marriage. The husband she loved so much isn't kind or comforting. After three miscarriages, she fears they will never have children, and he blames her for that."

"I'm sorry for your aunt. Her life must be difficult. She is fortunate to have you to console her. Fannie, we can't know the reason *Gott* chooses some of us to suffer in this world. He has a plan far beyond our simple understanding."

"I know that, but it worries me to see how easily love can blind us and lead us to mistakes. Connie loved the man she married, but he left her for another woman."

"For every sad story of broken love, you can find dozens, hundreds of people who have endured and grown old together with unwavering love for one another. My grandparents, my parents, your parents. I imagine even your grandparents in Florida will tell you they still care for each other. Am I right?"

"*Ja. Grossmammi* says *Grossdaadi* has the same twinkle in his eyes as she saw the day they met."

He tipped his head as he gazed at her. "I didn't know I should be watching for twinkling eyes. I'll keep that in mind from now on."

She felt the heat rush to her cheeks at his scrutiny. "Will you be at the school frolic on Friday?"

"Sure. Will you?"

She shrugged. "I'm thinking about it."

"*Goot.* I hope you come. It will do you good to get down from your horse and mingle with people for a change."

"I mingle."

"But you'd rather be riding."

"And you'd rather be playing ball."

"Ah, that's where I have the advantage. Someone will suggest we get up a ball game after the work is done at the school."

She chuckled. "Someone like you."

"Only if no one else suggests it first. I should be getting home. I just wanted to thank you for coming to my game tonight and explain about the other thing."

"I'm sorry I jumped to the wrong conclusion, and I'm sorry I didn't get there sooner to watch you pitch tonight."

"There will be other chances to see my fastball in action."

"I'm glad you stopped by." She was, and she didn't try to hide the fact. There was an ache in her heart because he wanted to be her friend and not something more, but she would learn to live with that.

He smiled. "I'm glad I did, too. It was nice to meet Fancy Stepper over there."

The colt was getting accustomed to his feet. Feeling

frisky, he tried a little jump that turned into a scramble to keep upright.

Noah and Fannie laughed at his antics. "Corker. I'm going to call him Corker," she said.

"That's a fine name for a horse with an attitude like his. *Ja*, it's a *goot* name. Would you like to ride home from church with me tomorrow, Fannie?"

A swirl of happiness made her almost giddy, but she kept a calm face. "I'd like that very much."

"*Goot*. So would I. *Guten nacht*, Fannie."

"Good night, Noah."

As he walked out into the dark, Fannie pulled her knees up and wrapped her arms around them. Noah hadn't been repulsed by her behavior, as she had wrongly imagined. He had been thinking of her feelings, not of himself. By jumping to the wrong conclusion, she had done him a disservice and spent an entire day feeling miserable.

Now that she knew they could be friends, a load had been lifted from her shoulders. She didn't have to worry about what to expect from him. His friendship was a fine gift and one she would cherish.

She didn't pause to wonder why the prospect of seeing her friend again tomorrow filled her with such eagerness.

Chapter Nine

Fannie rose early the next morning with a sense of excitement bubbling inside her. She was going to see Noah again soon. Recalling their evening in the barn left her feeling happy and hopeful. He was willing to be her friend, a dear friend.

As she entered the kitchen, the pale pink light of dawn provided a colorful view through the kitchen window over the sink. The few wispy clouds she saw promised a fine day.

She put the coffee on and grabbed the wire egg basket from the wall on the front porch. Keeping busy was a way to make the morning go faster. The dew was heavy on the grass as she hurried barefoot across the front yard.

Her parents kept a dozen laying hens. Their small henhouse was a movable pen and coop combined, painted white with a green roof to match the other buildings on the farm. It held two hinged nesting boxes with removable back panels that allowed for easy cleaning and access to the eggs. Happily, there were ten eggs, and all the chickens were accounted for. The rooster crowed his impatience to be let out. She opened the pen door and the flock raced out to roam the farmyard during the day and eat their fill of crickets and grasshoppers.

Fannie noticed the glow of a lamp down at the barn and guessed her father was already feeding the horses and making sure Willow and her colt were okay before they left for the church service. It was being held at the home of Luke Bowman. The family lived less than two miles away, so her family wouldn't have to make an early start.

Wiping her wet feet on the welcome mat, Fannie opened the door and saw her mother was up and getting breakfast ready.

"Did you see your father?" she asked, glancing over her shoulder at Fannie.

"*Nee*, but I saw a light in the barn."

"Tell him to hurry. We don't want to arrive late."

Fannie smiled. It was the same thing her mother said every Sunday there was a service. To Fannie's recollection, they had never been late, but still her mother insisted that they might be if her husband didn't hurry up.

Fannie's mother cut several slices of the ham that she had cooked the night before and transferred them into a skillet before packing the rest of it in a hamper. A light noon meal always followed the service. Each family brought enough food to share.

"I'll see if I can help him with the chores." Fannie put the eggs on the counter and started back outside, but stopped when she saw her father was already hitching a horse to the family buggy.

"Looks like he's finished. What do you need me to do?"

"Cut some lettuce from the garden and bring me in a half-dozen nice tomatoes."

Fannie pulled a kitchen knife from the drawer and went out to fetch the produce. Searching among the tomato plants for ripe fruit, Fannie smiled as she remembered the time Noah had shown her how he threw a baseball using a few tomatoes that made a satisfying splat when they hit the strike zone he had marked on the side of the house. They had been spotted by his mother, who had scolded them both for being wasteful.

"You seem happy this morning," her mother said, looking over the garden fence.

Fannie placed several ripe tomatoes in her bowl. "I was thinking back to some of my childhood scrapes."

What if her friendship with Noah grew into something more serious? Was she prepared for that? The idea of being courted in earnest didn't repulse her the way it once had.

"Remind me to share some of mine with you one of these days."

"*Mamm*, I can't imagine you getting into trouble, even as a child."

"Ha! With four sisters in our house we were always getting up to something."

"Like what?"

"Like tying someone's braids around the bedpost while they were sleeping."

Fannie gaped at her. "You didn't. Whose?"

"Mildred was the eldest and was always hogging the bathroom getting ready for school in the mornings. We thought we could have our turns before we untied her."

Fannie chuckled. "Did it work?"

"*Nee*, she hollered so loud that our *daed* rushed in to see who was being murdered. Needless to say, we never pulled that trick again."

"Did Mildred get the point?"

"She took even longer after that. Look at me, wasting time talking. I came out to ask you to bring in some green onions, too."

Fannie handed her the bowl of lettuce and tomatoes over the fence. "I'll be right in with them."

Her mother started to turn away, but paused. "You seem

more content today, Fannie. Did you patch things up with Noah?"

"We did." She smiled to herself.

"I'm so glad. Whatever the cause, I like this change in you. I'm so glad you and Noah have found each other. I may be getting ahead of myself, but I do love fall weddings."

"I'll get those onions for you." Fannie's excitement drained away.

It was one thing to imagine her friendship with Noah could blossom into a stronger relationship, but the reality was that when the summer was over, her pretend courtship with him would end, too.

Then she would have to pretend it didn't matter if he moved away to the English world—or if he remained Amish and chose to court another.

She pulled herself up short. That kind of thinking was selfish. She would be happy for Noah no matter where his life took him. A husband, even someone as progressive as Noah, would never accept her working for Connie.

Fannie and her parents arrived at Luke and Emma's place well before eight o'clock. Buggies and horses were already lined up along the corral fence. The bench wagon was being unloaded in front of the hardware store that Luke ran with his wife and his wife's two younger brothers.

The house was attached to the store by a covered walkway. Inside the building, the shelves of merchandise had been built with large casters that allowed them to be rolled back against the outer walls, making an open space where the benches were being set out.

Fannie followed her mother around to the entrance to the house and into the kitchen where the women were making preparations for the meal after the service. Dishes were being brought out; glasses were cleaned and stacked in rows. Coffee cups and mugs were arranged on the end of the kitchen counter. No meal after an Amish service was complete without plenty of piping hot black *kaffee*.

Emma took the hamper Fannie had carried in. "It's good to see you, Fannie. So, tell me, how is it going with you and Noah?"

"Fine," Fannie answered, feeling like a fraud each time she was asked about him.

"Just fine?"

"For now."

Emma bit the corner of her lip. "Lillian said the two of you had a quarrel. Give him a chance. The Bowman brothers are fine men. I almost didn't give Luke a second chance, but I thank *Gott* every day that I did. I couldn't be happier now."

"Noah and I worked out our differences," Fannie said to reassure her.

Relief filled Emma's eyes. "I'm happy to hear that."

"So am I," Rebecca said from behind Fannie. Apparently there was nothing secret about their courtship, except that it wasn't a real one.

The service lasted almost three and a half hours. Bishop Beachy was in fine form and gave a stirring sermon about forgiveness and the need to guard against pride. He and his ministers took turns preaching without notes. They spoke as God moved them.

Afterward, as the families filed out of the building, Fannie looked around for Noah. She had seen him when she came in, but he was gone from his place at the back when the service ended. She finally caught sight of him standing by his father's buggy, speaking with Rob and Simon Beachy. From their animated gestures, she guessed they were talking baseball.

Noah noticed her and nodded in acknowledgment. A grin lifted one side of his mouth and brought a light to his beautiful forget-me-not blue eyes. She smiled in return and went to join her mother and several other young women who were setting out lawn chairs in the shade of a large oak tree.

Her mother leaned close. "Will you be staying late with the other young people this evening?"

"I will be staying, but I'm not sure I'll be staying late."

"Someone is taking you home?"

"*Ja, Mamm.* Someone is taking me home."

Susan Yoder approached her. "We're getting up a volleyball game. Would you like to join us?"

"Sounds like fun, and I have some news to share with you." Fannie jumped up to follow Susan to where a dozen girls and young women were choosing sides as two young men strung the net for them.

Fannie gestured for the girls from her team to gather around. "Timothy Bowman and his wife are going to manage our team. We can start practicing again on Tuesday."

The girls clapped with delight. "Have you told Abbie and Laura?" Susan asked.

"I plan to ride over to their home tomorrow. We've missed an entire week of practice. That means we'll have to work doubly hard to make up for lost time."

"We could stay for an extra half hour each time we meet," Susan suggested.

"Only if you girls are willing to do that," Fannie said.

"I am," Pamela said, looking at her teammates.

They all agreed. Fannie couldn't have been more pleased with their dedication. The Amish Girls would ride again, and together they would showcase the wonderful horses of Stroud Stables.

After the game and the meal were over, a few of the families began leaving. Most would stay until late in the evening, visiting with one another. Fannie was taking the hamper and empty dishes back to her father's buggy when Noah caught up with her.

"Let me carry that for you." He reached for the hamper.

He took hold of it but she didn't let go. "I'm capable of carrying it."

"I know you are. I didn't offer because I thought you were infirm. I offered because I want to assist you and because my brothers are watching."

She glanced behind them. All four of his brothers were lined up along the porch staring in their direction.

He took the hamper from her. "They want to make sure you aren't still mad at me."

"Emma and Rebecca quizzed me this morning about our quarrel."

"What did you tell them?"

"That we had worked out our differences."

"*Goot* answer." He opened the buggy door and put the hamper on the backseat.

Fannie looked toward the porch and saw his brothers had been joined by their wives. Noah's parents and Fannie's parents were seated in the shade with glasses of lemonade in their hands, but they were staring in Fannie's direction, too. Everyone wanted to see how they were getting on. If this kept up, she would have to hang a sign around her neck announcing No Quarrel Today.

She sighed heavily. "I'm beginning to feel like a prize mare at the auction. Everyone in your family is looking me over. Next, they'll want to check my teeth. Luke and Emma will probably report back everything we do or say at the singing tonight."

He chuckled. "I have a solution, if you don't mind missing the party."

What was he up to? "I don't if you don't."

"Then just keep walking. Our getaway buggy is near the end of the row."

"You mean leave without telling anyone?"

"I do."

"What a great idea."

He reached for her hand. "You aren't the only one who has them."

She giggled and twined her fingers with his, feeling like a schoolgirl again, slipping away to play hooky.

They reached Noah's buggy and he helped her in. It took only a minute for him to back out of his parking space and set Willy in motion.

"Where to?" he asked when they reached the end of the lane.

"I don't care. Just somewhere where no one will ask how things are between us. I'm afraid I'm going to blurt out it was all a joke."

"I know the feeling. Want to go up to the overlook again?"

Fannie shook her head knowing it would get busy later. "Let's go to my family's picnic spot. No one will go there this evening."

"The Erb picnic spot it is. Do you mind if I pick up my fishing pole?"

"Not so long as I don't have to clean any fish."

"I will clean my own catch."

"And mine?"

He gave her a lopsided grin. "If you catch any. Fishing takes patience."

"And you think I lack patience?" She tried to hold back a grin and failed.

"Think? I know you do."

"Ha! We shall see about that."

After stopping at home to grab his fishing pole, Noah drove his buggy over to Fannie's place. She dashed inside to change out of her Sunday dress and grabbed a quilt for them to sit on. Noah drove them down to the creek on

Fannie's property feeling more lighthearted than he had in ages. While he unhitched Willy and left him to graze, Fannie spread out the quilt beneath a tree.

He settled on the blanket beside her and leaned back against the trunk of the tree. It was a beautiful sunny day with high, white cotton-ball clouds drifting across a blue sky so bright it made his eyes water to stare at it.

But it wasn't the sky that drew his attention. It was the sparkle in Fannie's eyes when she laughed at something he said or when she pointed out the antics of a squirrel in the tree overhead.

She pulled her knees up and wrapped her arms around them. "I do wonder what they are saying about us now."

"The squirrels?"

"*Nee*, our families."

"I'm sure everyone has an idea about where we went and what we are up to."

"Will Luke and Emma be upset that we didn't stay for the singing?"

"Luke understands. It wasn't that long ago that he was courting Emma."

She nodded toward his pole. "Aren't you going to fish?"

"Later. At the moment, I feel lazy and the grass under this blanket makes it wonderfully soft. This was a *goot* choice."

"*Danki.* This is one of my most favorite places in the whole world."

"It's a pretty place, all right." The trees were large with wide-spreading branches that let only dappled sunlight through. The murmur of the creek as it slipped over its rocky course provided a soothing sound, as did the birds and insects in the trees.

"I used to come here a lot. I would bring a book and

spend all afternoon reading when I was about twelve," Fannie said.

"Reading was Timothy's thing, not mine."

"What was your thing? Baseball?"

"Not at that age. I was a birder."

She looked at him in surprise. "A what?"

"A birder is a serious bird watcher," he said in a solemn voice.

"You're teasing me."

"Nope. I kept a log of all the species I identified. I still have it somewhere. Did you know there are more than one hundred types of common birds that call Ohio home?"

"I did not know that."

"I had a great-uncle who lived near the Killbuck Marsh. I used to go and stay with him for a few weeks each year. He got me started birding. He knew everything about birds. We would hike out into the marsh at dawn and spend the whole day trying to find as many species as we could. Each Christmas, he would send me a card with a beautifully drawn picture of one of the rare birds he'd seen that year. When he passed away, I sort of lost interest in it. Then I discovered baseball, and that became my passion."

"Oh, how I wish I had known that. To think of the names I could have called you. Birdbrain, featherhead, dodo bird. My cup would have runneth over with joy."

"I see where this is going. Revenge for carrottop."

"Pure and simple."

"Really? The name *Noah* didn't supply you with enough fodder for taunting?"

"It was a biblical name. It didn't feel right to make fun of you for that. Having the name *Fannie*, on the other hand, did bring out the worst in some of the boys."

"I never teased you about your name."

"Just about my looks. I don't see how that is any better."

He folded his arms and looked her up and down. "They have improved considerably over time."

"Coming from a birdbrain, that's quite a compliment."

"I knew I never should have shared that story. Do you still come out here to read?"

"I haven't in years. Riding and training horses takes up all my time now."

"Things change for all of us, I reckon."

"That is true. What will you do if you can't play professional ball?"

"Stay on the farm and work with my *daed* and brothers."

"As the youngest son, the land will come to you when your *daed* is gone."

"I hope I can be as good a steward to the land as he has been. What are your plans after the Horse Expo?"

"I'll keep working for Connie. If things go well for her, she'll employ me full-time."

"You truly love working with horses, don't you?"

"Do you think it's strange that I want to devote my life to it?"

"It's unusual, but then you've always been an unusual person. I mean that in a good way, before you get upset and resort to name-calling again. What will you do if Connie can't save her stable?"

"I don't know. It's something I can't consider."

"Isn't working with your father satisfying? You could always continue training his horses."

"I love my father and I enjoy helping him, but I want to train saddle horses, not just buggy horses, and I want to give riding lessons."

"Couldn't you do that at home?"

"My parents would object to having *Englisch* people coming in and out. You know how it is. I would have to conform to their Amish standards."

"My family does a lot of business with the *Englisch*."

"My parents are more old-fashioned in their beliefs than yours. They are already pressuring me to join the church. If and when I do, I will have to give up riding."

"Are you considering not joining?" He should have seen that coming, but he hadn't.

"Maybe. I don't know. I'm not ready to make that decision."

They were both on the fence about the most important decision young Amish adults had to make.

"Is there anything I can do to help?" he asked, genuinely wishing he could do something for her. He wanted to see her smile again.

Her eyes grew sad. "When you are a famous ballplayer and traveling to faraway cities, send me postcards so I can keep track of you."

"Sure," he answered quickly.

The only trouble was, he didn't want to go far away from Fannie. He'd never had someone he could share everything with, the way he could with her. Their make-believe courtship had sparked a true and deep friendship, for him, at least. He wasn't sure how she felt, but he hoped she felt the same.

Perhaps it was a foundation they could build into a real courtship one day.

If God wanted him to stay.

Chapter Ten

"You look like you have something serious on your mind, Fannie."

Sometimes Connie was too observant. Fannie had been thinking about Noah and her growing feelings for him, ever since their outing two days ago, but she wasn't sure she was ready to share them. "I was mentally preparing to start work with our new boarder. I have time before the group arrives for practice."

They were seated in Connie's office, a converted bedroom in her house, trying to make her income from riding classes cover the coming month's feed bill. It wasn't stretching. The expense of transporting eight horses and eight Amish girls to various fairs in the region had put a dent in their emergency funds. The rest was earmarked for the Expo.

Connie tipped her head to the side. "Is that all? Are you sure it isn't Noah that has you looking glum?"

Maybe it would ease her mind to share her feelings. "You guessed it."

"Want to talk about it?"

"Noah and I have gotten to be good friends. I've never said that about anyone but you. I think Noah understands me."

"Is that a bad thing?"

Fannie shrugged. "Of course not, but how do I keep from liking him too much?"

"Are you saying you're in love with Noah?"

"Maybe. *Nee*. I enjoy being around him. He's great company when we aren't fighting."

"By *fighting* I hope you don't mean he's abusive."

"Of course not. He's kind and he's funny. He teases me and makes me giggle."

Connie leaned back in her chair and twirled her pencil between her fingers. "Giggle. So you are half in love with him."

"Am I?" Was she?

"I'd say so."

"What do I do about it?"

"Fannie, if you can't commit to the relationship, you need to end it."

That wasn't what she wanted to hear. "Why should I give up being friends with him? He's a wonderful man."

"Because staying friends with him will be incredibly difficult. A woman's heart is made for love. I'm not saying a friendship between a man and a woman is impossible. I'm saying it's often the stepping-stone to love. How does Noah feel about you? Do you know? Has he told you?"

"He teases me like I'm his kid sister. I'm not sure how he feels, but it doesn't matter. We don't want the same things out of life. I won't let us become more than friends, but I won't give that up."

"More power to you if you can make that happen. The heart has a way of overlooking even the most difficult problems and tumbling you into love before you know it."

This wasn't getting her anywhere. "I should get to work. Are you going to come watch me?"

"Oh, like I would miss it. Let's go."

Fannie walked into Connie's arena ten minutes later with their new boarder on a lead rope. The black-and-white gelding kept his head high and flinched with every move she made toward him. Using the end of the rope, she swung it past him. He jerked away violently. She raised her hand quickly and got the same response. Anger made her press her lips together. The poor fellow had known unkindness, if not outright abuse, from someone.

Breathing deeply, she let go of her anger and concentrated on sending calm signals to the horse. She unsnapped the lead and let him loose. He took off at a run.

Noah entered the riding arena and saw Fannie with a tall paint gelding. The horse wore a halter, but Fannie didn't have him on a line. She was simply standing in the center of the arena as he galloped around it. She held a coiled lead rope in one hand. Noah leaned on the rail to watch her. What was she up to?

Fannie caught sight of him and grinned, but she kept her attention on the animal traveling around her.

Connie came over and stood beside Noah. "Fannie is very taken with you."

"I am taken with her myself."

"I can tell that you love her."

He drew back in surprise. He wasn't in love with Fannie. He cared for her. Deeply. But that wasn't love. Why did this woman think he was?

"We aren't that serious, but we have become very good friends." That much was the truth.

"I'm relieved to be wrong," Connie said.

"Why is that?"

"Because I believe Fannie will never be happy in a traditional Amish marriage. She's a woman who needs her freedom. She loves horses and she has a tremendous gift with them. She's what we call a horse whisperer."

"And what is that, exactly?"

"Someone who can communicate with horses on a level that few of us even understand. Plus, she is the best riding instructor I have ever met. Look at all she has done with her girls in such a short amount of time."

"You praise her highly."

"She has earned it."

"She thinks a lot of you, too."

He had never looked at Fannie's affection for horses as a gift. He had trained a number of them. He understood that it took patience and repetition to bring out the best in an animal. Connie clearly saw something more in what Fannie did.

Connie nodded toward the paint horse nervously pacing around the enclosure. "This is a horse I'm boarding. The owners brought him in yesterday. They recently purchased him for their daughter, but they say he's a problem for them to handle. He's head shy and difficult to catch."

"They chose poorly for their daughter."

"Not everyone who buys a horse is an expert. The previous owner should have alerted them to the issue. I suspect he wasn't an honest fellow. They thought the horse was simply spirited."

"Then they should get their money back."

"After Fannie explained to them why the horse was acting up, they decided that returning him to his former owner was not an option for them."

"I see. So they asked you to retrain the horse?"

"Fannie offered as soon as she saw what was wrong. See how the horse keeps moving? Their natural instinct is to fight or to flee. Their first choice is always flight."

"What is she doing now? Why is she just standing there?"

"Fannie is becoming the herd leader. She is going to show by her body language that she is a safe place."

When the horse came by she raised her arms and the horse moved away.

Perplexed, Noah said, "I thought she wanted him to come to her?"

"She hasn't invited him to join her herd."

Fannie continued to drive the horse forward until he had made a dozen laps around the arena. Twice, she closed the distance between them and forced the horse to switch directions. It went on for fifteen minutes.

Connie leaned closer to Noah after the horse had made several more circles of the arena. "Watch the horse's ears. See how he is keeping his inside ear toward Fannie. She is holding his attention while his other ear is listening to the rest of the building. When he starts slowing and moving his mouth, he's relaxing."

Fannie lowered her arms but kept moving more slowly. As she did, the horse began to close the distance between them as he circled her. When he was walking calmly, she turned her back to him and he approached within a few feet.

She took several steps away and the horse followed her. She turned left and he continued to follow close behind her. When she stopped to face him, he stretched his nose toward her and she rewarded him with a rub on the forehead.

"This is called joining. He has confidence now that she doesn't mean him harm. She's a safe place to be, and he'll remember that. He'll never forget the abuse someone gave him, but he can get past it now. Not all humans are bad."

"I thought I knew horses pretty well, but I see I have more to learn."

"If I can get this stable back in the black, Fannie is the one who can help me keep it that way. She has a job here for as long as she wants it. If she marries, she will have to give this up, won't she?"

"If Fannie joins the church, she will take a vow to follow the rules of our congregation, the Ordnung. Working outside the home is rarely permitted for a woman unless she is helping with her family's or her husband's business when she marries. Once the children come, she must give her family her full attention."

Connie gestured toward the middle of the arena. The horse that had been so fearful was resting his head on Fannie's shoulder. "Do you think she can give that up? I couldn't if I had her gift."

Fannie started jogging and the horse followed her. She darted one way and then another as he followed her every move in a game of tag. Laughing, she stopped and put her arms around his neck. The horse didn't flinch.

Noah realized he'd never seen Fannie so carefree. The half-formed idea that had been growing in his mind withered and died. If he didn't get picked up by a scout, he had been considering courting Fannie in earnest. She had an amazing way of getting inside his defenses. Just as she had done with the horse she was training.

Watching her doing what she loved, he knew he couldn't ask her to give it up. The most he could hope for was to continue their friendship. It was far better to accept that now. Before he made the mistake of falling in love with her. As she walked toward him, he was determined not to let his disappointment show.

Pasting a cheerful smile on his face, he opened the gate so she could come out and closed it before the horse came, too. The animal stood at the gate waiting for her to come back in.

Noah turned to Fannie. "Where did you learn to do that?"

"Do you remember me telling you about the fair I went to years ago?"

"Of course. The night your cousin died and *Gott* prompted Connie to step in and save you."

"While Maddy and I were exploring the fairgrounds that afternoon, I saw a man give a demonstration on this technique. He was amazing. They brought in three horses he'd never seen before, all with different problems, and he gentled each one of them. One in less than fifteen minutes. I knew I had to learn to do it. Then, well, you know my cousin was killed and I came home. I tried to show my father how it was done, but he said the old ways were best. He's not cruel to his horses, but he believes he has to show them he is in charge."

"That must have been frustrating for you."

"It was. Then I took this job working for Connie. After that, I was able to use what I knew and expand my education. Connie was as excited by the technique as I was. She purchased videos I could watch on her computer. We have even traveled to several events where—I don't call it horse training, I call it people reeducation—it was taking place. I learned something new every time."

"Will your friend react the same to me as he did to you?"

"He will if you are interesting enough."

Noah pretended indignation. "What's that mean? You don't think I'm an interesting fellow? What kind of thing is that to say to your beau?"

He opened the gate and stepped in with the horse, watching for any signs of agitation. He saw none. Instead of reaching for the horse, Noah walked a little way into the arena. The horse followed him after a brief hesitation.

Turning, Noah faced the animal, which still wasn't displaying any signs of agitation. He had his ears forward, his head was slightly lowered and his posture was relaxed. Noah held out his hand. The horse came forward to sniff him. After rubbing the animal's forehead, Noah took hold of his halter and led him back to Fannie. "He doesn't seem head shy to me."

"He was, wasn't he, Connie?" Fannie grinned at her friend.

"He jerked George off his feet when George took hold of his lead rope."

Connie came through the gate and clipped a lead to the horse's halter. The animal submitted meekly. "With a little extra people training for his owners, he should make a good family horse."

She led the paint away, leaving Noah and Fannie alone. Noah slipped his hands into the front pockets of his jeans. He was still in awe of what he'd seen. Fannie's famous temper was totally absent. "Timothy should be here soon. He wanted to be here before the girls began to arrive."

"I'm so thankful he has agreed to be our chaperone."

"He prefers the term *manager*."

"Manager it is."

"I have to say I'm really impressed with your gift, Fannie. I had no idea."

"Does it rank up there with your fastball?"

"Hmm, let me think. Nope."

"Oh! You are conceited, Noah Bowman."

"Ah, now you are the one looking for a compliment. Not very plain behavior, if you ask me."

"I didn't ask you. Don't you have somewhere else to be?"

"Are you two quarreling again?" The question came from Timothy, who was watching them both with mirth brimming in his eyes.

Noah winked at Fannie. "Not at all, *bruder*. Teasing is how we show our affection for each other, isn't it, dear?"

"Sure. And pigs have learned how to fly," she snapped back.

Noah chuckled. "I believe Hiram mentioned that."

Fannie closed her eyes and shook her head. "I have to go get Trinket. My team is arriving. Timothy, I can't tell you how much I appreciate what you are doing."

"It's all in the name of education. Mine, most of all."

Noah noticed George come in the far door, but at the sight of both brothers, he turned and walked out. Hopefully he understood the message. He wasn't to bother the girls again.

It didn't take long for the excited group of girls to offer Timothy their collective thanks and ready their mounts. When they were lined up by twos, Fannie called for the music to start and they rode out.

"I don't know much about this sport. I see the concept, but what are the challenges?" Timothy asked Connie, who had come back in to stand beside them.

"*Stay in line* is the first rule of a drill team. No matter what, the riders need to keep their positioning even and stay straight. It doesn't matter if the horse is trotting, pacing or cantering, the audience will only notice the spacing and unity of the group. The riders have to be ready to shift up or down to maintain the line. Riders on the inside of a turn have a smaller radius and need to hold back, while the horse and rider on the outside of the turn has to hustle. Notice how Abbie is lagging behind the group during turns."

"Abbie, keep up," Fannie called out.

"I'm trying."

"She's going to have to push her horse harder to make up that extra step," Connie said.

"Maybe not. Fannie, hold up a moment." Noah moved

out into the ring. He drew a line in the dirt with his boot and walked off a dozen paces before drawing a second line.

Fannie rode over with a scowl on her face. "What are you doing?"

"Measuring strides. Pamela, Abbie, I want you to trot your horses across the first line all the way to the second one at the same speed."

After the girls did as he asked, Timothy joined Noah to examine the hoofprints. Fannie swung out of the saddle. "I don't see what you're trying to prove. Abbie needs to push her mount harder to keep up."

Noah shook his head. "Misty needs to be the second horse on the inside of the pinwheel."

"We have the girls arranged according to their height. Having Pamela on the inside won't work."

"Then they need to trade horses. Is there a reason they can't?" He looked at the girls. They looked at each other and shook their heads.

"I'm not sure trading horses in the middle of the season is a good idea. Connie and I paired these girls with these horses for a reason. They have grown used to each other."

"Come look," he said. "Count the number of strides Misty took compared to Comet. See? Misty's stride is a good four inches shorter than Comet's. If we switch their places in the pattern, Abbie won't have to try so hard to keep up with the group."

"I see what you are saying." She didn't sound happy about it.

"If it doesn't work, it doesn't, and you go back to what you were doing."

She sighed heavily. "We can give it a try. Switch horses, girls. Zoe, start the music again. From the beginning, ladies."

The group went through the entire program without

pausing. Abbie was able to keep pace in the pinwheel and she was grinning from ear to ear when they finished. She patted her new mount's neck. "That was easier."

Noah walked up to Fannie's side and cupped his hand to his ear. "What was that, Fannie? Did you say *you were right, Noah*?"

She tried to hide a smile. "It pains me, but you were correct this time."

"Don't mention it."

"Any other suggestions?"

He tapped his lips with one finger. "Not at the moment, but I'm sure something will occur to me."

"Don't you have ball practice or something else you need to do?"

"Nope."

"Are you on call? Isn't there a fire somewhere?" She was struggling not to laugh.

"Nope."

"Can you just go away and leave us in peace?"

"You want me to go?"

"*Ja*, Noah."

"See how much better your communication skills have become, Fannie?"

"Are you going or not? Because I have work to do."

"Okay. I leave you and your group in Timothy's capable hands. Only there is one more thing."

Fannie rolled her eyes. "Tell me now before I die of curiosity."

"You want to showcase the horses' skills, don't you?"

"That is our entire plan in a nutshell."

"I saw you take some pretty impressive jumps on Trinket and on the gelding you were riding the other day. Why not add some jumps to your routine? Haflingers make fine show jumpers. You said so yourself."

Fannie opened her mouth and closed it again.

Noah turned to his brother. "I love it when I can leave her speechless."

Fannie was torn between feeling foolish that she hadn't thought of it and wanting to hug Noah for the suggestion. "You are right."

Noah cupped his hand to his ear. "What was that, Fannie? Did you just say I was right again? Twice in one day!"

"Yes, birdbrain, I said you were right again. Even a blind pig finds an acorn once in a while. However, I must admit it is an excellent idea," she added before he took exception to her quaint saying. He gave her a wounded look but kept quiet. She turned to Connie. "What do you think?"

"If we set them up in the center, you can use it as part of your entry. Say, four jumps of slightly increasing height?"

"We'll have to leave enough room for our pinwheel in the middle."

"Then that won't work."

"Set them around the perimeter, far enough away from your pattern area that they won't interfere," Noah suggested. "I assume the arena at the Horse Expo is larger than this one?"

Connie nodded. "Much larger. We don't want to detract from the flow of the ride. You girls can swing wide at some point and go over them. Perhaps at the end of the program."

"Will we be allowed to add jumps?" Susan asked. "Don't we have to follow the rules of the competition?"

"That's the beauty of it," Connie said. "We won't be competing in the drill team event at the Horse Expo. I've pulled in all the favors I could manage and even pressured some members of the Haflinger Association who were friends of my father to give us the breed spotlight. Our mission is to show the crowd and the country what awesome horses Haflingers are."

"What do you mean when you say 'show the country'?" Fannie asked.

Connie grinned. "The Expo is a televised event. You knew that, didn't you?"

No one spoke. She looked around the group and her smile faded. "Will that be a problem?"

Chapter Eleven

"It's going to be televised? Are you sure?" Lillian asked, looking from her husband to Fannie.

Seated with Noah and Timothy in Lillian's kitchen, Fannie blew out a deep breath. "That is what Connie told us. Do you think it will make a difference to the bishop? You don't think he'll put a stop to us again, do you?"

Timothy shook his head. "I'm not sure how he will feel about it, but we have to let him know."

"Sometimes it is better to ask forgiveness than permission," Noah said.

Timothy frowned at him. "This is not one of those times, little *bruder*."

"I thought I would offer it as a suggestion." Noah folded his arms over his chest.

"It isn't a bad one." Fannie could see the merit in it.

"They may be right," Lillian said, drumming her fingers on the tabletop.

"How so?" Timothy asked.

"Nothing has changed. The bishop has said these girls are not baptized and the rules of our church do not yet apply to them. People were taking pictures of you at the fair when the bishop was watching, weren't they, Fannie?"

"A lot of them were, but most people took pictures from a distance or from the side, so our faces weren't in them."

Lillian laced her fingers together and leaned forward. "Then Connie will have to insist that the television people do the same. No close-ups of the girls' faces. No mention of names. She must ask them to respect our religious beliefs. If they agree, I say there is no need to worry the bishop over this one small detail."

"And if they don't agree?" Timothy asked.

"Then we place the decision in Bishop Beachy's hands." Lillian sat back with a smile.

Timothy stared at Lillian in amazement. "I had no idea my wife was so devious."

Her mouth dropped open. "Husband, how can you say that?"

"I say it with great unease."

Lillian chuckled and leaned forward to pat his hand. "Have no fear. I will never deceive you, my love."

"You say that now, but what if *Gott* ordains that I am chosen to be a minister and then a bishop someday? Will you seek to keep other small details from my view?"

She shrugged. "I shall cross that bridge when I come to it."

Timothy looked to Noah. "Be cautious when you choose to wed, Noah. It can't be undone."

Lillian giggled. "As if you would undo our vows. I know you better than that. Fannie, are you coming to the frolic on Friday?"

"I am. My parents, too."

"It will be wonderful to finally have enough room for all our students," Timothy said.

Noah stood. "I hope we have plenty of willing hands to share the work."

Timothy rose, too. "I don't think we need to worry about that. All the children are excited about helping."

Lillian pulled a piece of paper from her pocket. "I had a note from my friend Debra Merrick. She is planning on coming. She's eager to begin teaching health and well-baby classes in the new wing and wants to do her part in getting it ready."

Debra was the local public health nurse. With Lillian's help, she had become well-known and well liked in the community after she and her brother helped raise money for the families affected by the arson fires. She held a well-baby clinic once a month and taught classes on food safety and other topics afterward. She took great pains to be respectful of their Amish beliefs. Fannie had met her several times and liked her.

"Are you ready to go, Fannie?" Noah settled his ball cap on his head.

"I am." She had ridden with him to Timothy's home to discuss what they should do about the Horse Expo being televised. She had been too upset to enjoy the buggy ride out, but she was looking forward to being alone with him on the ride home.

Outside, he helped her into the two-wheeled cart he had chosen to drive that day. It was the same type of cart she and her mother drove for short trips around the community when the weather was nice.

As they started up the hill, he glanced her way. "Feeling better about this now?"

"I am. If Connie can get the Expo to agree to our requests, I don't see a problem."

"Have faith that it will work out."

"I hope so. I truly do. We are so close to pulling it all together." She was almost afraid to believe it would happen.

"I was thinking."

"Not again, Noah. You know that strains your bird-brain." She tried not to giggle, but she couldn't help herself.

"Ha-ha! Why did I ever tell you that story?"

"Just to make me happy. What were you thinking?"

"Forget it."

"I want to know."

"I was thinking that your Haflingers have one more skill we could add to the program."

She tipped her head. "What skill would that be?"

"What are we doing right now?"

"They are wonderful horses, Noah, but they can't carry on a conversation."

"Be serious. What am I doing?"

"Annoying me?"

"Fannie! I'm trying to help. I'm driving a horse in harness."

Her mind began whirling with the possibilities. "A second act."

"Exactly."

"A driven drill team consisting of Haflingers."

"The same horses, driven by the same riders."

"Versatility is the mark of a horse trained at Stroud Stables."

"There you go. It doesn't have to be an elaborate program. Basically repeat the patterns you've already taught the girls, only in carts instead of on horseback. Are all the horses broke to harness?"

"They are. Connie insists on it because her Amish customers want horses to pull their buggies and carts. They aren't looking for riding stock, while her *Englisch* customers most often want ponies for their children to ride. The girls have been driving carts since they were five or six. They shouldn't have any problem."

"And you had the nerve to call me a birdbrain."

Fannie linked her arm through his. "I'm sorry. This is a fine idea. I can't wait to tell Connie and see what she says about it."

"I have my cell phone. Do you want to call her?"

Fannie was tempted but she shook her head. "*Nee*, it can wait. Good news is best shared in person."

"Spoken like a true Amish woman."

"*Danki.*" Fannie kept her arm linked through his all the way to Connie's farm.

Two days later, Fannie and her group practiced unsaddling their mounts and getting them into harnesses as quickly as possible. With two girls working together on each horse and the adults helping the youngest members, they soon had the time cut down to an acceptable amount.

Connie raised her hands. "The crowd will simply have to listen to music for a few minutes."

"Or you can be giving a short lecture on the breed history and characteristics," Fannie said. She knew people would find it interesting.

"Not me." Connie shook her head. "I can't speak in front of people. I get horrible stage fright, but I will give something to the announcer to read."

"You can stand on the back of a galloping horse in front of hundreds of people, but you can't speak in public?"

Connie gave her a sour look. "Everyone has some kind of phobia."

"Have you heard from the Expo people about our television restrictions?"

"I haven't, but I should hear something soon. I know some folks think I'm exploiting these young women to improve my financial standing, but I draw the line at asking them to go against their fundamental religious teachings on national television."

Fannie looked at her riders. "Are we ready to try this?"

They all agreed. The Amish Girls went through their main routine with ease while Timothy, Noah and Connie looked on. After the last pattern was complete, they swung out to take their mounts over the hurdles set up along the walls and then went out the open barn doors. Outside, the girls unsaddled their mounts and then harnessed them. It was time-consuming and before all eight horses were hitched to their prospective carts the girls were sweating and flustered. Once they entered the ring again, they were able to settle down and drive with precision.

Connie applauded loudly when they were done. "You make it look so easy."

Fannie stood in her cart. "Practice the same time next Tuesday. Remember, we are giving a show on Wednesday at the Mount Hope Horse Auction. Everyone should be here by nine o'clock. Connie will have a van to take us and a hauler to take our carts, so please drive your carts that morning. She will be taking the horses in her horse trailer. If the show goes well, we can skip practice on Thursday and plan on having one on Saturday at noon. I'm very proud of all you girls have accomplished. I couldn't be riding with a better group if I tried."

After the practice was over, Noah drove Willy home while Fannie rode beside his buggy.

"What did you think of it?" she asked.

"It was a little ragged at the end, but it's nothing that can't be smoothed over with a little more practice. I think the crowd at the Expo will be mightily impressed with the breed and with Connie's ability to train them."

"That's all I can ask," Fannie said with a satisfied smile.

When they reached her lane, she pulled to a stop beside him. "You're still planning on coming to the frolic, aren't you?"

"Of course. Will I see you there?"

She smiled and nodded. "I'll be there."

He touched the brim of his hat. "Until then."

Fannie trotted Trinket toward home, eager for tomorrow to arrive.

Noah was helping his brothers unload the lumber they would need at the school and keeping one eye out for Fannie and her family. Where were they?

"What's wrong with you?" Samuel asked.

"Nothing, why?"

"Then watch what you're doing. Two-by-fours go over there." He gestured toward a stack of lumber beside the school building.

"Right." Noah picked up the boards he'd added to the pile of siding and carried them to their proper place.

Two women came out of the school building. One was his sister-in-law Lillian. The other was an English woman, the county health nurse, Debra Merrick. A young woman in her midtwenties, Debra was dressed in a simple black skirt and a white blouse. Her low-heeled black shoes were sensible and sturdy. Debra's blond hair was cut short with curls clustered around her face. She was a pretty woman, but he liked Fannie's wild red curls better.

"Why do you call it a frolic?" Debra asked.

"The name just means a social and work event that takes place in our Amish communities," Lillian explained. "It can be anything from a quilting bee to a barn raising. Whatever needs doing, we ask for volunteers and they show up. Today, the men and boys get together to do a few hours work in putting up the new school wing, and we feed them. That's a frolic."

"Your good food is one wonderful thing I've discovered about Amish country. I've had to go up a dress size already, and I've been here less than a year."

Debra stared at the slab of concrete waiting to be covered. "Can you really get a building up today?"

"Noah, what do you think?" Lillian asked.

"The frame will be up by noon and the rest will be done by five if we get enough help."

"I'm willing to do my part. Where are the tools? I've always wanted to use a saw." Debra looked around.

Lillian steered her away from the lumber. "Let's make sure we have enough to feed everyone, and then we can help the men later."

The frolic was set to start at eight o'clock. Men trickled in until there was a crew of about fifteen. Fannie and her family finally arrived and Noah felt a surge of happiness at the sight of her. She wore a dark blue dress with a white apron, and for once she didn't have jeans and boots underneath. There was nothing to mark her as different from the other women gathered to work. All of them went inside the school building.

Some of the younger boys were playing with tools and trying not to cause mischief. Timothy took charge of them and put them to work. Paul came up to Noah carrying a case hung over his shoulder by a thick strap.

"What have you there?" Noah asked.

Paul opened the case and pulled out a microphone. "It just came today. It's my sound system. It operates on batteries as well as electricity. With this I can run an auction anywhere."

He switched it on. "Brothers and sisters, welcome to the Rider Hill School frolic." His voice boomed out clear and sharp, causing everyone to stop and look at him. The younger children came running up, begging him to say something else. He gave them turns speaking into it, to their delight.

Fannie's father stepped into the supervisor's role, walking around and keeping track of the progress, offering suggestions or instructions, sometimes cracking jokes to the crew. He made everyone feel that they had an important job, from the youngest boy swinging a hammer to the oldest man carrying siding.

At midmorning, he called for a break. Noah and his brothers gladly sat down to steaming black coffee, fresh-picked grapes, raisin bars, assorted cookies and tart lemonade. It was beginning to get hot. Noah lifted his wide-brimmed straw hat and wiped the sweat from his brow.

At noon, Fannie began setting out ham and bread for sandwiches. She looked his way and smiled sweetly. He narrowly missed smashing his thumb because he was watching her instead of what he was doing.

As he'd known they would, his mother and sisters-in-law produced a mountain of food in plastic bowls and jars. Along with paper plates and utensils, they placed everything down the center of the folding tables brought out of the school. There were fried chicken, German potato salad, pickles, pickled beets, stacks of brownies, whoopie pies, a jug of fresh lemonade and a jug of iced tea.

The bishop led the workers in a brief prayer of thanksgiving. Noah's mother made sure everyone had a heaping plate of food on his or her lap before she sat down with a plate of her own. She gazed out over the families gathered together. "It does my heart good to see so many people willing to help."

It did Noah's heart good to see Fannie get her plate of food and leave the group of women for the first time since she'd arrived. He followed her to the swing set beside the school and they each sat down on a swing. "Are you enjoying yourself?"

"I am. It almost feels like I'm back in school," she admitted with a shy smile. "Your brothers' wives have some funny stories to share about their husbands, but the bishop's wife takes the cake. If half of what she says is true, he is blessed to have her as his keeper. Twice this month she found his glasses on his mule's rump when he came in from the field."

Noah laughed. "Why there?"

"He claimed it was a handy flat spot to lay them so he could wipe the sweat off of his face, and he just forgot them."

"So mingling hasn't been so bad today?"

She swung gently back and forth. "It hasn't been this morning. Has anyone suggested a ball game later?"

"They have. It will be the annual boys against the men softball game. I will be pitching for the men's team."

"The underdogs?"

"We are not. The opposing pitcher is eleven, but I'm told he has a good arm."

She chuckled. "I can't wait to cheer you on."

"Are you going to be able to come to my regular game tomorrow? It's the last home game of the season. We'll be league champions if we win it and the next away game."

"I do plan to come. Our riding exhibition isn't until next Saturday. Which is good, because we need to practice with our carts. It was a great idea, Noah. I'm glad you thought of it."

It was gratifying that he had pleased her. He wanted to go on making her happy. "If I come up with anything else I'll let you know."

"And I have called you birdbrained for the last time. It was fun while it lasted, but the name doesn't truly fit you."

"Can I walk you home when this is over tonight?"

"I'd like that."

He rose and took her plate. Laying it aside, he said, "I have a little time before I have to get back to work. Would you like a push?"

"Now I really feel like I'm back in school." She giggled as she gripped the chains and lifted her feet.

As the men began their ball game against the boys late in the afternoon, Fannie joined Margret and her sister on a quilt in the shade where they could watch the game in progress. Margret was holding Rebecca's baby on her shoulder. The contented baby was trying to get his entire fist in his mouth and drooling excessively on his fingers.

"He's getting your dress damp," Fannie told her.

"I don't mind. Aren't babies wonderful?"

Fannie wrinkled her nose. "Not if one is drooling down my neck."

Rebecca returned to the quilt and sat down. "I can take him now."

"Is it all right if I hold him a little longer?" Margret asked hopefully.

His mother smiled. "I don't mind."

"He's such a good baby. It must be wonderful to be a mother." Margret patted his back and he burped loudly.

"He is *Gott*'s greatest blessing to me and Samuel. *Gott* willing, you will know the same joy someday."

"I pray you are right, but I'm not getting any younger, and there are many more single women in our community than there are single men because the boys leave as teenagers and don't return."

Lillian called to Rebecca from the school steps. Rebecca waved and rose to her feet again. "If you get tired of holding him, I'm sure Fannie will take him."

"I won't get tired," Margret assured her, smiling at the baby.

"When are you going home?" Fannie asked, desperate to talk about something other than babies. They were cute and they smelled good, but she wasn't ready to want one.

"I leave next week."

"I thought you were staying until the end of the month."

"My sister is staying longer. She has caught the eye of a young man from your church. The only two that struck my fancy are already seeing someone." She gave Fannie a sidelong glance.

Fannie gaped at her in surprise. "Do you mean Noah?"

"Have I offended you?" Margret asked quickly.

"*Nee*, I'm not offended." Surprised, yes, but she wasn't sure why she should be. Noah was a good-looking fellow from a nice family. He was hardworking and kind. Any woman would feel he was good husband material.

"Are you serious about each other?" Margret asked.

Fannie glanced to where Noah was standing in the batter's box as she pondered Margret's question. He was dressed plain today, with dark pants and suspenders over his muscular shoulders. He had taken off his hat in order to run the bases. She liked him best in plain clothes. They suited him. He took a swing at the first pitch and knocked it straight into the second baseman's glove. A groan went up from his bench. He turned to them and held his hands wide. "I'm a pitcher, not a hitter."

Fannie sighed. While she felt her relationship with Noah had grown in recent days, he hadn't said anything to that effect. "I'm afraid I may be more serious about him than he is about me."

"I hope that isn't the case," Margret said softly.

"Who is the other fellow?"

"Hiram, but your mother mentioned he is engaged to your sister. It seems I am too late in coming to Bowmans Crossing. The Erb sisters have snagged the best ones."

Fannie caught her lower lip between her teeth. If Noah hadn't been spending so much time with her, would he have discovered he liked the bishop's niece? Had her wild scheme prevented him from finding true romance? Or was he growing to care for her as she had grown to care for him?

Margret glanced Fannie's way. "There is talk that Noah may leave the faith. Are you aware of that?"

"He has not made that decision."

"So you have talked about it? Are you hoping to sway his decision by your affection?"

"*Nee*, I don't feel that would be right."

"And yet you continue to see him, knowing he may leave us."

"He is my friend, and I will support him in his decision."

"I'm surprised to hear you say that. Are you thinking about leaving the faith, as well? If he does?"

"There are many unanswered questions in my heart. If I choose to leave, it will not be because of Noah. What about you? Have you considered leaving?"

"I have already been baptized. I have no intention of leaving the Amish."

"But what if you never marry? What would you do then?"

"I have faith that God has a path laid out for me. I will do my best to accept His will. I long for love, marriage and children of my own, but if that is not to be, I will spend my life in service to my parents, my siblings and my community. There are many things an unmarried woman can do to make life better for all."

"But can you be happy?"

Margret laughed. "Of course I can be happy. Happiness does not come from outside of us. It comes from the inside. My uncle lost both his legs in a farm accident. No one would blame him for descending into bitterness, but he found inner peace and he is as happy as the next person. Perhaps more so, for he knows how close he came to losing his life. I think happiness comes from serving others. I don't think it comes from having the things we think we want."

Fannie glanced to where Noah was playing ball with his brothers. He seemed content today, but she knew questions about his place in the world troubled him. If she hadn't involved him in her courtship ploy, he would have had to end his *rumspringa* and make his decision. Would he have accepted his place among the Amish as God's will without testing his skill as a pitcher? As much as she hated to think of him going out into the world, she knew he needed to find out for himself.

Rebecca came out the school door and stood on the step. "Margret, can you give us a hand? Let Fannie hold Benjamin. It will only take a few minutes. You don't mind, do you, Fannie?"

Before Fannie could form a reply, the drooling baby was thrust into her arms. She sat him upright in her lap, but his head wobbled so much she thought he might hurt his neck. She pulled him close against her chest and cradled him in her arms. He stared at her with wide blue eyes that soon grew worried.

"Don't cry." Fannie searched for something to distract him. She used her bonnet ribbon to dangle in front of him, touching his nose and then pulling it away.

His frown disappeared. He grinned a wide toothless smile when his chubby fingers closed over the ribbon and he promptly stuffed it into his mouth. In a matter of seconds it was wet with drool.

Fannie smiled at him. "At least it's not my neck."

When Margret returned a few minutes later, Fannie reluctantly gave him back. Babies weren't so bad, after all.

* * *

"This is the first time in ten years that the grown men have lost to the schoolboy team in their annual game." Noah knew he'd be teased mercilessly when his ball team learned of it.

He sat down on the quilt beside Fannie. Most of the people who had come to the frolic were packing up and heading home. The new wing of the school was finished, except for the siding that needed to be painted, but that would be done by the schoolchildren after the start of the school year. "Timothy and Lillian are tickled with the amount of work that was done today."

When Fannie didn't reply, he glanced her way. She was staring off into the distance. He looked in that direction and saw the bishop helping his wife and nieces into his buggy.

"Margret is a very sweet woman," Fannie said without looking at Noah. "Have you taken the time to visit with her?"

"I'm too busy spending time with you."

"If we weren't dating, would you be interested in her?"

He leaned back on his arms and crossed his legs at the ankles. "If we weren't dating, you'd be in Florida, and I'd be hiding in the barn to avoid all the single women my mother had lined up for me to meet."

"I'm serious."

"Fannie, it's too late now to wonder what would have happened if we had made a different choice. If *Gott* has chosen Margret Stolfus to be my wife, it will come to pass."

"I reckon." She swiveled to face him. "What kind of wife are you looking for?"

"I haven't been looking for a wife, Fannie."

"If you were, what kind of woman would she be?"

"Funny, caring, loyal." *Everything you are.* Only he

didn't have the right to say that to her. "What kind of husband are you looking for?"

"If I ever choose to marry, it will be to a man who accepts me as I am. He won't want to change me. I'll want him to be kind, hardworking and not afraid to say he needs me. I hope that the things I value are important to him, as well."

Noah wasn't sure where this conversation had come from, but he saw Fannie was serious about it. "I reckon I want a woman like my mother. She laughs a lot and she is always trying to feed us. No matter what troubles arise in our home, she has food to make it better. In my opinion, her cinnamon rolls do the most good."

That coaxed a smile from Fannie. "Oatmeal-raisin cookies are my mother's treatment for what ails us."

"I suspect it's the love that goes in more than the ingredients."

"I'm sure you're right."

Paul came up to them, grinning from ear to ear. "I've just been hired for my first auction."

Noah looked around. "Who would hire you?"

"The *Englisch* nurse. Her brother's charity is holding an auction at the university where he teaches, and their auctioneer just canceled. I've got a job."

"That's *wunderbar*," Fannie said, enjoying his eagerness. "What are they auctioning off and when is it?"

"I don't know. I forgot to ask." He dashed away, leaving Fannie and Noah grinning at each other.

"Are you ready to go home?" Noah held out his hand.

Fannie nodded and allowed him to help her to her feet. Together they folded the quilt and he tucked it under his arm. Side by side, they started toward the road that curved around the school.

His brother Samuel drove by, nodding to them with a

knowing smile, but he didn't offer them a lift. Noah tossed the quilt in the back of Samuel's wagon as he went past. He was glad his brother hadn't offered them a ride. Noah wanted to draw out this day with Fannie. He didn't want to hurry it along in the least. She walked as slowly as he did.

"Don't you have ball practice tonight?" She slanted a glance his way.

"It won't hurt me to miss one practice."

"It won't?"

He smiled at her. "Not a bit."

It was twilight by the time they reached the covered bridge. Inside the dark arch, he stopped. Fannie turned toward him. He took her face between his hands. "I'm thinking this might be the right time and the right place, Fannie Erb. Are you busy?"

"Not at all." She closed her eyes and leaned toward him.

He pulled her close and kissed her. Gently at first, but with greater urgency when she responded in kind. The babbling of the river running beneath him, the sounds of the wind and the insects in the reeds all faded away until she was the only thing in his universe.

Any doubts Fannie had about her feelings for Noah vanished at the soft caress of his lips against hers. All she wanted was to move closer and closer still. She slipped her arms around his neck. He pulled her tight against him and held her in a powerful embrace. This wasn't at all like their kiss in the garden. That had been the kiss of a brash boy. This was the kiss of a man.

Her heart was pounding and her head was spinning by the time he drew away, ending the sweetest moment of her life. He didn't release her. He simply tucked her head beneath his chin and held her until his breathing slowed. "You are a remarkable woman, Fannie."

"I'm happy you think so."

"I'd better get you home."

She looked up at him. "Do we have to go?"

"*Ja*, we have to." He laid his arm across her shoulders and started walking with her tucked against his side.

"I'm not going to be busy *all* weekend," she offered.

He chuckled. "I'll keep that in mind."

Fannie walked in silence beside him, unsure what to say. Did this mean anything? Was he ready to remain Amish? Was she? Where did they go from here?

As they reached her lane, a buggy came flying past them.

"Was that Hiram?" Fannie asked, catching a glimpse of the stern-faced young man as he pulled out without acknowledging them.

"I think it was," Noah said.

"I wonder what he was doing at our place?"

"Maybe he's selling your *daed* some pigs."

She chuckled. "Let's go find out."

Before they reached the front door, Fannie saw her mother on the porch, weeping loudly as Fannie's father tried to console her.

"*Mamm*, what's wrong?" Fannie rushed to her side.

"I don't know how I'll ever be able to hold my head up in front of Hiram's family again. I can't believe she would do this to us."

"What are you talking about?" Fannie couldn't make sense of it.

Her father shook his head sadly. "Your sister has broken her engagement to Hiram. He had a letter from her today. She has met someone else in Florida."

Fannie's mother buried her face in her husband's shirt-front. "I never should have sent her to that place."

Chapter Twelve

❧

"I feel terrible. I don't know what to do." The next morning Fannie sat beside Noah on the bench in his mother's flower garden overlooking the river behind his house. She wasn't sure why she had gone to seek him out, but she needed to talk to someone.

"You couldn't know this would happen."

"It was all my idea. Now my sister's life is ruined. Poor Hiram. I can't imagine he will take her back. He must be humiliated. I was always making fun of him the way people made fun of me. How could I be so cruel?"

"I was as cruel in my comments as you were. The saving grace is that Hiram never heard our jests at his expense."

"That doesn't make them right."

"I agree, but all we can do is move forward and behave better in the future. And your sister's life is not ruined. It has taken an unexpected turn, that's all."

"I guess you're right."

"What are your parents going to do about Betsy? Are they sending you to take her place?"

"*Mamm* has gone to the phone shack to put a call through to my grandparents. Their landlady has a phone she lets them use. Once *Mamm* has had a chance to talk to them and to Betsy, she and *Daed* will decide what to do. If they want me to take her place, I will go. I've caused enough trouble for them."

She jumped to her feet and pulled the head off a sunflower. "This was such a simple plan. We both said we weren't hurting anyone. Why did it have to go so wrong? All I was trying to do was help my friend and look what happened."

"I know you're upset, Fannie, but I'd like to talk to you about last night."

He meant the kiss. Was he going to say he was sorry and it never should have happened? She couldn't bear to hear that from him. "I can't, Noah. I can't deal with one more thing." Throwing the crushed yellow petals to the ground, she ran out of the garden and across the field toward home.

At the house, she paused to catch her breath before she went in. Opening the door, she found her mother in the kitchen. Her face was blotchy, but she wasn't crying. Fannie sat in the chair beside her. "What did *Grossmammi* say? Did you speak to Betsy?"

She nodded. "I spoke to your sister."

"Is she coming back?"

"*Nee*. She wishes to remain and continue caring for my mother. She has promised to give prayerful thought to her engagement to Hiram. She has also promised to stop seeing the young man she met there. He is not Amish. I pray she comes to her senses and makes the correct decision."

"She will. She is a *goot* daughter."

Her mother clasped Fannie's hand. "You are my *goot dochtah*. I don't know what I would do without you. All things are by the will of *Gott*, but He is testing me and He is testing Betsy. I pray we may be found worthy of His mercy."

Fannie cringed inwardly at being called the good daughter. "I will do whatever I can to help."

Her mother rose slowly to her feet. "I am going to go lie down for a while."

Fannie had never known her mother to lie down in the middle of the day. "Are you okay?"

"I am weary today and I wish to rest, that's all. We have the big game to go to this afternoon."

"Why don't you skip the game? *Daed* can go by himself."

"We must keep up appearances. It wouldn't do to give people a reason to speculate on what is wrong. I'm sure the news will get around quickly, but perhaps Betsy will come to her senses soon and we can say it was all a misunderstanding. Besides, I know you want to watch Noah play."

"I watched him play ball at the frolic."

"Don't neglect him because of this. I want at least one of my children to be settled."

The front door opened and Anna Bowman came in. "Noah just told me. You poor dear. What can I do?" The two women embraced and Fannie slipped quietly out of the house. Noah had been right to send Anna. She was exactly who her mother needed now.

Later that afternoon, Fannie took a seat beside her father on the wooden bleachers set up along the third baseline. They had convinced Fannie's mother to stay home. She was still bursting into tears at the drop of a hat.

Noah and his team were gathered around their coach inside the wire enclosure that served as their dugout. Noah's team soon took the field and Fannie watched in amazement as Noah threw the ball with incredible precision and speed. This was nothing like the good-natured game she had watched yesterday.

She turned to her father. "Noah is very good, isn't he?"

"I have never seen the like."

"Do you think he could play for a professional team?"

"Maybe. An Amish fellow would have to give up a lot to follow that path. I've only heard of a few who have been good enough to make the major leagues, and that was years ago."

"The *Englisch* players, do they make a lot of money?"

"These fellows? *Nee.* They play for the fun of it. The professionals? I have heard they can earn millions, especially pitchers."

"Millions of dollars for throwing a ball? I should learn how to do it."

Her father laughed. "I wouldn't let your mother hear you say that. It's a shame Noah can't play for a few more years. It sure is nice to have a winning local team for a change."

"Noah could continue playing. I see no reason for him to stop."

"Are you saying you don't plan to wed this fall?"

She stared at her feet. "I'm not ready to marry so soon."

"Your mother gave me cause to think otherwise."

"I'm afraid that is wishful thinking on *Mamm*'s part."

She watched Noah walk in and take the ball from Walter, who met him halfway. They spoke briefly, then Noah returned to the pitcher's mound. Leaning toward her father, she said, "I hope you can explain this to me. I never liked baseball, so I never played. I know about strikes and balls. I know about outs and innings, but why does Noah nod at the batters?"

"He's nodding at the catcher, not the batter. Walter is giving him signals inside his glove for what kind of pitch he wants Noah to throw."

"Noah says Walter is the best catcher in the league."

"I'm not sure about that, but he's their cleanup hitter."

"What's a cleanup hitter?"

He looked at her as if she'd grown another head. "Are you jesting with me?"

"I wouldn't ask if I knew. Help me learn the game. Mother says I have to impress Noah the way she impressed you."

"Her cooking impressed me. A cleanup hitter is the fourth batter in the lineup. The hope is that several of the first three men will be on base when it's the cleanup hitter's turn. He is normally the most powerful hitter on the team and the one most likely to drive in runs."

"I'm sure Noah could be a cleanup hitter, too."

"His batting average is pretty low."

"Is that good?"

"It's okay for a pitcher. They aren't expected to be good hitters."

"I heard him mention that at the frolic."

When the inning was over and Noah's team came in, Fannie listened to the calls coming from the people in the stands. Some were for the players, calling out encouragement. Others were unkind suggestions, mostly made by fans of the visiting team.

Walter drove in two runs when it was his turn to bat, drawing cheers from everyone around her. As Noah approached the plate, Fannie rose to her feet, cupped her hands around her mouth and yelled, "Knock the hide off that thing. Knock it out of the park."

Her father yanked her back to the bench. "Do not be immodest, daughter."

"Everyone else is yelling."

Noah searched the stands and located her. She waved. He walked into the batter's box and struck out. Fannie leaned back on the bench. "That's too bad. He'll do better next time."

He didn't. At least, not when he came up to bat. He got

on base twice during the game, but never scored. Although she wasn't certain, his pitching seemed to decline, as well. She continued to call out her encouragement, in spite of her father's ire, but it made no difference. Still, the Fire Eaters won by a single run.

Afterward, she stood and waited for Noah to come out of the fire station. Walter walked by on his way in. He stopped when he caught sight of her and came over. "What did you think of our game?"

"I'm happy you won, but I'm no expert on baseball. Give me a horse and I'll list all his finer points and flaws. Did Noah play well?"

"I wouldn't call this his best game, but we won."

"Why wasn't it his best?"

"Honestly, I think it was because you were here."

"Me? What did I do?"

"I noticed he had a hard time keeping his head in the game. I think he was more interested in seeing what you were doing."

"My father was upset with my behavior, but it's hard not to yell for you men when everyone around me is yelling. I thought it was fun. I'm sorry I haven't been to more games. You are league champions now?"

"Only if we win our next game."

"You must be very pleased."

"It's a step in the right direction."

"Tell Noah I'm waiting for him, will you?" She was eager to see him. She wanted to share what she had learned about her sister's plans and to apologize for running away that morning. She'd chosen to leave rather than to show him her poor temper.

"You know Noah has been thinking about pursuing a professional ball career, don't you?"

She folded her arms over her middle and stared at the ground. "I know that."

"Are you trying to talk him out of it?"

Glancing at Walter's set face, Fannie realized he saw her as a threat to his dreams. "Noah must make his decision without influence from anyone. It is between him and *Gott*."

"He's the best pitcher I've ever seen. Don't let him throw his gift away."

Noah was toweling his hair dry when Walter sat down beside him. The room was full of men congratulating each other and laughing. A coveted title was only one game away. Walter gave him a sidelong glance. "You barely pulled that one out, my friend."

He'd been distracted by a loud redhead in the bleachers yelling his name and making him smile. "I wasn't on my game, that's for sure."

"I noticed." Walter was annoyed.

Noah shrugged. "Anyone can have a bad day."

"You've had an off week. You've never missed a practice before. Want to tell me why you weren't here yesterday?"

"I was at the school frolic." Noah didn't look at his friend. He could have made the practice if he'd tried.

"Until after dark?"

"I was busy."

"Busy with Fannie." It was a statement, not a question.

Noah smiled, thinking of the kiss on the bridge. "We're getting along pretty well."

"I thought you said it wasn't serious."

"It wasn't."

Walter arched his eyebrow. "But now it is?"

"Have you ever been in love?" Noah looked at his friend.

"No. Are you in love?"

Noah smiled. "I think I am."

"Does this mean you are ready to give up ball? If you are, I need to know. I have a lot riding on the next game and the state tournament if we get invited. This may be my only shot. If you can't help me get where I need to go, you have to tell me now. Don't leave me hanging."

Was he ready to give up ball? Noah realized if he wanted a life with Fannie, he would have to do just that.

No, he was getting ahead of himself. One kiss, no matter how wonderful, didn't mean Fannie wanted a life with him. She had her own dreams and her own decisions to make.

Yet even the remote possibility of spending a lifetime with her had him thinking twice about what it was that he really wanted.

"What's it going to be?" Walter asked.

Noah shook his head. "I won't leave you hanging."

"I hope not. We have been friends a long time. We've been through a lot together. You know how important this is to me. I thought it was just as important to you."

"I had an off night, but we won. As for the state tournament, it is up to the tournament committee to invite the teams they want to see matched up. Our success or our failure is up to *Gott*."

"I believe that just as you do, but my dad has a favorite Amish proverb he likes to quote. *All that you do, do with your might. Things done by halves are never done right.* Don't go after the next game halfheartedly or it's over. For all of us."

Walter was right. Noah had become so involved with Fannie's group, and with her, that he was neglecting the men who depended on him. It wasn't just a game to them, especially Walter. It was much more to him. Noah scanned the room. The honor of the fire company and the community was riding on the outcome of this season.

"I will heed your words and make sure that I pitch with all my might."

Walter patted his shoulder. "Thanks. Fannie seems like a sweet gal. She'll still be here when the season is over."

Would she? Or would she be on her way to Florida? He needed to see her.

She was waiting for him when he stepped outside, and his heart grew light at the sight of her smiling face.

He reached for her hand and she laced her fingers with his. "I had planned to ride with Walter, but would you like to walk home with me?"

"I would."

"Did you enjoy the game?"

She chuckled. "Couldn't you tell? My father was upset with me for my immodest behavior."

"I liked your behavior."

She pressed a hand to her chest. "I'm shocked."

"Why?"

"You have actually found something you like about me and you admitted it."

"A minor lapse of judgment."

She yanked her hand away. "I thought so."

He snatched it back. "I'm kidding. I like lots of things about you, Fannie."

She rolled her eyes. "Now you're kidding me."

"Nope, not even a little. A vain woman would ask me to list them."

He watched the indecision narrow her eyes, but then she shook her head. "I won't rise to your bait."

"You don't trust me?"

"I do. About as far as I can throw you."

He laughed. "I like that you aren't a vain woman."

* * *

And I like almost everything about you, she thought as he walked beside her. Each day her affection for him deepened.

"What did you find out about your sister?"

"*Mamm* spoke to her. She's reconsidering her decision to break her engagement, and she has promised not to see the man who prompted her choice. I won't be going to Florida. Betsy will be staying for a while."

"I'm glad of that."

"Me, too."

It was comfortable walking with him, hand in hand. The sun was a red ball hanging low in the west as it sank behind them. It cast their long shadows down the road in front of them. Fannie could remember her grandparents walking this way in the evenings. What would it be like to spend a lifetime holding Noah's hand?

"Fannie, what are we going to do about this courtship?"

"I have been wondering that, too. I hate to break it off now. My mother will be crushed."

"What if we don't break it off?"

Her heart tripped in her chest, causing her to catch her breath. "What are you suggesting?"

"We're getting along well, don't you think?"

"Surprisingly well, actually."

He chuckled. "I knew you were going to say that. Let's give it some more time. Let's make it a real courtship. What do you say?"

If she agreed, would he remain Amish? Would she be asking him to throw away his gift from God as Walter had suggested?

She bit the corner of her lip as she struggled to find the right thing to say.

Chapter Thirteen

On Wednesday afternoon, Fannie sat on Trinket, ready to lead her group through their program, but all she could think about was Noah's request to make their courtship a real one. Instead of saying yes, she had asked for some time to think it over. It was the memory of the disappointment that had flashed across his face that was keeping her up at night.

She told herself there was no harm in waiting, but she hadn't believed there was harm in her idea in the first place. That had been a false assumption. Fannie wasn't eager to create another set of problems.

Trinket shifted her weight, eager to get started. Their arena was an open field marked with reflective orange tape on thin metal rods, the kind used to hold electric fence wires. Hundreds of Amish folk were lined up behind the barrier, waiting for the draft horse auction to begin. Fannie and Connie had placed orange cones to mark the perimeter of their patterns so the girls didn't feel lost in the large area.

A heavyset man wearing an orange vest over his blue shirt came up to her. "Are you ready to begin?"

She nodded and rode over to where Zoe and Connie had the speaker system plugged in to a long extension cord. "It's showtime."

Riding back, she took her place and waited for the music to begin. The rollicking strains of the song began and Fannie said, "Now."

Because she was the first rider, she had no idea if the others were in line behind her until she made the first turn. She glanced back and smiled. The horses were in near-perfect step as they cantered across the field. Waiting for the pause in the singer's voice at just the right spot, Fannie wheeled Trinket left. The line of riders split four abreast, going in opposite directions with awesome precision. A few seconds later, the music stopped abruptly.

Fannie looked in Connie's direction. A tall man in a dark hat and suit with a long, shaggy gray beard was walking onto the field. He motioned to Abbie and Laura, who rode slowly to him. Fannie cantered over, too.

He sliced the air with one finger. "This is not permitted. *Dess* music of the *Englisch* is verboten. *Kumma.*" He turned on his heel and walked away.

Fannie looked to Abbie and Laura for an explanation, although she suspected she already knew the answer. Timothy came out to stand with the group. "What's going on?"

Laura looked ready to cry. "That's our grandpa. He is the bishop of our church. I'm sorry, Fannie. We have to go."

"Of course. Don't worry about it." She managed to smile at them, but inside she was seething.

She rode to Connie and motioned for the others to join her. "Start the music over. We'll finish with six."

Noah watched Fannie pacing across Timothy's kitchen and wondered if the floor would have a groove in it when she was done. He'd seen her angry, but not quite like this. "He just walked out and stopped our performance yesterday. His granddaughters were humiliated."

"He was doing what he believed was right," Lillian said.

"The girls hadn't told their family that they were riding to recorded music," Timothy added. "They thought if it was okay for the others, it was okay for them. However, Bishop Lapp leads a very conservative church, and even for unbaptized members, music is forbidden. I spoke to the man at length and he won't be swayed on this."

"So, this project is dead," Connie said glumly.

"Not necessarily," Lillian said. "Timothy, tell them."

"Lillian asked Debra Merrick to do some research for me and she came up with an alternative. She showed us a video of an Amish drill team where the leader signaled changes with a whistle. I spoke with Bishop Lapp this morning and he finds this acceptable."

Fannie stopped pacing. "A whistle instead of music. It won't work."

"Why not, Fannie?" Noah asked.

"All of us, including the horses are keyed into the beat. We don't have time to relearn our timing and signals. The Horse Expo is two weeks away."

Connie clasped her hands together on the red-and-white-checkered tablecloth. "What choice do we have? I had to prepay to reserve the hauler and motel rooms for us. I might get a refund on some of it, but not all of it."

Fannie moved to stare out the window. "Cut your losses and run, Connie. I'm sorry I ever got you into this."

Connie moved to put her arm around Fannie. "It was a fine idea. We've simply run into a stumbling block."

"Another one. What next?" She shrugged off Connie's arm and went outside.

Noah followed her. "Don't give up. You and your crew can do it. I have faith in you."

"I don't have faith in me anymore."

"Let me take you home." She was hurting and he had no idea how to help her.

"I'm sorry, Noah. I'd rather be alone." She paused. "I forgot to ask. Did you win your last game?"

"We did. We're the league champions."

"That's great. I guess I can give the whistle thing a try." She mounted her horse and rode away, leaving him aching to hold her and comfort her. Ever since he had asked to make their courtship real, she had been pulling away from him. Was it because she knew he might not remain Amish, or was it something else?

The members of Noah's ball team crowded into Eric's office and waited. The coaches of the teams that were being invited to the state tournament were to be notified by phone after ten o'clock on Thursday morning. It was ten fifteen.

"They aren't going to call." Walter pushed out of his chair and moved to the window.

"Have faith. We won our league." Noah, too, was beginning to doubt they would be contacted.

Teams qualified for the invitational by participating in regional tournaments held throughout the state. While finishing in the top generally guaranteed an invitation, it was up to the State Baseball Federation to determine invitees.

"There will be twelve teams in all. It takes time to call everyone." Eric drummed his fingers on his desk beside his smartphone.

"I need some air." Walter pushed past Noah and went outside.

Noah followed his friend. "Waiting is the hard part."

"Not playing will be the hard part."

"If we don't get called, there is always next year."

"You won't be pitching for us next year. Without your talent, we are only slightly above average players."

"That's not true."

"Isn't it?"

"What makes you think I won't be pitching again next year?"

"The girl."

Noah stared at his shoes. "I'm not sure I'm what she wants."

"But she is what *you* want."

"I'm trying to discover God's will for me. Is it Fannie? Is it a professional ball career? If that doesn't work out, will I come home and remain Amish because I've failed or because God wants me here? He has to show me the way."

Walter sighed. "Noah, maybe God wants you to make the choice. Did you ever think of that?"

Noah was saved from answering when he heard the sound of Eric's cell phone ringing. He and Walter grinned at each other and hurried back inside. Eric picked up the phone and listened. He gave them the thumbs-up sign and everyone cheered.

Noah slapped Walter on the back. "See? Faith."

"I can't believe it. This is my shot, Noah. I feel it in my bones."

"I pray you are right."

Eric stood. "Everyone is invited to my place for pizza. We need to celebrate."

The laughing group of men piled out of the office into the main bay of the fire station. Someone started honking the fire engine's horn.

Noah watched his teammates congratulating each other and realized there was only one person he wanted to share the news with as soon as possible. Fannie would be at her practice. He tapped Walter on the arm. "Can you run me over to Connie Stroud's farm before you go get pizza?"

"Aren't you coming with us?"

"I'll be over later. Save me a slice."

"Sure. Hop in."

Ten minutes later, Walter dropped Noah in front of Connie's barn. Noah entered the building and leaned on the rail. The team was lined up by twos. Fannie blew a whistle once and started forward. They were only a few paces along when Susan came up too quickly and had to pull back. Rose bumped into her and Goldenrod turned to the outside, breaking the pattern.

Rose got her horse back in line as Fannie blew the whistle and started to circle left. Sylvia had been holding back to let Rose regain her position. She turned too short and cut in front of Abbie. The resulting confusion made everyone stop.

Fannie whirled Trinket around and threw down her whistle. "This isn't going to work."

Noah stepped into the ring. "What's going on here?"

"What does it look like? We're riding without music and making mistake after mistake," Fannie snapped.

Sylvia looked ready to cry. Abbie and Laura were sniffling.

"We are learning to make our pattern changes when I blow the whistle, only we can't get it right." Fannie's voice shook with frustration.

He crossed to Fannie's side. "I'm sorry. Where is Timothy?"

"He's talking to Connie about where the girls should stay in Columbus. They are trying to find someplace less expensive and figure out how we are going to get the carts there."

"It turns out I'll be in Columbus at the same time you'll be there."

"Your team got the invitation?"

"We did."

She rolled her eyes. "You must be so thrilled. It's all working out exactly as you planned."

He pulled back. "You don't sound thrilled for me."

"Am I supposed to be?"

"I thought so. I thought you'd be happy for me. Maybe I was mistaken in your feelings."

"I guess you were. At least this stupid fake courtship can be over now. I can't tell you how happy that makes me."

"Fannie, I know you're upset, but don't take it out on me." He picked up the whistle. "It's going to take more time, that's all. You'll get it."

"We don't have more time. We've only got two weeks."

He handed her the whistle. "Everyone here will try their best. Stop being a baby about it and do the work."

She knocked the whistle from his hand. "That's easy for you to say. You won your season. You'll be pitching in the tournament of your dreams. I'm sure you'll be laughing at us as we make fools of ourselves in front of a thousand people. All our hard work will be for nothing. Connie will have wasted the money she's already spent on entry fees and motel rooms for us. I wish I'd never come up with this stupid idea, and I wish you'd leave me alone."

She kicked Trinket into a gallop and shot out the arena door.

Noah started after her, but Susan touched his arm. "Let her go. Let her blow off some steam."

"You girls are looking to her for leadership."

"And that's why she'll be back when she cools down," Susan said with a tiny smile.

He sighed. "You're right. I reckon she has to figure that out for herself."

The side door flew open and Zoe came running in. She gripped the railing, her eyes wide and frightened. "Come quick."

Noah started toward her. "What is it?"

"Fannie tried to jump Trinket over the south fence and they fell. I think she's hurt bad."

Noah vaulted over the railing and raced out the door.

Fannie was lying facedown in the grass just beyond the smashed board fence. Trinket lay a few feet away from her. He sprinted toward Fannie. *Please, Lord, let her be all right.*

Sliding to a stop beside her, Noah dropped to his knees as his first-aid training took over. There was blood on the side of her head and face, but she was breathing. Relief surged through his body and he started breathing again, too. He gently took her wrist in his hand to check her pulse. It was erratic but strong. *Thank You, God.*

He still didn't know how badly injured she might be, but he knew enough not to move her. Trinket was struggling to get up but couldn't. Blood covered her neck and front legs.

Connie arrived beside Noah. "How bad is it?"

"I'm not sure." He leaned down. "Fannie, can you hear me? Speak to me, Fannie."

"Trinket?" Her voice was a bare whisper, but it was the sweetest sound he'd ever heard.

"I'll take care of her," Connie said, moving to the horse. Speaking softly, she eased the mare's head back to the ground to keep her from moving. She quieted and lay with her sides heaving.

Connie pulled her cell phone from her pocket. "I'm calling 911."

"I'm so sorry," Fannie whispered. She closed her fingers over Noah's hand.

"Where are you hurt, *liebchen*?"

"I can't move—my legs." Her fingers went limp.

Noah squeezed them tighter. "Fannie, Fannie stay with me."

She didn't respond. *Please, God, don't take her from me. Not now, not before I've told her how much I love her.*

He leaned close and kissed her pale cheek. "I love you, Fannie. Do you hear me? I love you."

* * *

She had only herself to blame.

Her foolish, childish temper tantrum had cost her dearly.

Fannie lay inside the MRI machine at the hospital, listening to the thudding sounds it made. The doctor had explained that it would take detailed images of her spine and show what was wrong. It would tell them if she would walk again.

She was afraid to pray for herself. Afraid it was too late to ask God to heal her, but she prayed He would spare Trinket. Her poor, brave horse had done everything Fannie had asked and received only pain as a reward.

Fannie didn't remember anything after flying over Trinket's head until she woke up being wheeled into the emergency entrance of the hospital. She tried to look for Noah, but she couldn't move her head. Then she heard his voice telling her to lie still. The rest of her admission was a blur of bits and pieces, until now.

Finally, the hammering sound stopped and someone spoke to her from the end of the tunnel she lay in. Her bed moved backward, bringing her into the bright lights of the imaging room.

She couldn't turn her head away from their glare. A hard plastic collar around her neck prevented any movement. She closed her eyes as she was wheeled out. When her bed stopped moving, she swallowed against the pain the jolt caused in her back.

"We are here, Fannie." Her mother's voice made Fannie open her eyes again. Her parents were bending over her. There were tears in their eyes.

"Don't worry, *Mamm*. I'm fine." Fannie smiled to prove her point, but neither parent look relieved. "How is Trinket?"

Her father laid a hand on her head. "Noah told us Connie is taking care of her. The vet was on his way. As soon as Connie knows something for sure, she will call Noah and he will tell you. You are not to worry about your horse now. You are to get well."

The young doctor she had seen earlier came up to the other side of her bed. "I'm happy to say she is going to do just that if she takes it easy and does as we tell her."

"She will walk again?" Fresh tears poured down her mother's face.

"She has two burst-fractured vertebrae, but her spinal cord is intact. The bones are cracked, but none of the pieces are displaced. She won't need surgery. Her paralysis is most likely caused by what we call spinal shock. It can last a few hours to a few weeks after an injury like this. We are giving her anti-inflammatory medicine to relieve the tissue swelling and pressure. Other than a nasty concussion, we didn't find anything else abnormal. Fannie, can you wiggle your toes for me?"

She concentrated and moved her left foot a fraction.

"Good. The steroids are already helping. You are a very fortunate young woman. Our physical therapy department will fit you with a back brace that must be worn at all times while the bones mend."

"Will I be able to ride again?" Fannie whispered.

"Not for several months, but eventually, yes. I suggest you avoid having your horse step on your back in the future."

"Is that what happened? I don't remember. Trinket would never hurt me on purpose."

"I'm a horseman myself, so I believe you. I'm having the nurse give you something to help you rest. We will move you to a regular room when one is available. Expect to stay with us for at least three days. I know the Amish don't believe in medical insurance, so I will get you home as soon as I can."

The nurse came in and injected something into Fannie's IV. "This is going to make you sleepy very quickly."

Fannie's father held out his hand. "*Danki, Herr Doktor.* We are deeply grateful to you."

The doctor shook his hand. "I did my part, but God was looking after her."

When the man left the room, Fannie's mother leaned down to kiss her brow. "We are so thankful. Noah is waiting outside. Shall I have him come in?"

Shame blossomed in Fannie's heart. She remembered the cruel words she'd spoken to Noah. None of it was true. Yet God in His mercy had spared her life after all the deceit she had carried out. It was time to make a clean breast of it.

"*Mamm*, I have to tell you something first and I don't want you to be angry with Noah. He thought he was helping me."

Her parents exchanged puzzled glances.

"What are you talking about?" her mother asked.

"Noah and I are not courting. We never were. We made up the story so I could stay and ride in the drill team instead of going to Florida. I truly wanted to help Connie, but that doesn't change the fact that what I did was wrong."

"You lied to us?" Her mother drew back.

"I did. Please forgive me."

Her father's brow darkened. "And Noah lied to his family about this, too?"

"Yes," she answered softly, ashamed that she had suggested the scheme in the first place and had to lay any part of the blame at his door. "I'm so sorry."

"We will speak of this again when you are home." Her father put his arm around her mother's shoulders.

There was a knock at the door and Noah looked in. Relief filled his eyes. "You're awake."

"Come in." Fannie blinked and had trouble focusing on his dear face. She had so much to atone for.

"The doctor said it's good news. You're going to be fine," Noah said.

"Noah, I had to tell them."

He stepped inside. "Tell them what?"

"That we aren't courting. That we made it up."

"Fannie, I need to talk to you about us." He looked at her parents. "It's not what you think."

"I know how upset your mother will be and I am ashamed of my daughter's part in this." Fannie heard the disapproval in her mother's voice, but she couldn't keep her eyes open any longer. "I'm sorry, Noah, but now you are free."

He didn't want to be free.

The door opened behind Noah and a nurse came in. "We have a room for her now. If you'll wait outside for a few minutes while we get her ready, you can follow us when we leave."

Noah longed to tell Fannie his true feelings, but she was already asleep. He would have to wait. He held the door for Fannie's parents and felt their disapproval as they passed. Outside in the hall, they turned to him. He wanted Fannie to hear his words first, but it was her parents who needed to know his intentions now.

He took a deep breath. "What Fannie has told you is the truth, but it isn't the whole truth. I agreed to a pretend courtship because my parents were pressuring me to stop playing ball, join the faith and take a wife. I wasn't ready for that."

"I can't believe the two of you have deceived us this way." Belinda dabbed at her eyes with her handkerchief.

"It was wrong and I beg your forgiveness. But I want you to know my feelings for Fannie have changed. I am in love with your daughter. I kept up the pretense of a courtship because I wanted to be with her, not because I needed to convince you or my parents of my continued affections. I love her, and I pray that she loves me."

Ernest stroked his beard. "You aren't certain of my daughter's feelings?"

"Fannie and I quarreled before her accident. We both said hurtful things. You know her temper. I'm not sure she will believe me when I tell her how I truly feel."

Belinda gave him a watery smile. "Fannie is quick to anger and often speaks in haste, but I have seen a change in her recently. I believe it is because she has come to care for you, too, Noah, but Fannie can't be pushed into anything. She only digs in her heels."

The door to Fannie's room opened and two nurses wheeled her bed into the hall. Noah stood back to let them pass. He gently touched Fannie's shoulder, but she didn't open her eyes. One of the nurses said, "We are moving her to room 211. You can follow us, if you like."

They started down the hall with Belinda walking behind them. Ernest laid a hand on Noah's shoulder. "Fannie is a lot like my Belinda was when I first met her. Sassy, full of vinegar and determined to be independent. Like her mother, my daughter can be led, but she can't be driven. You have your work cut out for you."

"She is worth it. I can't imagine my life without her."

Chapter Fourteen

Fannie woke in near-total darkness. It took her a long moment to realize where she was. A faint light showed through the blinds covering a window beside her bed. The pain in her back was a dull ache. She lay still, not wanting to rouse it, and rubbed her sleep-blurry eyes with the heels of her hands. The hard collar was gone from her neck, but another brace encased her body from her chest to her hips. It was a pointed reminder of her foolishness and of God's mercy.

She had hurt a great many people with her bullheaded determination. Connie had invested her slim resources in Fannie's plan because Fannie convinced her she could make it work. She had lied to her parents and to Noah's family. She had turned her back on her responsibility to her grandparents, sending Betsy to care for them instead. When had horses become more important than her family? More important than her faith?

Shame sent her spirits lower. "I have learned my lesson, Lord," she whispered into the darkness.

Her path forward was clear now. She would beg the forgiveness of those she had wronged. She would strive to undo the hurt she had caused and humbly accept the physical burden of pain God had visited on her. But the pain in her body was nothing compared to the pain in her heart.

She loved Noah. Loved him enough to know that she was the wrong woman for him. He deserved someone better. She was barely trustworthy. She wasn't humble or meek of spirit. She was prideful and arrogant. Instead of turning to God for help, she had assumed she could supply the answers and win the day by herself. Noah did, indeed, deserve a better woman, and she would make sure she never hurt him again.

It was almost noon the next day when Noah returned to the hospital. He wanted to see Fannie alone. He needed to tell her how much he loved her.

The door to her room was open. He stopped just outside. Connie, Zoe and all the girls from the team were gathered around Fannie's bed.

"The girls don't think they can do this without you, Fannie. You're the leader," Connie said.

"I'm a poor leader. My actions yesterday were childish and irresponsible. I don't think you can do this without me. I *know* you can do it. Zoe, you have the routine down as well as I do and you're a better rider. If you don't mind dressing plain, Zoe, you will be a *wunderbar* addition to The Amish Girls."

"You want me to wear a bonnet? Isn't that against the rules or something?"

"I will loan you one of my *kapps*," Abbie said.

"You can wear one of my dresses over your riding clothes. No one will know you aren't Amish," Laura said with a giggle.

Zoe glanced around the room. "I don't feel right about pretending to be Amish."

Fannie reached toward her and took her hand. "You're

right, Zoe. You should never pretend to be something you aren't."

Abbie put an arm around her friend. "My *mamm* can make you a shirt out of the same material as our pink dresses. You can wear a white kerchief over your hair. That way you'll still match us, but folks will know you're *Englisch*."

Connie leaned down to her daughter. "Is that acceptable?"

"It sure is." Zoe nodded vigorously, clearly happy to be part of the group.

Fannie smiled at them. "I'm sorry I won't be there to help you practice. Susan, I want you to take over as the group leader. Timothy says he can supervise you six days a week, if that's what it will take."

"We won't let you down," Susan promised. The other girls all agreed.

"I know you will do your best. That's all anyone can do. Getting frustrated and angry won't help." She rapped on the brace encasing her upper body. "I know. I tried it and look where it got me. Ask *Gott* for help as often as you need it. He is listening."

"Why was *Gott* so unfair to you?" Pamela asked, a catch in her voice.

Fannie reached out to cup the child's face. "We can't know why bad things happen, but *Gott* has a reason. I believe He had a lesson for me to learn. My biggest mistake was not putting *Gott* first in my life. I didn't pray for guidance when I told Connie my idea for a drill team, not even when new problems arose. I thought I had to do it myself. I had to make it work. Worst of all, I didn't give thanks for you, my friends. I have been greatly blessed and I failed to be grateful." Her voice trembled and tears filled her eyes.

Connie laid her hand over Fannie's. "We should go, honey. You need your rest."

"How is Trinket?" Fannie asked quickly, wiping her cheek with the back of her hand.

"Trinket is recovering nicely. Fortunately, she didn't sustain any broken bones, just some deep cuts and bad bruises. Don't worry about her. We are taking good care of her, aren't we girls?"

"Very *goot* care," Zoe said in a bad Amish accent.

Noah stepped back as the girls left Fannie's room and thanked them for coming. They were being brave for Fannie's benefit, but he could see how upset they were.

Connie stayed beside him as the girls walked on. "I know she has been through a lot, but I'm worried about her. Keep an eye on her, will you?"

"She sounded fine to me."

Connie didn't look convinced. "I agree she said all the right things, but the fire in her eyes is missing."

"Don't fret. Fannie is a strong woman. She will bounce back from this."

"I hope you're right."

He dismissed her worry and opened the door to Fannie's room. "May I come in?"

"Hello, Noah." She smiled at him, but it didn't reach her eyes. She looked down at her hands clasped together on her brace.

"I'm glad to see you looking better. You gave me a terrible fright."

"I'm sorry for that." Why wouldn't she look at him?

He pulled a chair up beside her bed. "Fannie, I want to talk to you about us."

"It's a relief to stop pretending, isn't it? I feel like I've had a boulder lifted off my chest."

"That's just it. I'm not pretending anymore, Fannie. I'm in love with you."

She looked at him then, with sadness in her eyes. "I've

come to care for you, too, Noah, but not in that way. I care for you as a friend. I always will, but we must go our separate ways now."

"Nee." Noah couldn't believe what he was hearing. His heart sank at the blankness of her expression.

Fannie saw the confusion on Noah's face and hardened her heart against comforting him. She had done him a great disservice. He thought he was in love with her, but it was only pity and he would realize that soon enough. He deserved a better woman than she could ever be. "You aren't responsible for what happened, Noah. This was *Gott*'s will."

He shook his head. "I kissed you, Fannie, and you kissed me back. That wasn't the kiss of a friend."

"I'm sorry, Noah. I never intended to hurt you. I wanted our courtship to become real. Every time someone mentioned it, I was ashamed of what I had done. I was ashamed of making you a party to my deception."

"We started out together for the wrong reasons, but that doesn't matter now. I love you, Fannie. Nothing you say will change that."

"Then I have done you an even greater disservice than I imagined. Please forgive me."

He scooted his chair back. "You're tired. You're in pain. I should have waited until you were feeling better before I said anything."

"Please leave, Noah." She looked out the window.

"We can talk about this later. Don't shut me out, Fannie," he pleaded.

"When I'm recovered enough to travel, I'll be going to Florida and Betsy will be returning. I have neglected my duty to my grandparents. I see that now."

"What about Trinket? What about your friends?"

She stared at her clenched fingers. "My father will take

care of my horse. I have caused Connie enough trouble. The Amish Girls will ride without me and they will be fine."

"What about me, Fannie? How can I be fine if you can't even look at me?"

She forced herself to smile at him. "You had a purpose for joining me in our false courtship. That purpose still exists. *Gott* has given me an answer to my prayers. I accept it, even if it isn't the answer I wanted. I will take my vows when I return from Florida. You must find *Gott*'s answer for your life. Go to the state tournament and use the gift He has given you. To do less than your best would be wrong. If it is His will that you leave us and play professional ball, He will tell you."

"And if it is His will that I come home?"

"Either way, I will be happy for you, Noah. I will always be your friend."

"Fannie, I don't understand. I have come to know you and admire you, and I thought you returned my feelings."

"I admire your kindness. I admire many things about you, Noah, but I'm not the woman you need."

"I will be the judge of that."

He wasn't leaving. If he didn't go, she would break down and tell him she loved him. She closed her eyes. "After prayerful consideration, I realize you are not the man for me. I'm sorry. I'm very tired. Please go now." She turned her face toward the window, unwilling to watch him walk out of her life. When she heard the door close, tears streamed down her cheeks.

"Goodbye, Noah. I love you, too," she whispered.

Eric Swanson had been kind enough to take Noah to the hospital and then home. Noah didn't share any of his conversation with Fannie on the ride, but he was sure Eric knew he was upset. When they reached the farm, Noah stepped out of the car and looked back at him. "Would you like to come in?"

"Another time. Are you okay?"

"We'll see."

"Hang in there. She's going to be fine."

Noah nodded. Fannie was going to be fine, but he wasn't.

He found his mother in the kitchen when he entered the house. He had confessed his part in Fannie's fake courtship to his parents the night before. They had been shocked and dismayed by his behavior, but they forgave him and listened to the whole story without harsh judgment.

His mother pulled a pan of cinnamon rolls from the oven. Setting them on the table, she looked at him. "How is she?"

"She's okay." He took a seat at the table.

"And how are you?"

He raked his hands through his hair. "I don't know. I love her, but she says she doesn't love me. Where does that leave me?"

"Fannie has had a terrible experience, Noah. Give her time to heal. She will see things more clearly in time."

"I hope you are right." He pulled off a piece of cinnamon bun and popped it into his mouth. It burned, but he welcomed the pain. It took his mind off the ache in his heart.

His mother moved the pan away from him. "You never could wait for the frosting."

"I like them plain." He watched her make her glaze from powdered sugar, butter, vanilla and hot water.

"I like mine sweet and gooey." She stirred the mixture rapidly.

"*Mamm*, what would you do if I didn't join the church?"

"I'd never make you cinnamon rolls again," she said, without missing a stroke.

"I'm serious."

She stopped stirring to stare at him with deep concern in her eyes. "Are you actually considering this?"

"Maybe. I'm not sure."

She set her bowl down and took a seat across from him. "I would be brokenhearted, but I would accept your decision if that is what *Gott* wills for you. We must each serve Him in our own way."

He gave vent to his frustration. "How can I tell what His will is? I'm waiting for a sign, something to tell me what He wants from me. Am I to be a baseball player or a farmer? English or Amish? How do I know?"

Her expression softened. "My son, our Lord has given his children a great and terrible gift. The gift of free will. We get to choose our path. When we seek direction in our lives, we must pray for *Gott*'s guidance. But don't expect Him to put up a billboard that says This Way, Noah."

"It would sure be easier if He did."

She leaned forward and placed her hand on his chest. "*Gott*'s answer comes here, not to our eyes or our ears. Listen with your heart and you shall know His will."

Leaning back, she took up her bowl and spread some of the icing over a bun. She pulled it from the pan and broke it in two, offering Noah half. He took it and bit into the sweet, warm bread. "It's *goot. Danki.*"

"I learned a long time ago that *goot* advice goes down more easily with *goot* food. Have I helped you?"

He licked his fingers and nodded. His heart told him Fannie was the only one for him. He hadn't known that right away, but gradually he'd come to realize how much he loved her. Perhaps that was the way God would make known the path he was to choose.

* * *

"Noah is here to see you, Fannie." Her mother stood in the doorway to Fannie's room. Fannie sat in a rocker in the corner of her bedroom, looking out the window. She had been home for a week. Each day Noah had come to visit and each day she had sent him away, but it was becoming harder to do. She missed him so much.

"I don't want to see him. Tell him to stop coming." It hurt to say those words, but a clean break would be better for both of them instead of this painfully drawn-out process.

"As you wish." Her mother closed the door leaving Fannie alone. She blinked back tears and refused to let them fall.

Her door opened again, but it was her father this time. He stood staring at her with his arms crossed over his chest. "Aren't you done feeling sorry for yourself yet?"

She turned her face away. "I'm not feeling sorry for myself. My back aches, and I don't want company."

"Well, you are going to have my company until you agree to leave this room."

"I won't see him."

"He's not here. He and his team are on their way to Columbus. He left with his tail tucked between his legs like a scolded dog. Shame on you for treating him so. The boy is in love with you."

"He'll get over it, and he'll find someone better."

"Do you mean to say my daughter isn't good enough for him?"

"*Nee*, I'm not," she answered in a small voice, wishing her father would go away.

He came across the room and sat on the edge of her bed. "I can see that for myself. Noah deserves a woman with spunk. He needs a sassy gal to make him laugh and show him how wonderful love can be. He doesn't need a damp dishcloth of a woman like you."

"I'm not a damp dishcloth," she snapped back.

"Then stop acting like one. You made some mistakes. Welcome to life. We all make mistakes. Don't compound them by making things worse. That boy loves you. If we can forgive you, why can't you forgive yourself?"

"I don't deserve him."

"I see now. Your pride is getting in the way." He spread his arms wide. "Your sins are too great to be forgiven. Woe to Fannie Erb. Her heart is black as night. No one may love her."

"Don't make fun of me." He was beginning to annoy her.

"Someone should. Poor little Fannie fell off her horse and hurt her back. She can't ride, she can barely walk and she can't be nice to people who care about her. I love you, child, but I am more ashamed of you now than I have ever been in my life."

"What do you want me to do?" she shouted, then covered her mouth with her hand.

He stood. "The Horse Expo is the day after tomorrow and you are going. The doctor says you can travel."

She bit her lip. "They don't need me there."

He shook his head. "This isn't about you. It's about them. They want you there, Fannie. Doing something for someone else is the first step in your recovery. What do you say?"

He was right. It wasn't about her. Not anymore. She nodded. "They deserve my support. I'll go."

Her father came and took her face between his strong, calloused hands. "*Goot.* Noah deserves your support, too, Fannie. He's hurting. He doesn't deserve someone better. Do you know what he does deserve?"

"What?" Tears slipped from the corners of her eyes.

"Someone who loves him as much as you do." Her father kissed her forehead and left her room.

Fannie wiped her damp cheeks. Her father was right. She still hadn't learned her lesson. Instead of praying for God's guidance, she had assumed she knew best and had pushed Noah away. He had gone to his tournament and he might never come back. She bowed her head. "I'm sorry, Lord. I accept Your forgiveness and I pray it is not too late for me to tell Noah how much I love him. Please bring him back to us."

Chapter Fifteen

Noah stood lined up with his teammates in front of their dugout on the first baseline. The stadium wasn't full, but it held more people that he'd played in front of in his entire life.

"Don't be nervous. Keep your mind on the game," Walter said, a trickle of sweat slipping down his temple.

"I'm not the one who is nervous." Noah wasn't. There wasn't anything at stake for him. He scuffed the white chalk line with the toe of his cleats. If a minor- or major-league ball team recruited him, fine. There was little reason to go home. Fannie wouldn't even see him. How could he live across the road from her knowing she didn't want him when he loved her more with every breath he took?

"How is she?" Walter asked, looking his way.

Noah knew he was referring to Fannie. Everyone on the team had heard about the accident. "Home and mending, my mother tells me. Her drill team is performing at the Horse Expo across town tonight. I plan to get over there after our game and watch them. It's the least I can do."

Timothy had kept him informed of the group's progress. They were doing well using just the whistle, but they still missed their music. They were all worried about performing in front of such a large crowd. The event had been Fannie's dream. He hoped she would be there to see it, too. And he hoped he would have a chance to see her.

He hadn't spoken to Fannie since that day at the hospital. He'd stopped by her home daily, but she'd refused to see him. Her mother was apologetic, but Fannie wouldn't budge. She didn't want him. He was trying to accept that.

The game announcer's voice came over the PA system. "Please rise for our national anthem."

The crowd surged to its feet. A young woman walked to the pitcher's mound and began to sing. Her voice soared over the air in pure, clear notes without accompaniment. When the last word of the song faded away, applause burst from the crowd.

Walter clapped wildly. "The girl has some pipes. That's a tough song to sing a cappella."

Noah glanced to where nearly fifty members of his extended family and people from his community were seated together behind the dugout, eager to watch their hometown team play. Even Bishop Beachy was in attendance, although his wife wasn't. They had rented a bus to bring them all this way and they planned to travel to the horse show after the baseball game. Their plain dark clothes, white bonnets and straw hats made them stand out sharply from the colorful people around them. How many times had he heard them sing without music to praise God's name. Hundreds of times. He and Fannie had joined their voices at the singings for the young people, too. Could they do it again?

Noah slapped Walter's shoulder. "The singer has given me an idea. Bishop Lapp said no *Englisch* music, but singing is acceptable to us."

Noah hurried to where Simon Beachy was sitting on

the bleachers waiting his turn at bat. "Simon, do you have your cell phone with you? I left mine in the locker room."

Simon glanced up into the stands. "I kind of told my *onkel* I wouldn't use it when he's watching."

"You aren't going to use it, I am."

"It's in the side pocket of my jacket at the end of the bench. Check my messages for me, will you?"

"Sure thing." Noah fished out the phone and sat on the end of the bench as he dialed Paul's number. "Pick up, cousin. Pick up."

"*Hallo, wee gats*, Simon."

"It's not Simon, it's Noah. I had to use his phone. Are you still in the city?"

"I'm packing up now. We raised a lot of money for Debra's charity and I had a great time."

"*Goot.* Instead of going home, do you think you could take your portable speaker to the horse show?"

"Debra has planned on taking me there, but why bring my speaker?"

"I'll explain later. I've got a game to pitch. Find Timothy when you get there and tell him I'll call him as soon as I'm done."

"Is this about Fannie?"

"*Ja.* This is about her Amish Girls."

"*Mamm* heard from Belinda that Fannie will be there. The doctor has released her to travel."

Relief made Noah's spirits soar. He was going to see her today. He had one more chance to make her see how much he cared. "That is the best news I've had in weeks. *Danki.*"

Noah smiled as he ended the call. He tossed the phone to Simon. "No messages."

Simon slipped the phone under the bench and grabbed his glove. It was their turn to take the field.

Noah jogged out with Walter. "Three up, three down. That's the plan. I want to end this game as quick as we can."

Walter blew out a deep breath. "You won't get any argument from me. All I ask is that you make me look good. Captain says there are at least six major-league scouts here to check out the country boys."

Noah glanced to where his family was seated in the stands. By their simple life and commitment to God, they stood apart from others. They were in the world, but not a part of it. Living a simple life wasn't simple or easy, but they did it by caring for one another and sharing their burdens and joys.

As he wanted to share Fannie's problems and delights for the rest of their lives.

He had been wrong. He had a lot to go home to. His family and his Amish faith were gifts from God, just as surely as his fastball. He had been waiting for a sign from God to show him where he belonged. The sign had been in front of his eyes all along. He just hadn't seen it because he hadn't been looking for it with his heart. He belonged among the people he loved and cherished. No baseball career was worth giving them up.

A great lightness filled his heart. This was his decision, his God-given gift of free will, and it was the right decision—even if Fannie didn't want to be a part of his life. But he prayed fervently that she would.

The game didn't end as quickly as he would have liked. When it did, the Fire Eaters came out on top and were advanced to the next round. The following morning they would play the winner of the next game.

Back in the locker room, Noah quickly changed into his Amish clothes and pulled out his cell phone to call Connie, who gave her phone to Timothy. After explaining his plan, he hung up and grabbed his ball cap. He stuffed it in his bag and pulled his black Amish hat out.

Eric came in grinning from ear to ear. "Noah, I was just talking to an old friend of mine. He's a scout for the Pittsburgh Pirates these days. He talking to another player now, but he wants to meet you."

Noah drew a deep breath knowing he was about to disappoint his coach. "Walter is the fellow he should talk to."

Eric rested his hands on Noah's shoulders and gave him a shake. "He wants to meet both of you."

"That's great. I'm really glad for Walter, but I have made my decision. I won't be playing after this tournament is over. God has shown me the path He wants me to follow. I'm going home."

Eric's smile faded. "I'm sad to hear that, but I'm happy for you, too. I admire your choice."

Noah settled his broad black hat on his head. "*Danki.* Please excuse me. I've got to get to a horse show."

Fannie walked gingerly into the stands at the exhibition hall. Walking was still painful, and she had to use two canes to keep her balance. Her parents hovered on either side of her.

The music came up and a drill team emerged from the entrance onto the floor of the huge arena. There were ten boys and girls in sparkling cowboy costumes riding quarter horses with decorated saddles.

"Flashy," her father mumbled.

"They are not judged on their costumes, only on how well they ride," she reminded him.

"Are your girls going to be judged?"

"They aren't in the competition. They're going to be featured in the breed spotlight. It is Connie's intention to show how versatile Haflinger horses are."

Fannie's mother waved to someone behind her. "I see Anna and Isaac. They are coming this way."

Fannie closed her eyes. "Is Noah with them?"

"I don't see him, but all the rest of the family is here. His game must be over. I wonder if our fellows won."

Fannie wondered if God had given Noah the answer he longed for. She prayed he wouldn't be leaving them. She prayed she would have one more chance to mend the rift her pride had caused.

Noah found Timothy with Connie and the girls in the staging area. They were already on their horses. "Did you tell them?" he asked his brother.

"Ja." Timothy nodded.

"It's a wonderful idea. I don't know why we didn't think of it sooner. I could just hug you," Connie said with a wide grin.

Zoe moved her horse closer. She was wearing a dark pink shirt with white fringe along the sleeves and a white kerchief over her hair. Unlike the rest of the girls, her long blond hair hung down her back. "Since we're going to be using 'She'll Be Coming 'Round the Mountain' again, can we add my trick?"

Connie bit her lip. "I don't know, honey. It's so last-minute."

"We've been practicing. We can do it, can't we?" Zoe asked the other riders.

Everyone agreed.

"What trick is this?" Noah asked.

Timothy clapped a hand on Noah's shoulder. "You'll have to see it to believe it."

"All right," Connie said. "Get your other saddle, but hurry. Once around and then into the regular routine. Right?"

"You're awesome, Mom." Zoe wheeled her horse and galloped to the back of the staging area.

Timothy beckoned to Susan, who nudged her horse closer. "I think you should still use the whistle. The horses have gotten used to it."

She nodded. "Okay. Are there a lot of people out there?"

Connie patted her knee. "The only people that matter are on horses beside you. Remember, you are a team. Keep your eyes on each other."

They all nodded.

Paul came up to them carrying his portable loudspeaker. "Where do you want me?"

Noah looked around. "I need to find Fannie first."

"She's with her folks on the west side," Connie said.

"How is she?" Noah asked.

Connie smiled at him. "You should go see for yourself."

Noah rubbed his damp palms on his pants legs. "She may not want to see me. She may not want to do this."

Timothy gave him a shove. "You'll never know if you don't get in there."

He shrugged and started up into the stands. If she saw him, she didn't give any sign until he sat down beside her.

"What's up, *karotte oben*?"

Her gaze flew to his face. Her mouth dropped open and then snapped shut. "You know I hate being called a carrottop."

She didn't look upset. She looked almost happy to see him and his hopes grew.

"Sorry, I forgot. How are you?"

"Getting better. Did you win your game?"

"We did. Six to four. We play again tomorrow."

She looked down at her hands. "Were there professional scouts there?"

"They were."

"And what did they say about your pitching?"

"I didn't stay to find out. I had something more important to do."

She looked at him with a puzzled expression. "What was more important than the thing you've wanted for so long?"

"Helping you. The bishop said the group couldn't perform to recorded music. He didn't say anything about not using live singers. My cousin Paul has a mic and loudspeaker."

He gestured to the group coming in. Lillian, Mary, Emma and Rebecca came down to sit behind her with his brothers behind them. Paul sat down beside Fannie.

Fannie looked around at everyone. "I don't understand."

Noah took her hand in his. "We're going to sing with you, Fannie, but first I have to check and see if Connie is ready."

He rose to his feet, but she caught his hand. "Noah, why are you doing this?"

She was so dear to his heart. Didn't she realize that? "Because this is important to you."

"No, why are you doing this?"

He tilted his head to the side. "Don't you know, *liebchen*?"

Fannie's heart was pounding in her chest. "Maybe I do, but tell me anyway."

His grip on her hand tightened as he dropped to one knee beside her. "I'm doing this because what is important to you is important to me. I love you, Fannie. Even if you can't love me back, I still love you and I will never stop loving you."

Joy flooded her heart until she could barely breathe. With all her faults and shortcomings, he still loved her. The knowledge was humbling. "I don't deserve your love."

"I'm sorry. I can't change the way I feel. We'll talk about this later when we don't have such a large audience." He winked and hurried away.

Lillian put her arm around Fannie's shoulders. "Our Lord has filled Noah's heart with love for you, Fannie. You may not feel you deserve it, but *Gott* does not make mistakes. When Noah gets around to proposing, you'd better accept. We want you for our sister."

Tears filled Fannie's eyes as she looked at the women around her. "I'll give it serious consideration."

It would take her all of two seconds to say yes to him if he did propose. She loved him with all her heart and she would spend a lifetime trying to be worthy of God's great gift to her.

A few minutes later, Noah returned. "We're going to do 'She'll Be Coming 'Round the Mountain.' I will start, but at a slower cadence than the recorded song we were using. I want everyone to join in on the second stanza. The girls will come in on the second verse, so we'll speed up then and everyone will sing. I'll keep the time like this." He extended one finger and tapped the air.

Everyone nodded that they understood. "One more thing. Instead of 'driving six white horses,' we'll change it to 'driving six *wild* horses.' Okay?"

"Why?" Fannie asked.

"You'll see."

He raised a hand to signal the announcer in the booth above them and took the microphone from Paul.

The man's voice boomed over the arena's PA system. "Ladies and gentlemen, in our breed showcase this afternoon I'd like to welcome the Stroud Stables Haflingers and their riders, The Amish Girls. They are here to showcase the versatility of this breed. The Haflinger is also known as the Avelignese. The breed was developed in the mountainous regions of Austria and northern Italy during the nineteenth century. Some were brought to the US in the 1950s and the breed has been gaining in popularity since that time.

"Haflingers are relatively small and are considered a pony at 14.2 hands, which is 58 inches or less in height at the withers. These well-muscled ponies are remarkably strong. In fact, the winner of the pony pull yesterday was a pair of Haflingers from Holms County, Ohio. They pulled seventy-two hundred pounds a distance of ten feet ten inches to win the heavyweight division.

"They are always golden in color with white or flaxen manes and tails. The breed has its own distinctive gait described by enthusiats as energetic but smooth. If you haven't heard of Haflingers before, after today I'm sure you'll agree this is no ordinary horse and these are no ordinary riders. I'm pleased to present the Stroud Stables Haflingers and The Amish Girls."

"She'll be coming 'round the mountain when she comes." Noah's pure baritone voice poured out of the speaker. He nodded to Fannie.

She leaned in to add her voice to his. "She'll be coming 'round the mountain when she comes."

As they sang together, Fannie's heart grew light. She loved him so much. She couldn't wait to say those words to him.

She turned her attention to the arena entrance at the end of the stanza. The sharp crack of a whip shattered the quiet, and Noah motioned for his brothers and their wives to pick up the tempo and sing.

"She'll be driving six wild horses when she comes." Their blend of voices filled the air as horses and riders charged into the arena. They came six abreast with two singles in line behind them. Fannie saw Zoe on the first single horse. She was riding Misty. Abbie followed close behind her on Copper.

Zoe shot to her feet in a hippodrome stand. She was grinning from ear to ear and held a buggy whip in her right hand. She cracked it once as if driving the six horses in front of her and then waved to the stands as she raced past. The crowd erupted into cheers. Fannie could hardly believe her eyes. Zoe was a born performer.

After a thundering run around the perimeter, the girls slowed and broke into two columns as they began the routine Fannie had worked so hard to perfect. They did it beautifully, and in time with the singing, as Susan marked each change of pattern with a burst from her whistle.

It was a sight to behold—eight matching golden-caramel-colored horses with bright blond manes and tails stepping lightly in response to the Amish girls on their backs.

Fannie held her breath when they began their pass through the jumps, but every hurdle was cleared easily. When the last turn was made and the riders were leaving the arena, the crowd rose to its feet with deafening applause.

The announcer came back on when the noise died away. "Ladies and gentlemen, as impressive as that was, it's not all these girls and their horses can do. In a minute, we'll have a demonstration of their skill in harness. These will be the same horses and drivers with one exception. We will have one change of driver because the mother of the little gal who rides standing up tells us she isn't old enough to drive." The audience laughed.

Zoe came out leading Misty, who had been harnessed to a two-wheeled cart. She stopped in front of Noah and Fannie.

Noah leaned down to whisper in Fannie's ear. "Are you ready?"

"For what?"

"You started this wonderful crazy adventure. You must have a hand in the finish." He gently slipped his arms beneath her and picked her up.

Tears stung her eyes. "You want me to ride with you?"

"I want you to drive. After all, you can drive almost as well as I can."

She pulled back, a smile trembling on her lips. "Almost?"

"How about *just* as well?"

"*Ja*, Noah Bowman, that is more like it. I think you are beginning to understand me."

"Now that is a scary thought."

His brother Samuel opened the gate leading to the arena floor. Noah carried Fannie through and placed her tenderly on the seat of the cart. Zoe handed her the reins. Misty tossed her head, eager to be off again.

Noah covered Fannie's hand. "Are you sure you are well enough to do this?"

She gazed into his eyes. "As long as I have someone by my side to steady me, I will be fine."

He smiled. "Can I volunteer for the job?"

"I was hoping you would." Her heart was beating so hard that she was amazed he couldn't heart it.

"I want to spend a lifetime by your side, Fannie. You believe that, don't you?"

"I do. I love you will all my heart and soul, Noah Bowman."

His closed his eyes for a long second, as though savoring her words. Finally, he gazed at her tenderly. "Will you marry me?"

"Gladly. Oh, so gladly. *Gott* has chosen us for one another."

"If we weren't in front of so many people I would kiss you, Fannie Erb."

"Well, stop dawdling and get in so we can finish the program and find someplace more private."

He laughed as he went around and climbed in beside her. "That, my love, is your best idea to date."

Noah pulled his buggy to a stop in front of Fannie's house one month after her accident. Before he could get down, she was already out the door. She still moved stiffly in her back brace, but she wasn't letting it slow her any.

"You're late," she called out.

"You're rude," he snapped back, trying to stifle a grin.

"Just making sure you don't think I've mellowed."

"No chance of that, *karotte oben*."

She climbed in gingerly beside him. "You know I hate that name."

"That's why I use it."

She smiled and lifted her face for his kiss. He eagerly complied as she slipped her arms around his neck.

Kissing Fannie would never get old. The wedding couldn't come soon enough. They would finish their baptismal classes in another month and take their vows of faith soon after. The wedding would be the second Thursday in November. Not nearly soon enough.

Finally, he drew back. "You are making us even later."

"You've got a fast horse. You can make up the time." She pulled him down for another quick kiss, then straightened in her seat and made shooing motions with her hands. "What are you waiting for? Get a move on."

"You drive me crazy, woman."

"And you love it." She winked at him.

He flicked the reins. "What did I do to deserve this?"

She linked her arm through his. "You came to my rescue like a knight of old."

"Timothy would say that's proof you weren't paying attention in history class. There weren't any Amish knights."

Laying her head on his shoulder, she sighed. "But there were many brave Amish heroes, and I have one of my very own."

He headed Willy toward Connie's farm. "We aren't married yet. I could change my mind and court Margret Stolfus."

"You won't."

"What makes you so sure?"

"She married Hiram yesterday. Didn't you hear?"

"Are you kidding me?"

"Nope."

"That was one rushed wedding."

"I'm sure Hiram didn't want another fiancée to change her mind."

"How is your sister?"

"Happy as a clam at the seashore. All she can talk about in her letters is the wonderful Mennonite fellow she met at the beach. She wrote that she tried to stop seeing him as our parents asked, but her heart overruled her head. I expect they will marry soon."

"How do your parents feel about that?"

"She hasn't been baptized. They aren't thrilled that she won't be Amish, but an Old Order Mennonite is close enough. Apparently, the Amish community down there is more open. My grandparents both like him, so that helps. Betsy wants us to come visit them on our wedding trip."

"I had planned to take you to see your grandparents, but we are not taking Trinket with us and that is final."

"As you wish."

"Come again? Are you sick?"

"I'm simply agreeing with you."

"That's what worries me." He eyed her with concern.

"Have you heard from Walter?"

"Another happy clam. He's been signed to a minor-league team, but I know he'll be called up to the majors before too long."

"At least a few good things came out of our deception."

"Our one and only deception. From now on, we are walking a straight path together."

"I couldn't agree more."

He turned into Connie's lane. A horse trailer and pickup were sitting next to the barn. Zoe was waiting beside the truck cab. She dashed toward them. "I thought you would never get here."

Connie came around from the back of the trailer. "Calm down, Zoe. We have plenty of time. Help Noah stable his horse and then get your gear."

Zoe rolled her eyes. "It's been in the truck since I got up this morning, Mom."

As she and Noah led Willy away, Connie gave Fannie a gentle hug. "How are you?"

"Getting better every day. How are you?"

"Better than I've been in a long time. I sold three horses this week and two the week before. The two last week went to a therapy program run by a very nice, very cute single man who has asked me out. Oh, and I finally fired George. I hired a new guy full-time to run things while Zoe and I are on the road."

"Oh, Connie, I'm so happy for you."

"Aren't you going to ask me who the new guy is?"

"Do I know him?"

"Quite well," Noah said, grinning like the cat that ate the canary.

"You?" Fannie stared at him in stunned shock. "What about your family's business? The farm?"

"With my cousins moving here permanently, there is

plenty of help in the woodshop and on the farm. Besides, I'll only be two miles away if they need me. I've found I have a passion for Haflinger horses and a crazy woman who can tame a horse by turning in circles. As my wife, you will have to help me with my work. I expect there will be many times when we must ride together to exercise the horses. Perhaps we can even convince the bishop that horseback riding isn't worldly but a *goot* plain way to enjoy a family outing. You might want to think about where we should build our house."

Fannie leaned forward and kissed him. "I will."

Connie cleared her throat. "Our participation in the show impressed a number of people. Zoe tells me the video went viral, which I assume is good although it sounds horrible. I've been getting calls all week. Six more families have enrolled their kids in my riding classes, so you will be busy when you get out of that brace. I have you to thank for lifting some of the weight from my shoulders."

"I'm happy it turned out well for you."

"It didn't turn out too badly for you, either. He's a good man. You two will do well in harness together."

Zoe came running out of the barn. She opened the cab of the truck. "Let's go. I can't be late for my first paying gig. I'm so glad you are coming to watch me, Fannie. And you, too, Noah. I'm going to be awesome."

She leaned over to whisper to Fannie. "I'm trying to convince Mom to make us a mother-daughter act, but she's dragging her feet."

Connie shook her head. "I have created a monster. She's determined to become the best trick rider in the world and the halftime show at the Carlson rodeo will be her jumping-off point, if we get her there on time."

Noah opened the back door of the cab. "A very large goal for a small girl."

"One that I'm sure she will accomplish with *Gott*'s help," Fannie said.

Connie's smile faded. "I can't begin to thank the two of you for all you have done for us." She walked quickly to the driver's side of the truck and got in.

"Who would have thought our pretend courtship could open so many doors?" Fannie said softly.

Noah laid his hand on Fannie's cheek. "Do you know the most amazing thing about it?"

She shook her head.

He stroked her lips with his thumb. "It wasn't a pretend courtship at all. The Lord does move in mysterious ways."

"I love you, Noah Bowman."

"I love you, *karotte oben*."

"And I hope all your kids are redheads," Zoe said with a giggle before her mother shushed her.

* * * * *

If you enjoyed
THEIR PRETEND AMISH COURTSHIP,
look for the other books in the
AMISH BACHELORS *series:*

AN AMISH HARVEST
AN AMISH NOEL
HIS AMISH TEACHER

AN AMISH COURTSHIP

Jan Drexler

To Mrs. Harrington,
the kind of teacher I would like to be someday.

Soli Deo Gloria

Create in me a clean heart, O God; and renew
a right spirit within me. Cast me not away from
thy presence; and take not thy holy spirit from me.
Restore unto me the joy of thy salvation;
and uphold me with thy free spirit.
—*Psalms* 51:10–12

Chapter One

Shipshewana, Indiana
April 1937

"I'm so glad we aren't late," Aunt Sadie said as Mary turned the buggy into the farm lane.

Mary Hochstetter looked ahead, clutching the reins with damp hands. At least twenty buggies lined up along the barn like a flock of blackbirds on a telegraph wire and the lines of people moving toward the house were long.

So many strangers! But she must face them for Ida Mae's sake. She straightened her shoulders and glanced into the back seat to give her sister a reassuring smile. There was nothing frightening about attending the Sabbath meeting.

Ida Mae gave her a weak smile in return. "I'll be all right. After all, we already know the ladies we met at the quilting last week. The rest will soon become friends, too."

A boy stepped forward and grasped the horse's bridle. "I'll take care of Chester for you, Aunt Sadie."

"*Denki*, Stephen." Sadie climbed out of the buggy. Mary joined her, with Ida Mae right behind. "You're growing up so fast. I remember when your mother had to pull you out of mud puddles at Sunday meeting."

Stephen laughed, his voice slipping down to a deep bass and back up again. "That was a long time ago."

"Not to me, young man. The older I get, the faster time flies. You're a fine man, just like your father."

Sadie grasped Mary's arm to make sure she had her attention. "Here come the Lapp sisters, Judith and Esther, who you met at the quilting last week," she said. "That's their brother Samuel driving. They're our next-door neighbors." She leaned closer, dropping her voice. "And Mary, Samuel is a bachelor."

Mary shook her head. "I'm not looking for a husband."

"You never know what the Good Lord has planned."

Mary knew what the Good Lord had planned, and it was clear to her that marriage had no part of whatever He had in mind.

The Lapps' dusty buggy pulled up next to theirs and two young women jumped out. The man who was driving barely waited until they had stepped down before he started his horse forward to the buggy parking area. But just then Aunt Sadie's horse stepped sideways into his path.

Mutters and growls came from the buggy as it rocked under the weight of the man who jumped to the ground from the driver's seat, nearly landing on Sadie. He caught the older woman's arm to steady her.

"Sorry, Aunt Sadie." He waited until the older woman was stable again, then grasped his horse's bridle. "If someone hadn't left your buggy in the middle of the drive, I could have been out of the way by now."

"We just got here ourselves, Samuel," Aunt Sadie said. "There's no need to be in such a hurry." She turned to Mary with a satisfied smile. "I'm sure you and Mary will be able to straighten out the horses." She took Ida Mae's arm. "Let's go inside. I'll need your help."

Ida Mae gave Mary a helpless look.

"Go on in." Mary lifted her chin with confidence she didn't feel. "I'll be right there."

"It's going to take hours to get this mess straightened out." Samuel gestured toward the road where a buggy had just turned in, with another close behind it. "It's becoming a real log jam."

"Once I get Chester off to the side, things will clear up." Stephen took the horse's bridle and led him down the drive toward the barn, patting his brown neck.

As the buggy moved out of the way, Mary found herself face-to-face with Samuel Lapp. She felt her cheeks heat as he stared at her with dark blue eyes.

She leveled her gaze, focusing on the front of his coat. He was a solid wall in front of her, a man a couple years older than her own twenty-three years. His closeness sent her heart racing and she took a deep breath to steady her nerves. He wasn't Harvey Anderson. She bit her lip, forcing that thought out of her mind. Samuel was only an Amishman driving his sisters to Sunday meeting. There was nothing threatening about him.

Mary stepped to the side of the driveway so he could move past her.

"I think you can follow Stephen now."

He didn't budge.

"The way is clear."

Ignoring three more buggies that had driven into the barnyard, he still stared at her. Suddenly, his eyebrows shot up as if he had gotten a flash of insight. "You're that Mary Hochstetter that Sadie's been expecting."

"*Ja*, I am."

"From Ohio."

"*Ja.*"

He ran his hand down his short beard. "You're not what I imagined when Sadie said you were coming. I thought you'd be older, being her niece."

"Sadie is actually my mother's aunt." Mary glanced behind Samuel's buggy. Families walked toward the house, voices hushed as they separated into women's and men's lines. Stephen and two or three other boys had lined up the buggies in order and were unhitching the horses. The log jam had cleared.

She looked back at Samuel. "I should go in. Meeting is about to begin."

The corner of his mouth, visible above his short beard, quirked up.

"You're anxious to be rid of me?"

Now he was laughing at her, maybe even flirting with her. She drew herself up to her full height and looked him in the eyes, lowering her brow in the expression that always sent her younger brothers hurrying to do their chores.

He stepped forward to grasp his horse's bridle. "You're not only younger than I expected, but you're prettier, too."

Then he winked at her.

Mary stared at him, her fists clenched. What an infuriating man! Gruff and blustery until he found out who she was, as if any new woman he met would fall at his feet. As if she needed a man to run her life.

"Like I said, meeting is about to begin." She fought to keep her voice even.

"Go ahead," he said, gesturing toward the house. "I'll be in shortly."

But under her irritation, another feeling rose. That familiar twisting in her stomach that stole her breath. She swallowed, glancing around. The only other people in the barnyard were a few women on their way into the house. She would soon be alone in the yard with this man.

She shot another look in his direction, one that she reserved for her brothers' worst crimes, and hurried into the house.

She found a place on a bench next to Aunt Sadie and Ida Mae and took a deep breath, trying to forget that wink. No wonder he wasn't married. His beard only confirmed that he had given up looking for a wife. Only married men and old bachelors wore beards.

The worship began with a low, soft note sung by a man sitting on the front row. As the tune continued, she recognized the hymn from the *Ausbund* and joined in the singing with the rest of the community, settling into the familiar worship.

After the service ended, Mary followed Judith and Esther Lapp to the kitchen to help serve the meal.

"I can introduce you to the others," Esther said as she led the way through the lines of benches that the young men were already converting to tables for dinner.

"I'll never remember everyone's names."

Esther took her arm. "Don't worry. They don't expect you to. You'll learn them all eventually."

Mary joined in the work easily enough. The meal of sandwiches, pickles and applesauce was similar to what the folks would be having in her home church in Holmes County. Mary opened jars and poured applesauce into serving dishes while the other young women whirled around her, taking the food to the tables as the young men set them up.

"Hello," said a girl as she took one of the dishes Mary had prepared. "You're one of Sadie's nieces, aren't you? I wish I could have gone to the quilting on Wednesday.

I've been wanting to meet you ever since I heard you were coming."

Mary shook the jar she was holding to urge the last of the applesauce from the bottom. "I'm Mary. My sister is Ida Mae, over there helping with the rolls." She tilted her head toward the counter at the far end of the kitchen.

"I'm Sarah Hopplestadt. My mother said she met you at the quilting."

Hopplestadt? Mary sorted through the faces in her mind. "*Ja*, for sure. Isn't her name Effie?"

Sarah's face beamed. "It is!" She grabbed the filled serving dish and whirled away. "I'll be back with some empty dishes for you soon."

Mary watched her go as she reached for another jar. Sarah placed the applesauce on the table closest to the kitchen, in front of an older man. Across from him sat Samuel, red-faced with the tight collar fastened at his throat. He looked as uncomfortable as a cat in a room full of rocking chairs.

She shook her head at her own thoughts and glanced at him again. His brow was lowered and he kept his eyes on his plate, ignoring the other men around him. The confident man who had given her that exasperating wink was gone. He looked as out of place as she felt. She caught her lower lip between her teeth as she remembered how rude she had been before church. He might be a man, but he was also Aunt Sadie's neighbor. She quelled her shaking stomach. As much as she hated the thought of initiating a conversation with him, she needed to apologize.

As the men talked, their voices carried into the kitchen.

"Vernon Hershberger needs help with his plowing, I hear." The man sitting next to Samuel spoke, stopping the other conversations.

The man at the end of the table stroked his beard. "*Ja*,

for sure. His leg is healing after his fall last month, but he still isn't able to get around very well."

A man on the other side of Samuel, one of the ministers who had preached that morning, gestured with his fork. "We can all help him get his fields plowed and planted. Is Saturday a good day for everyone?"

Beards waggled as the men around the table nodded, but Samuel still looked at his plate.

"What about you, Samuel?" the minister asked.

The man sitting at the end of the table shook his head. "He's a Lapp. He won't help."

Samuel's face grew even redder. He leaned on his elbows, his hands clenched together, not looking at the men around him.

"I'll help." His voice was as low as a growl.

One of the men laughed. "Just like his *daed*. Today he'll help, but we won't see him come Saturday."

Laughter rippled around the table, and Samuel stood, backing away from the bench. He glared at the laughing faces, then turned to the minister. "I said I'd be there, and I will."

The minister held his gaze for a long minute as the laughter died away. "I believe you. We'll look forward to it."

Samuel nodded, swept his glance around the table again and then went out of the house.

Mary startled as Sarah appeared at her elbow again.

"That Samuel Lapp. I don't see why the men even invite him to help with the work."

"Why not?"

Sarah shrugged. "He rarely shows up, and then when he does, he doesn't do anything but stand around. His father was the same way."

"Perhaps he has changed. He seemed sincere to me."

"Maybe." Sarah picked up two more dishes of applesauce. "But this is a Lapp we're talking about. Some people never change."

As the girl walked away, Mary looked up to see Esther watching her. Samuel's sister had heard every word of their conversation.

"Esther..." Mary stepped across the kitchen and took her arm. "I hope you weren't offended by what Sarah said."

Esther plucked at her apron. "*Ne*. It's true." She looked at Mary, her narrow chin set firm. "But what you said is true, too. Samuel isn't *Daed*, and he can change." She glanced at the kitchen door, where Samuel had disappeared. "I just hope more folks come to see that."

Samuel Lapp charged out of the Stutzmans' house, ignoring everyone he passed. He'd hitch up the mare, find his sisters and head for home. He was a fool to think this morning would be different than any other Sabbath morning that he had attended the meeting.

His steps slowed. When was the last time he had come to the Sabbath meeting? A month ago? Two months? When he reached the pasture gate, he leaned on the post. Several of the horses started walking toward him, but his mare stood next to the water trough, ignoring him and the other horses.

A bay gelding stopped a pace away from him and extended his nose slightly.

"I have no carrots for you." Samuel spoke softly. Whose horse was this one? He eyed the sleek neck and the muscled haunches. Someone who knew horses and took good care of them.

The words of the men around the dinner table washed over him again. Even two years after his father's death, the Lapp legacy followed him no matter what he did. No matter how much he wanted to change.

He bent his head down to meet his fist, quelling the sick feeling in his stomach. Why should he even try? Men like Martin Troyer would never let him forget whose son he was. Samuel squeezed his eyes closed, seeing Martin's pompous figure at the end of the table once more.

Then the minister's words echoed over Martin's mocking tone. Jonas Weaver had said he believed him. He expected him to show up to help with Vernon Hershberger's farm work. The minister's confidence made Samuel want to follow through with his promise.

But *Daed* had burned too many bridges with his habit of promising help that he never delivered, and he was guilty of the same thing.

His father had lived on the edge of being shunned and put under the *bann*. How many times had the deacons stopped by the farm to talk to *Daed*? To reprimand him? And then he would promise to do better. He'd take the family to meeting for a month, maybe two. He'd promise to join in the community activities. He'd promise to stop the drinking...but then forget his promises.

Samuel rubbed his hands over his face. Could he face Martin again? Not when this slow burn continued in his stomach. The world was full of Martin Troyers who would never let him come out from under *Daed*'s shadow.

He leaned on the fence, watching the horses. They had lost interest in him and had gone back to cropping the grass.

When Bram had returned home after living in Chicago for twelve years, he had been able to avoid *Daed*'s legacy. His older brother had escaped the shame of the remarks and pitying looks and Samuel envied him.

The envy was worse than the shame.

When people spoke of Bram, respect echoed in their words. Respect Samuel had never heard when people spoke of their *daed*...or him.

As much as Samuel wanted to prove to the community that he wasn't the same man as his father, he had fallen short. Nothing he said made any difference. They treated him the same way they always had, as if a man could never change.

That girl with the brown eyes, Mary, was different, though. New in the community, she knew nothing about his past. Nothing to make her judge him. Perhaps if he could do something to earn her respect, the rest of the community would follow.

Samuel rubbed at his beard, remembering how Mary Hochstetter had stood up to him before church. If he could earn her respect, he wouldn't care about anyone else's opinion.

He picked at a loose sliver of wood on the fence post. It broke off and he stuck it in his mouth to use as a toothpick.

"Samuel?"

The woman's voice came from behind him. Unfamiliar. It wasn't Judith or Esther.

"Samuel Lapp? Is that you?"

He straightened and turned, facing this new challenge. But when he saw Mary Hochstetter standing next to the wheel of the last buggy in line, watching him, he felt his tense face relax into a smile.

"*Ja*, it's me."

She twisted her fingers together.

"When we met this morning, I was very impolite."

"Forget it." The words came out rough, and he cleared his throat.

She ran her hand along the wooden buggy wheel, brushing off a layer of dust. "I let myself form an opinion of you without learning to know you first. Sadie says I should be careful not to judge a book by its cover."

She smiled then, still watching the dust drift from the buggy wheel into the air. His heart wrenched at the soft curve of her lips.

"I wasn't very polite, myself."

"You were fine. I mean, you didn't do anything—" Her face flushed a pretty pink. "I mean, you were friendly." Her face grew even redder. "Except for…when you winked… I mean, I'm sure you didn't mean to be forward." She bit her lip and turned away.

Samuel resisted the urge to step close to her, to cover her embarrassment with a hand on her arm. "I think I know what you mean."

"I heard what you said in there." She tilted her head toward the house in a quick nod. "I think it is *wonderful-gut* that you want to help with that poor farmer's work. In Ohio, the community always works together when one family is having trouble."

He felt a flush rise in his cheeks at her words of praise. "We do that here, too." He couldn't look at her face. If she had heard what he said, then she had also heard the derisive remarks from the other men.

"That's good."

Samuel dared to raise his eyes, but she was fingering the buggy wheel again. As another little cloud of dust drifted to the ground, she glanced at him and smiled. "I must go help wash the dishes."

Mary walked back toward the house, turning once when she reached the center of the yard to give him a final glance. Samuel raised his hand in answer and leaned against the fence post behind him. She opened the screen door and entered the covered porch, disappearing from his view.

Samuel scratched his beard, running his fingers through its short length. Sometime after Bram had come back last year he had stopped shaving. A clean chin had been a sign of his single status, but last fall he had stopped caring. Stopped thinking that what he looked like mattered to anyone.

But now, his insides warm from Mary's kind words, he suddenly cared what she thought about him and his farm. Maybe he could earn her respect. Maybe he could hope to move out from under *Daed*'s shadow and become a member of the community the way Bram was.

He tugged at his whiskers, watching the screen door that had given a slight bang as Mary had disappeared. He tugged at the whiskers again. Maybe he would shave in the morning.

"Who would think that two nice girls like Judith and Esther would have a brother like that?"

Ida Mae leaned her arms on the back of the front buggy seat and tilted her head forward between Mary and Aunt Sadie.

All three of them were tired after the long Sunday afternoon at the Stutzmans', but they had enjoyed a good time of fellowship. All of Mary's fears had been for nothing. This new community had welcomed them with open arms.

"Samuel has a burden, for sure." Aunt Sadie turned to Ida Mae. "Don't be too quick to dismiss him, though. There's more to him than he shows us."

"Judith and Esther are nice girls, didn't you think so, Mary? Judith is going to bring a knitting pattern over this evening. She is so friendly."

"*Ja*, they both are. Is it only the three of them in their family, Aunt Sadie?"

"Their parents have passed on." The older woman's expression softened as she looked back over the years. "There were six children. A nice family, it seemed, until..." She glanced at Mary and Ida Mae. "I don't want to gossip. They were a nice family. Bram is the oldest. He left the community during his *rumspringa*, but his mother never gave up hope. Even on her deathbed she had faith that Bram would come back home."

"Did he?" Ida Mae watched their aunt's face, interested in the story.

"*Ja*, he did. Not until after she had passed on, but he did come back. He married a widow from Eden Township and lives down there with their children. A good Amishman, even after all his troubles."

Ida Mae leaned closer. "What about the rest of the family?"

"Samuel inherited the farm when their father died a couple years ago. The oldest girl...her name... I can't remember it. Maybe Katie? Anyway, she married a man from Berlin, Ohio. We haven't seen her since then. The next girl is Annie. She married a Beachey from Eden Township, the oldest son of their deacon. I go to quilting with her every other Thursday, and she has a sweet little boy."

Sadie's voice trailed off, smiling as she watched the roadside pass by.

"And the rest?"

"You've met them. Esther and Judith. They keep house for Samuel and have since Annie got married." She brushed at some dust on her apron. "I've tried to help those girls once they were on their own after their older sisters left home. I don't know how much they remember about their mother, but they were quite young when she died."

"What kind of help?" Ida Mae asked.

"We made soap together last winter, but I've also been longing to help them with their sewing. You've seen how worn their clothes are. They haven't made new ones for a couple years, and I don't think Katie or Annie taught them to sew. If we had fabric, we could have a sewing frolic, just the five of us."

Mary glanced at the smile on Sadie's face. "I think you would have a thing or two to teach us, too. We should invite them over."

"If they have time. They keep themselves at home most days. Our Wednesday quiltings are about the only time they get to be social with the rest of the women of the district."

"Maybe if we tell Samuel that we'll make new shirts and trousers for him, he'll like the idea."

"*Ja*, for sure." Aunt Sadie's chin rose and fell. "I'll talk to Samuel when he comes over tomorrow and make sure he encourages them to come."

Mary's stomach gave a little flutter at the thought of seeing Samuel again so soon. That flutter was very different than the clenching feeling she got when she thought of men like Harvey Anderson. She pushed it down anyway and cleared her throat.

"Why is Samuel coming over tomorrow?"

"He does my heavy chores for me." Sadie turned to her. "Didn't I tell you? He comes by to clean the chicken coop and cut the grass, and whatever else might need doing. He comes every Monday."

"Then Judith and Esther should come with him whenever he comes. We could have a sewing time every week," Ida Mae said. She was clearly excited about the idea.

They rode in silence for a while, and Mary watched the way ahead through Chester's upright ears. Now that she and Ida Mae were here, Samuel wouldn't need to bother doing Sadie's chores for her. She and her sister were more than capable of taking care of things without a man around.

As they passed the lane to the Lapps' farm, Mary glanced toward the house and barn. The odor of a pigsty drifted through the air.

Aunt Sadie had spoken of the Lapps as if they were a normal Amish family, but Samuel wasn't a normal Amishman. He had been pleasant enough at church, but some of the folks had spoken of him as if there was something very wrong.

"Why don't some of the men like Samuel? The women seemed to like Judith and Esther."

"Sometimes Samuel is too much like his father." Sadie's voice was so soft that Mary barely caught her words. "He is a troubled man. He learned some bad habits from Ira, but there is hope for him."

Less than a half mile down the road from the Lapps' farm, Chester turned into the drive of Aunt Sadie's place without any signal from Mary. Mary pulled up at the narrow walk for Ida Mae and their aunt to go into the house, and then she drove the buggy the short distance to the small barn. As she unhitched the buggy and took care of Chester, her thoughts went back to the Lapp family.

It wasn't unusual for sisters to keep house for their brother after their mother passed on, but both Judith and Esther were pale and worn, like they worked too hard. Mary smiled to herself as she brushed Chester's coat. Here she was, judging people before she got to know them again. The sisters seemed like nice girls. And since they were Aunt Sadie's closest neighbors, they would be able to spend much time together.

Their brother, though...

Mary turned Chester out into his pasture and hung up the harness.

Samuel was a strange one. Mary had never met anyone

quite like him. And what had Aunt Sadie meant when she said he was a troubled man?

Underneath the grouchy stares and gravelly voice, he was quite good-looking. And when she had apologized to him, he had been friendly. Even intriguing. And Aunt Sadie seemed to be very fond of him. He might be a puzzle worth figuring out.

Mary stopped her thoughts before they went any further. She wouldn't be the one to figure out the puzzle that was Samuel Lapp, so she should just forget about him. Forget about all men.

But she couldn't forget. It was too late. Her thoughts went on without her, down into that dark hole. Her skin crawled as if she could feel Harvey's sweaty palms through her dress, pressing close, and closer. She shuddered, willing the memory to disappear, but Harvey's hands groped and pulled. His breath smelled of stale tobacco and beer as he pushed his kisses on her.

Mary forced her eyes open, trembling all over. She concentrated her thoughts, trying to remember where she was—in Sadie's barn, hanging the buggy harness on its hooks.

Stroking the smooth leather of the harness, she focused on the buckle, the straps, the headpiece still damp from Chester's sweat. She kept her breathing even and controlled as she counted the tiny pinpoints of the stitching where the straps were fastened together until she reached one hundred.

Mary took a deep shaking breath. The memory had retreated to the back of her mind. She leaned her head against the warm wood of the barn wall. Someday those memories would stay buried. As long as she avoided men, she could forget the past.

But Samuel would be at the farm tomorrow, and she

would see him again on other days. Mary pushed at the shadows that threatened at the edge of her mind. A brother. The shadow retreated. She would treat Samuel the same as she treated her brothers. He wasn't Harvey Anderson.

Chapter Two

Monday morning dawned with the promise of a hot, sticky day ahead. On the way back to the house with the basket of eggs, Mary stopped by the garden to look for some early peas to go with their noon dinner. Noticing some stray lettuce seedlings among the beans, she bent to pull them out, but then saw how many there were. It was as if Sadie had planted the beans and lettuce in the same row.

She left the lettuce where it was and picked a couple handfuls of peas from the vines in front of her for lunch. Continuing on to the house, she paused at the sink in the back porch to wash up. The others were in the kitchen fixing breakfast.

"I want to ask Judith about the knitting pattern she brought over yesterday evening if the girls come this week," Ida Mae was saying.

Mary set the peas on the counter. "What is the pattern?"

"It's for stockings that you knit from the toe up, rather than the top down. I've never seen one like it. I was trying to figure out how it works last night, but it's beyond me."

"Margaret used to make stockings like that," Aunt Sadie said. She sat at the table, paring potatoes. "Margaret Lapp, Judith and Esther's mother. I have a pair of stockings she made. I'll show them to you…" Her voice trailed off as she dropped her knife on the table and started to rise.

Mary put a hand on her shoulder. "You can show us after breakfast. There's no hurry."

Aunt Sadie sank back down into her chair. "*Ja*. No hurry." She sat with her hands in her lap, a frown creasing her brow.

"What's wrong?"

The older woman startled and looked at Mary. "What was I doing?"

"You were peeling potatoes."

Aunt Sadie looked at the paring knife and potatoes on the table, her face vague. Then her brow cleared. "*Ach, ja.* The potatoes."

Mary glanced at Ida Mae. This wasn't the first time they had needed to remind Aunt Sadie of what she had been doing. In the six days since they had arrived, small lapses in their aunt's memory had been frequent. Perhaps their older relative did need them to take care of her, even if she wasn't ready to admit it.

They finished fixing breakfast in silence, each of them caught up in their own thoughts. As Mary scrambled the eggs, Ida Mae fried the potatoes and onions, the aroma filling the little kitchen.

Mary hoped the move to Indiana would be the healing balm her sister needed. The death of Ida Mae's young, handsome beau in a farming accident six weeks ago had been a terrible thing, and even though Ida Mae had put on a brave face this morning, grief still shadowed her eyes.

At least Ida Mae's tragedy gave Mary an excuse whenever someone questioned her own pale face and shadowed eyes. No one needed to know the real reason for her own grief, even her closest sister.

Mary set the table, laying the spoons next to the plates,

carefully lining them up next to the knives. One by one she set them down, her fingers lingering on the smooth handles. She missed, *ne*, she craved Ida Mae's cheerfulness. She relied on her sister to keep things going, to keep Mary's mind off the past.

Soon, though, Ida Mae would move on. She would meet a young man, get married, have a family of children and be happy again. The same dream that Mary had shared with her sister for so many years.

She blinked back tears as she straightened the fork she had just laid on the table. Ida Mae would see her hopes fulfilled, but not Mary. She laid another fork on the table. That dream belonged to an innocent girl with dreams of the future, and she had left that girl in Ohio.

The sun was already above the tops of the trees as Samuel walked to the barn. As he shoved the big sliding door open, he scanned the building's dusty interior, filled with equipment and clutter from days gone by. How would that Mary Hochstetter see *Daed*'s barn? Thinking about her coffee-brown eyes, so much like *Mamm*'s, pulled at something deep inside, something that reminded him of another time and another place.

A week, years ago, when he and his brother, Bram, had been sent to *Grossdawdi*'s farm in Eden Township. He must have been four or five years old. *Grossmutti*'s kitchen had been a wonder of cinnamon and apples and as much food as he could eat. *Grossdawdi*'s brown eyes crinkled when he smiled, and he had smiled often. The barn had been a wonderful place to play, with hay piled in the lofty mow.

Samuel relaxed against the doorframe, remembering *Grossdawdi*'s patient hands teaching him how to rub oil into the gleaming leather harnesses. His hand cupping

Samuel's head and pulling him close in the only hug he remembered.

He had never seen the old couple again, but he hadn't forgotten the peace that had reigned in their home. And one quiet glance of Mary's eyes had brought it all back.

Daed's barn had never been as orderly as *Grossdawdi*'s, even now when it was nearly empty. There hadn't been enough horses to fill the stalls since before *Daed* had passed on. Their driving mare spent her days in the meadow, too ornery for the girls to handle by themselves.

Samuel walked over to her stall and peered out the open side door to where the mare stood, one hip cocked and head down, drowsing in the afternoon sun as she swished flies with her tail.

Daed had left the barn a mess when he passed away two years ago. Broken harnesses still sat in a moldy pile in the corner and the unused stalls were knee deep in old straw. They had never been cleaned out when the work horses had been sold to pay off *Daed*'s debts. The cow was gone, too, and the bank barn's lower level was empty except for the mash cooker.

Every time he thought about trying to bring order to the chaos, Samuel felt like he was drowning in memories and past sins. Soon after *Daed*'s funeral, he had started clearing out the old, moldy harnesses and had found one of the bottles *Daed* kept stashed away. The smell brought back sickening scenes of *Daed* trying to hide the bottles from him with clumsy motions. When he found another stash among the straw in one of the empty box stalls, he had given up. Let the old barn keep its secrets.

Walking on to the horse's stall, he stopped at the stack of hay on the barn floor and pulled out a forkful. The mare poked her head into her stall, her feet planted firmly in the dried mud in the doorway between her pasture and the dim barn, watching Samuel. Her ears pricked forward as Samuel thumped the fork on the side of her manger to dump the hay off, but she didn't move. The horse was right to be suspicious. Samuel had never been overly kind to the beast. He had never been cruel, but had only followed *Daed*'s example.

Daed hadn't taken much time with the horses, using them until they were worn out and then buying new ones, and Samuel had always expected to do the same. He had never thought much about it until he saw the sleek horses in the pasture at meeting yesterday. His horse had looked sickly compared to them, and men judged a farmer's abilities by the condition of his stock. Anyone looking at his poor mare would know what the rest of his farm was like without even having to see it. They would know how he had been neglecting his legacy.

Samuel pulled the carrot he had brought from the root cellar out of his waistband. *Daed* had bought the mare cheap at a farm sale the year before he died. She had been strong enough, but with *Daed*'s lack of care, she had never become the sleek, healthy animal the other men at church kept.

He turned the carrot over in his hand. *Daed*'s horse, *Daed*'s problem. Except that *Daed* wasn't here anymore. Like everything else around the farm, the horse was his responsibility now whether he liked it or not.

"Hey there." Samuel kept his voice soft, and the mare's ears swiveled toward him. "Look what I have for you."

He broke the carrot in half and her head went up at the crisp snap. She stretched her neck toward him and took one step into the barn. He opened the gate and let himself into her stall.

"Come on, girl." He should give her a name, something

Daed would never do. Searching his memory of other horse names, he decided on one. "Come on, Brownie."

Not much of a name. He stretched the carrot out toward her, wiggling it between his fingers. She took another step forward.

"You'll like this carrot." He tried another name. "Come on, Mabel."

She snorted.

"All right then. Tilly."

She swiveled her ears back and then forward again.

"Have a carrot, Tilly." The name fit. He took a step toward her. "Come on, Tilly-girl. You'll like it."

He held the carrot half on his outstretched hand and she picked it up, lipping it into her mouth. She stood, crunching the carrot as he grasped her halter. He gave her the other half.

She pulled wisps of hay from her manger as he brushed her lightly. She needed more than just grass to live on if he wanted her to become the kind of horse the other farmers kept. Sadie kept oats on hand and gave Chester a measured amount every day, rather than the hit-or-miss rations he gave Tilly. Sadie's horse thrived on her care.

So he would need to buy oats for the mare. Samuel held up the old brush, inspecting the matted and bent bristles. And he needed to buy a new brush. And a currycomb.

Taking care of this horse was going to cost money.

When Tilly finished her hay, he turned her out into the pasture again and grabbed the manure fork. He hauled forkfuls of soiled straw out to the pasture and started a pile. Somewhere in the past he remembered a manure pile in this spot. *Mamm* had used the soiled bedding on her garden after it had mellowed over the winter.

By the time he finished emptying the stall and spreading it with the last of the clean straw he had on hand, it was time for breakfast. The aroma of bacon frying pulled him to the house.

The girls didn't look up when he walked into the kitchen after washing up on the back porch.

"Good morning." Samuel broke the silence, and Esther stared at him in surprise. He didn't blame her. When had he ever greeted her in the morning?

Judith placed a bowl of scrambled eggs on the table with a smile. "Good morning, Samuel."

He started to reach for the platter of bacon, then remembered. He waited for Judith and Esther to take their seats, and then bowed his head for the silent prayer.

He had never prayed during this time, but had always let his mind wander while he waited for *Daed*'s signal to eat. But this morning, as the aroma of the bacon teased his hunger, he felt a nudge of guilt. Did his sisters pray during this moment of silence?

After the right amount of time had passed, Samuel cleared his throat just as *Daed* had always done, and reached for the bacon.

"Some coffee, Samuel?" Esther stood at his elbow with the coffee pot.

Samuel nodded, his mouth full. She poured his coffee and then her own and Judith's. Her wrists, sticking out too far from the sleeves of her faded dress, were thin. The hollow places under her cheekbones were shadowed and gray.

Esther had been keeping house for him since Annie got married and before that had taken on her share of the work, just as Judith did now. Her brow was creased, as if she wore a perpetual frown at the young age of twenty-one. He had never noticed that before.

Not before he had met Mary. Tall and slim, Mary looked healthy and strong. Compared to her, Judith and Esther reminded him of last year's dry weeds along the fence.

Samuel shifted in his chair, the eggs tasting like dust in his mouth. The sight of the bacon on his plate turned his stomach. A sudden vision filled his memory. Sitting at this same table, watching *Daed* fill his plate with food, leaving just enough for the rest of the family to share between them. *Daed* eating the last piece of bacon every morning. And *Mamm* at the other end of the table, her face as thin and gray as Esther's, nibbling at a piece of toast.

Neither Judith nor Esther had taken any of the scrambled eggs but were eating toast with a bit of jam. Normally, Samuel would take two or three helpings of eggs and empty the platter of bacon. He pushed the bowl of eggs in their direction.

"I can't eat all of this. You take some."

Esther startled and looked at him, her eyes wide. "Did I fix too many eggs?"

He shook his head. "I'm just not as hungry this morning. You and Judith can eat them. Don't let them go to waste."

The girls glanced at each other, then Esther divided the last of the eggs between them. Judith dug in to hers eagerly.

"The bacon, too." Samuel pushed the platter in their direction. He had already eaten half of what Esther had prepared.

He drank his coffee, the bitter liquid hitting his stomach with a burn. The girls did without decent food and clothes...but whenever he had extra cash, he bought whatever he thought he needed. He stared at Esther's thin wrists. Just like *Daed* had done, he made his sisters make do with whatever was left over after he had taken what he wanted.

Samuel loosened his fingers carefully from his tight grip on the coffee cup. He had been so blind. No different from *Daed*.

"This afternoon I'll take you girls to town."

They exchanged looks.

"You don't need to do that," Esther said. "We don't need anything."

"I know you need groceries."

"We have no money."

"I'll take one of the hogs to sell at the butcher." Samuel drained his cup and rose from the table. "So make a list. I'm going over to Sadie's this morning, and then we'll head to town right after dinner."

Samuel took the path that led from the back of the barn through the fence row to Sadie's place. A well-worn path that he had traveled ever since he had been old enough to chore. *Daed* hadn't cared whether Sadie's chores were done or not, but *Grossdawdi* had drilled the habit of shouldering the responsibility into Bram and Samuel.

Grossdawdi Abe. Not the *grossdawdi* far away, *Mamm*'s parents, but *Daed*'s father. The old man had lived in the room off the kitchen for as long as Samuel could remember, until he became sick with fever fifteen years ago. *Grossdawdi* Abe had called Samuel and Bram into his room one afternoon when *Daed* was away.

"I want you boys to promise..." He had broken off, coughing, but then continued, "Promise me you'll look after Sadie Beiler. You boys are big enough to remember. Make sure her chores are done."

Then he had grasped Samuel's wrist and pulled him close.

"Promise me."

Samuel had nodded his promise. And he had kept his promise, even though Bram had forgotten. Every week, no matter what else happened, he was at Sadie's farm to do the chores he couldn't bring himself to do around *Daed*'s farm.

Choring on *Daed*'s farm brought too many memories to the surface, but when he worked on Sadie's farm, he could feel *Grossdawdi* Abe's approval. He did the chores for *Grossdawdi*, and for Sadie, and no one else.

Now that Sadie was elderly he made daily trips to her farm. Not to do the small chores that the old woman insisted on doing herself, but to make sure she was all right. Sadie was more frail and forgetful than she wanted to admit, so Samuel had taken it on himself to check the chickens after breakfast.

If the morning came when the eggs hadn't been gathered, he'd be there to make sure the elderly woman was all right. So far that morning hadn't come, but he still took the walk across the fields after breakfast each day. As far as he knew, Sadie had no clue that he made the daily visits.

On Mondays, though, she expected him to be there to clean the chicken coop and do some other heavy chores. She would meet him at the barn to visit for a few minutes before she went back to her work in the house and he went into the barn. Those Monday morning talks were more than just idle chats with his neighbor. Sadie reminded him of better times, when *Mamm* was still alive. Before *Daed* became a slave to drink. Talking with her made him think that there were still peaceful and happy places in the world.

Today, as he rounded the corner of the woodlot, Sadie was nowhere to be seen. Mary was in the garden, attacking the weeds with a hoe.

"You don't need to do that, you know."

She jumped as he spoke, but relaxed when she recognized him.

"Good morning to you, too." She straightened and gave him a smile. "And why don't I need to weed the garden?"

"I do the heavy chores for Sadie. I always have."

"But Ida Mae and I are here now, so we can take care of things."

Samuel stared at her. He had to admit that there had

been times when he had wished for someone else to take on the responsibility of watching out for Sadie, but now that Mary was offering, he didn't want to let it go. He clenched his hand, as if he could keep a wisp of smoke from slipping through it.

"At least I can clean out the chickens' pen."

She shook her head as she continued hoeing. "I've already finished that. Chester's stall, too."

Samuel looked around the orderly farmyard. "You've cut the grass?"

"Ida Mae did."

"Then I'll fix the hole in Chester's stall. Sadie told me about it yesterday and I said I'd get to it today."

Mary got to the end of the row and looked at him.

"You fixed the stall, too?"

"*Ja*, for sure." Her brown eyes twinkled in the morning sunlight. "My sister and I were taught to do all of the chores around the farm. *Daed*'s thinking was that everyone in the family needed to know how to do chores, from cooking breakfast to mucking stalls. So, we learned."

"And you've left me with nothing to do." Samuel felt the growl in his voice.

"There is something we do want you to do." Mary's face lit up. "We hoped you could bring Judith and Esther over for a sewing frolic. Just the five of us. Aunt Sadie knows so much that she can teach us, and we all need new dresses for summer." She twisted the hoe handle. "I'm sure the girls could make a new shirt or two for you, too."

Samuel scratched at his chin. The skin was itchy and irritated after being shaved this morning.

"I'll make you a deal."

Her eyes narrowed. "What kind of deal?"

"I'll bring my sisters over tomorrow morning, like you said, if you let me do some of the work around here. There are some fence rails that need replacing, along with a few other things, so I'll have plenty to do."

She pressed her lips together, as if relinquishing the fence mending was the last thing she wanted to do.

"All right," she said. "You can mend the fence. But bring your sisters, and any fabric they might have. Even an old dress we can make over into something new."

Esther's faded and ragged sleeve edge flashed through his mind. He would make sure his sisters each chose a dress length of fabric while they were in town this afternoon. Maybe he would sell two hogs. Then he thought of the shadowed look on Esther's face. She would appreciate the time she spent with Sadie just as much as he did.

He nodded. "We have an agreement."

Samuel stuck out his hand to seal the deal the way he would with another farmer and Mary hesitated, then slipped her slender one into his, her grip firm.

"Agreed."

Tuesday morning Mary came back to the house after the morning barn chores to find Sadie and Ida Mae already sitting at the breakfast table waiting for her.

"I didn't think I was that late," Mary said, slipping into her chair at the small table.

"You aren't." Sadie folded her hands in preparation for their silent prayer. "We have company coming this morning, so we got breakfast started early."

Mary bent her head over her own folded hands, struggling to force her thoughts away from Sadie's comment. After a brief, silent prayer of thanks, she raised her head. Sadie sat with her fork poised, waiting for her to finish.

"I had nearly forgotten that the Lapps would be here today." Mary cut a slice of sausage with the side of her fork.

"I'm glad Samuel is bringing the girls," Sadie said. "I always enjoy their company."

Ida Mae served herself some scrambled eggs from the bowl in the center of the round table. "Samuel looks different when he smiles. He was so gruff when we first met him, but then when he smiled, I nearly didn't recognize him."

Sadie sipped her coffee. "He looks much like his grandfather did, years ago. Quite good-looking."

"You knew his grandfather?" Ida Mae picked up the ketchup bottle. "That must have been a long time ago."

"I was only sixteen when he asked to walk me home from Saturday night singing."

Ida Mae stared at Sadie. "Did he court you?"

Sadie pointed at Ida Mae's eggs. "You're putting on too much ketchup."

Ida Mae put the bottle down. Her eggs were covered with the sauce.

Mary passed her plate to her sister. "Here, spoon some onto my eggs, then it won't go to waste."

Sadie took another sip of her coffee, staring out the window as if she were watching her memories through it.

"He was my only suitor. We courted for two years."

"What was he like?" Mary asked.

"Tall, with dark hair, just like Samuel. But careless. My *daed* didn't like him very much."

Mary took a bite of her eggs, trying to imagine Aunt Sadie's father. He had been Mary and Ida Mae's great-grandfather, and their mother had always described him as kind and loving.

Ida Mae finished her breakfast and leaned forward, folding her arms on the table. "What happened?"

Sadie sighed. "Abe—that was his name—liked to play practical jokes. One day he came to pick me up in his spring wagon, and he had whitewashed his horse." Sadie smiled, shaking her head. "That scamp. We had a good laugh over his white horse, until *Daed* saw it."

Mary picked up her coffee cup. "Then what happened?"

"*Daed* said the waste of the paint and mistreating the poor horse was the last straw." Sadie's eyes sparkled as tears welled up and she lifted the hem of her apron to wipe her cheek. "He told Abe not to bother coming around again. I would see him at Sabbath meeting, of course, but he never spoke to me again. He found a girl from the Clinton district a year later and married her."

"So he just forgot about you?"

Sadie smiled at Ida Mae. "*Ach, ne.* You see, when *Daed* left the farm to my younger brother, your uncle Sol, I didn't want to live there anymore. It was one thing to be an unwed daughter in my parents' home, but with Sol and his wife having one baby after another, I was more in the way than I was a help. Elsie didn't want an old maiden aunt telling her how to raise her children."

"You couldn't have been that old," Ida Mae said.

"That was thirty-five years ago. I was fifty and had nowhere to go."

"So what did you do?"

"Somehow Abe knew of my predicament. He gave me these ten acres and the church built this house and barn." Sadie sighed. "Even after all those years, with his family grown and grandchildren coming along, Abe thought of me."

They sat in silence, and Mary thought about Sadie's story. How much was Samuel like his grandfather?

Sadie stood and started gathering the plates from the table. "The Lapps will be here soon. I have some scraps of material we can use to make a quilt top. We may as well start the sewing lessons sooner than later."

Before the mantel clock in the front room struck eight, Samuel's buggy drove into the yard.

"Go out and tell him to put his horse in the pasture with Chester," Sadie said, pushing Mary toward the door. "And tell him we'll have dinner ready at noon, and he and the girls should stay."

Mary got to the buggy just at Samuel was tying the horse to the hitching post. "Aunt Sadie says to put your mare in the pasture."

"I didn't think the job would take very long. The horse can stand."

"We'll have dinner ready for you and the girls. Aunt Sadie says we're to have a good visit."

Esther climbed down from the buggy, followed by Judith. Each of them carried a bundle of fabric. "I'm glad we're going to spend the day. We need Aunt Sadie's help with our dresses."

As the girls went into the house, Mary couldn't contain her smile. "I'm so glad they found material to bring. I wasn't sure they would have any."

"We went into town yesterday afternoon." Samuel fiddled with the reins in his hands as if he wasn't sure what to do. He shifted his gaze toward the door, where the girls had disappeared. "I appreciate the offer of dinner. The girls will enjoy the visit, and I have plenty of work to do here."

Mary stepped back as he climbed down from the buggy. He was freshly shaven again today, and even with his worn work clothes, he was a fine-looking man. If Sadie's Abe had been anything like his grandson, she could understand why Sadie had fallen for him.

"I can show you where the repairs need to be done and where to put the horse."

He led the horse out from between the buggy shafts. "I know my way around. I've been helping Aunt Sadie since

I was a boy." He gave her a brotherly grin as he walked away. "I'll see you at dinnertime."

Mary watched as he disappeared into the barn. Sadie's story of his grandfather had made him more intriguing than ever.

When she went inside the house, she followed the voices until she found Aunt Sadie and the others in the sewing room. Judith and Esther had spread lengths of light-colored muslin on the cutting table.

"Samuel surprised us with the trip to town," Judith was saying, stroking her piece of pale yellow fabric.

Esther fingered her own light green piece. "For some reason, he said we needed new dresses." She looked at Sadie. "He has never noticed what we've worn before, but yesterday in town he kept piling things on the shop-keeper's counter. Fabric, flour and sugar, butter. He even bought a new crock, since our old one broke last winter."

Sadie fingered the edge of the fabric. "That must have cost a lot of money."

Judith nodded. "I think it did. But he had taken two of the hogs to the butcher shop and sold them. He kept say-ing he should have done it months ago."

Sadie looked out the window toward the barn, and Mary followed her gaze. Samuel had just opened the gate to the pasture and was letting the mare in with Chester. He glanced toward the house, and then went back into the barn. He looked like a man who was eager to start working.

"I wonder what has gotten into him," Sadie said softly, and moved her gaze from Samuel to Mary.

Mary caught her look and felt her face turning red. Sadie couldn't think that Samuel was trying to impress her. Romance seemed to be as far from his mind as it was from hers.

Chapter Three

Samuel straightened and thumbed his hat back on his head. Chester had punched a hole in the side of the stall, all right. After pulling off the scrap wood Mary had used to patch the hole and tearing away the splintered remains of the broken plank, he could see the extent of the damage. Mary might have thought her patch was adequate, but this needed more than a temporary fix. The entire board should be replaced.

He climbed the ladder to the haymow, nearly empty after the long winter. Sadie had some hay left, but someone would have to fill the mow again before the summer was too far gone.

Someone? Samuel rubbed at his bare chin. That someone should be him. Other years, the deacons had made sure the mow was filled, but he could do it this year.

On the other side of the haymow a stack of planks rose from the dusty floor. They had been left from when the barn was built years ago. *Grossdawdi* had said something about building a chicken coop out of them someday, but Sadie had converted an empty stall for her few chickens, cutting a door through the outside wall for them to use, and the coop had never been built.

Samuel picked up the top plank and stood it upright, thumping it on the wooden haymow floor to shake the dust off. From here he could see Sadie's little house through the loft door. The windows were open to the spring air, and voices drifted up to him. He could distinguish Mary's low voice, bubbling with laughter. He couldn't keep a smile away at that thought.

Judith's voice rose above the others, cheerful and eager. If he had known a length of fabric would make her this happy, he would have taken the girls to town long ago. Why didn't he? He thumped the board one last time. Because *Daed* wouldn't have. He didn't remember *Daed* ever taking *Mamm* to town. None of them went anywhere except for *Daed*. He kept everyone at home, where no one would see *Mamm*'s bruised face.

He gripped the board as if he could split it in two. He had been following *Daed*'s example like a wheelbarrow following the rut he had left behind. As if he had no power over his own actions. He hadn't treated Judith and Esther any differently than *Daed* had, and there was no reason for it.

How had Bram gotten free of *Daed*'s shadow? Or had he? Did his pretty wife live in fear of Bram's temper?

Samuel leaned his head against the board, closing his eyes against the ache in his head. No woman would ever live in fear of him. He couldn't be sure of controlling his temper, but if he stayed single and kept to himself, he could avoid *Daed*'s legacy in at least one area of his life.

He lifted the board and took it to the main floor of the barn.

Replacing the plank didn't take much time. He spent another hour giving Chester's stall a thorough cleaning, leveling the dirt floor and scrubbing the walls. The chickens' area, divided from the rest of the barn by a fence of wood slats and chicken wire, was already clean with fresh straw spread over the floor. Mary and Ida Mae were giving Sadie the help she had needed.

Movement in the vegetable garden caught his attention. Mary was there, picking lettuce. Samuel stood in the shadows just inside the door, watching the young woman in the garden. She bent, stooped and then straightened as she worked with a grace that drew him.

A few steps brought him close. Her back was turned to him as she leaned down to reach some lettuce that was tangled in the young bean plants.

"I've finished repairing the stall."

Mary jumped, whirling to face him. Her face was pale, and her hand clutched at the front of her apron.

"Are you all right?" Samuel took a step closer to her, but stopped when she moved away. "I didn't mean to scare you."

"Ne." She shook her head. "I mean, I'm all right. I just wasn't expecting anyone to be there. You surprised me."

Her hands trembled, and she clasped them together.

"Are you sure you're all right?"

She nodded and smiled, but the smile was stiff. "I'm picking some vegetables for dinner. Esther and Judith are having such fun with their new dresses. Aunt Sadie is teaching us all sorts of sewing tricks that I've never known before."

She chattered on as she turned to the peas. Her voice became more natural, and her trembling hands stilled as she worked. When she got to the end of the row, he lifted the basket of vegetables and carried them to the back porch.

After dinner, he would work on the pasture fence. A few loose boards near the gate needed to be tightened, and a few more around the perimeter needed to be replaced. When he finished with that, they would return home...

"Do you think they would want to come?"

Mary's question brought his attention back to her one-sided conversation. He was too used to ignoring his sisters' chatter.

"Where?"

"To the quilting in Eden Township on Thursday."

Samuel set the basket on the porch step. "Why would they want to go to another quilting?"

Mary's hands became fists that perched at her waist. "You weren't listening to me, were you?"

One look at her pursed lips, and he was done. Caught. He'd never be able to get anything by her.

"I missed the part about the quilting." He stared at her brown eyes. A trick he had learned from *Daed*. Put up a bluster. Make them think you are right, no matter what happens.

She met his stare, her eyes narrowing. He shifted his gaze to the peas, lifting one as if to inspect it for brown spots.

"You missed everything." She sighed and brushed some dirt off her apron. "On Thursday, the Eden Township group is meeting at your sister Annie's house. Aunt Sadie is planning to go, and we wondered if Judith and Esther would like to come along."

Annie. A pain he didn't know he held washed through him at the thought of her curly red hair. She had left…how long ago? Almost two years? It had been soon after *Daed* passed away. He hadn't spoken to her since, and he never even thought of taking the girls to visit her. Why had he ignored her after she left to marry the deacon's son?

Because *Daed* would have been angry when she went behind his back, and he had followed in *Daed*'s footsteps without even thinking.

"*Ja*." He made the decision quickly, before he could

think of all the reasons not to go to Eden Township. All the reasons to avoid mending the family ties. "And I'll drive you all in our buggy."

"You don't need to do that. We can take Chester."

"I'm going to drive. I have something to do down there, too."

Samuel lifted the basket and followed Mary into the kitchen. He needed to mend more than just the pasture fence. *Daed* had never apologized for anything he did, no matter how deep the wounds ran. But he wasn't *Daed*, and he wasn't going to act like him anymore.

He paused as Judith's and Esther's happy voices drifted into the kitchen from the back room. It was past time to apologize to Annie and her husband, and he had two days to prepare himself to face Bram.

"I can't wait until Thursday," Judith said.

The dress pieces had been cut out of the new fabric before dinner, and now, while Samuel mended the pasture fence and Aunt Sadie napped in her room, the girls sat together in the sewing room, each with pinned pieces to sew together.

"How long has it been since you've seen Annie?" Ida Mae asked.

"She left home two years ago." Esther snipped the end of her thread as she finished the shoulder of her dress, then tied a new knot to begin sewing the side seam. "She had met Matthew Beachey when he came to one of our singings, and they courted secretly for months."

"It wasn't a secret to us," Judith said.

Esther smiled, her sewing forgotten in her lap. "She was so happy with Matthew. When she came home from one of their buggy rides, we'd be waiting up for her. She'd tell us all about what they had done and where they had gone. Most often, he took her to his family's house after dinner to play games with his brothers and sisters in the evening, or he'd take her for a ride around Emma Lake. It sounded so romantic."

"Why was it such a secret?" Mary drew her thread through the seam. She had chosen the more difficult task of inserting the sleeves into the bodice of Judith's dress.

"She was afraid that if *Daed* had known she was seeing someone, he would have put a stop to it, the way he had tried to do with Katie." Esther's voice dropped, remembering. "Katie ran away with her beau to get married in Ohio, but Annie didn't want to run away. She didn't want to be separated from us."

Mary shifted in her chair. "But the bishop wouldn't allow them to marry without your *daed*'s permission, would he?"

"I don't know how Annie did it, but Bishop Yoder in Eden Township came here to talk to *Daed*, along with Matthew and Deacon Beachey. They wanted *Daed* to give his permission for the marriage."

Judith looked up from her sewing. "*Ach*, remember how angry he was?"

"He was so angry that Matthew left without Annie."

"I remember how she cried," Judith said. "She was afraid she would have to run away like Katie did."

"But Matthew came back when he heard *Daed* had died. It was after the funeral, but not too much time had passed." Esther sighed. "Samuel acted just like *Daed*, until Annie told him she was going to marry Matthew with his permission or without it."

"He stomped off to the barn then, didn't he?"

"But he gave her his permission first." Esther picked up her sewing again. "We haven't seen Annie since that day.

We didn't go to the wedding, and we never go to visit the Eden Township folks."

"But she lives so close," Mary said. "I can understand that you wouldn't see Katie, living in Ohio the way she does, but Annie is only a few miles down the road."

"Even so," Esther said, "we've never gone for a visit, and she hasn't come here." Esther stopped to thread her needle. "I hope we get to see Bram on Thursday. He's our other brother, and also lives in Eden Township."

"I do, too," said Judith. "I was only five years old when he left home, and I hardly remember him."

Mary sewed basting stitches in the right sleeve and then gathered them before she pinned the sleeve to the bodice. She had never met a family like the Lapps, where the scattered family members didn't try to see one another, even when they lived in the same area. But if Samuel had been as angry as the girls said when Annie left...

Rethreading her needle, Mary tried to imagine Samuel being angry. She had seen him embarrassed, and a bit grumpy, but angry? She imagined his eyes darkening, his mouth twisting, his hand reaching toward her... Her vision suddenly blurred, swirling so that she couldn't see the needle's eye. She took a deep breath and started counting.

There was nothing to fear from Samuel. He was a neighbor. Judith and Esther's brother. She would never be foolish enough to be alone with him in a secluded place. She would never let herself be at the mercy of any man again.

She started over. *One, two, three, four...* She fixed her eyes on the wooden planks of the floor in front of her toes. *Ten, eleven, twelve...* Her breathing slowed and she relaxed. *Twenty-five, twenty-six...*

Safe. She was safe in Aunt Sadie's home. Safe with the girls and Ida Mae, without any men around to intrude.

Except Samuel, and he would soon learn that they didn't

need him to do Sadie's chores any longer. Then she would only have to see him on church Sundays.

Esther's voice penetrated the hum in Mary's ears.

"What?"

"Did you enjoy church on Sunday?" Esther asked, looking at both Mary and Ida Mae.

"We did," Mary said. She forced herself to smile. "There were a lot of new people to meet, but other than that it was very much like church at home."

Judith giggled. "I saw someone taking notice of Ida Mae during dinner."

Mary exchanged glances with her sister, but Ida Mae shrugged, her eyebrows lifted.

"What do you mean? I didn't see anyone noticing me in particular."

The girl grinned, looking at their faces. "I can't be the only one who saw him. He couldn't take his eyes off you."

"Whoever it was," Mary said, "he was probably only looking at us because we're new."

Judith shook her head. "He was only looking at Ida Mae. I don't think he saw anyone else all day."

Esther leaned forward. "You have to tell us who it was."

Judith only grinned until Esther nudged her knee with her foot.

"It was Thomas Weaver."

"The minister's son?" Esther sat back in her chair. "Every girl around has been trying to catch his attention."

Ida Mae turned to Mary. Her face was mottled pink. "I… I'm going to check on Sadie. I'll be right back."

After she left the room, Esther said, "I hope we didn't say anything to upset her."

"It isn't anything to worry about. Ida Mae just isn't interested in getting to know any boys right now." She shifted the bodice in her lap and changed the subject.

"There were so many other young people at church on Sunday. I'm looking forward to getting to know the girls. Do you attend the singings?"

"Samuel won't take us, and he won't let us drive ourselves. I think he's afraid we'll end up the same way as Annie and Katie."

"But he lets you go to the quilting on Wednesdays."

Judith nodded. "That's because there aren't any boys there."

Esther stifled a giggle. "Can you imagine a boy at a quilting frolic?"

They all laughed at that.

Ida Mae came back into the room. "Sadie is sound asleep."

"I'm so glad," Mary said. "If she doesn't take a rest she gets overtired in the evenings and forgets things too easily."

"Everyone is glad you came to live with her," said Esther. "She shouldn't live alone anymore, not at her age. Too many things can happen."

"Like when she didn't come to church one Sunday last winter." Judith's face had grown pale. "The deacons went to check on her after the worship service was over. It turns out she had made a wrong turn on the way to meeting. They got here to her house just as she returned. She had gone all the way to Middlebury, but when she knew she had gone the wrong way, she let Chester bring her home."

"It's a good thing she has a smart horse," Esther said.

Mary and Ida Mae looked at each other. Mary saw the same alarm she felt reflected in her sister's eyes.

"That could have ended in disaster."

"But it didn't." Esther tied a knot in her thread. "The Good Lord was watching out for her that day."

What would they do if something like that happened

again? Mary rubbed her tired fingers. She and Ida Mae would have to watch Aunt Sadie very closely.

Samuel was at work early on Thursday, preparing for the trip to Eden Township. Tilly stood with a hind leg cocked, head down, her side to the morning sun as Samuel brushed her. The new bristles lifted the dust off her coat with little puffs that glinted in the sunlight. The mare's skin twitched in response. She was enjoying the pampering.

Samuel had curried and brushed her more in the last two days than he ever had before. He had even taken care of her hooves, trimming and polishing them until they shone. He stood back and inspected his brushing job. Her muscles could still use some filling out, but that would come with time. Meanwhile, her coat was beginning to take on the shine of a healthy animal. He didn't need to be ashamed of her when he faced Bram.

He left Tilly still basking in the sun as he went into the barn and put the brush and currycomb on their shelf with care. One thing he remembered from *Grossdawdi*'s barn was how clean and orderly everything had been. Each step he took in that direction was progress.

The old buggy stood in the middle of the barn floor, still clean from yesterday's washing. The wheels were worn, and should be replaced. The seats needed to be recovered, but the old blankets he had thrown over them would have to do for now. Even with as many years as the buggy had been around, though, the black lacquered oilcloth cover gleamed in the subdued light of the barn. Everything was ready for today's trip.

Samuel took off his new hat and ran his fingers through his hair. Everything was ready except him. The thought of seeing Annie again filled his stomach with something like a bundle of puppies, but Bram...

He whooshed out a breath at the thought of his last encounter with Bram at the barn raising last summer. He had been stupid, making idle threats that didn't mean anything, but Bram had responded like no Amishman ever did. He had drawn him close, like a brother would, but his grip had been hard on Samuel's shoulder, and his words dripped of danger. Samuel swallowed at the memory. He had never encountered anything like the tone in Bram's voice. The years his brother had spent working for gangsters in Chicago had hardened him.

Bram could be a dangerous man, but his life had changed since that hot day last summer. He had joined the church, married a pretty widow and was now a father to her three children. Was he any less threatening, though?

Samuel ran his hand through his hair again, making it stand up in spikes. He didn't have long to wait to find out. He planned to take the girls and Sadie to Annie's, where he would apologize to her and her husband. The puppies churned. That would be difficult enough. But then, once he learned where Bram lived, he would go to his farm and...what? Confront him? Try to make amends? Repair the broken places between them? It all depended on Bram's reaction.

He took a cloth and wiped a few stray specks of dust from the buggy, then led Tilly into the barn to harness her. Every clomp of her hooves on the wooden floor was one step closer to facing Bram. He tied Tilly to a post and stroked her neck.

"Well, Tilly-girl, it's going to be a day to remember."

Taking the harness from the hooks on the wall, he swung it onto the mare's back. She stepped away, but then stood quietly as he murmured to her. "So, Tilly, so. You know we're going for a drive, don't you?" Her ears swung back and then forward at the unfamiliar tone in his voice. He reached under her to grab a strap, and as he fastened the harness onto her, he kept talking. "We're going down to Eden Township today." He patted her rump as he walked around to her other side. "You'll like the drive. New places to see." Once the harness was on, he led her to the buggy and backed her into place between the shafts.

After she was hitched up, he led her out of the barn to the hitching rail next to the house. Esther was waiting for him on the steps, bouncing on her toes and grinning. He had to smile at her.

"You look like you're ready to go."

"For sure I am!" She ran down the walk toward the buggy. "I haven't seen Annie since she got married." She stopped when she reached him and looked into his face, suddenly sober. "You don't think she has forgotten us, do you?"

The litter of puppies in Samuel's stomach clambered over each other as Esther's words sunk in. He had been so concerned with his own meeting with Annie that he hadn't considered how Esther and Judith must be feeling. They were her sisters, separated from her through no fault of their own.

"I'm sorry." The words came out garbled, strangled by his swelling throat. As Judith joined them, he put a hand on each of his sister's shoulders and tried again. "I'm sorry that I haven't taken you to see Annie before."

Judith and Esther glanced at each other.

"We understand," Esther said. "You were angry—"

Samuel cut off her excuses. "But I shouldn't have been. I shouldn't have acted like I did when she wanted to marry that young man."

"Matthew."

Samuel squeezed Judith's shoulder in silent thanks for providing the name he couldn't remember. The name he had blocked. "Matthew." He nodded. "Matthew." The serious young man who had claimed their Annie. The puppies wouldn't settle down.

Judith shrugged his hand off her shoulder. "Can we go now? I can't wait to get there."

Samuel stroked Tilly's nose as the girls climbed into the buggy, ignoring their surprise at the changes he had made. He didn't have to go with them. He could send them over to Sadie's to ride with her. He didn't have to face Annie and Matthew. He could stay home. There was plenty of work to keep him busy.

He swallowed. He didn't have to risk Bram's rejection.

Tilly nibbled at his shoulder. It was the first sign of affection she had ever shown him. He patted her cheek and smoothed the hair under her bridle.

"Well, Tilly-girl, I guess it's time to face the lions."

He climbed into the buggy and lifted the reins. The girls chattered to each other in the back seat, talking about Annie and her baby. He rubbed at his freshly shaved chin as they talked. He hadn't thought that Annie would have a child. His nephew, from what the girls were saying.

Turning Tilly onto the road, he urged her into the quick trot she liked as they headed toward Sadie's house. As they turned in, he saw Sadie and Ida Mae waiting for them at the edge of the drive. The churning in his stomach eased as Mary stepped out of the house and joined them just as he drew the buggy up. She gave him one of her quiet smiles as Ida Mae climbed into the back of the buggy. He stepped out to help Sadie into the front seat.

"Good morning, Samuel." She clung to his hand as she put one foot on the buggy step. "It's a fine day for a drive."

"*Ja*, for sure."

He waited for her to move to the center of the seat so that Mary would be able to sit next to her, but Sadie waved him away.

"I'd like to sit here, if you don't mind. Mary can sit in the center, between us."

Mary shot a look toward her aunt, then walked around the back of the buggy with Samuel.

"You know why Sadie wants me to sit in the middle, don't you?" Mary whispered the words.

"Why?"

Mary stopped, out of sight of the others. "I think she's trying to push us together."

Samuel stared. Her cheeks were pink, and one wisp of hair curled around the edge of her bonnet, sending his thoughts down a path that led to tucking that wisp behind her ear. He gripped his suspenders to keep his hands still. "You mean like a matchmaker?"

"Shh." Mary turned away from the buggy. "Don't let her hear you." She twisted her fingers together. "If she sees that she isn't successful, then she'll give up. We just have to ignore her attempts to match us up."

"That sounds good to me."

Mary continued around the buggy to climb into the front seat and Samuel followed her. His plans didn't include a wife, and he should be glad that Mary had rejected the idea of the two of them making a match. So why did he feel like he had just watched something precious float away?

Chapter Four

The narrow seat on the buggy provided no opportunity for Mary to put any distance between her elbow and Samuel's. She finally gave up, resigning herself to the occasional bumps in the road that jostled her against his warm, strong arm. His muscles were tense as he handled the reins, so maybe he didn't notice when they made contact.

Sadie kept the conversation going with news about the neighbors as they made their way south.

"There's the Miller farm," she said as they passed a lovely shaded farmyard. Flowers lined the edge of the garden and some children were busy picking strawberries from the field next to the house. "They're Mennonite, and good neighbors." She went on without a pause. "And up ahead is the Jefferson place. They're *Englischers* and their family has lived here as long as ours." Sadie laid her hand on Mary's arm as she turned toward her. "My *daed* never understood Thomas Jefferson. *Ach, ja,* that was his name. No relation to the famous president, though. The man was a go-getter, never leaving things be. Now his son, Phillip, has the farm. You won't believe the bee he has in his hat."

Sadie fell silent and Mary exchanged glances with Samuel.

He grinned. "You're talking about the road paving he wants the county to do?"

Sadie nodded and set off again. "That's right! Pavement in the country! What trotting along on that hard surface will do to our poor horses, I don't know." She huffed as she settled back in her seat. "He just wants a smooth road for his fancy automobile, and wants the county to pay for it."

Samuel chirruped to the horse. "He says it will keep the dust down." His words were mild, but Mary could see his Adam's apple bobbing as he tried to keep from laughing.

Sadie crossed her arms. "There's nothing wrong with a little dust."

Samuel kept his voice calm, not letting the laughter emerge. "You just don't like to see progress."

"Of course not. Progress without wisdom isn't good for anyone. People like Phillip Jefferson can't see past the end of their own noses, and he has no thought of what unintended consequences this road of his might bring." Sadie sat up, her attention on the next farm. "There's the Zook farm. Good Amish folks, and now we're in Eden Township."

"Is that Levi Zook? I met him at a barn raising last summer," Samuel said.

Sadie shook her head. "*Ne*, his cousin, Caleb. Levi lives a few miles east of here." She leaned forward. "Matthew Beachey's place is just past this crossroad. Up there on the right."

Mary felt Samuel's body stiffen at Sadie's words. What must it be like for him to see Annie again after so long?

The other girls had been visiting in the back seat, but when Sadie pointed out their destination, Esther and Judith leaned forward to get a look.

"What a pretty place," Judith said.

"Look at all of the flowers. Annie always said gladiolus was her favorite, and she has planted a whole row of them."

Esther's voice sounded strained and Mary turned around as well as she could.

"Are you all right, Esther?"

She nodded. "I'm just so happy to see Annie again." She pointed, her arm extending between Mary and Sadie. "Look, there she is! Samuel, stop the buggy so we can get out."

"You can wait until I turn in the drive." Samuel's voice held a growl. His face was tense as he drove the horse toward Annie, who was waiting for them next to the gravel lane.

When he drew the buggy to a stop, Judith and Esther jumped out and into Annie's arms. The three sisters held each other close, none of them saying a word, until Annie pushed away from the embrace to look at the girls.

"You've both changed so much!" Annie's happy smile made Mary want to smile back.

As the girls launched into the story of everything that had happened since they had last been together, Annie looked toward the buggy, then back at her sisters. Samuel remained in his seat, watching the girls, but making no move to get out.

Sadie reached across Mary to poke his arm. "Samuel, it's time for you to say hello to Annie."

Samuel swallowed, his Adam's apple bobbing. *"Ja."* He sighed and secured the reins, but he didn't make a move to get out of the buggy.

Mary laid her hand on his arm. There must be some way she could help. The poor man looked like he was about to meet his doom.

"She's waiting for you."

Samuel looked past Mary and Sadie. Annie had glanced his way again, and had pulled her lower lip in between her teeth.

"Go on," Mary said. She pushed at his arm. "It's time."

His eyes met hers then, pleading with them as one of her younger brothers would do, but he climbed down from the buggy. Mary followed him and helped Sadie to the ground as she watched him greet his sister.

"Hello, Annie."

He stood back, but his sister reached toward him and grasped his hand.

"I'm so glad you came." Her eyes sparkled with tears. "I've missed you. All of you."

Sadie pulled on Mary's arm, and she led the way into the house with Ida Mae following.

"We'll let the four of them get acquainted again without us interfering."

Other buggies had already arrived, and as Mary stepped onto the porch, she could hear the hum of voices from inside the house. She swallowed down the thickness in her throat at the thought of all the strangers on the other side of that door, but she didn't have time to be nervous as Sadie walked in. They laid their bonnets with the others on a bed in the room off the kitchen, then followed the sound of women visiting.

The front room was filled with a quilt on a frame, and ten or twelve women sat around it, needles in their hands and all talking at once. Sadie led Ida Mae to three empty chairs on the far side of the quilt, stopping to greet the women they passed on the way.

"Good morning, Elizabeth." She grasped an older woman's shoulder. "These are my nieces from Ohio, Mary and Ida Mae." She went on to the next woman, a younger image of the first one. "And, Ellie, I'm so glad you're here. Meet my nieces."

Mary had hardly had a chance to greet Elizabeth when

she met Ellie's blue eyes. "I'm so happy to meet you. I'm Ellie Lapp."

"Lapp? Are you related to Esther and Judith?"

"*Ja*, for sure." Ellie's smile was relaxed and welcoming. "Their brother Bram is my husband, but I've never met the girls." She stuck her needle in the quilt and half rose from her seat. "Did they come with you? Are they outside?"

"They're talking with Annie. Samuel is there, too."

Ellie sat back in her chair. "Samuel came?"

"He said he had some business here in Eden Township, so he drove us down here this morning."

A little boy, about two years old, crawled out from under the quilting frame and pulled on Ellie's skirt. "*Memmie*, I'm thirsty."

Ellie cupped his head in her hand, a worried frown on her face. "*Ja*, Danny. We'll go to the kitchen and get a drink." She smiled at Mary, her brows still knit. "I'm so glad to meet you, Mary, and I hope we'll be able to get to know each other better."

She took the little boy by the hand and led him into the kitchen as Mary made her way to the chair next to Sadie and Ida Mae. For the first time, she wondered what business Samuel had in Eden Township. Whatever it was, it had Ellie worried.

Samuel let Tilly choose her own pace as he set off down the road toward Bram's farm. Annie's welcome had bolstered his courage enough to ask for directions to their brother's home, but when he saw Bram's wife peering at them through Annie's kitchen window, doubts began to crowd in again.

Meeting Bram wouldn't be as easy as seeing Annie again. His sister had always been quick to forgive and easy to talk to. Bram had never been easy to deal with.

Samuel stopped at a crossroad. Annie had said he would turn right after he passed over the creek, and he could see the wandering line of trees and bushes that marked the creek's progress through the fields ahead. Only one more mile before he turned onto Bram's road. When he clucked to Tilly, she shook her head and started off at a brisk trot.

He and Bram had never enjoyed the kind of brotherly love he saw in other families. *Daed* had pushed at them, and Samuel could hear his voice now. *"Bram can do it. Why can't you?"*

And then Bram would look at him with his superior, big-brother look that would spike Samuel's temper.

Whether it was pitching hay down from the loft or hauling buckets of slop for the hogs, Bram had always done it better, faster, easier.

Even after Bram had abandoned the family, *Daed* had kept goading at Samuel, pushing him to be the man Bram was.

But he wasn't Bram. He didn't leave. He had stayed and absorbed the brunt of *Daed*'s anger right until the end.

Samuel fingered the reins. Why hadn't he left? He could have followed Bram, but he shied away from the accusing voice in his head that said he had been too cowardly to strike out on his own. His eyes stung and he rubbed at them. He wasn't a coward. He was the good son. The one who had stayed home. But *Mamm* had still died.

Tilly trotted across the culvert over the stream and the next crossroad was in sight. A quarter mile west, Annie had said. His stomach churned with something. Anger? Resentment? Or was he only nervous?

Samuel pulled Tilly to a stop at the corner. He didn't have to turn. He could continue down this road, find a spot to rest until it was time to pick up the girls again and face Bram another day.

But he was done with putting things off. That's the way *Daed* would have handled this. He would have ignored Bram, pretended he didn't exist to punish him for taking off to Chicago all those years ago. If he was going to come out from his *daed*'s shadow, he needed to face Bram.

Make amends.

He turned the corner and headed west, keeping Tilly's pace to a slow trot, even though she shook her head in protest. Samuel kept the reins tight, holding her in. He wanted time.

The farm was on the left after he crossed another little creek. A *Dawdi Haus* nestled in the grass near the creek, with a flower garden in the front. The main house stood on a rise near it, and a white barn sat at the back of the lane. A field next to the lane was planted with corn, and the stalks stood nearly a foot high. A team of four matching Belgian horses grazed in the pasture beyond the barn.

Samuel pulled Tilly to a halt in the road. The horses in the pasture meant that Bram was at home, not out in the fields. He fought the urge to keep driving down the road and turned Tilly into the lane. Someone had seen him coming. An old man watched him from the porch of the *Dawdi Haus*, but Samuel followed the sound of metal hammering on metal that rang from the barn.

He halted Tilly near the barn door and climbed out of the buggy. The ringing continued. He tied the horse to the rail alongside the barn. No break in the rhythmic hammering from inside.

Looking around, Samuel spied the old man, who had walked up to the main house and stood on the front porch. He lifted his hand in a wave and Samuel returned the gesture. There was no alternative now except to face Bram. Wiping his hands on his trousers, he walked into the barn.

Just inside the door, he stopped to let his eyes adjust

to the dim light. Bram was at the end of the main bay, working on a plow, his back to the door. A boy stood next to him. The seven-year-old held his hands over his ears to block out the noise, but leaned as close to Bram as he could, fascinated by the work.

Bram stopped hammering and bent down to inspect his work. "You see here, Johnny," he said as he pointed, "that was the piece that had come loose. But now it's fastened in good and tight and should work fine."

Samuel walked toward them and the boy saw him.

"*Daed*, someone's here."

Bram straightened and turned, a welcoming smile on his face until he saw who it was.

"Samuel." His voice held a note of surprise.

"Hello, Bram."

Bram pulled off his gloves and laid one hand on the boy's shoulder without taking his gaze away from Samuel. "Johnny, we're done here. Why don't you go see if your *grossdawdi* needs any help?"

Johnny ran out the back door of the barn and Bram stepped closer.

"I didn't expect to see you."

Samuel tried to smile. "Annie told me where you live."

"You've been to Annie's?"

"I brought Judith and Esther to her house for the quilting this morning, and I thought I'd stop and see how you were doing."

Bram stared at him. "If I remember right, when I stopped by the farm last year you told me that I didn't belong there, and you didn't want to see me again."

Samuel took a step back. *Ja*, for sure, he remembered that day. Bram had been all slicked up in a gabardine suit. An *Englischer* through and through.

"You didn't look like you wanted to stay."

Bram stepped closer. "You didn't even let me go to the house to see the girls."

Samuel looked him in the eyes. "You weren't our brother anymore. You were some fancy *Englischer*. How did I know what you wanted from us?"

His brother looked down. "You were probably right." He rubbed at the back of his neck. "I was hoping to hide out at home, but when you sent me on my way, I had to make other plans." He smiled then, looking at Samuel again. "I should probably thank you for that. If you hadn't forced me to move on to Annie and Matthew's, I would never have met Ellie."

"But the last time we spoke, at the barn raising, you threatened me."

"*Ja*, well, I did, didn't I? You must understand, there were some dangerous men around and I didn't want you to get mixed up with them. I was hoping to scare you off."

Samuel felt the corner of his mouth twitch. "More dangerous than you?"

Bram's mouth widened in a wry grin. "Dangerous enough. But that's in the past. My life is different now. Better. Much better."

Samuel nodded, looking around at the neat, clean barn. "Life has been good to you."

"God has been good to me." Bram grabbed Samuel's shoulder and squeezed it. "What about you? How are things going for you?"

Samuel scratched at his chin, missing the whiskers. "Not as good."

"When I stopped by last year, it looked like the farm was doing all right."

He shrugged. "As well as when *Daed* ran it. The hogs sell, and that brings in cash when we need it."

"I'm sorry I wasn't there when *Mamm* died. How did *Daed* take it?"

"You don't know how she died? Annie didn't tell you?"

Bram shot him a look. "What do you mean?"

"*Daed* was drunk. He and *Mamm* were arguing." Samuel shut his eyes, trying to block out the memory of the shouts, *Mamm*'s cries. "She fell down the stairs and died three days later."

"Annie never told me any of this." Bram ran his hand over his face. "What do you think happened?"

"You know what *Daed* was like when he lost his temper."

Bram nodded. "Especially when he was drunk." He paused and their eyes met. "Do you think that had anything to do with the accident?"

Samuel shook his head. "I don't know. Sometimes I wonder if it wasn't an accident. I've gone over it in my head again and again. All I know is if he hadn't been drinking, he wouldn't have been fighting with her. But he drank all the time back then."

They stood in silence as Samuel relived the memories again, and felt the release of having someone to share his suspicions with. Whether or not *Daed* had shoved *Mamm*, causing her fall, or if she lost her balance, he would never know. He had never told anyone about what he had witnessed that day.

Finally, Bram sighed. "I'm sorry, Samuel. I left home because I couldn't take *Daed* and his temper anymore, but I left you alone with him. I shouldn't have done that. We should have faced him together."

Samuel shrugged. "You know *Daed*. He kept us working against each other so that we wouldn't work against him." Samuel stared at the barn floor as he realized just how strong their father's influence had been. "We were never friends, were we?"

Bram shook his head. "*Daed* always picked at me, asking me why I couldn't be more like you. He always did like you the best, you know."

Samuel stared. "What do you mean? He always told me that I should be more like you."

Bram stared back at him, then his laugh came out as a short bark. "That old rascal."

"It isn't funny. I've spent my life hating you."

"Same here." One corner of Bram's mouth still held a grin. "*Ach*, then, what do we do about it now?"

Samuel's thoughts whirled. What did he want? Could he be friends with this man when so many painful memories crowded in?

He stuck his hands in his pockets. "I'm not sure we can ever be brothers."

Bram had bent his head down, and now looked at him from under the brim of his hat. "Could we be friends?"

Samuel shrugged. "I don't know."

"Let's start with a truce, and then go on from there."

Bram stuck his hand out and Samuel looked at it. Calloused, strong, tanned by the sun. The mirror image of his own as he slowly took the offered hand. Bram's grip was sure. Firm. Samuel tightened his fingers and Bram's grip grew firmer. Samuel felt a grin starting as he met Bram's eyes.

"Truce."

Mary sat at the kitchen table while Ida Mae helped Sadie get ready for bed. They had quickly discovered that Sadie became confused easily at night, and more than once had gone to bed with her dress still on, or neglecting a final trip to the outhouse, so the two of them took turns keeping Sadie focused on her bedtime routine until she was finally settled and asleep.

But only half of Mary's mind was on Sadie and Ida Mae. She drummed her fingers on the table, echoing the rolling thunder of an approaching storm. The rain would be welcome, if they got any. Last year's drought was one for the history books, *Daed* had said often enough. But the thunder was outdone by the rising bubble of guilt that pricked at her conscience.

After the quilting today, Annie had sent some jars of canned asparagus and a loaf of bread home with Sadie. Mary hadn't thought much about it until this evening. While she had been washing up after supper, she had realized that Sadie's cellar was full of canned goods, and the kitchen cupboards held sacks of flour. Even baking powder and cinnamon. All items that were hard to come by at home.

The entire community was supporting Sadie, not only here in Shipshewana but even folks in Eden Township. They made sure she had enough food in her cupboards and plenty of staples to keep her comfortable. Even Samuel helped with her chores.

Ida Mae came into the kitchen, stifling a yawn. "It's been a long day, and I'm going to go to bed."

"Sit down for a minute, first." Mary used her foot to push a chair out from the table. "We need to talk."

Her sister yawned again, but sat down. "What about?"

"You know people give food and other things to Sadie. And the Yoders across the road bring a gallon of milk every day."

"Of course they do. Our church at home does the same for older people and others who can't work for themselves."

Mary nodded. "And that is the right thing to do, except that we're here now. Have you noticed that the Yoders used to send a quart of milk for Sadie, but now it's a gallon? Everyone has sent more food for Sadie since we came. They aren't only making sure Sadie has enough, but they're sending extra for us."

Ida Mae lifted an eyebrow.

"We can and should work for ourselves, and support Sadie, too. We should be helping to support the community, not taking aid that another family might need more than we do."

Ida Mae shifted in her chair as another roll of thunder sounded in the distance. "Are you suggesting we start farming? Or raising hogs like Samuel does?" She shook her head. "I don't think we could do anything like that and care for Sadie, too."

"I'm not sure what we could do, but there must be something. We will need to raise money to pay the property taxes, for sure, so we need a cash income."

"Could we sell vegetables by the road? Or baked goods?"

"Perhaps. But no one has money to buy such things, and we aren't on a main road to catch the attention of travelers." Mary tapped one finger against her chin. "Maybe we could plant fruit trees like we have at home. Apples always sell well."

Ida Mae rubbed her eyes. "It would take at least three years for the trees to give enough apples to sell. We can't wait that long, can we?"

Mary shook her head. She ran her finger along the edge of the table, her heart pounding at the possibility that she dreaded. "I suppose one of us could hire out as farm help somewhere."

"I wouldn't want to work for *Englischers*, even if you found someone to hire us. You wouldn't, either. Besides, we need to be here at home so we can take care of Aunt Sadie."

"You're right." Mary leaned back in her chair, glad that Ida Mae had found the perfect excuse. She couldn't imagine working in an *Englischer*'s house, possibly facing an *Englisch* man every day. And she wouldn't even think about taking a job in town, like she had at home in Ohio. She tapped her chin again. "The chickens are producing pretty well."

"Don't remind me. They're giving us so many eggs that we'll be eating custard every day." Ida Mae rolled her eyes and Mary grinned. Her sister hated custard.

"Maybe we can sell the extra eggs, or trade them for something at the store in Shipshewana."

Ida Mae covered her mouth as another yawn took over. "That sounds like a good idea. They won't bring in much money, but every little bit helps."

Mary stood. "You need to get to bed, and so do I. If you can stay here with Sadie tomorrow, I'll take the trip to town and make inquiries."

Ida Mae pushed her chair away from the table. "If you can sell those eggs, I'll be thankful."

"I'll see what I can get for them. The storekeeper might only take them in trade instead of buying them."

"Well, make a list of things we need, just in case he does." Ida Mae glanced at the stove. "Have you banked the fire yet?"

"I forgot. But go on to bed and I'll take care of it."

Rain spattered against the windowpanes as Ida Mae went up the narrow stairway off the kitchen. Mary opened the fire box on the stove. Coals glowed in the ashes, nearly out. If Ida Mae hadn't reminded her to check, they would have awakened to a cold stove in the morning. She set a small log in the ashes and added kindling to build the fire up. Blowing gently on the coals, she watched as the dry bits of wood caught the heat, then as the pulsing glow turned to flame. The fire licked at the log until it, too, was burning.

Mary sat back on her heels as she waited for the fire to

grow enough to keep the log smoldering all night. Watching the flames took her back to when she was a girl and helped *Mamm* build up the stove fire each morning. She had always loved feeding the fire and watching the flames take hold. The warmth of the fire fascinated her, and she still didn't understand where the heat came from. *Daed* said it was from the sunshine stored in the trees while they lived, but that didn't satisfy her curiosity. How did the trees do that? And why did the wood burn like it did?

She sighed and raked the coals close to the burning log. That was one mystery she would never solve. She shut the fire box door and closed the dampers. The log would smolder all night and leave a bed of live coals to start the morning's fire. As she passed the table on her way to the stairs, she turned down the lamp that hung from the ceiling until the flame went out.

Tomorrow she would take the extra eggs to town, but which store should she take them to? Rain pattered on the roof overhead as she felt her way up the dark stairs. And then the answer came to her. She would stop by the Lapps' farm on her way to town. Judith or Esther might know the best place for her to trade, and where she would get the best deal for the eggs. Hopefully the storekeeper would want to buy a few dozen every week, and their problems would be eased.

Mary shut her eyes against the thought of going to town and interacting with strangers. But she couldn't let things go on as they had been. She and Ida Mae would support themselves and Sadie, and help others with the surplus.

A low moan escaped. She would have to face the *Englisch* storekeepers in Shipshewana. Her knees grew weak at the thought. Where would she find the strength?

Chapter Five

The storms overnight had turned the hog pen into a morass of stinking mud. Samuel leaned on the top fence rail and plucked at a grass stem just out of the greedy sows' reach. The hogs milled around in the pen, rooting in the mud, stirring the mess into an ankle-deep slough. As he watched, one big sow dug under the feeding trough and lifted it until it rolled over, then grunted contentedly as she snagged bits of food that had been buried underneath it.

What would *Daed* do with this? Samuel rubbed at his forehead, trying to erase the memories that surfaced. *Daed* would send him into the mud to wrestle the trough upright and pour another bucket of slops in for the pigs, all while trying to keep from getting bitten or shoved down into the mud himself. Today, he would have to send himself into the pen.

No use putting it off. He climbed over the fence and waited for his boots to settle in the mud. Here by the fence it wasn't too bad. Samuel glanced at the sow that was trying to flip the feeding trough again. She was belly deep in the stuff. He headed toward the trough, one step at a time, the mud sucking at his boots. Fending off the rest of the sows that shoved at him, looking for the slops they knew he would soon give them, he grabbed the edge of the trough, set it upright and dragged it back to the fence.

Finally back on dry ground, he picked up a bucket to pour the slops into the mud-caked trough, but the sight of Chester pulling Sadie's buggy into the yard stopped him. Mary was driving, alone. He set the pail down and started toward the buggy. The only reason he could think of for Mary to drive over here by herself was that something had happened to Sadie. He quickened his pace to a trot.

He reached the hitching rail the same time Mary pulled Chester to a stop. Her smile of greeting faded as she stared at him.

Samuel panted, out of breath. "What's wrong? Is Sadie ill?"

She shook her head slowly, still staring. "I'm on my way to Shipshewana, and I thought the girls might like to go with me."

"So Sadie is all right?"

"For sure, she is. She and Ida Mae are spending the morning piecing a quilt top."

Samuel straightened his shoulders. He hated when his mind leaped ahead of him. "Then why are you staring at me?"

Mary blinked and moved her gaze to his face. "You're filthy."

"*Ja*, of course I am." He waved a dismissing hand, then caught sight of the mud. His hands, arms, shirt, trousers... every inch was covered in the muck from the hogs' pen. "The pigsty is deep in mud, and those sows had shoved their trough into the center of it all again."

"Do you fasten it to the fence?"

It was his turn to blink. "What?"

"The trough. Do you tie it to the fence so they can't move it?"

He had never thought of such a thing. *Daed* had never thought of such a thing…

"Here, I'll show you what I mean." Mary jumped out of the buggy and tied Chester to the rail before leading the way to the side of the pen where the buckets of slop were lined up.

Samuel had no choice but to follow. Surely she wouldn't get close to the hogs with a clean dress on. And shoes. She was wearing shoes to town.

Before his thoughts went any further, he followed her, catching up before she reached the fence.

"You want to be careful not to get muddy."

She looked at him, her eyes crinkling as she smiled. "Don't worry. I know my way around pigs." She pointed to the fence posts. "My *daed* uses pieces of barbed wire fencing and attaches the ends of the trough to the fence posts."

Samuel looked at the mud-covered wooden trough. "He must drill holes for the wire to go through?"

Mary nodded. "Four of them. One in each end and two in the sides near the corners. He strings the wire through them and then twists in onto the fence post. The barbs on the wire keep the hogs from fooling with it and getting it loose."

"That would do it, I suppose."

"And it would save you the trouble of climbing into the wallow with them."

He shot a sideways glance. *Ja*, for sure, she was laughing at him. He picked up the first bucket and poured the slops into the trough. The hogs squealed, fought and grunted as they buried their snouts in the mixture of cooked grain, garden refuse and sour milk.

"The girls said you sold a couple of the pigs last week."

Samuel nodded as he grabbed two more buckets of slops and went around the side of the barn to where the young pigs were kept in a separate sty. Mary followed him, picking her way between mud puddles. Smaller and thinner than the sows, these pigs ate as much as their mothers. By fall they would be filled out and ready to butcher.

He dumped some slops into their trough. "I took two of these to the butcher last week."

"Aren't they a bit underweight?"

Samuel glanced at her again. She knew her hogs. The butcher had said the same thing, but Samuel fed them the same food *Daed* had always done.

He turned to the final pen. "This is my boar." He heard the note of pride creep into his voice.

Mary leaned over the fence. "He's a big one."

"Over six hundred pounds, according to my calculations."

"Measuring his girth and length?"

"Ja." He shook the pail to get all the slops out of it and into the trough. This girl knew her hogs, for sure.

"It's time to sell him, isn't it? I mean, *Daed* would have sold him before he got too big to…do what boars need to do." Her face turned bright red.

"The sows are just as big, so there's no problem." And no money to buy a new boar. That was the real problem.

Samuel stacked the empty pails and led the way into the barn cellar. As he set them next to the mash cooker, Mary stepped to the cellar gate and looked out over the fields.

"Is all this land yours?"

"From the woodlot to the creek, and to Sadie's place on the other side. Fifty acres tillable."

"Why haven't you planted anything?"

He stared at her back. Maybe her *daed* had sent her to Indiana so he wouldn't have to listen to the constant questions.

"No plow. No work horses."

"You should consider it, anyway. Growing your own corn or barley to feed your hogs would save you money in the long run."

Samuel thought about her suggestion as she turned back to gaze toward the woodlot. He had purchased a neighbor's field of corn last fall, stunted from the drought and heat. Chopped and stored in the silo, the silage had fed the hogs through the winter. But now that source of feed was gone, and he was feeding them seed barley that had sprouted. The grain elevator in Shipshewana had sold it cheap, but it still cost something. What would he feed them when that ran out?

Shoving his hat back on his head, Samuel stepped up next to Mary and gazed out at the fields. Eighty acres stretched out, including the woodlot and the ten acres *Grossdawdi* had given to Sadie for her use. That left plenty to plant, but *Daed* had sold the plow and work horses years ago. Nothing had been planted in the fields as long as Samuel could remember. He had tried haying it once, but weeds had overtaken the land and there wasn't enough grass to make the work worthwhile.

It was a wasteland.

And he was spending the little cash he had to buy grain to feed his hogs. *Daed*'s way of doing things just didn't make sense sometimes.

Mary leaned on the top of the gate in Samuel's barn cellar. He stood next to her, looking out on the fallow acres of his farm. He was a confusing man.

On one hand, strong and solid. Comfortable. He was becoming a friend.

On the other hand, the way he kept his hogs was the most wasteful and lazy way she had ever seen. *Daed* kept his hogs in a field, not closed in some pen. And he let them graze in the pastures, moving them often so they wouldn't overgraze the grass.

"Where did you learn how to raise hogs?" She turned toward him as she asked the question.

Samuel shrugged, the caked mud on his shirt flaking off as it dried. "From *Daed*. I take care of them the way he taught me."

"At home, we pastured the hogs. They ate grass and other things in the fields, and being out in the sunshine helped them grow faster and better."

Samuel scowled. "They're doing fine. *Daed*'s ways have been working for years."

Mary bit her lower lip to keep the words in that she wanted to say. That Samuel was wrong, and perhaps his *daed* wasn't the best teacher. But that would only spoil their tenuous friendship, and it wasn't her place to tell a man how to manage his own farm.

He flicked at a glop of mud on his arm, then looked at her. "You never said why you're going to Shipshewana."

"We have some extra eggs, and I thought I'd see if any of the shopkeepers are interested in buying them."

"Eggs?"

"The hens are laying well, and we don't want them to go to waste."

"You can always can them. Save them for winter when the chickens don't produce so well."

Mary swallowed quickly as the thought of the quarts and quarts of canned eggs filling the cellar shelves made her stomach turn. "We already have too many pickled eggs. Folks have been very generous sharing canned goods with Sadie."

"I give our extra eggs to the hogs. They love them."

Mary glanced at the sacks of grain piled near the mash cooker. "You buy grain to feed the pigs?"

"When I can get it cheap."

"I still think you should raise your own grain." She bit her bottom lip before she said any more. He would think she was trying to tell him how to farm.

"I told you, I don't have the equipment to plant."

"I noticed the Yoders, across the road, have finished with their planting already. Ask if you can borrow their horses and plow."

Samuel rubbed at his chin. At least he wasn't getting angry at her suggestion.

"I suppose it wouldn't hurt to ask."

"If they aren't willing to help, there will be someone at church who will, for sure." She smiled, confident that he would take her advice. "You can ask tomorrow, when you help with the plowing."

"The plowing?"

"I heard you talking about it with the other men at dinner last Sunday. You haven't forgotten, have you? You promised you would be there."

Samuel rubbed at a spot of mud on his shirt. How he could worry about that one spot when the rest of him was caked with the stuff was beyond her.

When he didn't answer, she took a step closer. "You did forget, didn't you?"

"I didn't forget. But they don't want me there. It will be best for me to stay home."

Mary shook her head. Did he even hear what he was saying?

"If you don't go, you'll only prove that the one man was right. Remember? He said you wouldn't show up. You need to prove to him that he's wrong."

"Martin Troyer. And I can't prove that he's wrong." He looked at her from under his lowered brow. "He was right. Everything he said was true. You heard what he said."

Mary studied the man standing beside her. He looked just like a six-year-old boy waiting to be punished for some infraction as he stood with his thumbs threaded through his suspenders and one foot kicking at the dirt.

"Just because you haven't helped in the past doesn't mean you can't help tomorrow." This was the perfect opportunity to start over, to prove that he could change.

"I tried to help at a barn raising last summer." He straightened, rolling his shoulders as if he bore a weight that was too heavy for him. "They didn't want me there. Didn't want my help."

"I heard you tell the minister that you'd be there. You gave your word."

Samuel sighed and rubbed the back of his neck. "My *daed*'s word never meant anything. He never kept his promises, and they don't expect me to, either."

"You," Mary said, pointing her finger at his chest, "are not your *daed*. He isn't here, but you are. You don't have to follow in his footsteps." Especially when those footsteps are leading to ruin, she wanted to add. But she pressed her lips together, holding the words in.

He leaned on the top rail of the gate and looked across the fields, but didn't answer her. She left him standing there and made her way out of the barn, past the hogs and toward the house.

Judith stood at the clothesline, hanging dish towels. When she saw Mary, she stuck the last clothespin on the line and waved.

"I saw you talking with Samuel and hoped you'd come up to the house."

"For sure I will. The real reason I came was to see if you and Esther want to go to town with me." Mary kept her words casual, but her heart pounded. If neither of them wanted to ride with her, she would have to go into town alone.

"I'd love to go, but I'll have to ask Esther. I'm not sure what she has planned for today."

Judith ran up the wooden steps to the covered back porch while Mary followed. The porch held a washtub on a stand, with a wringer attached.

As Mary stepped into the kitchen, she felt like she had walked into a house from a bygone era. Sadie's kitchen was modern and clean, with linoleum floors and painted cabinets, but the Lapps' kitchen had not been changed in years. With no doors on the cabinets, the bare shelves were open to the room. A small table stood near the stove, barely large enough to seat more than four people. The floor, clean and smooth, was bare wood, with remnants of brown paint showing around the edges.

Judith led Esther into the kitchen from the front room. "We would both like to come with you, if you don't mind."

Esther's smile was contagious. "It will be a fun lark, won't it? Going to town twice in one week!"

"And Mary won't hurry us along so that we can't look at the things in the store, will you?" Judith's grin was as wide as Esther's.

Mary felt the tension drop from her shoulders. "We'll have a lot of fun. I want to sell or trade some eggs, and I thought you might be able to help me find the best store to do that."

"*Ach*, for sure. We'll have to ask Samuel, but I'm sure he'll say we can go. His dinner is in the oven," Esther said. She untied her apron as she turned toward a narrow stairway. "We'll just change to clean aprons and we'll be ready."

As the sisters ran up the stairs, Mary peered out the window over the sink. The hogs' pen and the barn filled the view. The barn needed paint as much as the kitchen floor did. The entire farm spoke of long years of neglect. Of poverty. Sadie had told them about Samuel's *gross-dawdi*, but not of his *daed*. Whatever kind of man he had been, Samuel seemed to be caught in the same habits he learned as a boy.

As Mary drove off with the girls, Samuel checked the angle of the sun. Not even midmorning yet.

Before he could talk himself out of it, he cleaned up on the back porch and changed into clean trousers. Scrubbing as much of the muck from the pigsty off his hands as he could, he rehearsed what he would say to Dale Yoder.

"Good morning, Dale."

He shook his head. He had never had much to say to his neighbor. These Yoders were Mennonite, and other than a wave when they passed on the road, he couldn't remember talking to the man in years.

"Fine day today, *ja*?"

At least the Yoders were Old Order Mennonite. They spoke *Deitsch* as plainly as he did, so they wouldn't have to worry about *Englisch* words coming between them. And he had known Dale since they were both boys in school. They weren't strangers.

He wiped his face with a towel, shoved his shirttail in and hauled his suspenders over his shoulders. *Daed* had never asked anyone for help. Never.

Samuel looked across the road toward the red hip-roofed barn. Mary was right. The fields had been plowed and planted. He hitched his trousers up and set his feet toward the road, wiping the sweat off his upper lip. His steps faltered as he reached the entrance to the Yoders' lane, and he stopped. Pulling off his hat, he ran his fingers through his hair.

"What's the worst he can do? Tell me to get lost?"

A boy riding a bike came down the lane toward him, gave him a wave and turned onto the road. Samuel hitched up his trousers again. If an eight-year-old could wave to him, he could talk to his neighbor.

He found Dale in the barn, cleaning the haymow.

"Good morning!" He shouted toward the high barn roof, hoping his neighbor would hear.

Dale looked over the edge of the mow. "Samuel Lapp? *Ach*, is there anything wrong?"

Samuel shook his head and stepped back from the ladder as Dale climbed down. "*Ne*, nothing wrong." He took a deep breath. "I need to plant some corn…"

The other man brushed some chaff off his trousers. "I don't remember the last time you folks planted anything."

"*Ja*, well, times are hard."

Dale looked at him, his eyes narrowed. "How have you been getting on since your *daed*'s accident? I've meant to come over but—"

Samuel held up a hand. "Don't worry about it. I didn't expect you to stop by after the way *Daed* treated you the last time."

He had forgotten until just now, but it all came back. Dale and his wife coming to *Mamm*'s funeral, and *Daed* throwing them off the farm in front of everyone.

"I'm sorry about that. *Daed* wasn't feeling well that day."

Daed had been drunk. But that wasn't the polite excuse for the way he had acted.

Dale led the way to a bucket of water placed under the shade of a sycamore tree in the yard. He took the cover off and offered a dipper of water to Samuel.

"So, you're going to plant some corn?"

Samuel smiled as the water slid down his throat. It had been flavored with ginger and tasted crisp and refreshing.

"I hope to. Someone suggested that if I grew my own grain the farm would be more profitable."

Dale nodded and finished off his dipper of water. "You're buying grain to feed your hogs?"

Samuel relaxed, leaning against the tree. Dale was just as easy to talk to now as he had been when they were boys. "When I can."

"Too bad the hogs can't forage on their own like the cattle do."

"Is that what you're raising these days?"

Dale gestured toward the eighty-acre pasture behind the barn where a good herd of steers grazed in the knee-deep grass. "The price of beef is high, and they're cheap to feed. I buy about twenty weaned calves at the Shipshewana auction each year, feed them on pasture for a few years and then sell them. I run about sixty head of the cattle on this pasture, buying and selling a third of the herd every year. It brings in a profit, and I don't have to fool with mixing slops for them like you do for hogs."

Samuel rubbed at his chin. Dale had a point.

"So then, you're planting corn?"

Samuel rubbed his chin again. "What do you feed the cattle during the winter?"

"Hay and silage. We're going to be mowing the back pasture next month and start loading the haymow."

"And you raise your own corn for the silage?" Samuel nodded toward the plowed fields between the house and the road.

"For sure. Raising our own feed for the cattle is necessary. Otherwise I wouldn't make any money doing it."

Samuel looked toward the cattle again and took a deep breath. Clean, sweet, fresh air filled his lungs. Dale had given him a lot to think about. If he grew his own grain, and pastured the hogs like Mary had suggested, would it make a difference? Could she have been right?

The thought strengthened his courage. He hitched his trousers up. "I came over to see if I could borrow your plow and team, if you're done with your planting."

Dale rubbed at the smooth bark of the sycamore tree. "I heard that your *daed* sold his equipment."

Samuel nodded, feeling his face redden. "He needed cash." For the next bottle. *Daed* had sold anything he could to buy the next bottle.

Dale's eyes narrowed again. "I've heard that you're just like him. Is it true?"

Samuel shoved down the sudden anger that had risen at Dale's words, but his jaw clenched.

"You mean, do I drink like he did? Just say it, Dale, and have done with it. You're wondering if I'm going to sell your team and drink away the cash."

Dale dipped into the ginger water again and held the dripping scoop as he looked at Samuel for a long minute. He drained the dipper and dropped it back in the bucket.

"I don't blame you for getting riled." His voice was mild. "But I had to ask. There are rumors, and I don't want to believe them. Now that I see you and talk to you, I can see that you aren't a slave to the drink the way he was."

"Rumors?"

Dale shrugged. "You know how people talk." He glanced at Samuel again. "I'll let you borrow my plow and team on one condition."

"Anything."

"I want to handle my own team, so I'll do the plowing and planting for you. In exchange, you give me ten percent of the crop."

Samuel chewed on his lip. Dale's suspicion rankled, but he had the upper hand and he knew it.

"Agreed. I'll buy the seed today."

"And I'll plow the field tomorrow. I'll be over first thing."

Samuel was supposed to help with Vernon Hershberger's plowing tomorrow. This could be the excuse he needed to avoid facing Martin Troyer and the others in the morning… but Mary was right. He had given his word.

"I'm busy tomorrow. Can we do it on Monday?"

Dale peered at him. "You're busy on a Saturday?"

"I'm helping a man from church with his plowing."

"You?" Dale grinned. "Maybe you're less like your *daed* than you look." He nodded. "Monday it is, then."

Mary guided Chester down the main street of Shipshe-wana, past the train depot and across the railroad tracks. On the corner of Middlebury Street and State Road 5 was a grocery store and Mary pulled into a spot along the hitching rail.

Even though Chester was standing quietly, she still grasped the reins as if she was driving. The store looked just like the one at home in Ohio. She glanced at Esther, sitting next to her. "Is this where you usually buy your groceries?"

"Samuel took us to a different store when we were here on Monday." Esther took the reins from Mary and secured them. "But we can try here."

Judith jumped to the ground on the other side of the buggy.

"I'll carry the eggs," she said as she reached for the basket in the back, "and you do the talking."

Mary's mouth was dry, but she felt better with Judith and Esther along. How could she have faced these *Englischers* without them?

She nodded and climbed down from the buggy seat. "Let's go in."

Mary led the way into the store with Esther and Judith following. A few men stood next to a display of tobacco, but didn't look up as they walked by. Mary headed straight to the counter at the back of the store where a woman waited for them.

"Good morning," she said. She eyed the basket Judith set on the counter. "I don't think I've seen you folks in here before."

Mary lifted her chin and smiled. She reached for the basket and pulled the towel off, revealing the eggs that she and Ida Mae had carefully washed that morning.

"I was wondering if you buy—"

"Nope. Never. The mister says we don't barter, and we don't buy except from our suppliers."

Mary felt her jaw drop at the woman's rudeness. She tried again. "But they're fresh, just gathered this morning."

The woman's head shook. "No it is, and no it will be." She smiled, but it didn't reach her eyes. "I'll be glad to sell you anything you need, though."

Mary's knees shook, but she straightened her shoulders. "No, thank you. I'm only interested in selling the eggs or trading."

The men's conversation had stopped and she heard footsteps heading their way.

"Anything wrong, Millie?"

The woman frowned over Mary's shoulder. "I told them we don't take barter."

Esther leaned forward. "Can you tell us if there's a store in town that would buy them?"

Millie started shaking her head, but the man behind Mary cleared his throat. She turned toward him as Judith picked up the eggs.

"You might try at the elevator. I heard they was buying eggs."

Mary kept her eyes focused on his shirt buttons and took a deep breath. "Thank you. We'll try there."

She followed Judith and Esther out the door, her knees shaking so much that she was afraid of falling with each step. She pressed her lips together as she felt the pounding in her head turn to a roaring. Not here. She couldn't faint here. She reached for Chester's tie as the girls climbed into the buggy and focused on the prickly hairs of the horse's chin. She counted silently, taking deep breaths. She had spoken to an *Englisch* man and nothing bad had happened. She would never need to talk to him again.

Fumbling with the tie rope, Mary climbed into the buggy and took the reins. By the time she sat down, her breathing had returned to normal and she could smile at Esther.

"Do you know where the grain elevator is?"

"Samuel went there on Monday. It's on the other side of the railroad station."

Mary clicked her tongue and Chester turned the buggy into the street again. A sudden thought made her stomach clench.

"The elevator," she said, trying to keep her voice from shaking, "is it owned by *Englischers*?"

"Mennonites." Esther pointed out the turn ahead. "They're a nice family, according to what Samuel said."

Mennonites. Mary pulled her lower lip in between her teeth. Perhaps dealing with Mennonites wouldn't be as bad as the *Englisch* men in the store.

She guided Chester to the hitching rail outside the grain elevator's office, next to a team of Belgians hitched to a farm wagon, and Judith jumped out of the buggy.

"I hope they take your eggs here, Mary." She looked up

at the tall storage towers that dwarfed the office building. "It doesn't look like the sort of place that you could trade them for anything, though."

"It won't hurt to ask," Esther said, climbing down next to her sister. "This is the only grain elevator in town, so it must be the one the man meant. And it is a feed store, also."

Mary finished tying Chester to the rail, clasped her hands together to stop their shaking, and led the way to the store. Dust was the first thing that greeted her. As she opened the door on its squeaking hinges, motes swirled in the sunshine that fell into the room ahead of the girls.

"*Ja*, well, I think you'll find we have the best prices around." A plain-dressed man stood behind the counter, speaking to an Amish farmer in a mixture of *Deitsch* and English. "On top of that, if you go to Elkhart to buy your seed, you'll have to factor in the cost of the trip." He glanced toward the door and smiled at the three of them. "I'll be right with you folks, if you don't mind waiting."

Mary smiled back, and she turned to look at the sacks of grain piled along the walls. Near each stack was a pail with a sample of what grain the sacks held. Next to the door was a display of Extension Office bulletins. Mary had just read the titles of the first two when the bell above the door rang, signaling the farmer's exit.

"What can I do for you?" the man asked. He was middle-aged, and wore his beard without a mustache, just like the married Amish men did.

Judith set the basket of eggs on his counter. "Do you buy eggs?"

He moved the cover aside and picked two of the eggs out of the basket and held them to the light that filtered in through the window. "We do, if they're top quality." He returned those eggs to the basket and picked up two more. "These look fresh."

Mary stepped forward. "*Ja*, they are. Gathered just this morning."

The man peered in the basket, and then at Mary. "Do you have any more?"

Mary swallowed down the quick flutter in her throat. "These are all we have today. Does this mean you want to buy them?"

"I'll buy all the eggs you can bring me." He reached under the counter for an egg tray and started transferring the eggs from the basket into it. "I have buyers from Detroit who stop in every Tuesday, and buyers from Fort Wayne on Fridays. They buy as many eggs as I can supply for them. They sell them to groceries in the big cities."

Mary's head spun. If she and Ida Mae could deliver two dozen eggs a week...

"Could you bring twelve dozen a week?"

She stared at him. "Twelve dozen?"

"Fifteen dozen would be better. I can't get enough eggs to make the buyers happy." He grinned as Mary's mouth fell open and reached for a brochure from the display of Extension Office literature. "Take this home and look through it. It explains how to raise chickens for egg production on a large scale. A lot of the local farm wives have started providing eggs and butter for the city markets to help their family's income."

Mary looked at the drawing of a chicken on the front as the flutter turned into a bubble. She did some quick calculations in her head. To get twelve dozen eggs a week, they would need at least twenty hens. Twenty-four would be better. Or even thirty. She and Ida Mae would need to build a larger henhouse, and buy feed for the chickens. It would be a lot of work, but would it be worth it?

She cleared her throat. "How much do you pay?"

"Ten cents a dozen, if they're as good quality as these."

Ten cents. Fifteen dozen a week would bring in one dollar and fifty cents. Six dollars a month. Mary flipped through the brochure until she reached a picture of a large henhouse. *Dimensions for seventy-five hens*, said the caption. The bubble expanded. She could do this, with Ida Mae's help. Visions of a clean, airy new henhouse and yard filled with contented chickens swirled through her mind.

"And if I could bring you forty dozen?"

The man leaned his hands on the counter, his brow knit as he looked her over. Wondering if she could deliver on her word, she figured.

"Now you're talking about going into business. That would be a mighty bit of work. You're sure your father won't mind?"

Mary smiled. Four dollars a week would be enough to pay all the household expenses and leave some cash to save. "Don't worry. We will enjoy the work."

He leaned forward. "You'll need a larger chicken coop, right? And fencing, feed, waterers? And more chickens?"

Mary nodded as the bubble deflated. She hadn't thought of the expense of going into this business. She would need boards and wire fencing for the new henhouse, and chicken feed. How much would it all cost?

"I'll loan you the money to supply what you need to get started. I'll front six dollars so you can buy the lumber, fencing and anything else you need. You should be able to pick up chickens at the livestock auction on Tuesdays, so you can build your flock up that way." He pointed a finger at the brochure in her hand. "But before you do anything, read up on what raising chickens on this scale demands. It isn't easy work."

"Why would you loan me the money?" Mary fingered the brochure, ready to hand it back to him. Her dream was slipping away as she considered the enormity of the project.

He waited until she looked up at him. "I have a daughter your age, and her family is struggling to make ends meet. She enjoys helping her husband by bringing in the income from her chickens, and she has worked hard enough to make it pay off. I'm sure you can do the same thing." He smiled again. "Besides, we both win on this deal. You sell your eggs, and I keep the big city buyers coming back."

He opened the drawer below his cash register and took out two dimes. "Here's your payment for the eggs you brought in today. Take the brochure home and discuss it with your family. Then the next time you come into town, you can tell me what you decide."

Mary rubbed the dimes together between her fingers as Judith picked up her empty basket and they headed for the door. Twenty cents, cash money. And this was just the beginning.

The girls were climbing into the buggy before Mary remembered. She ran back to the door and opened it.

"*Denki*, Mister… Mister…"

"Holdeman. Enosh Holdeman."

The bubble was back as she grinned at him. "*Denki*, Mister Holdeman. I will let you know what we decide."

Chapter Six

Saturday morning dawned cool and clear. A perfect day for spring field chores. Samuel frowned at the bright sunshine as Tilly trotted down the gravel road. Rain would have given him a good excuse to stay home.

Ahead, the Hershberger farmyard was crowded with horses. Some men had driven buggies, but a few had driven their plows, hitched to teams of Belgians or Clydesdales. Samuel chewed at his bottom lip as he glanced at the faces. Every one of those men had known *Daed*. Every one of them expected nothing more from his son. But Mary's words came back to him, and he rubbed the spot on his chest where her finger had pointed when she said them.

Mary was right. He wasn't *Daed*, and he didn't have to keep following in his footsteps. He turned Tilly in the drive and pulled to a stop alongside the other buggies. He considered unhitching her and tying her to the rope someone had strung along the shady side of the barn, but that meant he was committed to helping. Instead, he loosened her harness and left her standing in the shade of a tree.

He took a step toward the six men who had gathered in a group near the equipment, and then as he hesitated, he felt Mary's words prodding at him, as if she was poking that finger in his back. Taking a deep breath, he walked the rest of the way.

Martin Troyer was the first to spot him.

"Look who showed up."

As some other men stared at him, Samuel's steps faltered. Distrust clouded their features.

Jonas Weaver came toward him with a hand held out. "Good to see you, Samuel. We're just getting ready to divide the work, and we can use someone to drive Vernon's team."

Samuel glanced at the Percherons Jonas indicated. The giant horses stood quietly, but Samuel hadn't driven a team of work horses in more years than he could count. He glanced at the group of men. Martin Troyer and another man faced him with folded arms and lowered brows.

"I don't think driving a team is the right job for me." Samuel kept his voice quiet, but his words carried beyond Preacher Jonas.

"*Ja*, for sure." Martin Troyer stepped closer. "No job is the right one for you, is it?" He took the other men into his sweeping glance as he let out a short laugh. "Just like his *daed*. If he shows up, we still don't get any work out of him."

"Martin, that isn't fair." Preacher Jonas stepped between Samuel and the other men.

"You know it is. We know how these Lapps are. Lazy as the hogs that roll in that stinking wallow they keep them in."

Samuel's head pounded as he stepped toward Martin with his fists clenched. "I said I'd help. Tell me what you want me to do."

Martin laughed, and Samuel noticed smiles on the rest of the faces. "Give up, Lapp. You're cut from the same cloth as your *daed*. Make a big noise about how you are part of the community, and make promises to help, but then when the time comes—" Martin shrugged "—you're nowhere to be found."

"I'm here now." Samuel heard the growl in his own voice. *Daed*'s voice.

"Here, but are you sober?" Martin stepped closer and sniffed. "Can't tell. All I can smell is hog."

"I don't drink."

A quiet chuckle was Martin's response. He didn't believe a word Samuel said, so what was the use of trying?

Jonas's quiet voice cut through Samuel's growing headache. "We can't judge Samuel based on his father's actions." Jonas held up a hand as Martin started to protest. "Nor can we refuse to let Samuel help when he is willing."

Jonas turned to Samuel. "Why don't you think driving a team is the job for you?"

Samuel's hands clenched and unclenched. What did Preacher Jonas want? To make a fool of him?

"Forget it. Just forget it." He turned on his heel and headed back to his horse, anxious to be hidden by the line of buggies.

He fumbled with Tilly's harness as he heard footsteps approaching. The voices of the men drifted toward him as they arranged which team would lead the line of plows through the field. The footsteps stopped at the back corner of his buggy, but he ignored the intruder as he tightened the harness.

"What are you doing, Samuel?"

Preacher Jonas stood with his hands clasped behind his back, waiting for his answer.

"I'm going home. I'm not wanted here. You can see that as plainly as I can."

"Are you serious about wanting to help?"

Samuel rubbed the edge of the harness with his finger.

Why was he here? He felt Mary's prodding finger in his chest. He was here to prove that he didn't walk in his father's footsteps, but he had thrown a tantrum worthy of the Lapp name. He leaned his forehead on Tilly's flank. Would he ever escape *Daed*'s legacy?

Jonas stepped closer and laid a hand on Samuel's shoulder. "You aren't your father, Samuel. You don't have to act like him."

Samuel turned his head to face the preacher. "But I am like him. Don't you see? Whatever I try, I end up acting just like he would." He swallowed down the tightness in his throat. "It's no use, is it?"

"There's a verse in the Good Book that speaks to this. I'm sure you know it."

Samuel's gut clenched. "*Ja*, I know the one. Somewhere it says that the iniquities of the fathers are visited upon the sons to the third and fourth generations."

"But that isn't the end of the story." Jonas squeezed Samuel's shoulder, then stepped over to lean against the tree a few feet away. "When a father acts as yours did, he sets a poor example for his family. Then the children can suffer. But there is another verse in Deuteronomy that tells us that each one of us faces the punishment for our own sins."

"So *Daed* was right? He always said a person couldn't trust the Good Book because of all the contradictions in it."

Jonas shook his head. "There are no contradictions. Your troubles now might be because of your father's weaknesses, but that doesn't mean that you will face eternal punishment for them. You are your own man, and responsible for your own choices." He let these words sink in. "You can change the course of your life, and your family's life, by making the decisions your father couldn't. Your brother made that choice."

Bram again. The farmyard was quiet. The men and teams had gone out to the field.

Jonas straightened. "I need to join the others in the field. Vernon's team is waiting. You're sure you don't want to drive them?"

Samuel pushed the words out. "I can't."

"Think about what I said. With God's help, you can come out of the hole you've gotten yourself into. You can become a full member of the community, rather than a stray hanging around the edges."

Samuel eyed the preacher. His expression was as mild as ever, but his eyes burned with enthusiasm, as if he had just finished preaching a sermon.

"I'll consider it. I just don't know if it will do any good. The men won't give me a chance."

"Don't use that as an excuse." Jonas started back toward the barn and the waiting team. "There will always be Martin Troyers in your life. It's up to you to prove them wrong."

Samuel ran a finger between the harness and Tilly's warm side. Preacher Jonas was right, and if he was ever going to change Martin Troyer's opinion, it had to start today.

"Wait," he called to Jonas. "I'll drive the team, if they're well trained."

The preacher paused. "Why did you refuse before?"

Samuel glanced at the Percherons. "*Daed* sold our horses before he died, and I haven't driven a team since then. I'm afraid I'm out of practice."

Jonas grinned. "It's as easy as falling off a log with a team like this one. I'll help you refresh your memory, and then you'll be all set."

Samuel took the reins as Jonas handed them over and climbed into the seat of the plow. The thick leather straps molded to his hands and he gathered up the slack. One of the horses looked at him, as if he knew a stranger held the reins, but then, at Jonas's signal, Samuel called, "Hi-yup, there!" and the horses started toward the field.

Jonas jumped onto the step next to the seat and stood there as Samuel guided the team into the line of plows and engaged the blades. Martin Troyer kept his face straight ahead, but a couple of the other men gave him a friendly wave as he joined them.

"I don't think you need my help at all," Jonas said.

Samuel grinned. "Like you said, it's as easy as falling off a log."

Mary guided Chester through the crowded streets of Shipshewana. Tuesday morning meant the weekly auction, and folks from all over northern Indiana had flocked to town to either buy or sell goods. At the corner of State Road 5, she waited until the traffic cleared, then clucked Chester into a swift trot across the busy road.

Ida Mae leaned forward from the back seat. "Are you sure Mr. Holdeman will buy eggs again? You were just here on Friday."

"He said he would buy as many as I could bring him."

Sadie had been quiet during the trip to town, but as Mary turned into the Holdemans' parking lot she said, "I thought we were going to church." She turned toward Mary, her face pinched with worry.

Mary laid her hand over her aunt's. "You must have misunderstood me. I said we were going to town."

Sadie looked toward the feed store. "Why are we here? We don't buy things here."

Ida Mae and Mary exchanged glances. This seemed to be one of Aunt Sadie's bad days.

"It's all right." Mary picked up the egg basket and

climbed out of the buggy. "You stay here with Ida Mae while I go in to sell the eggs."

Walking into the elevator's office, Mary smiled at the sound of the bell over the door. The ringing had jangled her nerves on Friday, but today the bell sounded like an old friend. Mr. Holdeman came out of a back room, wiping his hands on a rag.

"Well, good morning. I thought you might be back today." He gestured toward her basket as she set it on the counter. "I'm glad you brought more eggs. The buyer from Detroit will be here this afternoon."

Mary smiled at his welcome. "I only have one dozen today, if that's all right." Much to her dismay, Ida Mae had opened one of the many jars of pickled eggs for their lunch yesterday instead of cooking eggs for breakfast. But between that and skimping on the eggs they used during other meals, they had ended up with a full dozen.

"Like I said before, I can take as many as you bring me." He started transferring the eggs from her basket to a tray. "Have you given any more thought to my offer of helping to expand your business?"

"We have. My sister and I will work on the project together."

He nodded. "I thought you would, so I've talked to Hal Stutzman over at the lumberyard. All you need to do is stop by there, and he'll see that you get the lumber you need."

"I don't know what to say…"

"Don't say anything." He opened the cash drawer for her dime and handed it to her. "Just bring more eggs."

Mary had already climbed back in the buggy before she remembered that she had no way to take the lumber home. She told Ida Mae about Mr. Holdeman's offer.

"Then we'll just have to borrow Samuel's wagon and come back tomorrow."

"We won't need to," Sadie said as Chester turned the corner by the auction barn. "Samuel's here already."

Samuel had just pulled his spring wagon into the driveway ahead of them, and the girls were with him. Pig snouts stuck out through the board sides.

Ida Mae leaned out of their buggy. "Judith! Esther!"

When the girls saw them, they spoke to Samuel and he halted the wagon while they jumped off and ran back to the buggy.

"It's a surprise to see you here," Esther said as she climbed into the back seat with Ida Mae.

"It's a surprise for us, too." Mary turned Chester into the field where lines of buggies and horses were tied along a hitching rail. "Did I see pigs in the back of Samuel's wagon?"

"He's taking them to the auction to sell so that he can buy seed corn."

Mary glanced at Sadie. She looked around with interest, as if she might see someone she knew. She seemed to have accepted that they were in Shipshewana this morning, rather than church. She turned in her seat to listen to the girls' conversation, and her face had lost the vague expression from earlier.

"What are you girls doing here today?" Judith asked.

"We're looking for some chickens to add to our flock," Ida Mae said as Mary pulled Chester to a stop along the hitching rail next to a bay horse.

"Then you decided to go into the egg business!" Esther grasped Mary's shoulder and gave it a squeeze. "That's exciting."

Sadie's face clouded again. "What business?"

"We talked about this yesterday, remember? Ida Mae and I are going to build a chicken coop and buy more chickens so that we can sell the eggs to Mr. Holdeman."

Her aunt smiled. "*Ach, ja.* I remember."

They went into the auction barn together, but Mary stopped just inside the entrance. The place was filled with people and noise, everything from cows bawling to horses neighing. All she could see were men in their summer straw hats and women in dark dresses. Old friends greeted one another with glad cries, while others walked along the aisles, peering at the animals for sale in the rows of pens.

Mary kept her hand in Sadie's elbow. "How will we ever find the chickens?" She had to shout, even though the other girls were gathered around her.

A man waved to get her attention. "Chickens are along the north side, over there."

She made her way through the crowds with Sadie, while Ida Mae followed with the girls. Nearly thirty cages of chickens were stacked in a corner, next to pens filled with hogs. Each cage held three or four chickens. She happened to look toward the pigpens as Samuel guided a pair of his sows through a gate and closed it behind them. He wiped his face with a handkerchief before he looked around and saw them. A smile appeared as his eyes met Mary's and he made his way over to them.

"You're looking to buy some chickens?"

"*Ja,* for sure," Ida Mae said. "Mary and I are going into the egg business."

He had leaned over to look into a cage of Rhode Island Reds, but at Ida Mae's words, he shot a glance at Mary. "The egg business?"

As she nodded, he gave Esther a couple coins. "The hogs and chickens won't be up for a while yet. Why don't you take Sadie somewhere a little quieter and get some lemonade for everyone?"

Esther gave him a quick hug. "*Denki,* Samuel. We will."

Samuel grasped Mary's elbow as the others left. "Not you. We need to talk."

"What about?"

He ushered her out of the aisle until they stood alongside the pen holding his sows. "What is this about going into business?"

"Just what Ida Mae said. We're going to add to our flock. Mr. Holdeman at the grain elevator said he will buy as many eggs as we can bring him."

Samuel crossed his arms and rubbed at his chin with one hand. He looked much better today than he had the last time she saw him. His clothes were clean, and he wore the new trousers Esther had made.

"You can't put many more hens into the chicken coop in Sadie's barn."

"I know. That's why we're building a new henhouse."

His eyebrows rose. "A new henhouse? How many chickens are you thinking about?"

"I think seventy-five will be enough."

"Seventy-five?" He leaned against the hog's fence. "I don't think you know what you're getting into."

Mary pressed her lips together and counted to ten before she spoke. The barn echoed as the auctioneer started warming up for the horse auction. As the noise rose, she stepped closer to Samuel so she wouldn't have to shout. She looked up into his face, waiting for the panic that being this close to a man should bring, but there was only irritation with Samuel's assumptions that she wouldn't be able to follow through on her plans.

"I know exactly what I'm getting into."

"A lot of work and bother."

"*Ja*, a lot of work. But Ida Mae and I can do it."

He looked toward the auction arena, and then back at

her. "Why? Are you bored? You don't have enough to do, taking care of Sadie?"

"I'm not bored. It's a way to earn a living. This is a good opportunity."

"You don't need to earn a living. There are plenty of single men around who are looking for a wife." He ran his thumbs up and down his suspenders. "Any one of them would be glad to marry you."

Mary's stomach seethed. "As if I'm some broodmare or sow, depending on some man for everything so that I can have a comfortable life?"

Samuel leaned toward her with amusement in his eyes. He was laughing at her!

"The man takes care of the woman and their children. That's how it is, and how it should be. You need to get married, not start a business."

Mary folded her arms around her middle. "That may be how it is for some women, but not for me." She bit her lip to hold back the sudden tears that threatened. The dream of a loving husband who would care for her and their family was gone. Long gone. She wasn't fit to be any man's wife.

Samuel tried to laugh at the set line of Mary's lips. She was as stubborn as Sadie, for sure.

"All right, all right. You don't have to get married." Samuel smiled as Mary's brows lowered. She reminded him of a setting hen, herself, with her mind focused on one idea. "But you don't have to worry about supporting yourselves. The church and our family have always taken care of Sadie. It doesn't make much difference if you girls are there or not."

"It does make a difference. Folks can't afford to give us as much as they have been. And there are other families in need." Her expression shifted. "Ida Mae and I are willing and able to work, but we need to stay on the farm to do it. Mr. Holdeman said that many of the farmers' wives are earning money this way."

"Holdeman." Samuel watched two men as they looked his sows over, but they moved on without asking any questions. "Holdeman is a fair businessman, and good to work with." He turned to Mary again. "I guess if you're determined to do this, I could help."

She allowed a smile then. "I hoped you would say that. We need to pick up some items at the lumberyard, but we don't have a wagon."

Her hands were clasped in front of her, and Samuel had the sudden urge to take them in his own. But his were calloused and worn. Dirty from handling the horse and the sows. Not worthy to touch her soft, slim fingers. He drew his fingers into a loose fist, hiding them.

"I'll be happy to help. We can swing by the lumberyard after the sale is over." He was gratified to see her nod her thanks. "Do you want to see if the others have found some lemonade?"

Mary glanced toward the cages of chickens. "I'd rather look at the chickens. I've never bought anything at an auction before. How do I know I'll get the ones I want?"

He followed her to a cage of Plymouth Rock hens. The black-and-white bars on their wings set them apart from the cages of White Leghorns next to them. "First, don't get your heart set on any particular lot."

"Lot?"

"Each cage is sold either singly or in a group. Either way, that's called a lot."

"So I don't choose one? I just wait to see which one I win?"

Samuel shook his head. She didn't have any experience, and yet she thought she could go into business?

"It isn't as easy as that. You need to choose the ones you want to bid on, but be willing to let them go if the price is too high. How much did you plan to spend?"

"I have two dollars. Will that be enough?"

"The way the prices went the last time I was here, you should be able to get a dozen hens or so. Which breed are you thinking of?"

"I like these Plymouth Rocks. They're the same breed Sadie already has. But the Extension Office bulletin said that the White Leghorns are better layers."

"Extension Office bulletin? What's that?"

"Mr. Holdeman had a display of them in his store at the grain elevator. There were bulletins on nearly anything you can think of when it comes to farming. Ida Mae and I read the one on egg production. It was very informative."

"So if the White Leghorns are better layers, why would anyone want to buy the Plymouth Rocks?"

She turned toward him. "Because the Plymouth Rocks are also good for meat. It depends on why you're raising them." Her eyes narrowed. "I thought a man would know that."

He shrugged as he felt his face heat. "*Mamm* and the girls always took care of the chickens. I've never had much to do with them."

"So perhaps going into the egg business isn't such a strange idea after all." She perched her fists at her waist.

Samuel grinned. "I already said I would help you, didn't I?"

She smiled back. "You did, but I wasn't sure if you still thought I would be better off letting someone else take care of me."

Samuel felt his grin widen. Mary was smart, and could keep up with his teasing. She turned back to the chickens and examined a cage holding a rooster. Why had he said that stuff about her needing to get married? If she married someone, he would never be able to talk with her like this. As long as she was single, he was free to spend as much time with her as he wished.

"I think I'll bid on these." Mary indicated the ten white hens. "Do you think I need the rooster, too? Sadie doesn't have one."

"Only if you want to raise chicks. The hens will lay just as many eggs whether there's a rooster around or not."

She smoothed her apron as she considered his words. "I guess if women can get along fine without men, then hens can, too."

She turned and walked toward another group of cages. Samuel followed her. Bantering with her was one thing, but this was going too far.

He grasped her elbow and turned her toward him. "What do you mean, women can get along—" He stopped when he saw the laughter in her eyes.

"I was only teasing you. I have to admit, men are convenient when there are heavy chores to do."

Folding his arms across his chest, Samuel planted his feet. "Haven't you known any men who were useful for more than chores?"

The light went out of her eyes as if he had blown out a flame. She sucked her lower lip in between her teeth. When she spoke, her voice shook like a willow in a storm. "Only my *daed*." She walked toward a large cage filled with six Leghorns.

Samuel swallowed. The look in her eyes…his mother had had that look.

He followed her again. In this corner of the sale barn, the noise was a dull roar. Everyone was focused on the horse sale, and no one paid any attention to the two of them.

"Mary, tell me. Has someone hurt you?"

She didn't look at him, but cleared her throat. "What makes you think that? Who would hurt me?"

She ended her speech with a little laugh, but he didn't believe her. *Mamm* had acted the same way, in the mornings at breakfast, even though Samuel had heard *Daed*'s voice through the floor berating her the night before. The averted gaze, the shaking voice. The denial that anything was amiss.

Something had happened to Mary. But if she wouldn't tell him the truth, wouldn't confide in him, he was as helpless as he had been as a boy. There was no way he could protect her.

Chapter Seven

After Samuel had unloaded the lumber and cages of the White Leghorn hens into the barn, where they would be protected, and taken Esther and Judith home, Ida Mae and Mary fixed a light supper of canned bean soup and some lettuce from the garden.

Sadie sat at the kitchen table, watching them work. "You didn't need to buy those hens."

Mary sighed. Some days Sadie required all the patience she could muster. "We've talked about this. Ida Mae and I need those hens to lay the eggs we're going to sell to Mr. Holdeman."

Her aunt muttered something as she picked an invisible piece of lint off the sleeve of her dress.

Ida Mae set the table with bowls and plates. "What did you say?"

"I said those white hens are evil. The speckled ones we have are good chickens."

Ida Mae sat next to Sadie and took her hand. "They aren't evil. Don't you think they're pretty with their white feathers?"

Sadie gestured toward Mary. "What is she doing here?

We don't need someone cooking for us. You're the only cook we need, Martha."

Ida Mae looked at Mary, and then back at Sadie. "Who is Martha?"

Sadie laughed. "Don't be silly. You're my favorite sister, you know that." She leaned toward Ida Mae. "Don't tell anyone else, but your cakes are the best around. Be careful, or that fellow from Holmes County will steal you away from us." Her finger, slender and slightly crooked, shook in Ida Mae's face.

Mary gripped the edge of the counter. "She thinks you're our *grossmutti*, Martha."

Ida Mae left Sadie at the table and stirred the pot of soup. "What are we going to do?" Her voice was a whisper, but Sadie heard her.

"Do? We're going to eat supper, that's what we're going to do. Send that other girl away and call the boys in from the barn." Sadie stood on shaky legs and walked to the silverware drawer. "I'll finish setting the table. You know the boys will be hungry when they come in."

Mary drew close to Ida Mae. "Let's just play along with her. We'll have supper, and then she'll be ready for bed. She'll be better in the morning."

Ida Mae nodded at Mary's suggestion, but she still wore a worried frown.

"The boys aren't eating here tonight. It's just us girls." She steered Sadie away from the drawer and back to her seat. "Mary is going to eat with us."

Sadie nodded and sat at the table, her expression vague once more.

She stared at the tablecloth while Mary dipped soup out for each of them and Ida Mae put the bowl of wilted lettuce on the table. The spicy vinegar smell of the dressing soothed Mary's nerves, and Sadie was quiet all through the meal. Perhaps the trip to Shipshewana had been too much for her aunt, but today had been a difficult day for her all around. When Sadie had eaten about half of her soup, she set her spoon down and folded her hands in her lap.

Mary nudged her sister under the table with her foot. "Why don't you go ahead and help Sadie get to bed while I do dishes? I want to get the chickens settled in before it gets dark, too."

"I think I'm going to go to bed right after Sadie," Ida Mae said as she rose and helped their aunt to her feet. "It's been a long day."

"It was fun to go to the sale again," Sadie said. She took Ida Mae's arm and her eyes were bright once more. "I don't think we've gone to the sale since we were girls, have we, Martha?"

"Sadie, you can call me Martha as long as it makes you smile." Ida Mae leaned down and kissed the top of the older woman's *kapp* as they headed toward the stairs.

Mary cleaned up the dishes in a few minutes, then went out to the barn. The sun was nearly gone, but the sky still held its light. She lit the lantern next to the barn door as she entered and peered into the stall that had been converted to a chicken coop. Sadie's hens clucked at the light, and peered out through their wire fence at the cages holding the new white chickens. Both groups started clucking at the disturbance Mary made in the quiet barn.

According to the extension bulletin, she would have to introduce the new chickens to the older ones gradually, or they would fight. Samuel had suggested lining the empty stall next to the chicken coop with chicken wire so the hens could see each other, but couldn't reach through to peck at the strangers. They had picked up some of the fencing at the lumberyard, and Mary rolled it out and started on the task.

As she worked, she thought of her soft bed and clean sheets. Ida Mae was right. It had been a long day. *Mamm* had taught her to take some time each evening to think of the worst part of each day, and ask the Good Lord for help with it. And then to think of the best part, and give thanks for it. As she hammered the staples into the wood to keep the wire fencing in place, she went over the day's events.

The worst part was easy. It was the crowds of people. Ever since... She stopped and reset the hammer. Ever since the attack, she had hated crowds. Especially crowds of strangers. It had been worse at home, before she and Ida Mae had moved here. There, she imagined she saw... She reached for more staples and braced the fencing again. Harvey. She whacked the staple with the hammer and positioned the next one. Harvey Anderson could be around any corner. The staple sank into the wood. If only she could make Harvey disappear as easily. Whack, whack, whack. Three staples in a row, and it was time to turn the corner.

The best part. What was the best part of the day? She hammered in a staple to hold the top edge of the fencing.

Buying the new chickens? Twelve new chickens to start building up their flock. That was a good part of the day. But was it the best?

She finished fastening the fence along the top rail of the stall, and then started the bottom row.

Samuel. The look in his eyes as he stared at her hands. As if... She straightened her back and stretched. As if he wanted to hold them.

Mary shook her head and hammered in five staples in a row. Her thoughts had no business dwelling on Samuel and what he might want to do. He was Judith and Esther's brother, that was all. A helpful friend. A man she could feel comfortable with.

The hammer slowed and she sat back on her heels. But

this change in him… Lately he had been kind rather than gruff. And he had asked if someone had hurt her. How could he have known? She hadn't told anyone her secret. No one knew. And yet Samuel had asked.

She couldn't tell him. Not that shameful secret. She couldn't tell anyone.

Her eyes pricked as she fought to hold back the tears. Harvey Anderson had taken everything from her. Her future. Her dreams. She wasn't fit to be a wife to any man.

She swallowed the knot that was growing in her throat and dropped the hammer onto the dirt floor of the stall. She had tried to convince herself that she could spend her life as Sadie had, unmarried but still a blessing to her community…but would that ever replace the life that had been stolen from her?

Samuel left the wagon in the center of the barn floor, still loaded with the sacks of seed corn he had bought at Holdeman's Feed Store. The two sows had brought in enough to buy the corn he needed, but just barely. He still didn't understand why they hadn't sold for more. They were in their prime, and had a few years left to produce litters of piglets.

He rubbed down Tilly and let her into her stall. The door to her pasture was open, and she walked out to the grass and rolled before settling down to graze. Samuel leaned on the stall gate watching her. Her coat gleamed in the rosy light from the setting sun and the chestnut color contrasted with the deep green of the grass. He rubbed his nose, letting the scene soak into his mind. Beauty. He had never thought of his farm being beautiful before. Work. Hard work. Care. Worry. Dirt. But not beauty.

By the time he reached the house, Esther and Judith had

supper ready. After the usual moment of silence, Samuel reached for the biscuits.

"We had so much fun in Shipshewana today," Esther said. She set a glass of water at his place and poured one for Judith. "I hope we can go to the sale again sometime."

"I'd like to have more time to shop. Did you see the glassware in the window of the department store?" Judith said.

She took the biscuits as Samuel crumbled one on his plate and reached for the bowl of gravy.

He looked at her, the gravy spoon in midair. "You're not thinking of buying new dishes?"

"*Ach, ne.* That would cost too much money. But I do like to look at them. They are so pretty."

Pretty. He looked around at the bare kitchen cupboards and gray, sooty ceiling over the stove. No one could call this kitchen pretty. Not like Sadie's kitchen, with the white cabinet doors to keep the dishes clean and the scrubbed floor.

"Perhaps you'll receive some dishes like that for a wedding present." Esther's voice held a smile.

Samuel looked from Esther to Judith. "Who is getting married?"

Judith looked down at her plate and Esther's smile disappeared. "No one, Samuel. I was only saying when the time comes for Judith—"

"That time will never come." Judith cut a bite of her biscuit covered with gravy with the side of her fork. She shrugged. "No fellows will come here to court one of us."

Samuel looked at them again, the steaming food on his plate forgotten. "Why not? Katie and Annie both found husbands."

He didn't remind them of how hard it had been for both of their older sisters to go against *Daed*'s—and his—

wishes. They had disobeyed, sneaking out to attend Youth Singings in neighboring districts, meeting boys.

Judith pressed her lips together, making him wonder if she had ever thought of sneaking away to a singing.

"But their beaus never came to the house." Esther pushed at her food with her fork. "No one wants to come here."

"There's no reason why a boy shouldn't stop by." An unsettled feeling rumbled in Samuel's stomach. "I mean, if he's the right type of boy."

He stuck his fork into a biscuit. As far as he was concerned, no boy would be the right type for one of his sisters.

Esther and Judith exchanged glances. "It's the hogs."

Samuel had just taken a bite and he let Esther's words sink in as he chewed.

"What about the hogs?"

Judith wrinkled her nose. "They smell."

He let out a short laugh. "Of course they smell. They're hogs."

Esther leaned forward. "But they don't smell good. They smell terrible. The neighbors complain about it."

"Not to me they don't."

His sister bit her lip, as if she was afraid to go on.

"Why don't I hear the complaints?"

Judith squirmed in her seat. "They know what a short temper you have."

He felt his face heating and he gritted his teeth to keep his voice even. "I don't have a short temper."

The girls glanced at each other, but didn't say anything.

"Who said I have a short temper?" The words came out as a bark, but Samuel didn't care. He hit the table with his fist to make them look at him. "Who said it?"

Judith's face mottled pink as she ran from the table and up the stairs. Esther dared to glance at him.

"Sometimes..." Her voice was quiet and her face was as pink as Judith's. "Sometimes you act just like *Daed*."

Samuel stared at his hand, clenched and ready to strike the table again. He swallowed and loosened his fist. *Ach, ja.* Just like *Daed*. Why did he even try to deny the rage that boiled inside him?

"Esther..." His voice failed. He cleared his throat. "Tell Judith I'm sorry. Go find her and tell her to finish her supper."

She sat in her chair on the opposite side of the table, holding her elbows, staring at her plate...the table...anywhere but at him. Looking just like *Mamm*.

"You're right." She raised her eyes at his voice. "Sometimes I'm too much like *Daed*, and I hate it."

He left the table and went into the front room. Lighting the lantern on the table, he walked over to *Daed*'s desk along the wall. It was an ancient piece, with a lid that closed. He unlocked it with the key that was left in the lock and opened the lid, pulling out the supports as he lowered it to make the desk surface. He hadn't opened this desk since *Daed* died. Hadn't wanted to face him or anything he had left behind.

Bringing a chair over, he sat down and reached for a small black book. A diary. Opening it, he saw *Daed*'s scribbled handwriting.

Worked in the woods today. Got paid ten cents.

Samuel looked for the date. January first, nineteen thirty-five. The year *Daed* had died.

The next two days were blank. Then the fourth day: *Worked in the woods. Ten cents. Went to town.*

Samuel flipped forward to May. The month before Daed died.

Sold ten pigs. Paid off note at Harmon's.

Samuel shifted in his chair. Harmon's was the store in Elkhart that sold liquor.

Sick today. No work.

The next week was blank. Then: *S asked about selling the hogs. Wants to try cattle. Told him to...*

Samuel closed the book and buried his face in his hands, elbows on the desktop. He had forgotten that day. *Daed* had gotten angry when the subject of cattle was mentioned. Took after him with a hay fork and Samuel hadn't come home until after he was sure *Daed* was in bed.

He opened a drawer. It was filled with *Daed*'s diaries. Small leather-bound books, each with the year's date on it. He flipped through the one dated nineteen thirty-one. The year *Mamm* had died. He stopped when he got to October twelfth.

Margaret died today. Funeral tomorrow.

Nothing more. The next page was blank. The following one said: *Old sow farrowed out of season.*

The following pages held sporadic notes about the farm or work he had done, but *Daed* had written nothing more about his wife of twenty-five years.

Samuel got the old tin waste basket from its place by Esther's...*Mamm*'s...rocking chair and dumped the diaries into it. He went through the papers in the cubbyholes. Bills of sale. A mortgage on the farm. Lists of debts. Samuel put the bills that had been paid off into the trash. The mortgage paper went back into the slot it had come from.

When the waste basket was full, he took it out to the burning barrel next to the boar's pen by the barn. Taking a match from his hat brim, he struck it on the side of the barrel and held the match to the first piece of paper. A receipt from Harmon's. The fire licked at the edge, then as it caught, Samuel dropped it into the barrel. He added the papers, one at a time. When they were burning, he opened the first diary and tore out the pages. He dropped them into the flames, then threw in the cover. When the diaries were all in the barrel, he turned the waste can over and shook it so that every last scrap went into the flames.

The flames lit the darkness around him.

Scrap wood was next, from the pile he kept next to the barrel. He fed the fire slowly, watching the flames eat up the papers and leather-bound diaries. Watching *Daed* disappear.

Mary turned the buggy onto the road and gripped the reins firmly as Chester set off toward town. If only her knees would stop shaking. This was her first time to go to town alone since the attack. But she was only going to Shipshewana, she reminded herself. No need to be nervous.

It had been a week since she and Ida Mae had purchased the new hens, and she had four dozen eggs in her basket. The chickens were beginning to settle into the new chicken coop Dale Yoder had built for them, using the lumber from Enosh Holdeman, and Mary was determined to pay off her debt as soon as possible.

Ida Mae had asked why she didn't get Samuel to build the new chicken coop and Mary still didn't have an answer. She glanced toward the Lapp farm as Chester trotted by, but there were no answers there, either.

It wasn't that Samuel wouldn't have done the work for them, but… Mary loosened her hold on the reins as Chester's pace became steady. But what? Was it because of the expression on Samuel's face every time she saw him during the past week? It had to be only her imagination that Samuel had guessed her secret.

Perhaps she had asked Dale because then she wouldn't have to defend her actions to Samuel.

Either way, the new henhouse looked just like the picture in the extension brochure. A roomy building with nest boxes and a large outdoor pen for the hens to scratch and peck all day long. The White Leghorns and Sadie's Plymouth Rocks had finally learned to accept each other, and the hens lived in as much harmony as sixteen chickens could.

As Mary drew closer to town, she suddenly remembered that Tuesdays were the day for the auction. Dozens of buggies filled the roads, and she had to let Chester pick his way through the crowds to the far side of town and the grain elevator and feed store. She tied Chester to the rail outside the feed store and reached for the basket of eggs.

Facing the door, she smoothed her apron and checked her bonnet. She would do her business with Mr. Holdeman and then return home. Nothing could be more simple.

She frowned at her shaking hand as she reached for the doorknob, and walked into the store. The bell chimed and she took a deep breath.

Mr. Holdeman came out of the back room. "Hello, Mary. Good to see you again. How are those new chickens?"

"They are doing well and beginning to lay eggs." She set the basket on the counter and took off the towel.

"Then you must be making them feel at home."

Mr. Holdeman reached for a tray and transferred the eggs, counting as he went.

"Four dozen even." He opened the cash drawer. "And here are your forty cents." He laid the money on the counter.

Mary shook her head. "I want to use the money to start paying off my loan."

"Are you sure?"

As Mary nodded her head, the sound of peeping came from the back room. Mr. Holdeman thumbed over his shoulder.

"We just got in some baby chicks, and I have a dozen that aren't spoken for yet."

The peeping continued and Mary looked past the grinning man to a cardboard box on a table. Little beaks poked through the holes.

"Besides, if you use all your income to pay back the loan, you won't be able to continue growing your business until it's paid off."

He got the box and set it on the counter next to Mary's dimes. He opened the lid and Mary couldn't help herself. She reached into the pile of chicks.

"They're so little." She picked up one of the fuzzy black-and-yellow balls. Plymouth Rock chicks.

"Just a day old. All they need is warmth, food and water. In six months, they'll be laying for you. An extra dozen eggs a day for a nickel's investment now."

"Five cents?" Mary ran a finger along the fuzzy back.

"Five cents for the chicks. Another nickel for the starter feed I sell. Enough to keep them going until they can be put in with the older chickens." He picked up another one of the chicks. "Don't forget, they need to be kept warm, so keep them in a box by your stove for the first couple weeks."

She couldn't help smiling at the tiny things. Returning the chick to the box, she said, "All right. Take the thirty cents to start paying the debt, and the last dime for these wee things."

"You carry the box of chicks and I'll get your bag of starter feed."

He followed her out to the buggy and put a heavy bag in the back seat. Mary frowned at Mr. Holdeman. It had to weigh at least fifty pounds the way he had hefted it.

"Are you sure that big sack of feed is only five cents?"

"Well, you caught me on that." He held up a hand as she started to protest. "Take it as a gift from me. You and your sister remind me of my own daughters. Think of it as an investment in your business."

"*Denki*, then. And I'll be back on Friday with more eggs."

He waved as she turned Chester toward the street again. The chicks peeped louder as the buggy lurched onto the road and Mary felt a giggle tickling her throat. She smiled at the frantic peeping that settled down as soon as Chester was on the pavement of the city street.

As she stopped at the corner of State Road 5, a familiar wagon on the opposite side of the intersection turned to the right, heading toward the sale barn.

"Hello!" Samuel waved as his horse made the turn. "What are you doing here?"

Mary wasn't about to shout across the intersection to answer him—the other drivers were already laughing at Samuel—so she turned Chester to follow Samuel's wagon down the road and into the driveway leading to the auction. She pulled up to the hitching rail next to the other buggies like she had last week, then headed toward the livestock area behind the barn where Samuel had disappeared.

As soon as she started through the line of wagons waiting to turn into the lot behind the sale barn, she was sorry. The men were all farmers, and none of them spoke to her, but she could feel them staring as she strained to see Samuel's wagon among the others.

She was ready to turn back to her buggy when she saw him standing on the seat of his wagon, looking through the crowds. She waved to get his attention, and he jumped to the ground and started toward her. When he reached her side and took her elbow, she nearly grasped his hand, she was so relieved to see him. He led her back to his wagon and helped her onto the high seat.

"Wait here while I unload the hogs."

She smiled her answer and settled herself, looking around. A few other women sat with their wagons like she was doing, while their husbands or brothers unloaded the stock they were hoping to sell at today's auction. The noise made calling from one wagon to another impossible, so she nodded to the ones who waved to her, and waited.

Samuel had a wagon full of hogs. In a crate by himself was his boar. The rest of the wagon bed was packed with the animals standing head to flank, pressed against each other so they wouldn't fall during the trip. Mary counted them as Samuel backed the wagon to a chute leading into the larger pens outside the barn. Twenty-three pigs. His entire stock, including the sows.

She grabbed his sleeve as the wagon halted. "Are you selling all of your hogs?"

His smile was grim. "That's right. No more hogs for me."

"Then what will you do?"

"I'm buying weaned steer calves." He gestured to another wagon that was unloading into a pen across the way. "Like those. Half grown, ready for pasture."

He went around the wagon and opened the back gate. As he guided the hogs down the chute and into the pen, Mary noticed the difference in his features. With every hog that clambered down the chute, Samuel looked a little bit happier. A little more relaxed. When the wagon was unloaded, including the crate with the boar, Samuel drove out of the livestock yard and back to the field where she had left the buggy.

As he pulled the horse to a halt, he turned to her. "You still haven't answered my question. What are you doing in town today? Buying more chickens?"

"I came to sell eggs to Mr. Holdeman, and I did end up buying some chicks."

"You're really going into this egg business, aren't you?"

He jumped down from the wagon and gave her his hand to steady her climb down. "I saw the new chicken coop the other day."

"Ida Mae and I are enjoying the work. The new chicken coop just makes things easier."

He leaned against the wagon, more relaxed than she had ever seen him. She smiled at how much he reminded her of her brothers. But he was more than a brother, he was a friend. A good friend.

"I guess we're both starting new projects." The corner of his mouth twitched. "Since we're both here, and I have some time before the hog sale starts—" he ran his thumb up and down his suspender "—I don't suppose you'd like to have lunch with me at the café."

At the thought of lunch, her stomach rumbled, turning the twitch into a full grin. "I think I had better take you up on the offer before I faint from hunger."

He offered her his arm and she took it. A friendly gesture demanding nothing in return.

She smiled up at him as they walked across the grass toward the café, her hand safe in the crook of his elbow. She hadn't been this relaxed with a man in months. If only every day could be like this.

Chapter Eight

No-church Sundays were the best days of the month. Samuel leaned on the gate enclosing the twenty-acre pasture holding the young steers. A day with no work, no trip to a church meeting, no demands.

He leaned down to pluck a grass stem and chewed on the sweet end. The young steers had settled into their new home easily enough. After he bought them at the auction, Samuel had spent last week strengthening the existing fence and using the old hog fencing to divide the pasture from the corn field. Dale had planted the seed corn on Wednesday, and now all he had to do was wait for rain.

The pasture had everything the cattle needed except water. He had a well near the barn, but had to pump the trough full three times a day. He could use a larger watering trough, but until he sold the cattle there was no cash to pay for it. So, he pumped. He threw the grass stem away and plucked another. Maybe he should try fixing the old windmill.

"Samuel! Dinner is ready."

Esther's call was faint, drifting from the house to the barn. He could see her in his imagination, standing on her tiptoes to get as close to the kitchen window as she could, and calling to him. *Mamm* had called to *Daed* the same way, every dinnertime that he could remember.

When he reached the front of the barn he saw Sadie's horse and buggy tied to the hitching rail by the back door. The surprise would have sent him into a bad mood a few months ago, but now... What had changed? He quickened his pace toward the house. The difference was simple. He looked forward to seeing Mary.

Mary, her sister and Sadie had brought a big bowl of potato salad and some cold ham. Esther had set the table for the six of them, and they crowded together in the kitchen. Another reminder of the past, when all his sisters and Bram lived at home. He squeezed into his seat against the wall and pushed away the prickly memories.

Sadie sat next to him, then fussed. "This chair is too short for me, Mary. Will you trade places?"

"I'll give you mine, Sadie," Esther said, jumping up and picking up her chair to move it around the table.

But the older woman waved her away as Mary moved from one seat to the other. "That's all right. This will work fine." She sat down with a smile and a slight wink in Samuel's direction.

Mary leaned over. "She's up to her tricks again," she said, keeping her voice low.

Samuel shrugged. "It doesn't matter. I don't mind if you don't."

That brought a smile as she turned away and concentrated on straightening her silverware.

After dinner, Samuel took the chairs out into the shady part of the yard while the girls cleaned up the dishes.

"There is something different around here," Sadie said as she made her way through the rough grass toward him. "What have you changed?"

Samuel nodded in the direction of the bare dirt patches next to the barn. "I sold the hogs."

"That's it." She nodded, satisfied. "That change certainly improves the place." She gestured, taking in the farmyard and the fields beyond. "With the hogs gone and cattle in the pasture out there, the farm looks more like it did when Abe was alive."

Samuel had sat on a chair near hers, leaning on his knees, but when she mentioned his grandfather he had to ask, "Why was *Daed* so different from *Grossdawdi*?"

Sadie didn't answer right away. She watched the cattle make their way to the shady corner of the pasture, then turned to him. "Sometimes folks make decisions that take them down wrong paths." She waved at a fly that had landed on her apron. "Your *daed* was full of rebellion as a young man. Hated the farm and everything about it. But when Abe became ill, he seemed to settle down. Came back to the farm. Married a fine girl. Started a family." She patted his hand. "Your *mamm* was a good woman, you know that?"

He nodded and waited for her to go on.

"But that rebellion seemed to continue under the surface, and then the drinking started." Her smile dimmed and her eyes became moist. "But I don't need to tell you this. You remember what he was like."

Samuel reached into the grass to pick a dandelion and twirled it between his fingers. "Do you think I'm like him?"

"In some ways." Sadie's head tilted as she watched him. "You look a lot like him. But you act more like Abe. You remind me more of your grandfather every year."

A buggy turned into the driveway, followed by a second, larger one. As they pulled up, Judith and Esther ran out of the house.

"Annie!" Esther said. "It's *wonderful-gut* to see you."

Samuel rose from his seat and helped Sadie to her feet. Another surprise. His stomach turned as he saw Bram's family climbing down from the second buggy. A truce with his brother was one thing, but was he ready to spend the afternoon visiting with these folks from Eden Township?

"Samuel, good to see you." Annie's husband walked toward him, hand outstretched, and Samuel had no choice but to welcome him with a firm handshake.

"Glad you stopped by—" Samuel paused, trying to remember his name.

"Matthew." The shorter man grinned, his brown eyes bright and his brown beard bobbing as he nodded his head. "When you stopped by to see Annie a couple weeks ago, you made her so happy. She's been bubbling with joy ever since."

Samuel looked from Matthew to Annie. She and her sisters stood in a circle with Mary and Ida Mae, fussing over the little boy Esther held in her arms. They both seemed to have forgotten the day Samuel had thrown them out of the house.

Bram's wife joined the group and Bram headed toward him and Matthew, carrying a young boy and trailed by a girl and the boy Samuel had seen when he stopped by their farm. Would he ever remember their names?

Bram nodded at Matthew and Samuel as he came close. "We hoped you would be at home this afternoon. Ellie and Annie wanted to visit."

His brother's voice held a note of caution.

"*Ja*, sure, we're glad you came." Samuel worked up a smile. "Look at the girls over there. Who would they have talked to if you hadn't come?"

The little girl pulled at Bram's sleeve and he stooped down, setting the small boy on his feet.

"May we see the cows?" She pointed toward the pasture.

"That is up to Uncle Samuel. They're his cows."

Samuel swallowed as the girl's big brown eyes turned toward him. Uncle. He was an uncle to these children. Four of them, and from the looks of Annie and Bram's wife, there would soon be two more.

"You can look at them from the fence, but don't go into the pasture. These are young steers, and not very friendly."

"Johnny, will you take Susan to see the cattle? But listen to Uncle Samuel."

As the children ran toward the barn, Bram grinned. "You sold the hogs?"

"How could you tell?"

Bram took a deep breath. "The whole place is different. The hogs were—"

"Dirty? Smelly? Stinking?"

His brother nodded. "All three. What made you change?"

His stomach turned again, facing Bram's questioning. Why couldn't he just leave it alone? Nobody invited him to come by and poke his nose in where he wasn't wanted. Then he looked past the men at the circle of women, still standing at the edge of the drive, talking up a storm. He would be polite and make the best of things for their sakes. He could do that.

"It just seemed like a good thing to do." He started toward the house as the girls drifted their way. "I'll get some more chairs so we can visit."

Bram started after him. "I'll help."

Samuel turned on him, his stomach clenching. "I can do it." He felt the growl creeping into his voice. "Stay here with the others."

His brother took a step back, a troubled frown on his face. "Sure, Samuel. If that's what you want."

He stalked into the house. He didn't need Bram's help.

He didn't need Bram telling him what to do. He didn't need Bram in his life at all.

Stomping up the stairs to fetch a couple chairs from the girls' rooms, he glanced out the window toward the group on the lawn. Judith and Esther were smiling. Annie laughed at something Ellie had said. Even Mary looked at ease and happy.

Why did he have this anger surging inside him?

Samuel sat on one of the chairs and buried his face in his hands.

There was a wall between him and his brother. Something about the man set his nerves on edge. Always had. But it seemed that Bram didn't feel the same way, laughing and joking with the others. Leaving him out.

Samuel rubbed his hands over his face again. Sadie was wrong. He was too much like *Daed* and not at all like *Grossdawdi* Abe.

Mary kept a close eye on Sadie as the afternoon wore on, but she seemed to keep her energy, participating in the conversations and even walking with Ellie's youngest, Danny, to see the cows in the pasture.

They hadn't had another bad day like the Tuesday they had all gone into Shipshewana together, but she and Ida Mae had been vigilant about keeping their aunt rested, and they hadn't tried an outing like that one since.

As the Eden Township folks prepared to head home later in the afternoon, Annie took Mary aside.

"I was glad to see you visiting the family this afternoon."

Mary had to return Annie's infectious smile. "My sister and I have gotten to be friends with Judith and Esther."

"That's good." Annie smoothed her apron over her rounded stomach. "When I was at home, we didn't see people from outside the family very much. Once *Mamm* passed away, we didn't go anywhere except to church." She gave Mary's hand a squeeze. "I'm so happy they have friends close to their own ages."

"They've been good friends for us, too." Mary glanced at Ida Mae as she and Sadie chatted with Ellie. "It's difficult to move to a new area."

Annie nodded. "For sure, it is."

As the families got into their buggies, Annie gave Mary a quick hug. "*Denki*. And whatever you're doing for Samuel, it's working."

"I'm not doing anything for him. We're just getting to know each other."

Annie laughed. "As long as I've known him, he has never sat and visited with folks the way he did today." She looked around and took a deep breath. "And the farm is so pleasant. I've never seen it looking so…so…right." She beamed when she found the word she wanted, then climbed into the buggy with Matthew.

After the buggies had disappeared down the road, Mary looked for Samuel, but he had disappeared.

"He went to get Chester for you," Judith said. "Unless you aren't ready to go home yet."

"We had better get Sadie home before she gets too tired." Across the yard Sadie struggled to pull a chair toward the house, but Ida Mae stepped in to help her. "We should stay and help you straighten up, though."

"Don't worry about it," Judith said. "We had a good visit, and you're right. Sadie needs a rest. If she stays here, we won't be able to stop her from helping."

Samuel came from the direction of the barn with Chester and hitched him to the buggy. When he was done, he headed back toward the barn without saying a word. Mary seemed to be the only one who noticed, though, as Sadie and Ida Mae were saying their goodbyes. Samuel disappeared into the barn, but Mary could see him lingering near the doorway, as if he was watching them. Back to his old grumpy self.

Mary waved to him, but he only turned away. She climbed into the buggy next to Sadie. They called goodbye to the girls as they started the short drive home.

Sadie sighed. "Now that was a fine visit."

"I was surprised to see Annie and Bram and their families come by," Ida Mae said from the back seat. "They haven't been here before, have they?"

Sadie shook her head. "Not since Annie was married, I think. But she loved the idea when I suggested it."

Ida Mae leaned forward. "You suggested it?"

"When we were at Annie's for the quilting. I told her that the girls would love a visit some Sunday afternoon. They need to be close to their family."

Mary shifted the reins to her left hand and gave Sadie's shoulders a hug. "You're always so thoughtful. I'm glad we came to live with you."

She left her arm around Sadie as Chester turned into the drive without any direction and stopped at the end of the walk leading to the back door.

Ida Mae jumped out of the buggy and reached up to help Sadie down. "I think that horse could go anywhere without a driver. He just reads our minds and takes us where we want to go."

Sadie chuckled. "Anywhere he wants to go, you mean. He knows it's time for his oats." She walked to the horse's head and patted his nose before heading up the sidewalk.

Her steps were halting, as if walking was difficult. Chester headed toward the barn and his supper, but Mary's mind was still on Sadie. Perhaps it was time for her to start using a cane. She would hate to see the elderly woman suffer from a fall when they could prevent it.

After taking care of Chester for the night, Mary checked on the chickens. The new henhouse still smelled of fresh sawed wood and whitewash. The hens gathered around her when she let herself into their yard, knowing the routine as well as she did. She filled their waterers as the hens chose their roosting spots, then she closed the door and latched it. No foxes would get these chickens.

The sun still lingered in the sky as she went in the back door, but Ida Mae had lit the lantern over the kitchen table. Sadie sat in her chair, leafing through a magazine as Ida Mae stirred a pot of soup on the stove. Mary stifled the sigh that rose. She didn't want to complain about the bounty of food in the cellar, but this was the third time they were having canned bean soup in the last four days.

Ida Mae had also brought a jar of canned peaches up from the cellar and Mary picked it up. Bits of cinnamon stick and cloves floated in the juice.

"Spiced peaches? This is a treat."

"I found them with the jars of regular peaches, and I thought they would make a nice change." Ida Mae reached into the cupboard for a bowl to pour them in. "I have to say, though, that it will be nice when the garden starts producing. My mouth has been watering for fresh tomatoes."

"And we haven't had any since September." Mary bit her lip as memories from last fall flooded her mind. It was September when she had pestered *Mamm* and *Daed* to let her take a job in town, at the little diner next to the hardware store. If she hadn't taken that job, she would never have met Harvey Anderson. She gripped the edge of the counter as gray clouds swirled, and she counted, silently, staring at the edge of the cabinet.

"You're doing it again." Ida Mae had her fists balled on her hips and was staring at her.

The swirls disappeared as Mary faced her sister. "Doing what again?"

Ida Mae glanced at Sadie, who was ignoring them, and leaned closer to whisper, "Every so often, for the past few months, your face goes blank and you look like you're going to faint." She bit her lip as her eyes welled with tears. "You're scaring me. What is wrong?"

Mary took a step back. "I'm all right. It's nothing for you to worry about."

"But I do worry. First I lose Seth in that horrible accident, and now I'm afraid that you're going to have an apoplexy or something." She wiped her eyes with the corner of her apron. "I don't want to lose you, too."

Mary tried to smile as she took Ida Mae's hand and squeezed it. "I'm not going anywhere."

Her sister held on to her hand. "But you already have. We used to talk about everything, but now…"

"You're right." Tears filled Mary's eyes and she blinked them away. When they were girls, she and Ida Mae shared all their secrets. Their dreams. Every moment of their days. "I've never let you talk about Seth."

"And we've never talked about what happened to you."

Mary swallowed. "What happened to me?"

"When you came home that day in February with your clothes all dirty, and you had been crying. I waited for you to tell me, but then…well, Seth's accident, and then moving here to Indiana…" She held Mary's gaze and didn't look away. "I miss how close we used to be. Whatever happened, we need to talk about it. It has put a wall between us, and I don't want it there anymore."

Mary took a deep, ragged breath. Her secret was a bur-

den that weighed her down, but could she share it with
Ida Mae?

"After supper. We'll talk after supper."

When Sadie's buggy disappeared down the road, Samuel turned his attention to his chores. The afternoon had
been torturous, sitting with the family and pretending everything was going well.

After he poured oats into Tilly's feed box, he went to
the pump and started filling the water trough again. The
steers crowded around as the fresh water gushed from the
spout, and Samuel's sour mood lifted. The steers were a
good investment, so far. They grazed on the rich spring
grass during the day, relieving him of the chore of cooking mash and making slop for the hogs. The oppressive
atmosphere around the farm had lifted with the clean odor
of the pastured cattle. The change had been a good one.

As he pumped, he thought back on the afternoon. Bram
had been friendly. Pleasant, even. He and Matthew had
visited together the way longtime friends did, with inside
jokes and speaking of folks Samuel had never met. Was
that what had turned his mood sour?

The trough finally full, Samuel lowered the handle with
a clang. He leaned on the fence and watched Tilly push her
way through the herd of cattle to get some of the water.
After dipping her nose into the cold water, she lifted it and
looked at him, water dripping from her chin.

"Hello, Tilly-girl." Samuel kept his voice soft, in the
tone she liked.

She took a step closer and laid her chin on his shoulder, soaking his shirt. He patted her cheek and smoothed
the hair along her neck under her mane. Her affection over
the last few weeks continued to take him by surprise. He
had never had an animal that liked him. *Daed* had never

allowed dogs on the farm, and the barn cats were all half wild. Tilly's willingness to be near him hammered against that place in his head that told him that animals were only dumb creatures, created to be used. Nothing more.

He stroked her neck once more. *Daed*'s voice again. He tuned it out.

Had it been *Daed*'s voice that had made his temper rise this afternoon? Made him see Bram and Matthew as enemies?

Tilly stuck her nose back in the water for another drink and Samuel headed toward the house. He picked up the two chairs remaining in the yard and carried them inside, his mind still on the afternoon. He still didn't know what had bothered him so much about the afternoon visits from Bram and Matthew and their families. The girls had enjoyed spending time with them.

Maybe it was the bond he had seen between the folks from Eden Township. He was the odd one out. Again.

And he hadn't said goodbye to Mary.

Esther and Judith were working in the kitchen as he walked in.

"Supper will be ready in a few minutes."

Samuel set the chairs around the table. "I'm not hungry." He was too restless to sit and eat.

Esther glanced at him, looking more like *Mamm* than ever.

"I forgot to send Sadie's bowl from the potato salad home with them. Would you take it over when you go in the morning?"

Samuel grabbed the bowl. "I'll take it over now. The walk will do me good."

As Esther and Judith exchanged glances, he could tell that his attempt to keep the growl out of his voice hadn't been successful. *Ja*, he needed the walk over to Sadie's.

He took the path through the fields. Darkness had fallen while he had been in the house, and now only a pale gray sky remained of the day. Light glowed from Sadie's windows, and he could see the three women in the kitchen. Mary gathered dishes from the table as Ida Mae helped Sadie into the back bedroom. He knocked on the door, and Mary hesitated.

"It's only me," Samuel said. "I have Sadie's bowl."

She opened the door. "*Denki*. I had forgotten that we took it over to your house this morning." She took a step back. "Do you want to come in?"

Samuel leaned in. "I don't want to disturb your supper."

Mary waved him in. "We've finished, but there are a few spiced peaches left. Sit down and I'll get a dish for you."

Samuel hung his hat on a peg near the door and sat down. Sadie's kitchen was always bright and clean, but this evening, in the lamplight, it was an island in the dark.

He smiled as Mary set the peaches and a spoon in front of him. "These smell delicious."

Mary sat in a chair next to him. "I don't know who made them, but they are very good."

Cutting into the peach half with the edge of his spoon, Samuel took a bite and nodded as the sweet juice filled his mouth.

"Good. Very good." He took another bite and looked at Mary. "I didn't come over only to return the bowl."

Her eyebrows went up.

"I guess I need to apologize. I never thanked you for coming over today, and bringing dinner to share."

"We had a lot of fun getting to know some more of your family."

Samuel moved the rest of the peach half around in the juice. "*Ja*, well, they were a surprise."

"You don't sound like it was a pleasant surprise."

He peered at her. "I didn't expect them to be there, that's all."

"I watched you talking with Bram and Matthew. They get along well together."

The restlessness came back at the mention of the two men and he pushed away from the table. "They do. The peaches were good."

She followed him out to the back porch. "What did I say to chase you away?"

He turned his hat over in his hands, then stuck it on his head. "Nothing. It's nothing."

"It's Bram and Matthew, isn't it? They're friends with each other and you feel left out."

"I'm not some schoolboy who wasn't chosen for the softball team."

"But you are Bram's brother, and you don't act like you are."

His throat constricted and his words came out as a growl. "We're not brothers. We only happen to have the same parents."

She was silent then, and he turned to leave. But she came after him.

"Wait."

He stopped at the bottom of the porch steps and looked up at her. The scent of cinnamon and vanilla wafted toward him.

"No matter what has gone on between the two of you in the past, you have to admit that Bram is trying. He came over to see you today. Doesn't that tell you he wants to be friends?"

"You don't know what it was like, growing up with our *daed*."

She came down one step and her head was even with

his. "I don't know what it was like for you growing up, but Sadie has told us some things about your family. I understand that your father was a hard man to live with."

He shrugged. "You're right."

"But that is the past."

He felt a weight drop off his shoulders at her words. She was right. He took her hand in his. "And I'm not my *daed*."

She didn't pull her hand back, but squeezed his, leaning close. "You're not your *daed*."

If Mary thought Ida Mae might forget the promised talk, she was wrong. When she came back inside after saying good-night to Samuel and making a final check on the chickens, Ida Mae was sitting at the kitchen table with a pan of light brown fudge and two cups of mint tea.

Ida Mae smiled when she saw Mary. "Remember how we used to sneak downstairs after *Mamm* went to bed and made fudge?"

"Where did you find the sugar?" Mary slipped into her chair and took the spoon her sister offered her.

"I used some from the sugar bowl, and then added some honey. I couldn't find any chocolate, though, so it's a vanilla fudge."

Mary spooned some of the warm candy into her mouth. "Mmm. More like caramel."

"I cooked the sugar and butter together before I added the milk, but I wasn't sure how it would turn out."

"Perfect."

Ida Mae took a bite on her spoon and held it up, admiring the rich color. "So. Tell me what happened last February."

Mary swallowed as she turned her cup of tea around on the saucer. "It is something terrible. Are you sure you want to hear?"

Her sister put her spoon down and took both of Mary's hands in hers. "I'm here to listen. And it can't be as terrible as what I've been imagining."

Mary looked at her and Ida Mae sucked in her lower lip. "Or maybe it is."

"There was a young man. A boy, really." Mary took a deep breath. "He worked at the store next to the diner where I worked last winter."

"I don't remember any Amish boys working there."

"He wasn't Amish."

Ida Mae waited for her to go on.

"He…was friendly at first." She swallowed. "And he would ask me to meet him in the alley behind the diner after work. He said he would buy me a soda pop."

"Did he?"

"The first time." Mary remembered the fuzzy feeling of the pop sliding down her throat. "I liked it. It was orange."

"But then?"

"We met every Friday night, after the stores closed, and before I walked home. He was funny. Told jokes. When he tried to put his arm around me one time, I told him I couldn't do that. And he laughed and said I'd learn to like it."

"Did he stop?"

"That time he did. But then the next week he told me how pretty I was, and how I should take off my *kapp* so he could see how long my hair was…" She stopped. Her voice was shaking and Ida Mae squeezed her hand.

"Were you in love with him?"

"Maybe." Mary blinked back the tears that sprang into her eyes. "I don't know. I don't think so."

"Did he kiss you?"

Mary couldn't look at Ida Mae. "He did much more than kiss me." Tears tickled her cheeks as they tracked down to her chin. Her voice shook, but she kept on, feeling the burden of her secret lift as she shared it with her sister. "That night in February, he wouldn't stop. He wouldn't listen to me. He pushed me down to the ground…"

Ida Mae scooted her chair over and pulled her close in a hug. "Shh. It's all right. You don't have to tell me more."

"Every time something reminds me of it, I…" She hiccupped. "I start shaking, and I feel like I'm going to faint."

"What can I do to help you?"

Mary leaned her head on her sister's shoulder. "You've been through a terrible time, too. How can I ask you to help?"

Ida Mae pushed Mary up and looked into her eyes. "Because we've both been through terrible things. We need each other."

Mary swiped at her cheek. "And I've been shutting you out. I was afraid that when you learned how shameful I had been…"

"What is shameful about being a victim?"

"If I hadn't asked *Daed* to let me work in town, and if I hadn't been so friendly with…with Harvey…" She swiped at another tear. "I know I led him on, making him think I was a different kind of girl—" She sniffed. "I'm so ashamed of what I did."

"Don't." Ida Mae's lips pressed together. "Don't blame yourself. I've been blaming myself ever since Seth died. I wanted to go on a picnic with him that day, but I never told him. If I had made him go with me, he wouldn't have been in that accident."

Mary shook her head. "Seth's accident wasn't your fault. You didn't know he was going to fall into that machine."

"*Mamm* finally convinced me of that, just before we left home. But don't you see? You're trying to blame yourself for the terrible thing Harvey did. It isn't your fault. It's his."

"But if I hadn't…"

"Don't make excuses for him." Ida Mae brushed a lock of Mary's hair behind her ear with a tender touch. "He made you trust him. He took something that didn't belong to him. It isn't your fault."

Mary squeezed Ida Mae's hand. "Tell me again, which one of us is the older sister?"

"Will you tell Samuel?"

"Why would I tell him?"

Ida Mae shrugged. "You are good friends with him, aren't you? And the way he looks at you…"

Mary's stomach turned. "What do you mean, the way he looks at me?"

"He's in love with you."

"He can't be." Mary shook her head. "He can't."

"Why not?"

"Because I'm never going to fall in love. I'm never going to get married."

Ida Mae twined her fingers in Mary's. "Is that what you really want? What about the dreams we had as girls?"

Mary watched her sister's face as Ida Mae struggled to keep a smile. "Have you given up on yours, now that Seth is gone?"

She shook her head. "Seth was the best thing that ever happened to me. I still can't imagine living my life without him. But then I think about Ruth, in the Good Book. Her husband died, but she was faithful and honored her mother-in-law, and look what happened to her." Her smile became peaceful. "She married a good, honest man who loved her. Don't you think God could have something like that in our future?"

"For you, for sure." Mary smiled at her sweet sister. God would have another young man who would be perfect for Ida Mae.

"And for you, too."

Mary shook her head. "Not for me. No man wants a woman like me for a wife. I'm content with what He has given me. Sadie and I will be happy together."

Ida Mae squeezed her hand again. "Samuel may have something to say about that."

Chapter Nine

It was Thursday morning, and Samuel had propped the chicken coop doors open while he cleaned out the litter and mess from the winter. He had let the chickens run into the yard to scratch and feed on whatever they found, and they clucked with every bug they ate. He leaned on his shovel in the doorway and watched them.

While he still had the hogs, the hens had stayed in their yard. The hog wallow with its flies and leftover slops was too tempting for the hens, but it was a dangerous place for them. More than one chicken had ended up being a meal for the hungry sows.

He went back to shoveling soiled bedding into the wheelbarrow, but his conversation with Mary on Sunday evening kept intruding, just as it had all week. Did Bram want to be more than friends? Could they be real brothers? Could they leave the past behind them? The idea was tempting. Starting over. Clearing out the old and starting fresh.

After the chicken house was cleaned out, Judith and Esther brought out a bucket of sudsy water and some old brushes, and the three of them scrubbed the roosts, nesting boxes and floor.

Judith coughed. "Do you think the hens will appreciate all of our hard work?"

"We will when we come out to gather the eggs in the morning." Esther gave the roost another swipe, then swished her brush in the bucket.

When they finished, Samuel gave the floor a final rinse with a pail of clean water and they retreated to the fresh air of the barnyard. The girls went to change their clothes while Samuel got the bucket of cracked corn to scatter for the hens, grinning at their eager clucking.

Just as he finished, Sadie's buggy came up the lane and stopped outside the house. Setting the empty pail inside the henhouse, he met Mary just as she stepped down. He frowned to banish the smile. She didn't need to know how happy he was to see her. Since she and Ida Mae had taken over his chores at Sadie's, he missed seeing her every day.

"What brings you by?"

She waved a paper. "I got a letter from Ellie."

Ellie? "Bram's wife?"

"She said on Sunday that she had a hen sitting on some eggs, and she would give me some of the chicks when they hatched."

Samuel couldn't stop his grin. She looked like a young girl, she was so excited. "She wrote to tell you they have hatched."

"She said I could come and get them, but I don't know where they live."

"So you want me to take you?"

"Would you be able to? I have a dinner packed, since it's so late in the morning. We can eat it on the way."

Samuel crossed his arms. "What if I'm busy?"

"Then Esther or Judith could go with me. But I thought you would like to see your brother." She leaned closer to him and lowered her voice. "I thought you'd like to show him that you aren't always as grumpy as you were on Sunday afternoon."

Scratching his jaw, Samuel eyed Mary. Her cheeks were dimpled, as if she was laughing at him.

"Was I that bad when they were here?"

"Not that bad, but not as friendly as you could have been. Sadie says you've become a new man over the last few weeks."

"Humph." He tried to scowl, but Mary's smile broke through. "All right. Let me change out of my work clothes, and then I'll take you. Come on in and visit with the girls while you wait."

Mary went into the kitchen with Judith and Esther while Samuel washed up on the back porch. As he changed into clean clothes in his room off the kitchen, he could hear their voices, but couldn't make out the words. Were they talking about him? About how Sadie said he had changed?

He looked down at the soiled work clothes he had piled on the floor and tucked his shirttail into his clean trousers. If only getting rid of his unpredictable temper was as easy as changing his clothes. He had fought that temper all Sunday afternoon, but it hadn't shown itself since. Would seeing Bram again start it all over?

Not if he could help it.

Samuel paused before he opened the door leading to the kitchen. That was the problem. He couldn't help it. He fingered the doorknob. *Mamm* would tell him to pray about his temper, and for help as he talked to Bram this afternoon. Could he do that? Would the Good Lord even listen? He raised his eyes toward the ceiling.

"God, if You're there," he whispered, "help me keep my temper today. Don't let Mary see me at my worst."

No answer.

When he opened the door, a trio of faces met him.

"We're going to go over to Sadie's while you and Mary visit Bram and Ellie." Esther's smile was brighter than he had ever seen it. "Mary said they're sewing a new quilt top today, so we're going to help."

Samuel looked from one to the other. Before Mary and her sister had moved here, Esther and Judith had never visited their neighbor. They rarely left the farm, except to go to church or a quilting.

Esther's face fell. "Unless you don't want us to."

That's when he realized he was frowning. "*Ach*, I want you to. I'm glad you're going."

"We'll be home before supper," Judith said.

"If you want to eat supper there, that will be fine. I'll fix something for myself when Mary and I get home."

The girls stared at him.

"What's wrong? Have I sprouted wings or something?"

Judith chewed on her lower lip. "Do you know how to fix your supper?"

"For sure, I do." Samuel looked around the kitchen. How hard could it be? "There's a loaf of bread, and we have butter in the cellar, right? I'll fix myself a sandwich."

Esther grinned. "If you're certain you don't mind..."

He flapped his hands at them. "Go to Sadie's. Have fun. Don't worry about me."

Judith squealed and ran up the stairs to her room and Esther gave him a quick hug before heading to the front room, where she kept her sewing basket.

Samuel grabbed his hat from the hook by the door and looked at Mary. She was smiling as she followed him out the door.

"That was very nice of you," she said, as she climbed into the buggy seat. She sat on the passenger side and handed him the reins as he climbed in.

He shrugged his shoulders. She didn't need to make it sound so noble.

"It wasn't anything. I just thought they would have fun." He turned Chester onto the road and they headed west.

"Think about it," Mary said. "When is the last time the girls ate supper someplace besides home?"

Samuel searched his memory. "I have no idea. They always stay at home."

She nodded. "They stay at home because they need to take care of you. You just gave them an entire afternoon of not having to worry about you."

He felt a frown lowering his brow. "I'm not such a bother."

"Maybe not, but you're there. You need to be fed, your clothes need to be washed, your house needs to be cleaned…"

Samuel raised a hand to halt her words. "I understand." He grinned at her as he turned Chester south at the next intersection. "So I did a good thing?"

She smiled and leaned back in the seat. "*Ja.* A *wonderful-gut* thing."

Mary relaxed in the seat and watched the scenery go by. Chester trotted along, his hooves tapping out a comfortable rhythm on the road. Buggy wheel tracks stretched along the dusty ribbon as far as she could see. She still hadn't gotten used to the straight-as-arrow roads and flatland of her new northern Indiana home.

"So, Sadie has been talking about me?"

Samuel's voice startled her out of her thoughts.

"Not in a bad way." Mary brushed some dust off her skirt. "She likes you very much, you know."

He sat a little straighter. "That's good, because I like

her, too." He used the whip to brush a fly off Chester's back. "She has always been good to me, even when…"

His voice trailed off, as if he thought he had said too much.

"Even when what?"

"When *Daed* was at his worst." Samuel glanced at her. "Has Sadie told you about him?"

"Only that he could be difficult, and that he had some problems."

Chester trotted on.

"*Daed* was a drunk."

Samuel had said it quietly and with no emotion. It took a minute for Mary to realize what he meant.

"You mean he drank alcohol? How often?"

"All of the time. But sometimes he got angry when he drank. Those were the bad times." He looked at her. "Sadie always knew, somehow, and would come up with some chore for Bram and me to do at her place, to give us an excuse to be away from home."

"What about the girls?"

"*Mamm* took care of the girls. She protected them."

Mary bit her lip and stared at the side of the road. She couldn't imagine a family like that. A sudden thought made her stomach clench.

"Sadie has said that you had learned some bad habits from your *daed*…"

"You want to ask me if I drink?"

She nodded.

"*Ne*. Never. That's one thing Bram and I agreed on when we were young. We promised each other that we would never touch alcohol."

"Has it been hard to keep that promise?"

He shook his head. "Not for me. I have a bad enough

temper that I never want to add drink to it. I saw what it did to *Daed*, and to *Mamm*."

They rode in silence until they passed the next intersection. Mary tried to imagine what a young Samuel had been like. She didn't have to imagine the warm refuge Sadie had given him. She had felt that welcoming safety herself.

"Enough about me. Tell me about your family."

Mary smiled. "*Mamm* and *Daed* have always been good parents. *Daed* is a minister in our church. There are eight of us children. I'm the oldest, and then Ida Mae. We have another sister and five brothers."

"Do you all get along?"

"Sometimes the boys squabble, but *Daed* puts a stop to that. Whenever they start arguing, he gives them a chore to do."

He chuckled. "That sounds like a good idea." He nudged her with his elbow. "What about you? What brought you to Indiana?"

Her insides went cold and she rubbed her fingers together. "You know. We came to take care of Aunt Sadie."

"Sadie has a lot of relatives who could have taken care of her. Why did you and Ida Mae come?"

Mary's finger began to hurt, so she rubbed a different one. "Ida Mae's beau died in an accident. She wanted to move here, where the memories wouldn't be so fresh."

Chester's hooves clip-clopped on the gravel while she waited for Samuel's next question. Ida Mae had said she should tell him her secret, but she couldn't. She couldn't face the shame of telling him.

"Why did you come? You must have had a beau, too, didn't you?"

He watched her, waiting for her answer. Then he smiled when she shook her head.

"I… I don't have a beau. I thought Ida Mae would need me to be with her."

"Was it hard to leave home?"

"Ne…ja…"

Her throat filled as she panicked. He must think she was lying. She turned slightly away from him as she watched a herd of cows in a field. He had been open with her, telling her about the hurts from his past. But this secret…it was too fresh. And Samuel was still a man. She couldn't tell him, and she couldn't lie.

He laughed. "Which was it? Hard or easy?"

She could feel the wall between them, tall and thick as if she had built it out of bricks. She had nearly lost the close relationship she had with Ida Mae because of keeping her secret. Would she ever be able to be close to anyone, any friend, as long as she hid her past?

"Something happened, back in Ohio. Something that made me want to leave home." She took a deep breath as he took her hand in his. "Please don't ask me to tell you."

"I know someone hurt you. I can see it in your eyes sometimes."

Mary nodded. "Someone did hurt me, but it is over. I will never see him again."

"Him?"

His face was growing red as he stared at her.

"Please don't ask me any more about it. It's in the past, and I want to leave it there."

Chester trotted past Annie and Matthew's house. Matthew's work horses grazed in the pasture next to the barn.

Samuel sighed and sat back in the buggy seat. "If you don't want to talk about it, that's all right. But if you ever need someone to listen to your story…" He smiled at her. "Sadie is a good listener. And if you don't want to tell her, then I hope I can be as good a friend as she is."

Mary smiled her thanks as Chester crossed the next intersection.

Samuel pointed across the fields with his buggy whip. "There's Bram's place."

"By the creek? It's pretty, isn't it?"

"Ja." He sighed again. "Very nice."

As Samuel drove up Bram's lane, he felt that envy creeping back in. The house and barnyard were neat and orderly, and early summer flowers turned the yard into a lovely riot of color. Bram's wife, Ellie, stepped out onto the porch to greet them, and the two older children came running from the barn. What had Bram done to deserve this kind of life?

But he tamped down the irritation as he pulled Chester to a halt at the hitching rail by the house. He wanted this day to be a good one for Mary, and if he didn't control the direction of his thoughts, he would spoil it for her.

Mary jumped down from the buggy as soon as it stopped and went to greet Ellie. As Samuel tied Chester, the oldest boy approached him.

"Hello, Uncle Samuel."

"Hey there, Johnny."

Behind the boy, the little girl, Susan, peeked at him. He smiled at her, and she grinned back. Maybe Bram had never told them about his brother and how grumpy he could be.

"What have you two been up to today?"

Johnny thumbed over his shoulder. "We're helping *Daed* in the barn. Bessie is having a calf soon, so we're building a special pen for her."

"You're helping Bram?"

"Ja, for sure. I always help him."

The boy's chest swelled as he said this, and Samuel

looked past him as Bram emerged from the barn. Their *daed* had always said that boys got in the way, and they would learn as they got older. But Johnny had been helping the last time he was here, and this time, too. That was something Bram had never learned growing up, and another reminder of just how far his brother had slipped out from under their father's shadow.

Bram joined Johnny and Susan, putting a hand on each of their shoulders.

"Samuel. I didn't expect to see you today."

Samuel tilted his head in Mary's direction. "Mary didn't know how to get here, so she asked me to drive. She said Ellie had written to her about some chickens."

"*Ach, ja.* The chickens." Bram tousled Johnny's hair. "And we're building a calf pen in the barn. Do you want to join us?"

"Can we play with the baby chicks?" Susan asked, looking up at Bram.

"For sure." Bram turned to Samuel as they ran to their mother. "I guess I've lost my helpers."

"Are they any good? I mean, you know how *Daed* said we were never a help to him."

Bram started back toward the barn and motioned for Samuel to follow him. "I've come to realize that *Daed*'s way wasn't the best way. What did we learn from the way he raised us?"

Samuel rubbed the back of his neck as he walked. "I suppose we didn't learn much."

Bram gave a short laugh. "I learned a lot of things I wish I hadn't. Like how to fear him, and how to be a bully. I learned how to get out of work by finding the easiest way to do things rather than the best." He picked a stalk of grass growing next to the barn door and snapped it in two. "I don't want Ellie's children—my children—to learn the same from me."

"But…" Samuel stopped and picked his own grass stalk. "How did you do it?"

"What?"

Samuel gestured around them at the barn, the yard, the sounds of the children calling to each other. "How did you know that there was any other way than what *Daed* taught us?"

Bram leaned against the doorway of the barn and crossed his arms. "I suppose the first time I thought I could live differently was when I bought a horse from Ellie's father, John Stoltzfus. You haven't met him yet, have you?"

Samuel shook his head.

"Some homes are like ours was. You just feel like you have to leave. To get away. The Stoltzfus farm is what a home should be. It reminds me of that time we visited *Mamm*'s parents when Annie was born. Do you remember that? The two of us spent a week with them."

Samuel smiled as the memory came back again. "It was a good week, wasn't it?"

"I want my home to have that same feeling of welcome. Of peace. So, I have spent a lot of time with Ellie's parents and their family, and I try to love and discipline my own family the way John does his."

Bram walked over to the half-built calving pen. "Would you hold the other end of this board while I nail it on?"

Samuel picked up the end of the board and held it while Bram hammered some nails into the other end. They worked together as Bram finished building the pen, then picked up a few nails that had fallen onto the floor.

"Now we're all set for Bessie to have her calf." He grinned at Samuel. "I appreciate you giving me a hand."

Samuel shrugged. "For sure. You would do the same for me, wouldn't you?"

Bram studied him. "I would. Because that's what brothers do."

"And we didn't get into an argument, even though you did use three nails where I would have used two." Samuel felt a grin starting.

"Two would have gotten the job done, but three makes it more secure." Bram grinned back as he put his tools away. "I was surprised to see that you had company when we got to the farm on Sunday. I'm glad the girls have friends." He turned to Samuel. "Or is one of Sadie's nieces more than a friend?"

Samuel felt his face heating. "What do you mean?"

"You know what I mean. You and Mary seem quite friendly today, with you driving her down here and everything."

Samuel's stomach started turning as if the puppies were back, raising a ruckus. "I don't intend to be too friendly with anyone."

Bram closed his toolbox. "Why not?"

The churning in his stomach closed in on itself. "I'm too much like *Daed*."

"Who said?"

Samuel shrugged. "Everyone. I could see it in your eyes when you stopped by the farm last year. Men at church just laugh when I say I want to do something to be part of the community. And…" And his temper. Always going off when he least expected it.

"And you storm off when things don't go your way," Bram finished for him. "I saw that on Sunday afternoon." He wiped his hands on a rag and tossed it on the workbench. "You don't have to be that way. Look at you now. You aren't angry with me, are you?"

Samuel shook his head. Bram was right. At other times, he would have closed off the conversation by now, with all of Bram's prodding.

"You're changing. I can see it."

"But not enough. I can't control my temper, and I can't ask any woman to live…to live like *Mamm* did."

Bram stood at the barn door, combing his fingers through his beard and watching a pair of barn swallows dance over the corn field.

"One thing I've learned is that if you try to change on your own, it's nearly impossible."

"How else can I do it?" Samuel could feel his temper pulsing.

"Ask God to help you."

"As simple as that?" His words came out with a growl, but then he remembered. His prayer that morning had been for God to help him keep his temper, and here he was, talking with Bram, and his temper was controlled.

"As simple as that."

Samuel looked at him sideways, not sure how to ask the next question. "You believe that God will do that?"

Bram grinned, still watching the swallows. "I know as sure as I'm standing here that God will do that if you ask Him."

Chapter Ten

Mary held the box of chicks on her lap as Samuel drove home. The fifteen Rhode Island Reds from Ellie would be a welcome addition to the young flock.

They passed Annie's house and continued north, but Samuel was silent. Ever since they had left Bram and Ellie's, he had stared straight ahead through Chester's ears as if she didn't exist.

"The chicks are a wonderful gift, don't you think?"

Samuel grunted.

"Ellie has nice children. She said they love Bram, and he is a good father to them."

Samuel rubbed the side of his nose.

"The children certainly like having the old folks around. They are Ellie's first husband's aunt and uncle. Did you know that?"

No response. Mary sat back in her seat and watched the roadside.

When Samuel pulled to a stop at an intersection, she tried again.

"What did you and Bram find to talk about?"

He looked at her as if he had forgotten she was there.

"Hmm." He clucked at Chester to signal him to go on. "We talked about the children."

He had finally given her a response.

"What about them?"

Samuel glanced at her. "Bram wants to raise them differently than how he and I were raised."

"I'm sure you'd want to do the same thing if you had children."

He nodded. "If I ever have children."

"You don't think you'll find a nice girl to marry and raise a family?" Mary's fingers grew cold. Had Samuel given up on the same dream that she had?

"I never thought about it much. I've always thought I was too much like my *daed*, and I didn't want to have a family like his."

Mary remembered the sad tone of his voice as he had spoken of his father on the way to Bram and Ellie's farm.

"You don't have to be like him. Bram isn't."

He lowered his brow. "I'm not Bram."

"You aren't your *daed*, either. I've told you that." She shifted in her seat to look at him. "Who are you, Samuel?"

"I'm not sure." He glanced at her again. "I've spent too much time trying to not be *Daed*, I guess."

He drove past his farm and on to Sadie's. When he turned in the drive, a strange buggy was tied near the house.

"Who could that be?"

Samuel's voice was a growl. "That's Martin Troyer's rig."

He pulled to a stop in the drive behind the other buggy. "I'll take care of Chester if you want to go in to see your visitor. Esther and Judith might be eating supper here, too."

Mary shook her head. "*Ne*, I'll go to the barn with you." She clutched the box of chicks, thankful for their presence. "I have to get these peeps settled in."

She had no idea what Martin was doing there, but she wanted to put off going into the house as long as possible. She would find a way to keep busy in the barn or the henhouse.

Samuel nudged her with his elbow as he clucked to Chester to continue to the barn. "Don't you want to keep those chicks in the house until they're older?"

Mary looked down at the box. "I forgot that I need to keep them by the stove for a week or so. But I still want to check on the other chickens."

"Martin might be waiting for you." Chester walked into the barn and stopped. Samuel got out of the buggy and reached for the chicks so Mary could climb out.

"Why would he do that?"

Samuel shrugged, not meeting her eyes as he handed the peeping box back to her. "He's a bachelor, and there are two single women living here."

Mary stared at him. "You don't mean that you think he came courting?"

"You won't find out until you go in."

As Samuel started unhitching Chester, Mary glanced back at the house. The sun was lowering into a bank of clouds in the west and Ida Mae had lit the kitchen lamp. If she was fixing supper already, that meant Sadie had invited Martin to stay. Her knees started to shake at the thought of a man sitting at their cozy kitchen table. Unless…

"Samuel, would you stay to supper?"

He had hung the harness on its rack and was brushing Chester.

"You want me to eat with Martin Troyer?"

She didn't want to beg, but Samuel's presence might keep the conversation off the subject of exactly why Martin Troyer was visiting a home with two single women.

"Please do. We can make a party of it, with your sisters

and Sadie." She smiled, willing her chin to stop quivering. "You can visit with Martin."

"What makes you think Martin and I have anything to talk about?" He opened Chester's stall and led him in.

"Please, Samuel. For me."

He looked at her then, his eyes dark in the shadows of Chester's stall. He met her in the center of the barn and took the box of chicks.

"All right. I'll stay for you." He carried the box under one arm and took her elbow with the other. "For you, I'll even try to control my temper."

When Mary stepped into the kitchen, the first thing she noticed was Ida Mae's face. Tight and pale with a pained smile. Judith and Esther sat on either side of her, and Sadie was at the end of the table watching Martin, who sat with his back to the door.

"My farm is quite large," he was saying, "and I have a full barn of dairy cows. My brother and I work the farm together."

Samuel hung his hat on the peg next to Martin's and planted his hand in the small of Mary's back, propelling her forward to the empty chair at the end of the table.

"Good afternoon, Martin," he said as he pulled the kitchen stool over and placed it at the corner between Mary and their visitor. "I was surprised to see your buggy here."

Martin smiled at Mary before turning to Samuel, his eyebrows raised. "No more surprised than I am to see you here."

Martin leaned forward so he could see past Samuel's bulk and catch Mary's eye. "As I was saying, my brother and I have a dairy farm. And to be plain—" He broke off and glared at Samuel before scooting his chair up. "Neither one of us is married." He grinned. "Just a couple of bachelors. And we thought we should learn to know you girls a bit better."

Samuel shifted on his stool and moved the box so it cut off Martin's view of Mary. She looked up at him and he gave her a wink.

Ida Mae grabbed Mary's hand under the table and squeezed hard enough to send shooting pains up her arm. Judith and Esther were both scrunched small in their chairs, looking at their laps. None of them looked happy. How long had Martin been here?

"I don't think—" Mary started.

But Martin kept talking. "We thought a picnic on Saturday would be a good way to get acquainted. Just us four. You could pack some fried chicken, and potato salad. And Peter loves boiled eggs." He scooted forward again to see around Samuel. "What do you think?"

Mary exchanged glances with Ida Mae. There had to be a reason for them to decline.

"This coming Saturday?" Samuel said, placing a hand on Mary's shoulder. "I was going to ask Mary to spend the day with me."

He squeezed her shoulder, letting her know he was giving her an excuse to refuse the invitation, but Mary wouldn't make any commitments without talking to Ida Mae.

Martin's teeth ground together. "I don't see what concern this is of yours, Samuel Lapp. Isn't it time for you to leave?"

Mary glanced at Sadie. The older woman was quiet for once, watching the exchange between the two men with a little smile, as if she was enjoying herself.

"I was invited to stay for supper." Samuel's voice was quiet, without the hard edge Martin's frown invited.

Martin looked from Mary, to Ida Mae, to Sadie. But

none of them said anything. The aroma of roast ham filled the kitchen, and a pot of potatoes boiled on the stove. If Ida Mae hadn't invited him to supper, Mary certainly wasn't going to be the one to do it, no matter how rude it looked.

Shoving his chair back, Martin finally stood and reached for his hat.

"I'll come back another time, when you aren't so busy," he said, stepping toward the door, "and when you're ready for better company." He glared at Samuel.

"You're welcome anytime," Sadie said. "Isn't he, girls?"

"For sure," Mary said. She got up to close the door behind him. "Anytime."

Martin turned as he reached the top of the steps.

"Think about my invitation."

"I'll let you know what we decide."

Martin looked from Mary to Samuel, still sitting on the stool with his back to the door. "If I were you, I would think hard about the kind of company you keep." His voice was quiet, so it wouldn't carry back into the kitchen. "I can offer you a much better life than a Lapp can."

Mary forced a polite smile. "I'll keep that in mind."

"And I will be back on Thursday for your answer. I've been watching you at church, and I like how you care for Sadie. You seem to be a good Amish woman, just the type of girl I want to be my wife. We'll do well together."

A sickening turn to her stomach forced Mary to clutch at the doorknob. "You are wasting your time. I don't intend to marry."

He gave her a self-assured grin. "We'll see about that." He stepped off the porch and untied his horse. "We'll see."

Mary watched him leave, willing her knees to stop quivering. When she had seen Martin at church, she had no idea that he might have been watching her. The thought made her stomach turn again. He didn't seem to be the type of man who would give up his suit easily.

Even though he had been invited to supper, Samuel had no intention of outstaying his welcome. Once the sound of Martin's buggy wheels disappeared down the drive, Samuel set the box of chicks on the table and took his hat from the peg by the door.

"I'll be getting home. I don't want to horn in on your hen party." He grinned at Judith's giggle.

Mary, still standing by the door, brushed his sleeve with her hand. "You can still stay, even though Martin left."

"I have work to do at home, but I'll do your chores before I leave."

Mary followed him out the door. "You don't need to do that."

She seemed nervous. Had Martin's visit frightened her? He started toward the chicken house on the far side of the barn and she followed.

"I heard Martin talking to you as he left. Did he insist that you and Ida Mae go on that picnic he had planned?"

"He said he wants to marry me."

Samuel put his hands on his hips, facing her. "You can't think that Martin Troyer would make a good husband. What made him think you would consider such a thing? How many times has he visited you? How much have you talked together?"

"I don't know." She shook her head. "I've never even talked to him before."

A dull roar started in Samuel's ears, echoing the thunder that rumbled in the distance. "He wouldn't just ask you out of thin air." But why would Mary lie to him?

"He said he had been watching me at church meeting, and he liked what he saw. I guess he and his brother want to spend time with Ida Mae and me to convince us to marry them."

Samuel rubbed his day's growth of whiskers. Martin Troyer. If that man came courting his sisters, he would throw him out on his ear. He was old enough to be their father.

"I hope you told him to forget the idea."

She drew herself up to her full height and her eyes narrowed. "Why?"

"Because he's not the man for you."

She took a step closer to him and he backed away. "You are not the one to tell me who I should consider and who I shouldn't, Samuel Lapp. You are not my father or my brother."

"But I'm…" What? Her friend? He leaned toward her. "I don't want to see you make a bad decision. You don't know this man like I do."

"Aren't you the one who told me I should get married rather than start a business?" Her eyes narrowed farther. "Maybe I should think about taking your advice."

Had he said that? He stared at her. Probably, and she remembered even if he didn't. But she couldn't…she wouldn't marry that bully.

He wouldn't let her.

"Go on in the house and visit with the girls. I'll do your chores for you."

She shook her head. "I'll do them. I don't need you or any other man telling me what to do."

Samuel's face grew hot in the cool evening air. The wind whipped in a moisture-laden gust. "I said I would do your chores. You need to learn to accept help when it's offered."

Her fists perched on her hips. "You're telling me what to do again."

He held his hands up in surrender. "All right. You do it your way." He took two steps back as the thunder rumbled again. "I told the girls to stay all night if it's still storming after supper." He turned to take the path home. "But don't forget what I said about Martin."

Glancing back, he saw her silhouette in the dusk, her fists still on her hips, watching him go. He took off his hat and slapped it against his leg as he walked. That woman was the most stubborn female in the world. He had known sows who were easier to handle than her.

Reaching home, he went to the barn to do his chores. The first task was pumping the water trough full. As he pumped, he watched the sky. Clouds gathered in the west, blocking the last pale blue of the sky. A flash of lightning lit the darkness with a brief glow. He counted the seconds before the quiet rumble of thunder reached him. By the time the rain started, he should be in the house for the night.

He finished filling the trough, then went into the barn. As he poured a cupful of oats into Tilly's feed box, she came in from her pasture. She sniffed the grain, then pushed against his chest with her nose before taking a mouthful of the oats. She raised her head, watching him as she chewed. He closed her door to keep her in out of the storm for the night, and fastened the shutters on the windows. He gave Tilly a last pat before leaving the barn. After he blew out the lantern and hung it from the hook by the door, he checked the latch on the big main doors, then headed to the house.

The wind had picked up, and the storm was closer. Lightning flashed again, followed by a crack of thunder. He watched the storm as it rolled in, the black clouds building on each other as the wind pushed them, backlit by lightning that was nearly constant. A picture of his building temper.

As the first large drops plopped on his hat, he ran the rest of the way to the back porch and cover.

He shut the back door against the storm and hung his hat on the hook. The house was quiet and still. Heat radiated from the kitchen stove as Samuel lit the lamp above the table. He grabbed a towel and took out the Dutch oven. Even though he had told her he would fend for himself, Esther had made a potpie. A thick crust, golden brown, covered the chicken and gravy. The aroma of stewed chicken filled the kitchen when he poked the crust with a fork.

Taking a dish from the cupboard shelf, he cut into the crust and laid it on his plate. Then he spooned the rich gravy, chicken and vegetables over the crust and held it close, breathing in the aroma.

Sitting at the table, he lifted a forkful of his supper, then paused. He was alone in the house. He couldn't remember the last time he had been alone in this house, if he had ever been. Someone had always been here… *Mamm*, one of his sisters, Bram…

The doorway to the living room was an empty hole, black between flashes of lightning. His bedroom door was shut, and the door to the back porch was, too. The kitchen light showed the bottom three steps going up from the doorway next to the stove, but then darkness lurked beyond the lamplight.

He ate the food on his fork, his chewing loud in his own ears between the rumbles of thunder. The storm passed overhead, leaving behind a steady rain that could last for hours. The girls would stay at Sadie's tonight, and he was on his own.

Washing the dishes took no time, except for the minutes he spent watching raindrops hit the window, then slide down to the sill. Over and over, one after another. Just like the generations of Lapps who had lived in this house. Abe's father had built the house nearly a hundred years ago. Then *Grossdawdi* Abe, then his own father, and now him. Who would live here after him?

Samuel wiped out the Dutch oven with an oiled rag and set it on the stove. Banking the fire, he left the kitchen. He took the lamp with him into the living room and found the new *Farm and Home* magazine. Settling into the rocking chair with the lamp on the table beside him, he leafed through articles about shearing sheep, the new electric fence someone in New Zealand had developed, poultry waterers and a different butchering technique for hogs.

Tossing the magazine onto the table, Samuel leaned back in the chair, rocking himself with his toe. The house was quiet. Too quiet. But when Judith and Esther married and moved away, this would be his life. Quiet evenings alone in the dark, silent house.

As the wind picked up, the old house creaked, as if it was complaining about the quiet, too. The house was full of memories. So many folks had been born and died within these walls.

He pulled his thoughts back from that road. Very few of his memories were good ones, but there had been some worth thinking about on a stormy night. Like when he was small, and *Daed* would come in from doing chores in the winter, laughing as Samuel and Bram would rush to lick the snow off his coat sleeve before it melted. He remembered *Mamm* in the kitchen and the warm stove on cold mornings. He remembered jokes, stories, games…he remembered that there had once been life in this house. Life that was gone now, and no one could bring it back.

Leaning his head back against the rocker, he closed his eyes. Sadie's kitchen had been full of that life this evening, and the girls were there enjoying it. And Mary... His eyes popped open. He couldn't let Mary wed that Martin Troyer. He couldn't. But how could he stop her?

The storm hit with a rush of wind carrying big, plopping drops of rain. Mary ran from the barn to the house, but by the time she reached the back porch, she was soaked. Her *kapp* hung by its ties from her neck, and her hair clung to her wet skin in long, dripping ropes. She lifted her skirt and apron together and wrung out a few drops of water, but it was no use. She needed to change into dry clothes before supper.

She opened the kitchen door into a world of light and happy conversation. Esther and Ida Mae were laughing over something as they sprinkled chopped raisins into cake batter. Judith sat at the table while Sadie showed her how to do a knitting stitch. They all looked up when Mary came in.

"You're wet," Ida Mae said. "Is it raining that hard?"

"For sure it is." Mary stepped over to the stove and spread her hands out to the heat. "And with the storm as strong as it is, Judith and Esther will be staying the night with us, *ja*?"

"We were just talking about that. Supper is nearly ready, but you have time to change." Ida Mae tilted the bowl so that Esther could scrape the cake batter into the pan. "Put on your nightgown and some warm socks."

"To eat supper?"

Judith grinned. "Why not? No one will be here except us."

Esther nudged Mary aside with her elbow so she could put the cake in the oven. "Perhaps we should all put our nightgowns on. Ida Mae said you had an extra one I could borrow."

Sadie laughed. "That sounds like fun. I haven't done anything like this since I was a girl."

By the time everyone met back in the kitchen, the thunderstorm had passed overhead and left a steady rain. Ida Mae dished up ham and scalloped potatoes while Judith and Esther set the table. Sadie sat in her usual place, with a quaint *kapp* on her head.

"What are you wearing, Aunt Sadie?" Judith asked.

"My night *kapp*. I know girls don't wear them anymore, but I don't feel dressed without one."

Mary had combed and braided her wet hair, and the other girls had long braids hanging past their waists, too. Ida Mae had been right. Mary had gotten her long flannel nightgown from her chest and loaned her summer cotton one to Esther. The warm, dry fabric felt wonderful against her chilled skin, and the warm socks were beginning to take the icy feeling out of her toes.

In fact, between the warmth of her nightclothes and the filling heat of her supper, Mary began to get sleepy as she sat at the table, listening to the conversation. But then Judith mentioned Martin Troyer's visit.

"Are you going to go on that picnic he invited you to?"

Ida Mae glanced at Mary, then shook her head. "I'm sure he and his brother are nice men, but…" She bit her lip.

Mary felt a guilty nudge inside. She had only thought what Martin's invitation meant to her. She hadn't considered Ida Mae's feelings at all. Was her sister ready to spend some time with a man?

"I'm not too sure about Martin," Esther said. "He always seems to be bragging about something."

"His brother, Peter, is a hard worker, but that's all I know about him." Judith cut her ham into bites. "He's very quiet, and doesn't enter into conversations much."

Mary took a biscuit and spread some jam on it. "What do you know about them, Sadie?"

"Like the girls said, Martin is a talker and Peter isn't. Martin was right about their dairy farm, though. Their father started it, and the boys have taken it over and are doing well with it. They're hard workers, for sure."

Ida Mae leaned back in her chair. "You called them boys, but Martin seemed to be pretty old."

"He may seem that way to you, but to me he's still a boy." Sadie tapped her finger on pursed lips. "He must be Samuel's age...*ne*, that can't be right. Martin's mother was a Zook, but not related to the Eden Township Zooks. She was Myron's Betza's sister..." Suddenly Sadie smiled. "Martin was born the same year as my brother Solomon's youngest. So, that would make him forty years old, and his brother, Peter, must be thirty-eight."

Martin Troyer was the same age as *Daed*. "And they are both bachelors?"

Sadie nodded. "The dairy farm has kept them busy. Too busy for starting a family, it seems. I'm not sure what put it into Martin's head that he should come courting."

Ida Mae stood and started gathering the dirty dishes. "No one said anything about courting. Martin only asked if we would want to go on a picnic."

Mary rubbed at her finger. Ida Mae hadn't heard her conversation with Martin on the back porch. But she seemed to be interested. Perhaps they should accept the invitation, for Ida Mae's sake. But Mary's stomach clenched. She couldn't think of marrying Martin Troyer. She would never put herself in the position of being alone with any man again. Especially an overbearing man like him. But what did Ida Mae think?

Judith and Esther took Sadie into the front room while

Mary and Ida Mae washed the dishes and *redd* up the kitchen for the night.

Ida Mae chewed her bottom lip as she shaved soap flakes into the dishpan. "Do you think we should go on the picnic with Martin and Peter?"

That was the comment Mary had been waiting for. It sounded like Ida Mae was in favor of getting to know the two men better.

She poured warm water into the dishpan and kept her voice casual. "If you would like to." She smiled as Ida Mae glanced at her. "It's an opportunity to get to know them better. And who knows? We might even like them."

"Would you consider marrying a man so much older than you are?" Ida Mae swirled the dishrag in the water to melt the soap flakes.

"It happens pretty often," Mary said, thinking of the number of families she knew where the husband was several years older than his wife. "Especially when the man is a widower and has young children to care for."

"But these two have never been married. What if there is something wrong with them? How many girls have they tried to court that have turned them down?"

Mary couldn't tell if Ida Mae was worried about the men's characters, or if she felt sorry for them.

"Sadie said they have been working very hard on their farm. It sounds like they would be good providers."

Her sister chewed on her bottom lip again as she washed the five plates and handed them to Mary to dry.

"I guess we could go on the picnic. What would it hurt?"

It was Mary's turn to chew on her bottom lip. She could do this for Ida Mae. She would do anything to see her sister happy and looking toward the future again.

"You're right. What would it hurt?"

Chapter Eleven

Samuel couldn't listen to Preacher William's sermon that Sunday morning. Martin Troyer sat two rows in front of him, next to Peter, and two rows in front of them, on the women's side, were Mary and Ida Mae. It seemed that Martin and Peter weren't listening to the sermon, either, since they were both staring at the girls. He recognized the slow burn of jealousy for what it was, and didn't care. Martin had no call to be thinking of marrying a girl like Mary.

At least Mary didn't notice. Her attention was on the preaching.

Samuel forced his attention back to Preacher William's droning voice. It was too bad preachers weren't called on the basis of their speaking ability. Focusing on the sermon, Samuel heard him stress that a man must die to sin and be united with Christ.

Samuel's gaze drifted to his hands, calloused and with a bruise on one thumb where he had hit it with a hammer yesterday. Yesterday. When Mary and Ida Mae had gone on that picnic with the Troyers and he had heard the Troyers' buggy going by on the road. He flexed his fingers, feeling the dull pain of the bruise creep into the palm of his hand.

The congregation shifted in their seats as Preacher Wil-

liam sat down and Preacher Jonas stood. The first thing
he did was to read from the German Bible the story of
how the Pharisee, Nicodemus, had talked with Jesus in the
garden at night. Samuel tried to think of something other
than the familiar words, but Jonas's voice wasn't the kind
you could ignore.

Preacher Jonas had a habit of looking the people of the
congregation in the eyes as he spoke, and for some reason,
he focused on Samuel this morning. Samuel shifted on
the bench and glanced behind him. Every man's gaze was
focused on the preacher. When he looked back at Jonas,
the preacher had shifted his focus to the other side of the
room, but then came right back to Samuel.

"Ye must be born again," said Jonas with a smile.

A smile on the man's face? After Preacher William had
only talked of death?

Samuel focused on his shoes, polished for this morning's meeting. The messages in the sermons were confusing. He glanced at Mary. She watched Preacher Jonas,
sitting straight on the bench, her hands in her lap. He
looked at Martin. He was also watching the preacher, as
if the man was talking only to him.

Tapping the bruise on his thumb, Samuel kept his gaze
focused on the black coat in front of him, waiting for the
preaching to end.

Dinner after the preaching was intolerable as Samuel
watched Martin watch Mary. The man was blatant in his
attentions to her, even rising once to help her carry a heavy
platter to one of the tables. He should be embarrassed,
mooning on like a lovesick cow.

Samuel snorted and left the house. He would wait for the
girls by the buggy, and then they could go home. Maybe
he should have stayed home today and let the girls ride

with Sadie, then he wouldn't have had to witness that display of Martin's.

He leaned on the Hopplestadts' pasture fence. Conrad was one of those farmers who never let anything on his farm look run-down, but the pasture fence had been repaired badly. Samuel bent down to examine it. The broken fence wires had been patched with baling twine, and the patch was nearly worn through.

"Hello, Samuel."

Preacher Jonas's voice took him by surprise.

"Preacher." Samuel shook the hand the other man offered.

Jonas leaned on the fence next to Samuel. "You barely touched your dinner, and now you're out here by yourself instead of visiting with the rest of the congregation." He turned to look at him. "Is everything all right?"

Samuel shrugged. "For sure, everything is fine."

"That's good." The preacher looked out over the pasture. "The grass is good and rich this year. Not like last year at all."

"We've had some good rain."

"*Ja*, for sure. We have much to be thankful for."

Samuel picked at the broken bit of fence wire.

"You seemed uncomfortable during the sermon."

"Preachers notice things like that?"

The older man laughed. "*Ja*, for sure." He gestured toward the horses in the field. "When you look at these horses, what do you see? A bunch of animals? Or do you see that some are grazing and some are standing, drowsing in the sun? It's like that when you're in front of a congregation. We see who is paying attention to our words, who is thinking of something else and who is fighting to stay awake."

"So, which one was I?" Samuel grinned. At least he wasn't sleeping.

"You seemed to be listening at first, but then you were trying hard not to listen."

Samuel didn't answer.

"I had to ask myself, why? Why is Samuel Lapp trying so hard to ignore God's word?"

"It wasn't God talking, Preacher. It was you."

"When I read from the Good Book, I'm reading God's words. And when I expound on those words in a sermon, I pray that I'm communicating God's message to His people."

Samuel picked at the fence again. "I'll tell you why. It seemed that Preacher William had one kind of message, and then you were saying the opposite. How am I supposed to figure out who is right?"

Jonas picked a stalk of grass and started pulling off blades. "The messages weren't contradictory. They go together, like a hand in a glove."

"So we die, and then are born again?"

The preacher smiled. "That's right."

"Who? Who could die and then come to life again? You're not making sense."

Jonas sighed. "Have you ever listened to a sermon in your life, Samuel?"

Samuel dug into a clump of grass with the toe of his shoe.

The preacher grabbed his shoulder and gave it a squeeze. "Try listening to the entire sermon the next time, all right?"

Samuel nodded. "I'll try."

Jonas shook his head. "No one can ever accuse you of being a liar." Then he laughed. "I just wish all church members were as honest with themselves as you are." He plucked another blade of grass. "In a few weeks we'll have the church council meeting. Someone has asked that you be disciplined."

An icy hand clutched at Samuel's stomach. Disciplining meant standing before the congregation and being asked to repent.

"What for?"

"We've received an accusation that you are harboring ill will toward another church member." Jonas paused, then said, "Is this something you need to repent of before the congregation?"

"Who am I supposed to be angry with?"

"Martin Troyer."

Samuel sighed. "I guess it is no secret that his words goad me to anger, but I don't wish him ill."

"You would not rejoice if his dairy cows became ill and he couldn't sell the milk?"

Samuel's eyebrows rose. "Is that what I'm accused of saying?"

"Something similar."

"I have never thought such a thing, and I certainly never said it."

Preacher Jonas threw the grass stem away and leaned on the fence post, staring out at the horses. "Then we have one man's word against another's."

Samuel's temper rose. "You can't believe this—"

Jonas interrupted him with a raised hand. "I don't know who to believe, but I've never known you to be other than truthful."

"Tell me, is it Martin who made this accusation?"

The preacher shook his head. "And at this point, I don't want to tell you who did."

Jonas sighed again, his shoulders bent as if he carried the weight of the entire congregation on them. With a start, Samuel realized that was exactly the burden he bore.

"Preacher William, Bishop Kaufman and I need to discuss this. But I hope you will do everything you can to make amends with Martin. You are brothers in Christ, and must act that way. I will say the same to Martin."

Samuel shifted his feet. He was being asked to do more than just talk to Martin. He must support him in his work and find a way to be friends with the man. Must he even encourage Martin's courtship of Mary, like a friend and brother would?

"Is something wrong?"

"There's a girl…"

Jonas nodded. "I thought there might be when I saw the direction of Martin's thoughts this morning." He glanced at Samuel. "What are your feelings for Mary?"

"I don't have feelings for her. I just want to make sure she's happy, and safe, and that she marries someone better for her than Martin Troyer."

Jonas laughed. "But you don't have feelings for her."

Samuel shook his head. He didn't—couldn't—harbor any feelings for any woman.

The preacher clapped him on the shoulder. "I hate to tell you the bad news, but it's obvious to me that you are in love with her."

"Love?" His voice turned into a growl. "I'm not in love with anyone. I just don't want Mary to be hurt."

Jonas grinned. "Maybe if you tell yourself that enough, you might believe it. But I think you're wrong." He leaned closer to Samuel. "Ask yourself this, then. How will you feel when you are at her wedding if you aren't the groom?"

Samuel glared at him. This preacher had a knack for reading his mind.

Monday morning dawned with a glorious blue sky.

"A perfect day for laundry," Sadie said. She stirred the

tubful of white clothes with an old washing bat. Mary thought it was probably a hundred years old, as stained and warped as it was, yet Sadie wielded it like she was David fighting the giant laundry tasks.

Ida Mae ran an apron through the wringer and dropped it in the basket for Mary to hang on the line.

"It feels like it might get warm enough today to set out the tomato plants. What do you think, Mary?"

Before Mary could even think of an answer, a farm wagon turned into the lane. Her stomach sank when she saw Martin Troyer driving. Peter rode in the back of the wagon with a cow.

"Good morning!" Martin pulled his team to a stop and climbed into the wagon to help Peter. "We brought you a present."

Mary and Ida Mae both stared as Peter and Martin unloaded the cow from the wagon. Martin handed the lead rope to Mary. Meanwhile, Sadie had come up behind them.

"That's a cow," she said.

The Jersey stared at Mary with huge brown eyes as she chewed her cud.

"It's a cow," Ida Mae said.

"*Ja*, for sure." Martin grinned. "A cow."

"Y-you said y-you could sell b-butter along with your eggs," Peter said. He smiled as he watched Ida Mae.

"We thought you could put her to good use." Martin said, petting the animal's neck. "And the butter would bring in a good income, just like you said."

Mary shook her head. "We can't pay you for her."

Martin grinned wider. "We don't want to sell her. We're giving her to you." He glanced at his brother. "Right, Peter?"

The other man nodded, his eyes still on Ida Mae. "*Ja, ja, ja*. She's a p-present."

"Do you want us to help you get her settled? You have a stall for her, don't you?"

Sadie took the rope from Mary. "We can put her in the second stall, and she can share Chester's pasture." The old woman started toward the barn, the cow following her.

Mary looked from Sadie's retreating back to Ida Mae, who shrugged.

"We don't know how to thank you," she said. "But we really can't take her—"

Peter climbed into the wagon and Martin followed him. "You have to take her. She's yours." He clucked to the team and turned them around in the space in front of the barn. He waved as the wagon passed the house on the way down the drive. "We'll see you again soon. We're looking forward to another picnic."

Ida Mae slipped her arm through Mary's as she stared at the retreating wagon. "What are we going to do now?"

"I guess we have a cow. We'll have to ask Sadie if she has any milking equipment, because that cow will need to be milked this evening."

They started toward the barn.

"Do you know anything about taking care of cows?" Ida Mae asked.

"I know as much as you do, and that's from helping *Daed* do the milking. But beyond the day-to-day feeding and milking, I don't know what to do with her."

"She'll need to be freshened sometime…"

Mary stopped her sister's words as they entered the barn. "We'll worry about that when the time comes."

When the time came, they would need to find a bull. And then decide what to do with the calf. And then… Mary shook her head. One step at a time.

Sadie had let the cow into the stall next to Chester's and

was patting her nose. "Nice *Schmetterling*. Good *Schmet-terling*."

Mary and Ida Mae exchanged glances.

"Sadie," Mary said, keeping her voice even, "why are you calling her a butterfly?"

Sadie grinned at the girls. "I know she isn't a butterfly. I thought *Schmetterling* would be a nice name for her. Her eyelashes are so long, just like a butterfly's wings."

"I feel funny, accepting a gift like this from Martin and Peter," Ida Mae said, stroking Schmetterling's face. "We hardly know them."

"You'll get to know Peter, and then fall in love with him," Mary said. "You know he wants to marry you, and that's why he gave you the cow."

Ida Mae's mouth dropped open. "I'm not going to marry Peter. It's Martin who wants to marry you. He brought the cow to you."

Mary shook her head. "And I'm never going to marry Martin, no matter how many cows he brings us."

"Then you need to make sure he knows that."

"I've told him." Mary shrugged. "He won't listen to me."

Sadie stroked the cow's soft ears. "Those Troyers never listen to anyone. Once they have their minds made up, they're going to get their way, unless someone steps in to stop them."

Ida Mae groaned and covered her face with her hands. "Is there no way to get out of marrying them, then?"

"You won't have any trouble with Peter," Sadie said. "Martin is the hardheaded one. Once Mary has dissuaded him, Peter will follow."

"How can we convince Martin?" Mary asked.

Sadie smiled, looking as crafty as a fox. "I don't think

you'll need to worry about that. Meanwhile, we have a cow, and we need to take care of her."

"Do you have anything like a milking pail? Or a stool?"

"I have all that in the cellar, in a box in the corner. I had a cow until a few years ago, and milked her every morning and evening. She was a fine cow, but not a Jersey like this one. Jerseys give rich milk, and we'll be able to make a lot of butter to sell."

Mary's mind started churning. How much butter could she make from Schmetterling's milk? If her milk was as rich as Sadie said, probably more than enough to pay for the cow's keep. She scratched Schmetterling's ears. She would have to find a way to thank Martin, without making him think it was time to start planning a wedding.

"Chester's pasture is too small for both animals, though. Can we make it bigger?"

"Ach, ja." Sadie gestured out the back door of the barn. "Abe gave me ten acres. All we need to do is move the fence back behind the barn. We can go all the way to the line of trees along the fence row back there, where it was before I sold my cow." Sadie started out the side door of the barn. "Come along and I'll show you."

She led the way around Chester's pasture to the far side, walking between the new chicken coop and fence. When she reached the corner fence post, she stopped.

"Who has been plowing back here?"

The space between the back fence and the tree line had been plowed in neat rows, and corn shoots were already growing in the black soil.

"Samuel said that Dale Yoder was going to plow a corn field for him. He must have thought this was part of Samuel's farm."

"We need to let Schmetterling graze. She needs a pasture." Sadie's brow puckered as she tried to think through the problem without success.

Mary gave her shoulders a quick hug. "Don't worry about it. We'll fence in the space and she can eat the corn shoots until the grass grows again."

Ida Mae took Sadie's arm and turned her back toward the house. "Let's finish our laundry and get out the milking pail to use this evening. And Mary is right. We'll just move the fence and use the field. Samuel probably doesn't know that Dale planted it."

Mary hung back as Ida Mae and Sadie walked toward the house. The corn shoots fluttered in the slight breeze. They would need to fence off about three acres on the end of the planted field that stretched from here to behind Samuel's barn. Moving the fence wasn't something the three of them could do on their own, but she could ask Samuel to help. They would have a good laugh over Dale's mistake.

She hoped.

Samuel gave the pump handle one last push, sending a spurt of water into the watering trough. He wiped his forehead with his handkerchief and leaned back against the fence post, looking up at the derelict water pump tower again. When the windmill had stopped working five or six years ago, *Daed* had left it where it stood. Winds had battered the mill blades and a few hung from the broken spokes.

If he could get the windmill going again, he'd save himself a lot of work.

Shoving his hat back on his head, he walked over to the sixteen-foot tower and pushed against it, then pulled on it. Steady as the day it was built, years before his time. He put a foot on the crossbar, hearing *Daed*'s voice in his head.

"You boys stay away from that tower. First thing you know, one of you will fall off and break your leg."

Samuel grinned. *Daed* had been right. Bram had climbed up about ten feet before he missed his footing. He didn't break his leg, but he was bruised and sore. Neither of them had said anything about the fall, though. Bram said that *Daed*'s punishment for disobedience would be worse than the bruises he already had.

Testing the steadiness of the tower once more, Samuel started the climb. Right about where Bram had fallen, rungs had been nailed to the vertical tower beams to form a ladder. The rest of the way up was easy, and he soon reached the top. He pried the cover off the gearbox. He had never seen how the mill worked, but it shouldn't be too hard to figure out. Opening his knife, he pried away some of the old hard grease, crusted with dirt that had blown in over the years.

Reaching over to the vanes, Samuel tried moving the wheel, but the complex tangle of gears didn't budge. It was frozen tight. The mill had worked once, though, and maybe he could get it working again. He scraped dirt and rust away from the nuts and bolts, checking for any damage. It looked like it only needed to be taken apart and cleaned. If he could get the gear mechanism down to the barn, he could do the job properly.

"Samuel!"

Mary was below him.

"What are you doing up there?"

"Checking to see if the windmill can be fixed." He started down the ladder.

"Do you think you can do it?"

Her skirt swirled around her legs as the wind freshened, and she stood with one hand shading her eyes against the sun. He had never seen a prettier girl. He dropped to the ground and grinned at her.

"Well? Do you think you'll be able to get it going?"

"*Ja*, for sure." Samuel wiped his greasy hands on his handkerchief and tucked it back in his waistband. "It's dirty and the vanes need repairing, but I think I can do it."

"It would sure help you keep the watering troughs full, wouldn't it?"

He patted the tower. "It sure would." Then he turned his attention to Mary. "What brings you here today?"

"We have a cow, and we need your help."

Samuel had started walking with her toward the barn and his toolbox, but now turned and stared at her. "A cow? Why did you buy a cow?"

Her eyes shifted away from his. "We didn't buy it. It was a gift."

He could guess who the gift was from. "A gift? With strings attached?"

"I don't think so."

She answered so quickly that he could tell the possibility was on her mind.

"You should have refused to take her."

"We tried." Her gaze went from the cattle in the field to the windmill. "But they wouldn't hear of it."

"And 'they' are the Troyer brothers?"

Mary nodded and finally met his eyes. "Sadie thought we should keep her, since there's no arguing with a Troyer, as she put it."

Samuel started toward the barn again and Mary came after him.

"We'll get a lot of good butter from her milk, and we'll be able to sell it along with the eggs."

"So you're still determined to make this business idea of yours work?"

Her eyebrows went up. "For sure, and it's working already. We're paying back the money Mr. Holdeman loaned us for the lumber and supplies, and we're making a bit extra, too. The chickens are doing well, and in a few months when the new chicks are grown, we'll have even more eggs to sell."

Samuel went to his workbench and opened the toolbox, but she followed him, moving around so she could see his face.

"I plan to go to the auction again tomorrow to buy more hens. Having the cow means that we'll be able to support ourselves that much sooner."

"You don't need to do all that work. I can support both of our families. That's the way *Grossdawdi* Abe wanted it, and that's the way it will be."

She stared at him, her lips pressed together. He found his gloves, put them in the toolbox and went back outside, the heavy wooden box bumping against his knee as he walked. She trotted behind him to keep up, but he didn't shorten his stride. She wasn't going to listen to reason.

"But I don't want you to support us. Ida Mae and I can take care of Sadie on our own. We don't need your help."

Samuel had reached the base of the windmill tower, but at her words he turned back. "You need my help," he said, pointing his finger and jabbing with every word, "and you're going to accept my help. I can do this. I can take care of all of us."

"I don't want your help." She spoke through gritted teeth.

A sudden thought almost made him laugh. "Then why did you come over here?"

Mary's face grew red and she stamped one foot. "All right. I came to ask for your help. But as a neighbor, not... not as someone who has to take care of us."

He turned around and leaned against the tower. "What do you need my help with?"

"We need a bigger pasture since we have both Chester and Schmetterling."

"Who?"

"The cow. Sadie named her." She swiped at a lock of hair that had escaped her *kapp*. "We need to move the fence to enlarge the pasture. It shouldn't be too hard."

Samuel set his toolbox on the ground. "And just where are you going to move the fence? The new chicken coop takes up the only space."

"We want to use the back part of Sadie's land. Dale planted corn there, but I'm sure it was a mistake. He must not know where your land ends and Sadie's begins."

"There was no mistake." Samuel rubbed the back of his neck. *Grossdawdi* Abe had handled the transfer of the land for Sadie's use, but the deed was clear. The ten acres still belonged to the Lapps. Sadie must not have told Mary of the arrangement.

"You told him to plant corn on Sadie's farm?"

"Actually, it isn't Sadie's land."

Mary stared at him for a full minute, her eyes widening, then narrowing as she took this information in.

"Sadie said it is. It was her idea to move the fence to make a larger pasture."

"You're not going to ruin good acres of growing corn."

She bit her lower lip. "I'll admit, it isn't the best pasture, but the grass will grow back."

Samuel felt the pounding in his ears before he heard it. His fists flexed. There must be a way to solve this problem before he lost his temper completely. He sent a quick look up at the white clouds hanging in the deep blue sky. Count to ten. He could hear *Mamm*'s voice echoing from his memory. She would tell her boys to count whenever they started one of their many fights.

"One...two...three..."

He glanced at Mary, who was staring at him with her eyes wide. He forced the muscles in his face to relax into a more pleasant expression.

"Four...five...six..."

"What are you doing?"

"Counting to ten. Seven...eight..."

"Why?"

He clenched his teeth. "Because it's better than yelling at you."

"Why would you yell at me?"

"Because you aren't listening to reason." His voice rose and he finished counting. "Nine...ten."

"Do you feel better?"

"*Ja.* I feel better." His voice was a growl.

"Then you'll help us move the fence?"

"*Ne.* I won't help you move the fence!" He started counting again as she turned on her heel and walked away.

Chapter Twelve

After leaving Samuel in the barnyard, Mary stormed along the path leading to Sadie's house. She had never met such an overbearing, stubborn, pigheaded man in her entire life. She knew men could be pushy and high-handed, but Samuel Lapp put all of them to shame.

She slowed when she reached the corner of their barn and paused to catch her breath. Sadie would not understand why she was so upset, and that could make the day end up like a buggy with a wobbly wheel. She and Ida Mae had discovered that keeping their lives calm and peaceful was the key to helping Sadie get through the day without becoming confused or anxious.

Once her breathing slowed, she went into the house. She followed the sound of humming through the kitchen and into the sewing room. Ida Mae sat in the rocking chair, putting the last stitches on a quilt block.

She looked up when Mary stepped into the room. "What has you all flustered?"

Mary pressed cool hands to her hot cheeks. "Does it show so much?" When Ida Mae nodded, she plopped onto the other rocking chair. "Where is Sadie?"

"Lying down for a while. She might be sleeping."

"We have a problem."

Ida Mae laid her sewing in her lap. "What kind of problem?"

"Samuel says that field behind the barn isn't Sadie's."

"Whose is it then? Sadie is sure it's part of her farm."

Mary shook her head. "Samuel thinks it is his, and he has this notion that it's his job to take care of us. Something about his *grossdawdi*. He says he won't help us at all."

Ida Mae picked her sewing up again. "How is he going to take care of us if he doesn't help us?"

Mary pushed her foot against the floorboards, sending the chair into an agitated rocking. "That isn't what I meant. He isn't going to help us move the fence because he says the corn field is his. He wants us to give Schmetterling back to the Troyers and stop trying to support ourselves." Mary got up and paced to the end of the room and back. "If I didn't know better, I would think he regards us as two more of his sisters, under his thumb and at his beck and call."

Ida Mae laid the finished quilt block on a pile of other blocks on the table and picked up two small triangles to stitch together.

"And if I didn't know better," she said, threading her needle, "I would say he thinks of you as much more than another sister."

Mary spun on her heel to face her sister. "What did you say?"

"Shh. Don't wake Sadie." Ida Mae twisted the thread around her needle to make a knot. "I think he's in love with you."

Mary sank into the rocking chair again, shaking her head. "He can't be."

"You haven't seen the way he looks at you." Ida Mae

took five tiny stitches in her seam and pulled the thread through. "And I've seen the looks you give him."

"I don't give him looks."

"You might not think so, but you do."

"But…" Mary bit her lower lip, then went on. "You know that I am never going to marry anyone. How can I? No man wants a woman with my…past…for his wife." She bit her lip again to keep the welling tears from falling.

"So you're not denying that you have feelings for him."

Mary slouched back in the chair and rocked it gently. A swaying branch outside the window caught her eye. She didn't want to think about her feelings for Samuel. She wanted things to go on the way they had been. When did life get so difficult?

"All right. I think I like him." She rocked her chair harder. "At least I do when he isn't being so…so…"

"…much like a man?" Ida Mae grinned at her.

The grin swept Mary's melancholy mood away and she smiled back. "Even so, I'm never getting married."

"Martin Troyer would marry you, even if he knew… what happened. It wouldn't matter to him."

Mary shuddered at the thought of being married to Martin. The thought of his hands holding hers, of being alone with him… Dark clouds swirled and she took a deep breath. "I can never, never marry Martin. He wouldn't be…patient, or tender or thoughtful. He only thinks about himself."

"And you know this from one short picnic?"

With a nod, Mary leaned forward in her chair. "You have seen how he treats Peter. If he can be so thoughtless and selfish with his brother, how do you think he would treat a wife?" She leaned back and rocked again. "Any woman married to him would be little more than a slave."

Ida Mae looked up from her sewing. "I'm so glad we don't have to go on another picnic with them."

"Are you sure you want to refuse Peter so quickly?"

Ida Mae threw a scrap of cloth across the space between them as Mary covered her mouth to keep a burst of laughter from escaping. Then she looked at Ida Mae's red cheeks and couldn't help it. They both giggled with hissing whispers.

"Don't wake up Sadie!"

Ida Mae laughed. "I… I'm…not the one…who's making all the noise." She glanced at Mary and the giggles started again.

"We have to tell Martin and Peter that there will be no more picnics," Mary said when she finally caught her breath.

"You'll have to do it." Ida Mae's face was bright pink from laughing.

"Why me?"

"Because if I tell Peter, it won't do any good. Martin will never pay attention to what he says."

Mary nodded. "Martin won't listen to either of you. But what makes you think he'll be any different with me?"

"You're strong and stubborn. You'll make him listen."

"I'm not sure being stubborn will be enough." Mary sighed and laid her head against the back of the chair. "Do you think we should give back the cow?"

"After Sadie already named her? I don't think we'll be able to."

Mary rocked while Ida Mae sewed in silence for a few minutes. The sound of a buggy horse clip-clopping on the road drifted in the open windows. The trotting horse slowed, then stopped.

Ida Mae put her sewing on the table. "Someone is here."

She went to the back door while Mary stayed sitting in the rocker.

Voices drifting from the kitchen told her that their visitor was Effie Hopplestadt calling on Sadie. Since the season had turned to early summer, the weekly quiltings had ended until after the garden produce was stored away in the fall. But Sadie's friends still dropped in on her regularly.

Sadie must have heard Effie come in, because her voice joined the others, but Mary still sat and rocked. She should get up and greet Effie, but her mind kept going back to Ida Mae's comment that Samuel was in love with her.

Mary closed her eyes. Samuel wasn't in love with her. If he was, he wouldn't have argued with her the way he had this morning. But if someone had to be in love with her, he wouldn't be a bad choice. Much better than Martin Troyer. That man caused her thoughts to go down dark paths.

Samuel, though... Even if they did argue, she still looked forward to talking to him every day.

A smile crept its way onto her face as she gazed out the window. *Ja*, she looked forward to seeing him again.

Samuel's mood worsened as the sun sped toward noon. After Mary left, he climbed the tower and unfastened the wind wheel from the shaft, lowering it with a rope until it lay on the ground in three pieces. Then he worked at the bolts holding the gearbox to the platform until they finally came loose and the gearbox was ready to follow the wind wheel to the ground. He tied the rope firmly and lowered it, bracing himself on the ladder.

Only then did he let himself look toward Sadie's farm, but Mary wasn't coming back to apologize.

"Leave it to her to find a way to ruin the corn field," he said to Tilly as he climbed down the ladder. "She'll probably move the fence herself, and get hurt in the process."

His feet touched the ground and Tilly's ears swiveled back and forth.

Samuel untied the gearbox from the rope, lifted it and started toward the barn.

"Don't look at me that way, Tilly-girl. I know you're on her side."

He glanced back once to see Tilly standing with her hip cocked and her ears swiveled toward her tail. *Ja*, those women stuck together.

Once the gearbox was on the workbench, Samuel spent the rest of the morning dismantling the gears and shafts and cleaning the old grease off the mechanism. Kerosene helped dissolve the gummy residue and he soon had the pieces apart and cleaned.

After dinner, he got his grease pot and started putting the machine back together.

"Hello, Samuel."

Samuel turned to see Preacher Jonas.

"Esther told me you were working in the barn cellar."

"Good afternoon and welcome."

Samuel grabbed a rag to clean his hands but Jonas stopped him.

"Don't let me keep you from your work." He stepped closer to see what Samuel was doing. "I didn't know you could repair machines like this."

Samuel held a bolt up to the light to check the size. "I've never tried before. But the windmill hasn't worked for years and I thought it was worth seeing what was wrong with it." He set a gear in place and tightened the bolt.

Jonas watched as Samuel placed another gear so that it interlocked with the first one. Cleaned and with fresh grease, the pieces went together easily.

"Where did you learn how to do that?"

"Rebuild a gearbox?" Samuel shrugged. "I just remember where the pieces go." He set the shaft in place and turned the mechanism. "It looks like it's working." He tightened a couple of the bolts and spun the shaft. The gears moved like clockwork.

He picked it up and started toward the mill tower. "I could use your help."

"For sure. What can I do?"

"I'll climb up with the rope while you tie the gearbox and wheel pieces to the other end. Then I'll be able to haul them up as I need them, without having to climb up and down this tower."

Jonas helped as Samuel reassembled the windmill mechanism and reattached the wheel. He climbed down the tower and released the brake, and both men watched as the mill turned into the wind and picked up speed.

"You're certain you've never fixed a windmill before?" Jonas asked.

"I've never fixed any machine before."

"You seem to have a knack for it. That would have taken me a week of fruitless toil, and then it still wouldn't run."

Samuel's chest warmed at the other man's words. Praise for a job well done. He had never heard anyone say anything like that before. Not to him.

He cleared his throat and wiped the grease off his hands. "You didn't make the trip over here to help me with a little chore."

Jonas was still watching the mill turn in the wind. "I came to tell you that your name won't come up at the council meeting. Your accuser will be repenting instead. It turns out that he was spreading a tale to get attention for himself."

"Who?"

"Peter Troyer." The older man looked at Samuel as he

said the name. "Don't harbor hard feelings toward him. He is truly repentant for the trouble he caused."

Samuel waited for the roar in his ears and the pounding in his head that always signaled that his temper was flaring, but it didn't come. Instead, he saw Peter's face in his mind, a little bit homely and perpetually sad.

"I'm not angry with him. But I feel sorry for the man. He is always in his brother's shadow." Samuel rubbed at a stubborn grease spot on his left palm. He knew what it was like to live in someone's shadow, never seen for who he was. Always judged by someone else's actions.

"I hope that you will tell him that you forgive him after he repents in front of the church."

Samuel nodded and Jonas watched the mill again.

"I wonder if you'd do something else for me."

"For sure."

"Some of the others in the community have windmills that are giving them problems. Vernon Hershberger for one. His mill creaks and groans with every turn, but with his broken leg, he can't hope to climb the tower to fix it. There are other older members, too, who could use the help of someone who knows what he's doing. Would you consider going around to the different farms? Give a hand to whoever needs it?"

Samuel shrugged. "That shouldn't be any trouble. I'll go over to Vernon's in the morning and see what's going on there."

That put a smile on Jonas's face. "You know, the Samuel Lapp of a few months ago would have found some excuse to stay home."

"The Samuel Lapp of a few months ago didn't know he had anything to offer." Samuel grinned back. "Anything I can do to help, I'd like to."

Jonas clapped him on the shoulder before he started

back toward his buggy. "Someone has been having a good influence on you. You should keep spending time with her."

Samuel's grin widened. Perhaps he would invite Mary to go to the Hershbergers' with him tomorrow. That would help them get past their disagreement about the fence.

On Tuesday morning Samuel pulled into Sadie's drive. Those puppies were back in his stomach, rolling over each other as they tried to fight their way out. He laid a hand on his waist to try to quiet them down, but then Mary came from the henhouse with a basket of eggs and they started all over again. She blushed when she saw him but continued to the house without a greeting.

Samuel climbed down from the buggy and met Mary at the door, opening it for her.

"Mary, I—"

She walked into the house without even looking at him. Sadie peered out the open door from her seat at the table and beckoned him into the kitchen. When he shook his head, she came out onto the porch, closing the kitchen door behind her.

"What are you doing out here?"

"I was going to talk to Mary, but she doesn't seem to want to see me."

"You're going to let a little thing like that stop you from talking to her?"

Samuel shrugged. "What can I do? She just walked right by without even looking at me."

"You need to go after her. Don't let her treat you like that."

He grinned. "This is your niece we're talking about, not some misbehaving horse."

Sadie's eyes twinkled. "You go after her. She wants to see you, but she's afraid for some reason."

"Probably because I yelled at her yesterday."

The elderly woman patted his arm. "So the two of you had a disagreement. That won't stop you." She turned to go back into the house.

"Stop me from what?"

But she continued into the kitchen as if she hadn't heard him. He had no choice but to follow her.

Ida Mae was washing dishes, but Mary was nowhere to be seen. The basket of eggs sat on the kitchen table.

"Good morning, Samuel," Ida Mae said. "Do you want me to find Mary for you?"

His teeth ground together, but he couldn't decide if he should get angry or not. "If you just point out the way she went, I'll go find her."

Ida Mae grinned. "Back there," she tilted her head down the short hallway off the kitchen. "She went into the sewing room."

Samuel hung his hat on the hook by the door and headed that way. As he passed Sadie's seat at the table, she smiled and sipped her coffee.

The room was airy and bright. A table for cutting fabric was in the center, and near the window were two rocking chairs. Mary stood at one of the windows as if she was waiting for him.

"Why didn't you talk to me?" Samuel stopped, cautious. "You walked right past me as if I wasn't there."

"I won't talk to you until you apologize."

Samuel put his hands on his hips and stared at the floor. *One...two...three...*

"Oh, no, you don't." Mary stepped across the room toward him. "You stop counting and apologize to me."

He gritted his teeth. *Four...five...*

"Well?"

Bah! Women!

"I apologize for…" Samuel scratched his head. "What am I apologizing for?"

"For being pigheaded and not helping us move the fence so Schmetterling could have the larger pasture she needs."

Samuel met her eyes. Instead of the stormy anger he expected, she was almost smiling.

"You didn't move that fence on your own, did you? Because if you let that cow destroy my corn—"

"There is no need to get upset. We haven't moved any fences. Not yet."

The light coming in the window made her face glow as she turned toward him. She was beautiful.

"Samuel, are you going to apologize or not? That's why you came over here, isn't it?"

She had him so turned around he was surprised he could remember his own name.

"I'm going over to Vernon Hershberger's to repair his windmill. I thought you might want to come along."

"Why would I want to go watch you look at a windmill?" Her toe started tapping. "Especially since you haven't apologized to me yet."

Samuel stifled a groan. A noise from the kitchen sounded like Sadie laughing.

"All right, all right. I apologize for…" He raised his eyebrows at her.

"For refusing to help me move the fence."

His eyebrows went down. "I apologize for making you angry so that you stormed off." His own toe started twitching. "Now, will you come with me or not?"

She crossed her arms and looked out the window. Her cheeks became pinker by the minute. Her profile was perfect, with her nose turning up a bit at the tip. He could watch her all morning.

"I need to go into Shipshewana today to sell the eggs we've collected."

"We can go to Shipshewana, too. We'll make a day of it."

Her eyes narrowed as she turned to him. "What do you mean?"

"We'll take a picnic for a lunch we can eat at the park in town. And then if I get done at Vernon's early enough, maybe we'll take a drive down by Emma Lake before we come home."

"Why?"

He shrugged, wanting her to agree to the outing, but refusing to force her into it. "We're friends, aren't we? And I don't want us going on the way we did yesterday."

"So we're just two friends spending the day together?"

Samuel grinned. "Maybe I'll make you climb up Vernon's windmill tower with me."

"I won't climb any tower, but I'll go with you. Who knows? We might even have a good time." She started toward the kitchen. "I have to clean the eggs and pack a picnic first."

Samuel watched her skirt swish around her legs as she went down the hallway.

"I'll wait."

The drive to Vernon Hershberger's farm, just a mile or so south of Shipshewana, was enjoyable. Mary had sold four dozen eggs and a pound of butter. At this rate, she would have her debt to Mr. Holdeman paid off in only a couple months.

Samuel didn't speak much as he drove, but when they went by a pasture with some mares and foals, he pointed them out to her.

"There are a bunch of new work horses for someone."

One of the youngsters trotted along the fence as they passed, nose in the air.

"They are very cute, aren't they?"

He nodded. "They look fine. The dams are in good shape, which means the foals should be healthy and strong."

Mary remembered the empty stalls in Samuel's barn. "Do you think you'll ever have a team again?"

He was silent as they went past the horses and came to a field filled with growing corn. "I haven't thought much about it. Horses cost money, and there isn't very much of that for anyone these days."

Samuel turned Tilly into the next farm lane. Mary didn't have to look for the windmill. The contraption creaked and groaned from the top of the tower next to the barn.

"This is the Hershbergers'?"

"*Ja.* Are you ready to climb that windmill with me?"

Samuel jumped out of the buggy and reached for Mary's hand to steady her as she climbed down. His grip was firm, but tender.

"I think I'll visit with Myrtle and the children while you're working."

He grinned. "If you're sure you want to."

Mary spent the time visiting with Vernon's wife while Samuel worked on the windmill. Vernon could get around with his crutches and had gone outside to watch Samuel.

"What can I do to help?" Mary asked. She picked up Myrtle's toddling one-year-old who was about to fall into the table leg.

"If you can just hold her while I get this bread in the oven, that would be *wonderful-gut.*"

Myrtle slid five loaf pans in the oven and closed the damper to keep the heat regulated. Just as she straightened up, a crash of wooden blocks came from the front room, along with a crying voice.

"It never ends," Myrtle said.

Her smile kept Mary from being too worried as they went into the front room, where Troy and David, two and three years old, were playing with blocks. Troy's face was red with anger as Myrtle sat next to him and took the little boy on her lap.

"See?" she said, pointing at the blocks. "David is setting them back up again. There isn't anything to cry about."

"He cries because I knocked his tower over," David said.

"Why did you do that?"

"Because he knocked my barn down."

"Did pushing his tower over help you fix your barn?"

David sat back on his heels, shaking his head.

"You both need to put the blocks away. It's nap time."

The boys obeyed and then followed Myrtle up the stairs.

"I'll be right back," she said.

"Don't hurry."

Mary held the little girl, Rosie, in her arms, rocking her gently. The baby settled in against her shoulder and grew heavier with every minute. Soft breathing told Mary that the little girl was asleep.

She stood in the middle of the room, swaying slowly. She took in the two comfortable chairs, the heating stove along the wall, the toys set neatly on shelves, and the table between the chairs with a copy of the Good Book and the *Christenflicht*, the book of prayers. The aroma of baking bread drifted in from the kitchen, and from the stairway came Myrtle's soft voice as she helped the boys into their beds for their afternoon naps.

Tears welled in Mary's eyes and she buried her nose in Rosie's curls. This had been her dream. The home, the children, the husband…a man who cherished her and their life together. Lately she had felt the pull of that dream again, but she pushed it away. A man like Martin would never be part of her life. And Samuel…if he knew her secret, he wouldn't want to go beyond being friends. She breathed in the little-girl scent and closed her eyes. Somehow she would have to learn to be content loving other people's children.

After Myrtle took Rosie into the downstairs bedroom to lay her down, she came back to join Mary.

"*Ach*, nap time is my favorite part of the afternoon," she said, dropping into a chair. "Sit down and we can have a nice, uninterrupted visit. I miss the weekly quiltings, even though I didn't make it very often this winter. I was glad to meet you and your sister at the last one, though. How are you getting on with Sadie?"

"We're adjusting." Mary took the other chair and relaxed. "Sadie usually doesn't need much care at all, but we're there in case she does need us."

"I'm happy you came today, but I was surprised to see you with Samuel Lapp." Her face turned bright red and she laughed. "I guess Samuel is the one I'm surprised to see. When Preacher Jonas stopped by yesterday and told Vernon that Samuel would help him with the windmill, I had a hard time believing it."

Mary's mind went back to her first Sunday in Shipshewana, when Martin bullied Samuel about helping Vernon with his plowing.

"The men got the fields plowed and planted?"

"They did it all in one day. It is such a blessing to be part of a close church like ours. With Vernon's injury, we would never have been able to get all the work done."

Myrtle sat up and looked out the window. "There's Samuel climbing down the tower." She stood up. "Let's go see if he's done."

Mary followed her friend out into the barnyard, where Samuel and Vernon stood, watching the wind wheel spin in the breeze without any squeaking or moaning. Vernon turned as his wife came to his side.

"Listen to that quiet," he said. "No more shrieking during storms."

Samuel stood with his arms crossed, and Mary could tell he was pleased.

"You could have engaged the brake if it got too bad."

Vernon shook his head. "I thought about it, but we need the pump to keep working. Myrtle couldn't spend her time out here pumping water, and I have been in no shape to get around, either." He hobbled the two steps over to Samuel and put out his hand. "*Denki*, Samuel. You have a gift for working with machines. I had no idea."

Samuel shook Vernon's hand. "Neither did I, until I tried to repair my own wind pump."

"I appreciate everything you've done."

Mary watched Samuel's face as his expression flitted from denial to acceptance and then to irritation as his brow lowered. Was it so hard for him to accept the thanks of a friend?

Samuel finally nodded and turned to get in the buggy, pushing Mary ahead of him.

"Goodbye, Myrtle." Mary waved as she stepped into the buggy. "I enjoyed our visit."

Myrtle waved as Samuel slapped the reins on Tilly's back and headed down the lane toward the road.

"We left awfully fast."

Samuel still didn't say anything, but drove with his gaze set on the road ahead.

"That was a good thing you did, using your skill to help Vernon and Myrtle. But why did we leave so quickly?"

"I don't like it when folks start thanking me like that,

as if I'm something special." Samuel hunched his shoulders. "I suppose you're used to it."

Mary let his words sink in as Tilly trotted south. Samuel was right. There were things she did well, and she helped others whenever she could. But she never thought about it beyond knowing that was the way the people of the community lived together.

"That feeling you get when you help others might be new to you," she said, laying a hand on his arm, "but I think you'll learn to like it."

Chapter Thirteen

Samuel kept driving south until they reached the county road leading to the little town of Emma. As he turned Tilly at the corner, he dared to glance at Mary. She had been silent for the last two miles, ever since she said he might learn to like helping others. With a sigh, he concentrated on the road ahead again.

She couldn't know how wrong she was. He was a Lapp. He had seen the surprise in Vernon's eyes when they arrived at the farm. And then the man had been so suspicious that he had watched Samuel's every move. Nothing had changed. He still lived in *Daed*'s shadow.

"It's such a beautiful afternoon," Mary said.

He nodded.

"Look how green everything is. Summer is getting close."

"It's green because of the rain we've had, and the warm nights. It makes the grass grow."

She nodded, smiling at him. "That's what I said. Summer is getting close."

He felt a grin coming in spite of his sour mood. "Emma is just ahead. Do you want to stop at the store for a soda pop?"

Mary stiffened. He felt it in her elbow that brushed against his as they sat next to each other in the buggy seat.

"There's nothing wrong with a soda pop, is there?"

She took a deep breath, her eyes closed.

"Mary?"

Her eyes flashed open and she stared at him. "I... I guess we could have a soda."

He pulled Tilly to a stop outside the general store. "What flavor do you want? Grape? Orange?"

Her hands shook. "Not orange. Grape. Or strawberry. Anything but orange."

Samuel hesitated before taking the bottles of pop from the cooler on the store's broad front porch. Something was wrong. Mary sat in the buggy seat, staring at her lap. Her lips were moving as if she was reciting something to herself, or...counting. She continued her strange behavior as he used the bottle opener on the outside of the cooler.

He went into the store and laid a dime on the counter, nodding to the clerk, then hurried back to the buggy.

"Here you go."

She stared at the bottle of grape soda he handed her.

"I chose grape. It's my favorite."

Mary finally took it from him, but she didn't drink it. He turned south and drove out of town to the little lake that lapped against the shore, just yards from the road. He slowed Tilly to a walk. Mary still hadn't taken a drink of her soda, and she still hadn't said a word.

She startled when he drove Tilly off the road into the grass where someone had set up a bench under a tree. He pulled the hitching weight out from under the buggy seat and fastened it to Tilly's bridle. The short rope would allow the horse to graze in the shade while he and Mary talked. He went back to the buggy and held Mary's pop bottle while she climbed down, then he led her to the bench. It was time to find out what was going on.

"Now," he said as he handed the bottle back to her. "Tell me what's wrong."

She stared at him. "Who said anything is wrong?"

"As soon as I mentioned getting some soda pop, you changed. You haven't even taken a drink." He tipped his own bottle up to drain the last of his grape soda. Just as he thought, she was going to deny that anything was amiss.

She passed her bottle from one hand to the other.

He leaned toward her. "Whatever it is, it's making you into someone other than the Mary I know. I've suspected for a long time that someone has hurt you, and now it's time for you to tell me about it."

She shook her head. He took the bottle from her and set it next to her on the bench.

Samuel tried again. "My *mamm* was a wonderful, gentle, kind woman." Thinking about her made his eyes itch. "But she was the victim of *Daed*'s temper."

Mary looked at him.

"She never told anyone, but we children knew." He cleared his throat. "I wonder how different her life would have been if she had confided in Sadie, or her parents or someone."

Mary sniffed. "I've told Ida Mae about it."

He was right. There was something wrong.

"I'm glad you told your sister, but it's still bothering you, isn't it?" He scooted closer to her. "We're friends, aren't we?"

She nodded.

"You can tell me anything. I want to help you."

"Ida Mae said I should tell you, but you'll never want to see me again." Her voice was raspy, almost a whisper.

He slid so he was next to her on the bench and took her icy hands in his. "I don't think you could say anything that would cause that."

She glanced at him. "It's terrible."

"I thought it would be."

She chewed on her bottom lip.

"Why is the soda pop a problem?"

"He…he bought some for me. Orange."

He? Samuel's head started pounding, but he kept his voice quiet.

"Orange soda?"

She nodded.

"Who is he?"

"A man…a boy I met when I worked at a diner back home."

"An Amishman?"

She shook her head. Samuel squeezed the cold fingers and sat back a little, relaxing. She was only embarrassed because she had let an *Englischer* buy a soda pop for her. The way she had been acting, he had thought the problem was much worse.

"There isn't anything that bad about sharing a soda pop—"

"We didn't just sh-share a soda." She took a deep, shaky breath. "He…took advantage of me. He forced himself on me."

She pulled her hands from his grasp and walked down the grassy lawn to the edge of the lake, but Samuel couldn't move. Could he have heard her right? This wasn't about sharing a soda with an *Englischer*.

Ice filled his arms, his legs, his core. Everything was frozen as he watched her stand on the shore of the lake with her back to him. He sank his head into his hands and a moan escaped. What could he say to her? How could she live after experiencing that… The ice fled as quickly as it had formed and the anger came roaring in. His fist slammed on the bench, knocking the soda bottle off, spilling the grape pop onto the ground, where it disappeared into the grass.

Never to be recovered.

Mary still stood looking out over the lake as he walked up behind her and grasped her shoulders with both hands. He pulled her back against him.

"It wasn't your fault." He whispered the words, close to her ear as his cheek brushed her *kapp*.

A tear dripped from her chin as he put his arms around her.

"You don't have to be nice to me. I can guess what you must think." She stepped away from his embrace, but he grasped her hand.

"I don't hate you."

She sniffed. "But now, every time you look at me, you'll think about what happened. What I did."

A stone dropped in Samuel's middle. If he ever needed the Good Lord to hear his prayers, now was the time. He needed to say whatever she needed to hear.

He turned Mary around and tipped her face toward his. "*Ne*, that isn't true. Every time I look at you, I'll think about what a strong woman you are. You have suffered, and survived, and you will never suffer like that again. I promise."

She buried her face in his shirt and he held her close, tucked under his chin.

Mary kept her arms folded tight as she rode in the buggy, her knees pressed together and as far away from Samuel as she could get. If they were closer to home, she would get out and walk the rest of the way, but the only thing worse than sitting in the same buggy as Samuel would to be alone. Vulnerable.

Why had she told him her secret? Mary chewed her

lower lip. She knew why. The soda pop had brought back such strong memories. Memories that clamored for release. And in a way, she felt better. A tight knot inside her had loosened and she could breathe easier.

But things would never be the same between the two of them. Samuel would never feel relaxed and comfortable around her again.

Thunder rolled from the west, and the breeze gusted, rocking the buggy. Samuel urged Tilly to a faster trot and glanced at Mary, the creases around his eyes showing that he was concerned. Even worried.

"A storm is coming, but I'm going to try to make it home before the worst of it hits."

Lightning flashed in the distance and Tilly's ears went back. Samuel kept a firm grip on the reins and paid attention to his driving instead of her.

Tilly jumped at the next crack of thunder, and Samuel leaned forward, concentrating on his driving.

"That storm is getting closer. Will you roll down the rain curtains? I don't want to risk taking my hands off the reins with Tilly as skittish as she is."

Mary untied the rolled curtain on her side and lowered it, snapping it into place all the way down. But to reach the other one, she would have to get past Samuel somehow.

"Do you want me to drive while you do your side?"

He shook his head, his gaze on the road ahead. "Here." Samuel lifted his arms so she could climb over him, under the reins, but she hesitated. "Come on, scoot over there before Tilly gets spooked again."

She had no choice. She ducked under his outstretched arms and stepped over his legs while he slid to her spot on the buggy seat. Now she could reach the curtain and fasten the snaps, and they were closed in the cozy buggy just in time. Big raindrops pelted the roof.

Samuel said something, but she couldn't hear him over the noise.

"What?" she shouted.

He leaned toward her and spoke close to her ear. "We're almost to our farm. I'm going to stop there until the storm is over and take you home after."

She nodded, showing she understood. Tilly trotted faster, but Samuel still gripped the reins, keeping her from breaking into a full gallop. If she panicked, they would be in trouble. But Samuel's firm grip told the horse he was in control and she trusted him.

Samuel turned up the lane, past the house and on to the barn.

He pulled Tilly to a stop in front of the closed barn door. "You hold her until I get the doors open, then let her go in. Whatever you do, don't let go of the reins."

Mary nodded, grasping the leather reins in shaky hands. Just as Samuel unfastened the rain curtain, lightning flashed again, sending Tilly into a half rear, her front feet striking at the barn door. Samuel sent Mary a worried look, but she smiled, trying to look confident.

Samuel opened one of the doors, and then the other, sliding them out of the way. As soon as the opening appeared, Tilly tried to leap into the shelter, but Mary was ready for her. Bracing her feet, Mary leaned back on the reins, keeping the frightened horse under control. Tilly walked into the barn, straining at the reins the whole way, but Mary didn't let up until Tilly reached the gate of her stall and Samuel took her bridle, stopping her.

Mary climbed down from the buggy and shook her arms, releasing the tense muscles. The barn echoed with the pounding rain on the roof high above them, but Samuel grinned at her in the dim light. He looked triumphant, as if they had defeated a monster rather than escaped a rainstorm.

"You did a *wonderful-gut* job," he shouted. "Will you close the doors while I take care of Tilly?"

Mary slid the big doors closed while Samuel lit the lantern to chase away the shadows. He unhitched the buggy, then removed Tilly's bridle and slipped a halter over her head. Tying her to the hitching post, he got a towel from a pile nearby. He crooned to Tilly as he wiped her face dry and gave her an old apple from a bucket. He cared for her as tenderly as he would a child.

As tenderly as he had held her when she confessed what had happened. Samuel didn't seem to hate her, and hadn't turned away from her, even when he had learned the worst about her.

Shivering, Mary moved toward him, craving the security of his strength and the warmth of his company.

"Can I help?"

"For sure. I'll take the harness off while you rub Tilly down."

"She's soaked through to the skin. Do you have some warm mash for her?"

"I'll heat some up in the barn cellar." The thunder boomed, sounding like the center of the storm was above their heads. "If the storm ever lets up."

They worked in silence since talking was nearly impossible with the rain pounding on the roof. By the time Mary had toweled off Tilly's back and was working on her front legs, the rain had eased. Samuel had hung the harness on its pegs and had wiped each strap, then he grabbed another towel and started rubbing down Tilly's hind legs.

When they were done, he led Tilly into her stall and poured a measure of oats into her feed box while Mary opened the small door next to the big barn door. The thunder and lightning had passed, but rain still poured down in steady streams. Samuel joined her and peered out.

"Look there." He pointed to the west, where a shaft of sunlight had broken out of the clouds. "The storm is nearly over. We'll wait for a few moments, then we can go to the house."

Mary shivered in her damp clothes and Samuel moved closer. Was he going to hold her in his arms again? Part of her recoiled from the thought, but another part remembered his solid strength and the complete safety she had felt by the lakeshore. The first time she had truly felt safe in months.

He knew her secret, but he hadn't shunned her. His acceptance had softened her heart and she leaned toward him, longing for his strong arms around her.

Samuel, standing behind her, rubbed her upper arms, then pulled her close.

"You're cold." His breath was warm and moist in her ear.

"Not very cold."

"Enough to give me an excuse to put my arms around you."

She turned in his arms and looked up at him. She had to know, to hear him say it again. "Do you want to do that, knowing…what you know about me?"

He wiped at her cheek with his thumb. "I told you, I don't blame you for what happened."

It was too good to be true. "You say that now, but what about the future?"

"I've told you about my *daed*."

She nodded.

"What you went through has left you wounded. What *Daed* did to my *mamm* left its mark, too."

Mary saw the pain on his face as he relived the memories. His arms dropped to his sides as he gazed out the door at the rain.

"Sometimes it was a black eye. Once it was a broken arm. Other times the bruises were hidden, but I knew they were there." He sighed. "I wish I could have helped her."

"You were only a boy."

"I'm not a boy anymore." His hand shook as he reached for hers. "I couldn't protect *Mamm*, but perhaps I can stand between you and your past." He didn't look at her, but shut his eyes, as if pushing away his own memories.

Mary drew back a little, looking into his face. "I've told you that you aren't your father, and this is proof. He didn't protect and care for your mother, but when you heard of my problem, that's the first thing you wanted to do." She reached up and traced a line down his cheek to his chin. "You are a gentle and tender man, Samuel. And I… I trust you to take care of me."

He looked at her then, his smile grim. "Don't trust me too far, Mary. I may not be my *daed*, but—"

She rose on her toes and kissed his cheek. "You aren't your *daed*. I see a lot of Bram in you, and from what Sadie says, your *grossdawdi* Abe, too. I do trust you."

He kissed her then, pulling her to himself and claiming her with a kiss so light she almost didn't feel it. The kisses continued to her cheek, her ear, and then he tucked her under his chin, surrounded by his arms.

"I will try my best."

Samuel picked his way around mud puddles the next morning. Last night's storm had been powerful, and it had brought plenty of rain. Tilly stood in the pasture, her side to the rising sun, hip cocked and head down. Her ear flicked at a fly, but there was no other movement.

The stock watering trough was full, so Samuel threw

the brake, disengaging the windmill. The wheel would still spin in the wind, but wouldn't pump the water, wasting it.

The next chore was cleaning the harness after the soaking it got in last night's rain. Samuel pushed the big barn doors open and pulled Tilly's harness down from its pegs. He laid it on the workbench and grabbed the can of saddle soap off the shelf, setting to work. Methodically, he detached each piece of harness and rubbed the soap into it, cleaning and conditioning the leather. As he worked, his mind drifted right back to Mary.

He had told her that he didn't hate her for the attack, that she wasn't to blame. But that unknown man…had he been punished for causing Mary such grief? Did he even know how much he had hurt her? Someone should do something. He should do something.

Rubbing harder at the harness, he pushed that thought from his mind. Samuel stretched and rolled his shoulders, trying to relieve the tension that had crept in. He wanted to protect her, but who was he protecting her from? She hadn't said who her attacker had been, only that it was a young man in Ohio. No wonder she jumped every time a strange man came near. She was worried that the scoundrel would try to follow her to Indiana.

By the time he finished cleaning the harness and had put it away, he had run through five or six possibilities of what would happen if a strange *Englischer* started nosing around. And by the time he finished cleaning Tilly's box stall he had imagined every outcome, from Mary's panicked flight to another community where he would never see her again to her welcoming smile when the man showed up.

When that scene flitted through his imagination, he slammed his fist into the post next to the stall, making the entire barn quiver.

Suddenly, he had to see Mary. Last night, after the
storm, he had walked her home. But even though she had
let him hold her hand, there had been no more kisses. He
had to know...had he imagined the sweetness of holding her in his arms? The closeness he had felt was something he craved. He wanted to be that close to her again.
Every day.

He washed quickly in the watering trough, splashing
water in his hair and scrubbing his hands. A tune found
its way out in a whistle as he strode along the path. His
steps quickened as he imagined the smile that would light
Mary's face when she saw him.

When he reached Sadie's, Martin Troyer's buggy was
in the yard and voices came from the barn. He headed that
way, but stopped just outside the door. Martin was inside
with Mary facing him.

"I told you. Ida Mae and I won't go on any more picnics
with you." Her voice sounded strained. Tired.

Martin took a step closer to her. "The picnic isn't important. I've learned everything about you that I need to
know. I'll ask Bishop to announce the wedding next week,
and we can marry in July."

Even from this distance, Samuel saw the panic in
Mary's eyes. She shook her head.

"I've been waiting a long time to find someone like
you," Martin said. His voice had become tender, almost
petulant. "You will be the perfect wife for me. You're
young and strong. We'll have a big family with plenty of
sons and daughters to carry on after me."

Mary shook her head again as Martin stepped closer
and took her hand. "I don't want to marry you."

"You'll have everything you need. And when your sister marries Peter, you'll even have her close by."

Martin grasped her shoulder, but Mary shrugged his

hand off and stepped back until she was pressed against the center post.

"I won't marry you." She shook her head. "I won't."

"Why not?" Martin stepped closer to her, trapping her against the post. "Don't you see? You're perfect for me." He traced the line of her jaw with a stubby finger.

Mary wrenched her face away from him.

Samuel had seen enough. He stepped into the barn.

"I think she has refused you, Martin."

The older man jumped at the sound of his voice, dropping his hands and taking a step away from Mary. The grateful look on her face gave Samuel the courage he needed.

"I think it's time for you to leave."

"This isn't any concern of yours, Lapp." Martin's face grew red. "This is between me and Mary."

"It is my concern, because Mary and I are friends." Samuel felt the familiar, tight burn pushing its way into his head, but ignored the warning. "I heard her say she doesn't want to marry you, but you aren't listening to her."

Martin turned toward Samuel as Mary moved away from him, toward Chester's stall.

"She's a woman who needs someone to take care of her." Martin's voice rose as he spoke. "I can do that for her better than anyone, whether she thinks so now or not. She'll learn."

Samuel's head throbbed. He took a step closer to Martin, clenching his fists.

"She's a woman who knows her own mind and she will marry the man she chooses."

Martin laughed. "And who will that be? You? That just proves what I was saying. She needs someone to help her and guide her so she doesn't make a terrible mistake."

Samuel grabbed Martin's shirt and yanked him close.

"The mistake would be marrying you, Troyer." The words roared in his ears. Over Martin's shoulder he saw Mary let herself into Chester's stall, putting a barrier between them.

Martin tried to push him away, but Samuel's grip on his shirt was too tight.

"When she accepted the cow, she accepted me." Martin's eyes narrowed as he leaned toward Samuel. "It has already been decided and there is nothing you can do about it."

Samuel lifted his fist, pulling Martin up with it. The other man's feet scraped the floor as he tried to regain his footing. "Take the cow and leave."

Martin's face hardened. "You're just like your old *daed*, Samuel. Just like him. You're a bully and always will be." His lips thinned as he dropped his voice to a whisper. "And Mary knows it. You've lost any chance you had with her."

Samuel's grip loosened on Martin's shirt and he backed away. His heart was a heavy rock plummeting toward his feet. Martin was right. He was his father's son.

Martin straightened his shirt. "Mary can keep the cow. She'll come around."

Samuel looked toward the stall where Mary stood, staring at him with eyes wide.

Martin pushed past him. "*Ja*, for sure. She'll come around."

Samuel barely heard the other man leave. He only saw Mary slip through the outside door of the stall and disappear.

Chapter Fourteen

Mary ran around the end of the barn, wiping away tears as she went. Slipping through the gate into the pasture, she ran to the far corner, where a creek cut through and trees grew in a small grove. She jumped across the narrow stream and pushed her way through the branches until she reached the fence, hidden from prying eyes.

She had never seen Samuel when he was angry. Not like this. She bit her knuckle raw when the memory of his uncontrolled rage washed over her. If that anger was ever directed at her, she would be helpless. As helpless as she had been in the barn with Martin. As helpless as she had been in the alley... She sank to the ground as the tears overwhelmed her. Cold mud seeped through her dress, and she welcomed it, trying to keep the memories at bay. But like a barn door flung open in a stormy wind, the carefully tied and bundled thoughts flew where they would.

Samuel's angry shouts. Every groping touch of Harvey's hands. The hot look in Martin's eyes. The stones of the alleyway pressing into her back. Damp, steaming breath on her neck... She tried to wrench her thoughts away, but they wouldn't obey her. She couldn't stop the tears. Her hoarse sobs took over, wrenching her body until she was sick, and still they continued until she gave up fighting against them.

Until every one of the memories had flown through her consciousness, leaving her empty of everything except the shame. The dreadful shame. The shame that made her want to bury herself in the cold mud.

She knelt on the ground, her forehead against a tree, but her thoughts went no further than the hollow pit deep within her.

"God in Heaven…"

How could she even pray? She had no words.

"Mary!"

Samuel was calling her. Looking for her. She wiped one cheek, and then the other, trembling. How could she face him?

"Mary?"

She looked up at his voice, tender and quiet. He had found her hiding place. He dropped to his knees beside her, but she turned away from him.

"Leave me alone." She buried her face in her hands. "Go away and leave me alone."

A dead stick cracked as he moved closer.

"I'm so sorry—"

"Samuel…" Mary swallowed. She was going to be sick again. "I told you to go away. I don't want to see you."

"What I did back there—" He sniffed as if he was trying to hold back tears. "I lost control, and I'm sorry."

She stood with jerky movements. She hadn't been afraid of Samuel since she learned to know him, but now his angry expression filled her mind, blotting out the man kneeling before her.

"You think you're going to fix this, but you aren't. Don't try. Don't ask about it. Don't talk about it."

His face grew pale. Her hands shook and she clasped

them together. She hadn't made him angry, she had hurt him. Her heart wrenched, but she couldn't…she couldn't reach out to him. She couldn't survive when his expression twisted into the hunger she had seen on Martin's face. And it would change, because he was a man, with the same hunger for what every man wanted. The clawing, grasping hunger…

She turned and ran, splashing through the creek and to the house. Ida Mae and Sadie were in the kitchen, but she flew past them and up the stairs, slamming her bedroom door shut and throwing herself on the bed.

The tears flowed as if she had never cried before. Her stomach roiled. She covered her head with her pillow and sobbed into the quilt on her bed. She would never, never know the tender love of a man. Never know what it was like to be cherished as someone's wife. She would never be anyone's mother. In one horrible night, Harvey Anderson had stolen that from her, and Samuel had only proven that she could never trust any man.

Anything good that might have come out of her friendship with Samuel was gone. Destroyed. Because every time he held her close, she would relive the horror of his rage against Martin.

The sobs ended, but the despair remained. She threw the pillow off her head and sat up, wiping her hot cheeks with the heel of her hand.

"Are you all right?"

Ida Mae had pushed the door open far enough to peek through.

Mary shook her head, making it throb.

"I'll get you a cool cloth, and we'll talk."

Mary took a deep breath. "I don't want to talk."

The door pushed open farther and Sadie walked into the room. "Go get a towel." She waved Ida Mae away and sat on the bed next to Mary, sighing as she lowered herself onto the mattress.

"You didn't need to come all the way upstairs."

"I find it difficult, but not impossible." Sadie smoothed the hair off Mary's forehead. "You need us, so we came."

Ida Mae came back with a damp towel and Mary held it on her face, drinking in the coolness.

"How did your dress get so muddy?" Ida Mae asked.

Mary had forgotten the mud. She stood, moaning as she saw that the mud from her dress had soiled the quilt. She buried her face in the towel again.

Sadie pulled her back down to sit on the bed again. "Tell us what is wrong."

"I'm all right, really."

"Your *kapp* is crooked," Ida Mae said. She reached to straighten Mary's *kapp* and the hairpins fell out.

Sadie brought a small stool closer to the bed. "Sit here and I'll brush your hair while you tell us what is wrong."

Mary succumbed to Sadie's attention and relaxed on the stool, fingering the towel she still held. Sadie took long strokes with the brush that eased away all the remaining tension, leaving Mary as weak as the towel in her hands. She gave it back to Ida Mae and picked up her *kapp* from the bed where Sadie had laid it. Mary turned it in her hands. She had worn it for as long as she could remember, from the time she was a little girl. Every woman she knew wore a *kapp*, only to be removed at bedtime, and she had done the same...until the night Harvey had attacked her. Then it had fallen off as she struggled with him.

She fingered each pleat in the fine fabric.

"Sadie, why do we wear our *kapps*?"

"It is a sign of our submission to God and to our fathers or husbands. It is a sign of our humility."

Humility. The concept was as familiar to her as her

kapp. It went hand in hand with submission…she held back a shudder as she considered ever needing to submit to a husband. She was right to remain single.

Mary shook her head. "I don't feel very humble, or very much like submitting to any man."

Sadie chuckled. "Whether you feel humble or not, you must act that way. God calls us to always put others before ourselves. To obey. To serve. And to put Him above all." She finished brushing and started gathering Mary's hair into a bun. "We are to enthrone Him, not ourselves. The *kapp* is the symbol of that submission, of putting ourselves under His authority."

She took Mary's *kapp* and pinned it in place with the last of the hairpins.

"What if it doesn't work?"

"What do you mean?" Sadie sat down on the bed again and Ida Mae joined her.

Mary bit her lip and glanced at Ida Mae.

Her sister grasped her hand. "I told Sadie what happened to you. I know you wanted to keep it a secret, but Sadie asked what was bothering you—"

Mary patted her sister's knee. "That's all right. I'm glad you both know." She drew a deep breath that caught at the end. She wouldn't start crying again.

"I mean," she said, looking at Sadie, "the *kapp* is that sign, but doesn't that mean that God is supposed to protect us?"

Sadie's eyes grew wet and she bowed her head.

"*Ach*, Mary, you're learning what submission to God truly is."

She raised her head again and took Mary's hand in her own worn one. Mary stroked the soft, fragile skin with her thumb.

"You are asking where God was when you needed him

the most." She grasped Mary's hand tighter. "He was right there with you, suffering with you. And He is with you now, ready to help you understand. Our Lord suffered and died so that we could come to Him and be forgiven of our sins."

Mary shrugged. "I've heard that my whole life, in church and at home. What does that have to do with what… what happened?"

"When you can forgive that man for what he did to you, you will begin to understand the forgiveness God extends to us." Sadie leaned closer. "Humble yourself, and submit to what God is teaching you through these circumstances."

Mary pressed her lips together, thinking of Samuel's angry face as he had held Martin in his grip. "How can I do that? How can I just forgive and forget like nothing ever happened?"

Sadie shook her head. "You will never forget. But you must forgive, whether the man who attacked you is repentant or not. Forgiving him has nothing to do with him, and everything to do with you. Let God turn this terrible event to your good rather than making you fearful and bitter."

Mary sniffed. Fearful, *ja*. She had lived in fear ever since that night. But bitter? Unbidden, memories came of harsh words to Ida Mae, and to Samuel. Uncharitable thoughts about Sadie. And Martin…she had reserved her most bitter thoughts for him.

She gave Sadie's hand a gentle squeeze before releasing it.

"I think I need to spend some time alone."

Sadie gave Mary a gentle hug, then she and Ida Mae left the room, closing the door quietly behind them. She sat, considering Sadie's words. Forgiving Harvey…that would take more strength than she possessed, but perhaps she could in time.

But Samuel was different. She would see him often, perhaps daily. He had asked for her forgiveness. Could she do that? Could they ever be friends once more?

Mary changed her soiled dress for her clean one and lay down on the bed again. Tears came, but not the anguished, violent tears of earlier. These tears fell like a gentle, cleansing rain until she fell asleep.

On Friday, Samuel was surprised to see Ida Mae drive Chester up the lane to the house. He met her at the hitching rail and caught Chester's reins to hold him while Ida Mae stepped out of the buggy.

"You're on your way to town?"

Ida Mae smiled at him. She was nearly as pretty as Mary, with blue eyes instead of brown. But some unnamed sadness haunted her expression most days.

"I'm taking the eggs and butter into Shipshewana, and I thought Judith or Esther would like to go with me." She glanced toward the house. "Mary is brave enough to make the trip by herself, but not me. I'd rather have company."

"I haven't seen Mary for days." Not since she had told him to leave her alone. And he had, even though he worried about her every minute. "Is she feeling all right?"

"She has been staying close to home, taking care of the chickens and everything. And the cow, Schmetterling, takes a lot of her time."

He backed away. "I see."

Ida Mae took a step closer to him. "Sadie thought you might like to stop by sometime. Maybe tomorrow?"

Samuel rubbed his chin. "Sadie thought so?"

Ida Mae just smiled and started toward the house with Samuel following.

"What about Mary? Does she want me to come by?"

Mary's sister paused. "She hasn't said so, but I think

she misses you. I think she would like to see you again."
She put her hand on the doorknob, then turned to him.
"Tomorrow. After morning chores are done."

Samuel headed back to the barn and the work that was
waiting. Sadie and Ida Mae both thought Mary wanted to
see him, but he knew better. He had seen the frightened
look in her eyes. She feared what he had become when he
let the rage take over.

He took the manure fork from its place on the wall and
headed toward Tilly's stall, but stopped when his vision
became too blurred to see where he was going. He wiped
at his eyes with the back of his hand. The weight of what
he had done bowed his shoulders as he opened the gate to
the stall. He stared at the soiled straw. What was the use?
Why even try to clear it out? It would only have to be done
again tomorrow.

For the first time, he understood *Daed*'s need to drink.
To obliterate the pain of what he had become, what he had
done. What hope was there if he couldn't control the rage
that lurked inside him?

A call came from outside the barn. "Samuel?"

Bram. What was he doing here? Samuel wiped his eyes
again and picked up the manure fork before Bram walked
into the barn.

"There you are." Bram voice was pleasant. Carefree. "I
was passing by on my way to town and thought I'd stop
in to say hello."

Samuel shoved the fork under the straw and lifted, bal-
ancing the load. If he didn't turn around, if he didn't look
at Bram, maybe his brother would get the message that he
didn't feel like talking.

"Esther sent me out to get you. She has some bread fresh
out of the oven, and she put a pot of coffee on. She thought
you'd like to take a break while we visit."

Samuel grunted as he carried the loaded fork to the manure pile outside. When he came back in, Bram was waiting for him, leaning on the stall gate.

"If I didn't know better, I'd think you were back to your old self."

Samuel glared at him. "I never stopped being my 'old self.' I'm the same as I've ever been."

A frown passed over his brother's face. "What has happened?"

Samuel shoved the fork under the next section of wet, soiled bedding and carried it out to the pile. Bram was still waiting for an answer when he came back in.

"Who says anything has happened?"

Bram reached over the gate and grabbed his sleeve. "Put the fork down and talk to me. You're as grumpy as an old hen."

"I'm not grumpy. This is just the way I am."

Bram stared at him and Samuel gave up. He leaned the fork handle against the side of the stall and faced Bram.

"I lost my temper and acted as bad as *Daed* ever did. Worse."

"So you slipped back into his old habits."

Samuel nodded. "I can't trust myself not to do it again."

"Is that why you've stopped keeping company with Mary?"

"Esther's been talking about me?"

Bram rubbed his thumb along the top of the gate. "Actually, she asked me to stop by and talk to you. She's worried about you."

Samuel shrugged, trying not to care. "There's no reason to be worried. I'm a Lapp. Our father's son. It's just the way I am."

"I used to think you were, too. But as we've gotten reacquainted I can see that you're nothing like him."

Samuel picked at a loose splinter on the wall of the stall. He couldn't look his brother in the eye. "How can you say that?"

"We both know what drove *Daed*. It was the alcohol. I don't know why he drank, but he did, and it controlled him." Bram reached over and grasped Samuel's arm. "You aren't like him. You can ask for help. You can control your temper."

A short laugh escaped. "Obviously, I can't. You weren't there." Samuel shook his head. "You didn't see the look on Mary's face when I threw Martin out of the barn." Just like *Daed*, he had ruined everything that was good in his life.

Bram's eyebrows rose. "Mary? So you do care about her."

"If I did, I ruined it when I lost my temper." He leveled his gaze at Bram. "You know I can't ask anyone to live the way *Mamm* did."

Bram didn't answer right away and Samuel didn't blame him.

"So you made a mistake."

"A big one."

"Have you asked for forgiveness?"

Samuel picked at another splinter in the wood. "I thought so. But Mary hasn't spoken to me since then."

"Not from Mary. From God."

It was Samuel's turn to be silent. He hadn't asked God for help, and he hadn't asked Him for forgiveness, either. It was no use, anyway.

"You haven't, have you?"

Samuel shook his head.

"Then you have some work to do. Ask God for His forgiveness and His help. Then go apologize to Mary. Ask her to give you another chance."

Samuel bowed his head. "I can't risk it. I know that

eventually I'll lose my temper again. It's best that Mary and I just call it quits. She'll find someone else." Even as he said the words, he felt them knife through his heart.

"You can't give up, Samuel. Let God take control of your temper and your life. Submit to Him." Bram squeezed his arm, then pushed away from the gate. "I'll leave you to it."

Samuel watched him leave. Bram was wrong. There were just some things a man couldn't trust to anyone else, even God.

Samuel woke before the sun came up the next morning. It had been a long night as he spent several sleepless hours arguing with God. Every time he had made up his mind to ignore Bram's advice and give up on Mary, Bible verses and snatches of sermons would echo in his mind. The theme of all of them was trust.

He finally gave up, sitting on the edge of his bed and reaching for his clothes. He would give God one more chance. He would trust Him with Mary's safety and his own sanity. Glancing at the ceiling, he had said one simple prayer. "Help me."

But he still wasn't in a hurry to face Mary. He dawdled at his chores and breakfast until Esther took his plate away.

"Whatever it is you don't want to do, just get it over with."

He pushed himself away from the table. "That's easy for you to say."

She piled his plate on top of hers and Judith's and took them to the sink. "So what is it that you don't want to do?"

"I need to go over to Sadie's, but I'm not sure Mary wants to see me."

Her eyebrows rose. "You don't think Mary wants to talk to you?"

He shrugged and took his hat from the peg. "I guess I'll find out."

Esther's giggle followed him out the door and down the steps. He stalked down the worn path through the fence row. Esther could laugh all she wanted, but she hadn't seen Mary's face when she told him to leave. He couldn't see any way back to the friendship they had shared before.

When he reached Sadie's yard, the only person in sight was Ida Mae, working in the garden. When she saw him, she pointed in the direction of the new chicken coop.

Samuel walked in that direction, following the sound of excited clucking and Mary's voice calling to the hens. As he rounded the corner of the chicken coop, she saw him and fell silent.

"Good morning," Samuel said.

She finished spreading the rest of the grain over the ground, then came out of the pen, closing the gate behind her. "I didn't expect to see you."

"I know." He ran his thumbs up and down his suspenders. "The last time we spoke, you told me to leave you alone. Do you still mean it?"

Mary swung the empty grain bucket in her hand. "I don't know."

"Ida Mae said she thought you missed me." He took the pail from her and set it next to the gate. "Do you want to go for a walk? Just down to the creek?"

She bit her lip, and then shrugged, never looking at him. He held the fence wires apart for her, and then he looked at the pasture. Instead of stopping at the corn field, it extended all the way to the woods, the fence enclosing a good three acres of his corn field. The young corn plants were gone, and he could imagine how the cow and Chester had found them sweet and tasty.

"When did you move the fence?" He struggled to keep his voice even.

"Dale and his son came over and did it for us yesterday afternoon. He said he was sorry he had planted corn on Sadie's land."

Samuel started counting inside his head, hoping Mary wouldn't notice. "On my land. Dale planted the corn on my land."

She faced him. "Aren't these three acres part of the ten that your *grossdawdi* gave to Sadie? She said it was."

"He gave her the ten acres to use, but we still own it. Someday, when Sadie is gone, this land will be part of our farm again."

Mary stared at him. "Does Sadie know this?"

"She did at one time. But the way she forgets things, I have no idea what she believes."

"Then it sounds like we should move the fence back."

Samuel had lost track of his counting. He didn't need it. He was in no danger of losing his temper. "The corn is already gone, and you are right. You need the pasture for the cow." He lifted his hat and wiped his brow. The day was growing warm. "There's no use making Sadie upset. *Grossdawdi* would never have wanted that to happen."

Mary was quiet as they continued to the corner of the pasture where the creek cut through. "He must have loved her very much, the way he made sure she was taken care of." She plucked a wild carrot flower and twirled it between her fingers.

"I think he regretted what happened between them. Even though he had married *Grossmutti* and was happy with her, he always had a soft spot for Sadie."

They had reached the creek and Mary jumped across it. Samuel followed her.

"Are all the Lapp men like that?"

Samuel watched her profile as she leaned against a sycamore tree. If she never loved him, it didn't matter. He would still care for her and protect her.

"I think they are."

She picked some more of the wild carrots and started making a chain of the flower stems.

Samuel plucked one of the flowers and let it bounce at the end of its stalk. "I came to apologize. I… I lost my temper the other day."

Her hands stilled, holding the half-finished chain.

"I frightened you, the way I lost my temper with Martin."

She nodded. He picked the flower in his hands apart. "I don't know why I lost control. I was angry about what you told me…what happened to you…and then when I saw Martin…"

Mary wove another flower into her chain.

"I had the thought that I could go and take care of that man in Ohio. Make him pay for what he did."

Her eyebrows went up. "That wouldn't change anything."

He shrugged. "I only want to fix things, to make it better."

She plucked a flower. "Even if you wiped Harvey off the face of the earth, it wouldn't change what happened. I still have to live with…with the shame." She bit her lip. "No one can make this better."

He moved closer to her and brushed a fly off her shoulder. She tensed.

"Maybe you need to go on with your life. Leave those memories behind you."

"I tried that when I came here. It doesn't work."

"You came here to hide. To escape. Not to go on."

She finished the flower chain and turned it between her fingers.

"You're right. When Sadie invited Ida Mae and me to

come here, I jumped at the chance. Anything to get away. But the memories followed me." She dropped the flowers onto an old tree stump. "It's no use."

Samuel leaned toward Mary, catching a scent of chicken feed and fresh straw. "What can I say to make things better?"

She turned away from him, toward the house. "Nothing. Don't say anything."

As she walked away, Samuel waited as a hot stone burned in his chest. But it wasn't anger. The stone settled. A weight of sorrow only Mary's forgiveness could ease.

Chapter Fifteen

A week later, the thunderstorms were still coming almost every day.

On Thursday night, a storm had kept Samuel awake until nearly midnight. And then sometime during the night, another storm blew in, the rolls of thunder bringing Samuel fully awake again.

His bedroom was close and hot with the windows closed. When the earlier storm had come through, he had gone around the house, slamming the sashes down against the rising wind. As he had stumbled back to his bed, he had heard the girls closing the windows upstairs.

Thunder boomed again, only seconds after the last roll. Samuel held his clock up to the faint light coming through the window. A flash of lightning illuminated the dial enough for him to read it. Three o'clock.

He settled back into his pillow and tried to sleep again, but to no avail. Between the thunder and Mary...

Samuel sat up, planting his feet on the throw rug next to his bed, and ran his fingers through his hair. Mary had filled his thoughts for the past week. More than that. Ever since she had first come from Ohio.

A loud boom shook the house and Samuel jumped to

his feet. Lightning had struck something close. His first thought was Sadie's barn, and he got dressed as quickly as he could. Shoving his feet into his shoes, he found himself praying, "Not Mary. Protect Mary…"

He ran out the kitchen door, past Esther and Judith standing at the bottom of the stairway in their nightdresses and out to the back porch. The glow that met him was what he had feared, but Sadie's barn was safe. The glow was coming from his barn. The lightning had struck the cupola and flames were tailing in the south wind. The smoke stung his eyes, even from across the barnyard.

Esther had followed him to the porch. "Samuel! The barn!"

He pushed her back. "I know. I know. Stay back. I'm going to get as much out as I can."

"The roof is burning. It's going to fall in."

He heard Esther's words screaming after him, but he was already at the barn door. Tilly was inside, shut in her stall to keep her safe from the storm, but now she was trapped.

The barn door latch stuck. He hit it with his fist, then rammed the door with his shoulder until it broke. By the time he reached Tilly's stall, the haymow was on fire. Embers drifted down around him. He stared at the thick tree trunk, the center post that carried the weight of the whole structure. Flames ran down it, toward him.

Tilly's scream brought him to his senses, and he swung her stall door open. She ran past him, eyes wide and white in the firelight, out the door to safety.

A crash from above made him look up. One end of the roof had caved in. Waves of heat washed over him. He ran for the harness and threw it onto the buggy. He made a grab for the buggy shafts, but there was another crash and the wall of heat and flames threw him backward. He scrambled toward the door, watching in horror as the lacquered roof of the old buggy burst into flames.

He turned and ran out the door, his eyes on his sisters. Their white nightdresses waved in the wind. The wind that was sending flaming sparks toward the house.

The cattle. Samuel turned to look toward the pasture. The windmill was burning, standing like a torch, and in its light, he could make out the steers in the far corner of the pasture, huddled together. Upwind of the fire, they would be safe.

He grabbed Judith in one arm and Esther in the other, holding them close. The fire roared and he shouted so they could hear him.

"Go to Sadie's house. I'm going to go to the neighbors for help."

"We need to get dressed!" Esther tried to pull away from him.

"It's too late. Look!"

As they watched, the fire engulfed the old, rotten shingles of the roof. The house would be gone before they could do anything.

"Go to Sadie's," he yelled. "You'll be safe there."

Esther grabbed Judith's hand and the girls ran down the path. The path he had taken so many times. He started down the lane toward the road, toward Dale Yoder's, but a strange noise made him look back. The roaring had turned to a groaning sound as the old barn twisted, then collapsed on itself. The apple trees between the barn and house were burning, and the chicken coop… Samuel sank to his knees as the chicken coop disappeared in the flames.

It was too late. Too late to save anything.

As the fire claimed the house, Samuel struggled to his feet and retreated from the blaze. He thought of all the things that the fire was consuming. The room where he and the other children had been born. *Daed*'s old desk. *Mamm*'s rocking chair. The kitchen table.

He buried his face in his hands. The steps that had claimed *Mamm*'s life.

And now the fire was destroying everything. Everything.

Another crash as the roof of the house collapsed into the second floor, and then he felt ashes pelting him.

Looking up, he stared in disbelief as the rain began to fall. Heavy, wet, raindrops. He held his face up to the cleansing rain, letting it cool his burning skin.

A distant pounding woke Mary up. The first thing she saw was light on her bedroom ceiling. It couldn't be the dawning sun. The light was too red...

Fire. She sat up in bed and reached for her robe. Through the top pane in her window she could see the angry red flames pulsing against black smoke. Fear stabbed like lightning when she saw that Samuel's barn was on fire.

When she opened her bedroom door, the pounding was louder. Someone knocking at the back door. She ran down the stairs just as Sadie opened her bedroom door.

"What is going on?"

Mary continued through the kitchen to the door. "There's a fire at Samuel's."

Judith and Esther were at the back door in their nightdresses.

"Come in, come in." Mary opened the door and ushered them into the kitchen, where Sadie had already lit the lantern above the kitchen table.

The girls clung to each other as Sadie pumped water into the coffee pot. Ida Mae appeared at the bottom of the stairs.

"What is happening?"

"Our barn caught on fire." Esther coughed, then went on. "Samuel went into the barn to let Tilly out—" She coughed again.

Samuel. Dread filled Mary with a cold spiral. If something happened to Samuel—

"Is Samuel all right?"

Judith nodded. "He got Tilly out of the barn, but the fire was so hot…"

"…and it spread to the house."

Sadie handed Esther a glass of water and sank into one of the chairs. "The house?"

"Everything caught fire so quickly, there was nothing we could do." Esther took another swallow of water. "Samuel wouldn't let us go back in to get our clothes, or anything."

Mary slipped out the back door as they continued talking. Esther and Judith would be all right. Sadie and Ida Mae would take care of them. But Samuel…

She ran down the path toward the Lapp farm in the rain, her bare feet slipping in the mud. Where was Samuel?

When she came through the opening in the fence row that opened into the Lapps' farmyard, she stopped. The scene in front of her was horrific. The barn was gone and only a pile of smoldering rubble remained. The house… two walls still stood, but they were burning, even in the rain. The rest was a pile of black beams and crazy angles. One pane of glass hadn't broken, but reflected the flames. Smoke and steam rose everywhere.

The rain let up as the storm moved on, but Mary couldn't see Samuel anywhere. She walked toward the destroyed house, careful not to get too close. Smoking embers lay all around, and she was barefoot. When she reached the lane that led from the road, past the house and to the barn, she stopped. As the brief shower of rain ended, the remaining house walls burned stronger, lending light and heat.

"Samuel! Where are you?"

Her voice met silence.

The wind pushed the storm to the east and the morning sun lightened the sky behind the breaking clouds. The gray, predawn glow revealed more of the destruction…and a man hunched in the lane. Mary picked her way through the debris until she reached him. She knelt and laid her hand on his back. He didn't look at her.

"Are you all right? Are you hurt anywhere?"

His shoulders shook as if he was crying in deep, silent sobs.

"Samuel, it's me, Mary. Talk to me."

He stood and pulled her to him in a strong hug, and she realized that he wasn't crying, he was…laughing?

"It's gone." He gestured with one arm to take in the scene before them. "It's all gone."

Mary took a step back. "Why are you—"

"Laughing?" He hiccupped, then laughed again. "It's gone." The laugh turned into a sob, and he reached for her again. "I'm not going insane," he said into her ear as he held her close. "It's just that this farm…the memories…the work…it's all gone."

Mary looked into his face. The growing light was reflected in tears that streamed down his cheeks.

"I know. It's terrible."

He shook his head. "Not terrible."

"But you've lost everything." Mary couldn't look at the destruction the fire had caused. She jumped when one of the house walls fell in with a crash.

"There it goes, burning up like chaff." Samuel watched, sober now, as the greedy flames fed on the newly exposed beams.

"But the barn, the house—"

Samuel shook his head. "The girls are safe, and Tilly is grazing over there along the road. What have we really lost?"

"What will you wear? What will you eat? The fire has burned up everything." She stared at him. Did he lose his mind along with everything else?

"You don't understand."

He turned them both away from the fire, toward the rising sun in the east. Mary heard horses trotting on the road. The neighbors had seen the smoke in the morning light and were coming to help.

"At first I thought that my life was over. You're right, we lost everything. But I also lost this burden. God freed me from *Daed*'s legacy, and now I can go my own way. I can start over new and fresh. Clean. All the things that were holding me back are gone."

Samuel cupped her cheeks in his large hands, gazing into her eyes.

"I'm glad you came. I've been wanting to tell you how sorry I am. Can you forgive me for being so overbearing and stupid?"

Mary searched his face, looking for any sign that he had lost touch with reality, but she only saw weariness and peace. She nodded and he smiled.

"You're the most beautiful sight I've ever seen." His thumb traced her cheekbone. "Don't you have anything to say?"

She felt her own smile answering his. "Only that I'm sorry, too. When the girls came to the house and told us about the fire, and that you had gone into the burning barn—" Tears sprang into her eyes. "I was so afraid for you. What if I lost you, and I had never told you—?" She bit her lower lip. Amish girls didn't say the things she wanted to say to Samuel.

He lifted her chin. "Never told me what?"

Mary straightened her shoulders. She didn't care what she was supposed to do or not do.

"If I never told you that I…love you, I would be sorry for the rest of my life."

He leaned close and brushed his lips against her cheek. "It's all right. I'm all right."

"But we've wasted so much time with my silliness."

"It wasn't silliness." He tugged the braid hanging down her back. "I'm just glad you aren't going to marry Martin."

She pulled her braid out of his grasp. "Who says I'm not?"

He grinned and brought her close to him again. "I do."

His kiss was tender, yet demanding. As if she was the only answer to his longings.

But he broke off the kiss all too soon.

"Folks are coming, and we shouldn't be together like this. You had better go home and get dressed."

Mary looked down. She had forgotten she was still in her nightclothes.

As she left, she heard Dale Yoder ask, "Samuel, is everyone all right? Where do you need me to help?"

When she reached the opening in the fence row between the two farms, she glanced back. Buggies had crowded into the lane and more were stopped along the road. Even an automobile was making its way to the farm. Cleanup was already under way.

By midmorning, the barnyard was crowded with neighbors and church folks. Mary, Sadie and the girls had made a batch of doughnuts and had brought over baskets full of them, along with pots of coffee.

Samuel leaned against a makeshift table someone had put together out of lumber they had brought and held a warm doughnut in his hand, but he had no appetite. Once the initial shock had worn off, the reality of the fire began to set in. There was no feed for Tilly or the cattle. It had been destroyed. There were no clean trousers for him to change into, so he wore his wet, ash-encrusted pants with holes burned in them where embers had landed. He had thought he would wash the grime off his hands...but the soap was gone. The bars of soap Sadie had helped Judith and Esther make last winter.

Everything they had worked for was gone. Every bit of food they had stored. The chickens. The hams hung from the beams in the cellar. Everything gone.

He took a bite of the doughnut, but it tasted like ashes.

"Here's some coffee for you." Mary held out a steaming cup. "You need to eat and drink something."

Samuel took the cup she offered, looking into her eyes. "Are you all right?"

Her brows peaked. "I should be asking you that question."

"You looked upset this morning."

"I was." She broke off a piece of his doughnut and popped it in her mouth.

He leaned into her strength. The moment when she had come to find him in the midst of the chaos was the point he clung to as his world collapsed around him.

He brushed a crumb off her chin. "I would never be able to survive this without you."

She held him with her gaze. "You won't need to. I'm here."

Samuel let his gaze scan the crowd of people. Some were carrying buckets of water to the areas of the house and barn that were still smoldering. Others picked through the rubble, but found nothing worth saving.

Mary threaded her hand through his elbow. "I was concerned because I didn't know where you were. I didn't know if you were hurt or not." She squeezed his elbow. "And here you were. You had lost everything."

Samuel sipped the hot coffee. "Not everything." He pressed his elbow against his side, trapping her hand. "I didn't lose you."

She smiled and ducked her head. "I'm not that important."

"Now that all of this is gone—" he gestured toward the ashes "—I can see what the most important things in my life are. The girls are safe, you're safe. Nothing else matters."

Another buggy pulled up the lane. Bram and Matthew got out.

Mary took his cup and the doughnut. "You need to go talk to Bram."

"I know." He glanced at her. She looked very kissable in the morning light. "The coffee was good."

Matthew spotted Samuel and made his way toward him, but Bram stood in the lane, staring at what had been the house and barn.

Samuel met Matthew halfway across the yard. "I wasn't expecting to see you this morning." He shook Matthew's offered hand.

Matthew gripped Samuel's shoulder. "I don't think you expected any of this, did you?"

Samuel shook his head. "How did you folks hear about the fire?"

"News travels fast. Someone told Bram, knowing it was his family's farm, and Bram stopped by to get me. We came to help." Matthew glanced at the crowds. "At least, to do what we can."

"I'm not sure what there is to do. As far as I can tell, there is nothing to be saved except the livestock."

Matthew's eyes widened. "You lost everything?"

"Everything."

Bram joined them. "I can't believe this. How did it happen?"

"During the storm last night, lightning hit the cupola on the barn, and the place went up faster than I could think."

"The house, too?"

"The wind blew embers from the barn to the house. The roof must have been dry and rotten, it caught so quickly."

Bram stared at what was left of the house. "All those memories."

"You still have the memories," Matthew said. "No fire can erase those."

Bram turned away from the devastation. "You're right. The important thing is that you and the girls are all right."

"We're safe." Samuel couldn't look toward the ruined house.

"Were you able to save anything? Clothes? Anything?"

"Only the clothes we were wearing. The girls were in their nightdresses." Samuel gestured toward the circle of women gathered around Judith and Esther. "The clothes they are wearing now are borrowed."

Preacher Jonas came toward them. "Samuel, this is terrible. How are you holding up?"

The reminder of just what had happened overnight made Samuel's knees weak. "It has been a long morning."

Martin Troyer's farm wagon joined the other buggies and wagons along the road, and the Troyer brothers jumped down. The morning was about to get a lot longer.

"You will have the help of the community when you're

ready to rebuild," Jonas said. "I've had several offers already."

Samuel's mouth went dry. He hadn't thought of rebuilding yet…and he never would have expected the community to help.

Jonas stepped across the yard to greet another church member, but Bram pulled Samuel aside.

"That's something, isn't it?" Bram's voice was low, meant for only Samuel to hear. "Would they have stepped forward so quickly when *Daed* was alive?"

Samuel shook his head.

"You're changing things." Bram gave him a brotherly squeeze around his shoulders. "You're becoming part of the community."

"*Daed* always hovered around the edges, didn't he?"

"Like a dog waiting for scraps." Bram shook his head. "I don't know what made him be the way he was, but you've shown that you aren't like him."

Samuel spied Martin coming toward him. "Here comes trouble."

Bram's eyebrows went up. "Why?"

"We've had some words about Mary. Martin Troyer is convinced he's going to marry her."

"What does she say about that?"

Samuel grinned. "She's a strong one. Refused him with no way to misunderstand her meaning, but he still insists it's going to happen."

"Is he jealous of you?"

"Most likely."

Martin stopped several steps away from Samuel, raising his voice as he spoke so that everyone could hear.

"Sorry to hear about the tragedy, Lapp."

Samuel faced him. Out of the corner of his eye, he could see Mary watching them. "Not so much of a tragedy, Martin. We only lost the house and barn. The family and the livestock survived. We're thankful."

"I've heard folks saying that you're going to rebuild."

"I haven't thought too much about it yet, but I suppose we will."

Martin took a step closer. "So at the end of it, you'll have a nice new barn to replace the old decrepit one that stood here yesterday."

Samuel shifted his feet. What was Martin getting at?

Preacher Jonas stepped forward. "Are you suggesting something, Martin?"

Martin turned from one side to the other, perusing the audience he had gathered. "I'm just saying that it is nice for Samuel Lapp—" he emphasized the last name "—to enjoy a new house and barn while the rest of us are struggling so much in these hard times."

Samuel heard the accusation in his voice. "I didn't have anything to do with this fire."

"Of course you would say that." Martin grinned, his gaze shifting to Mary and then back. "But we have to wonder, don't we? You were saddled with a real burden when your old father died, and you've been losing ground every year." He took another step closer. "So tell us, Samuel, did you wait for a storm in the middle of the night to set the fire so you could blame it on the lightning? Or was it just a happy coincidence?"

A few voices protested at Martin's accusation, but not enough. Samuel looked around at the small clusters of men talking among themselves. Not enough.

Preacher Jonas stepped between Samuel and Martin. "That is a pretty serious accusation, Martin. There is no proof that Samuel had anything to do with the fire."

Martin's grin faded, then strengthened as he found a few supporters in the crowd. "There isn't any proof that he didn't, either. It seems that this should be a matter to look into."

Jonas quieted the crowd's response to Martin's suggestion. "It was an accident, Martin. This rumor that you're trying to spread needs to stop."

Martin took a few steps back, a satisfied look on his face. Samuel's pulse thumped as Martin joined his friends near the farm lane. If Martin was determined to follow through with his threats, knowing the truth might not be enough to stop him.

Chapter Sixteen

Mary packed the used coffee cups into the baskets the doughnuts had been in and swept crumbs off the makeshift table onto the ground. The crowds had cleared out once Preacher Jonas had come up with a plan to begin preparing the old building sites for the new barn and house. Work would begin tomorrow morning. Saturday.

With a gasp, she remembered that this was Friday, the day to take her carefully gathered eggs to town for the buyer. The butter would keep until next week, but the six dozen eggs waiting in the cool cellar wouldn't be fresh by Tuesday. Ida Mae would have to put up with more puddings and custard. And they would have to pickle most of the eggs. With a sigh, Mary resigned herself to the chore she hated.

"Good afternoon, Mary."

"Martin." He had walked up while she had been thinking about the eggs.

"Can I give you a hand with anything?"

She leveled her gaze at him. "If you want to help me, you can take back that accusation you made about Samuel. You know he didn't set this fire."

He smiled with a touch of a leer. "I don't know that,

and neither do you. This is just the kind of stunt a Lapp would pull."

"You don't need to run Samuel down. No matter how you feel about him, it makes no difference in how I feel about you. I've told you that I won't marry you."

Martin put a false pouting expression on his face. "You keep saying that."

"Because it's true."

"You won't find a better situation than I can offer you."

He started ticking off the reasons on his fingers, but she interrupted him.

"I don't care what you can offer me, because you can't offer me what I want."

"And what is that?"

"To be left alone." She picked up the basket full of coffee cups and carried it to the buggy. Chester stood, still hitched to it, head down and tail swishing.

Martin hurried after her. "You don't mean that."

She turned on him. "Don't tell me what I mean." Too late, she remembered her manners. She started over. "I want you to leave me alone. Forget about me."

He spread his hands with an imploring gesture. "But I gave you a cow."

"You can have her back." Mary walked back to the table to get the next basket.

"You don't like her?"

Mary sighed and turned toward him. "I like the cow. She is very useful. But if accepting her means I owe you something, then you can have her back."

Martin's eyes narrowed. "You want her, but you don't want her. It's time to stop playing games. Bishop Kaufman is going to announce our wedding at church on Sunday. We're going to get married."

An icy trickle went down Mary's back. "I'm not going to marry you, and you can't force me."

Martin stepped toward her and Mary looked for help, but no one was near. He grabbed her hand and pulled her close. His breath smelled like cheese.

"When we are married, you will learn to control what you say. Now—" he wrenched her hand and tears welled "—tell me what I want to hear."

She looked him in the eye. "I will not marry you. Never."

He tightened his grip, but she refused to back down. When Harvey Anderson had forced her against her will, she had been weak. She had caved in to his demands. She had given him control.

But she wasn't that girl anymore.

"Leave now, Martin, and don't come back. I won't marry you, and my sister won't marry Peter. You need to look somewhere else."

Over Martin's shoulder, she caught sight of Samuel walking toward them. Martin turned to see what had captured her attention.

"So that's it. You've chosen that Samuel Lapp over me." He shoved her away. "You deserve whatever he gives you. Peter and I will stop by your place to pick up the cow on our way home." He glanced behind him again. Samuel had almost reached them. "I will enjoy watching you suffer as his wife the same way his mother suffered. Being married to a Lapp is no way for a woman as fine as you to spend her life, but that's your choice."

He walked off toward his wagon and Mary ran to Samuel. He held her close, but she didn't cry. Martin Troyer wasn't worth crying over.

Samuel held her for a moment, then pushed her back,

searching her face. "What did he do? What did he say to you?"

Mary wiped her eyes and laughed. "He said I deserve what I get when I—"

She stopped, biting her lip before the rest of the sentence could escape.

"When you what?"

"Never mind. He's taking Schmetterling back." She looked up at Samuel's puzzled face. "I'll miss the poor cow, and I'll miss the butter we made from her milk, but I won't keep her on Martin's terms."

"He still wants you to marry him?"

"I think I've finally convinced him that I won't."

Samuel picked up the basket of coffee cups and carried it to the buggy, sliding it in the back next to the first one.

"I'm not sure he's going to give up that easily."

"He'll have to get used to it." She sighed and rolled her tired shoulders. "Do you think anyone will listen to his silly accusation?"

"That I set this fire myself?" He shook his head. "I don't know. Some people will believe anything bad they hear about the Lapps, and Martin has his supporters."

"But you've been working so hard to change that ever since the day you helped with the plowing. How many farmers have you helped with their windmills? And didn't you say you spent all day Wednesday at the Hopplestadts' last week, helping build a new fence?"

"It might not make any difference if Martin insists on spreading his rumors."

Mary folded her arms. "If the church won't help you rebuild because of Martin, then we'll do it ourselves."

He grinned. "You and I are going to build a barn?"

"We have Judith, Esther and Ida Mae to help, too."

"Four women and one man are going to build a barn and house without anyone else helping?"

"Why not? You know how, don't you?"

Samuel shook his head and leaned against the buggy. "I don't see Sadie and the girls anywhere."

"They went home a while ago. Sadie was getting tired."

"You and your sister take good care of her." He scratched at the day's growth of whiskers on his chin. "I have to admit, I had my doubts when you first moved here."

"But then you realized that someone else is just as able…even more able to care for her like she needs than you are."

The corners of his mouth twitched and he shrugged. "I've gotten used to it."

He waved to Preacher Jonas as he drove down the lane toward the road, the last of the neighbors to leave after the long day.

"What time are folks coming in the morning?"

"An hour past dawn. That will give everyone the time to finish their chores at home, and then we start clearing out the debris from the barn and house."

"Judith and Esther are staying with us, but where will you sleep tonight?"

"Sadie said I should sleep in her barn. The girls were going to make a bed for me in the loft."

Mary closed the side door of the buggy. "Do you have anything else you need to do here? You could ride home with me."

"I need to make sure the pasture fence is tight. I don't want the cattle wandering off. I also need to check on Tilly. Dale Yoder put her in with his horses. I'll walk over when I'm done."

It was time for her to go home, but Mary didn't want to

leave Samuel alone. She was running out of things to say, though. She stalled one more time.

"Have you thought about rebuilding? What kind of house and barn you'll need?"

Samuel turned to her. "That's been going through my head all day. We need a home, the three of us, but I want to build for the future, too."

"What do you mean?"

He shrugged. "I may decide to get married someday. So, the house will need an upstairs for the children, and a room downstairs."

Mary remembered the day he told her he would never get married. What had changed his mind?

Then she thought about the house she grew up in back in Ohio. "A big laundry porch would be nice. And a cellar."

"And the house should be large enough so we could host church without crowding everyone in too much."

"A modern kitchen, with a pump at the sink."

"With room for a big table."

Mary's eyebrows rose. "Why does it have to be big?"

"For all of the children. I don't want my children squeezed so tightly on a bench that one might fall off during a meal."

"Just how many children do you think you'll have?"

Samuel's eyes were soft and warm as he watched her face. "As many as we can."

She leaned closer to him, drawn by the breathless tone in his voice. "And who will be the mother of all these children?"

He smiled and put his arms around her, pulling her close. "We'll have to see about that."

His kiss, gentle and warm, grew deeper until he broke it off. Then he tucked her under his chin.

"We'll have to see."

* * *

Samuel reached the farm just before dawn, after downing a quick cup of coffee and a couple slices of bread and butter in Sadie's kitchen. The air reeked of ashes and soot, damp and acrid. It was the only odor he could smell all through the night. Even the strong cup of coffee hadn't washed it away.

As the rising sun turned the sky rosy pink, the devastation stood out black against the surrounding grass. He peered into the old cellar, something he hadn't been able to bring himself to do the day before. Underneath half-burned beams and floorboards, the canning shelves lay strewn on the dirt floor, every jar broken.

He choked back a sob when he saw *Mamm*'s rocking chair, charred but still together, hanging upside down from a beam. He ventured onto unsteady boards to retrieve it and set it on the ground. He smoothed the seat, wiping ashes off. One arm was burned and blackened, and one of the rockers was broken, but the rest was in one piece. How had it escaped the fury of the fire? Perhaps it could be repaired. He set it to the side, underneath the maple tree in the front yard.

A steer's bawl from the pasture pulled him away from the house, and he made his way through the orchard, past the shell of the henhouse, to the pump. The watering trough had escaped the fire, but it was dry. He set to work, pumping by hand, turning his back on the skeleton of the windmill and the barn. The steers crowded around, all of them shoving their way in to the fresh water. He pumped hard, working out all the anger and frustration. All the grief. Why did he have to be the one to lose everything?

But at the same time, the relief still lingered. He had tried to push it away, knowing he shouldn't be happy about anything, but the relief of knowing he would never again have to look at the stairway where *Mamm* died. And the barn roof... *Daed*'s death had been just as sudden as he had fallen from that height. Those constant reminders of his failures were gone.

As he finished filling the trough the whisking sound of buggy wheels on the gravel road made him turn around. Preacher Jonas was the first to arrive, along with Paul Stutzman and Conrad Hopplestadt. They tied their horses along the fence away from the burned house. Samuel met them as they crossed the lane to survey the damage.

"Good morning, Samuel," Jonas said, shaking his hand. He sighed. "It doesn't look any better this morning, does it?"

Samuel shook the other men's hands. "Not at all. Except that it seems the fire is out. I haven't seen any smoke from either building."

Conrad gestured toward what remained of the house. "Will we start here, or at the barn?"

"The barn can wait. I only have the one horse, and she's happy sharing Sadie's barn. And the steers won't need shelter. But my sisters need a home, so I thought we'd start there."

Jonas peered into the black hole where the house had once stood. "Are you planning to use the same cellar?" He looked around the barnyard. "There's a nice spot for a house up there on that rise by the maple tree. It's closer to the road, but it will bring the house up and away from the barn."

Samuel nodded. "That would be a good place. And someone suggested a larger cellar, with a window or two. It would be a better cellar for the girls." Sadie had made that suggestion the night before. A light and airy place for the girls to work.

Paul Stutzman rubbed at his beard. "You're going to

build a new modern house?" His eyebrows rose as he looked at Samuel. "This fire seems to be a mixed blessing, allowing you to move up in the world."

Something in Samuel's stomach gnawed at him. He had hoped Martin's accusing words from yesterday would be forgotten.

Jonas ignored Paul's comment. "So we have two things to take care of. First we need to do something with the old cellar, and then we need to dig a new one."

Samuel pushed a blackened board in the cellar with his foot. "We could fill in this cellar with the debris from the house and dirt from digging the new one."

"We should let the rest of the house burn down to ashes, then," Conrad said, pushing on a beam. "Some of this is still pretty solid, but not good enough to reuse it."

More buggies pulled in, and soon the yard was filled with as much activity as it had been the day before. Several of the men got together with ropes and maneuvered the larger pieces of the house into a pile and set it on fire. Smoke billowed into the air once more as others gathered loose boards and pieces to throw on the burning pile, but Samuel saved the rocking chair.

He was carrying the chair to Sadie's barn when he met Mary and the girls on their way to the farm. Each had a covered pan in their hands.

"That smells like breakfast," Samuel said.

"We thought you would all be getting hungry about now," Judith said.

"And we had plenty of eggs to use." Ida Mae grinned at Mary, who was bringing up the rear. "So we made scrambled eggs and sausage."

"What did you find?" Esther asked. "Is that *Mamm*'s chair?"

Samuel nodded. "I think I might be able to fix it."

Tears stood in Esther's eyes, and Samuel suddenly realized that he hadn't been the only one to lose everything. He might be glad some of the reminders of *Daed* were gone, but Esther and Judith had so few memories to hold on to.

"When I do repair it, it will be yours."

Esther's face brightened. "That would be wonderful. *Denki*, Samuel."

They went on their way, but Mary stopped him before she passed by. "That is very thoughtful. Esther will cherish that chair."

The glow from Mary's praise lasted until he rejoined the workers at the farm. Several of the men had brought tools, including picks and shovels, and had started in digging the new cellar.

"Samuel," Preacher Jonas called. "Come help me mark out the walls."

When Samuel reached the work site, Martin was there.

"You finally showed up to help?" Martin's face was twisted in a sneer.

Samuel glanced at Jonas and chose to ignore Martin. The preacher had already put one stake into the ground, but waited for Samuel to place the other corners. Once the stakes were in, they threaded a string around them, forming a square.

Martin's sour stare made Samuel doubt what he was doing. Should he make the house so big? He paced off the area he had marked out. The cellar would be under the kitchen. It didn't need to be large to store the vegetables and canned goods, but if it was bigger, Esther and Judith could do laundry down there in the winter months. He could see it in his imagination, clean and bright with whitewashed walls and windows to let light in. New shelves lining the walls, filled with jars of canned goods. The washtub set in the center of the room with clotheslines strung from the ceiling.

He glanced at Esther and Judith, serving plates of eggs and sausage to the hungry workers. How many times had they apologized to him because the laundry was still hanging in the kitchen at dinnertime on rainy days? And Mary... He looked at the size of the cellar he planned. He couldn't ask her to work in a dark, cramped hole in the ground.

Samuel felt the corners of his mouth ease into a smile. The idea had crept up on him until he couldn't think of anything else. This new house would be Mary's. And his. This house would be for their family...if she would agree.

All through church, Mary struggled to keep her mind on the worship service. After dinner was the council meeting, and she had heard rumors that Martin Troyer was planning to bring something before the church. But he couldn't request for a wedding to be announced without her permission, could he?

She shivered, even though the day was warm. No one could force her to marry against her will, she reminded herself. No one.

Finally, the sermons were over and Bishop started the low tones of the final hymn. Mary closed her eyes as she sang, knowing the words by heart. They spoke to her anxious thoughts. God was her salvation, her protection, the rock of her faith. He never changes, never wavers. When the hymn ended, she was at peace.

After a hurried dinner, the members of the church met again in the house. The usual business of the council meeting was finished, including Peter Troyer's repentance for the rumors he had spread, and folks were shifting restlessly on their benches when Martin stood up to speak.

He glanced in Mary's direction, but she averted her eyes, dreading what he might say.

"I have approached Preacher Jonas about this, and the bishop, but neither of them seem to think what I have to say merits any discussion by the members of the church."

Preacher William stood. The old man swayed a bit, and his voice was raspy, but the congregation respected his age and wisdom. "If Bishop and Preacher Jonas have heard what you have to say, then why do you bring it up in the council meeting?"

Martin shifted from one foot to the other, but pressed on. "I want the church to place Samuel Lapp under the *bann*."

At first, Mary sighed with relief. He wasn't going to bring up any pending marriage. But then his words sunk in. Place Samuel under the *bann*?

"The *bann* is a very serious matter," Preacher William said, raising his hand to call for silence. "What do you accuse Samuel of doing?"

"Samuel Lapp, like his father before him, has repeatedly taken advantage of the goodwill of this congregation. I think he set the fire that destroyed his house and barn last Friday morning to have us build a new one for him."

Bishop Kaufman stood and raised his hands, quieting the murmuring that had broken out at Martin's words.

"This is not the time to discuss this, Martin."

"Then when is the time?" Martin's face reddened as he faced the bishop. "I've tried to bring this up the right way, by going to Preacher Jonas and you, but you won't do anything about it." He took a step toward the bishop and pointed an accusatory finger at Samuel. "This man is taking advantage of the congregation just as his father did before him, and you won't do anything about it."

Bishop laced his fingers together and bent his head. "Sit down, Martin."

Martin looked around the congregation. "Who agrees with me? Shouldn't we look into this travesty? Will we endure more years of bowing to the whims of the Lapp family, bailing them out of trouble wherever their foolish choices lead them?"

Esther, sitting next to Mary, buried her face in her hands. Sadie put her arm around Judith and held her close.

Bishop, his voice as mild as ever, repeated his request. "Martin, sit down and we will discuss this matter." He turned toward Samuel. "You may stay and face your accuser, or you may leave. It's up to you, but I recommend that you stay."

Samuel sat with his head bowed. "I'll stay."

"Before we open our discussion," said Bishop, his head still bowed, "I ask that we enter into a time of silent prayer."

Mary closed her eyes, but couldn't pray. Martin's accusation couldn't be true…but she remembered Samuel on the morning of the fire. His seeming joy in the face of tragedy. Could it be that he did set the fire on purpose? And just as quickly, her thoughts rebelled against the idea. She hadn't known Samuel very long, but he had never given her any reason to doubt that he was completely truthful. He wouldn't destroy his farm. He couldn't.

After the prayer, Bishop Kaufman opened the discussion. Martin made his accusation again, and a couple men added their opinion to support him.

Then men started speaking in support of Samuel, including Preacher Jonas.

"I've gotten to know Samuel quite well over the years," Jonas said, "and I've seen the changes he has made since he lost his father in the accident two years ago. I have never known him to lie, or to twist the truth to his advantage. I think we can trust his version of the cause of the fire."

Other men rose to speak of his willingness to work on their windmills over the past few weeks, volunteering his time to repair or service them before the summer heat came. Samuel fidgeted in his seat when Conrad Hopplestadt rose to tell how Samuel had helped him repair his pasture fence, and had even supplied the fence wire to do the job right.

Then Sadie rose from her seat and Bishop gave her a nod of acknowledgment.

"I know it isn't the custom for women to speak in council meetings, but I've never been much for custom." She smiled as the congregation laughed at this, then became serious once more. "I've known Samuel his entire life, and I knew his father before him. I've never known Samuel to be anything but caring and honest. He has done his best to fulfill his grandfather's desire to care for me into my old age, and he has been a good neighbor and a good friend." She nodded in Samuel's direction, then addressed Bishop Kaufman again. "I don't believe he could set fire to his farm on purpose. He respects his legacy too much to destroy it."

She sat back down while the congregation's voices murmured all around them.

Bishop held up his hand for quiet and turned to Martin. "Do you still want us to vote on whether to place Samuel under the *bann*?"

Martin looked at the faces of the congregation. The men who had supported him during the discussion averted their gazes, then he looked at Mary. She turned her face away, unable to look at him any longer.

"I withdraw my accusation." His voice was quiet. Defeated.

Bishop raised his hands over the congregation once more. "Let us pray."

As the bishop led the people in a prayer of repentance and reconciliation, Mary glanced at Samuel. His head was bowed, fingers steepled in front of his face, and tears flowed freely. How could she have ever doubted that she loved this man?

Chapter Seventeen

By the beginning of July, the new house was finished. After pouring the cement walls for the cellar, the framing had gone up in a single day. Samuel had chosen to make it a larger version of Sadie's house, with two bedrooms upstairs and two on the main floor. The downstairs rooms had removable partitions to open the space for Sunday meeting when it was their turn to host. He and Bram spent most of their time during June plastering the walls and putting down floors. They had been joined by Matthew, when he could come.

Samuel had spent most evenings building furniture in Sadie's barn after working on the house all day. The first thing he did was repair *Mamm*'s rocking chair, making new pieces to replace the charred arm and rocker, and staining the wood a dark brown. Esther was delighted when it was finished, and insisted on putting it in the bedroom she shared with Judith immediately.

"You don't want to wait until we can put it in the new house?" Samuel had asked.

She had shaken her head. "I want it with me. When I sit in it, it's like *Mamm* is with me."

Samuel had built a table with two chairs and two long

benches, and two more chairs for the living room. He had also built two bedsteads for Esther and Judith, and a large one for himself. He had smiled as he had measured the wood for the headboard. Large enough for two people, husband and wife.

One or two evenings a week, he took Mary for a buggy ride. Sadie had thought it was scandalous that they would take her closed buggy to court in, and arranged to borrow a proper courting buggy with an open top for them to use. Mary had agreed, so Samuel drove her down the back roads and up the main roads between Shipshewana and Topeka in the open courting buggy. They went all the way west to Goshen, and as far north as Pretty Prairie, near the Michigan state line. Every evening ride was filled with conversation and laughter as he got to know her better.

And as the month wore on, Mary lost that strained look in her face that had been with her since she had come to Indiana. She was happier than he had ever seen her.

When the house was done and the furniture in place, Samuel took Mary to see it for the first time.

"Why have you kept it a secret?" Mary slipped her hand into his as they ambled down the path through the fence row.

"I wanted it to be a surprise."

"You let your sisters go over already, and even Ida Mae."

He shrugged. "I wanted to hear their opinions about certain things."

"But not mine?"

Samuel stopped in the yard where they had the best view of the new house. It stood on a bit of a rise in the afternoon sunlight next to the shady maple tree. The siding was white, and white shades hung in every window, each of them pulled halfway down to keep the house cool in the afternoon heat.

"It looks just right," Mary said. "And look! You already have a garden planted where the old house was."

"I thought that would be the best way to use that space. It's already level, and the ashes in the soil will make everything grow well."

She hugged his arm. "New life out of ruin," she said. "How appropriate."

"Do you want to go inside?"

Mary let go of him and ran to the back steps and into the back porch.

"This is a wonderful washing porch."

"For summer."

"Esther and Judith will be able to use it in the winter, too, if you cover the screens with boards to keep the weather out."

He grinned. He couldn't wait for her to see the cellar.

Mary led the way into the kitchen, running her hand along the new shelf with the modern cabinets above it. "You built the cabinets yourself?"

"What did you think I've been doing all month?"

She opened the oven door and lifted the stove lids. "Where did you find such a beautiful stove?"

"At an auction. It was a bit rusty, but nothing that couldn't be polished off."

She continued through the kitchen to the bedroom off it, in the same spot as Sadie's room was in her house. When she saw the big bed he had placed there, her face grew red and she drew back into the hall.

Samuel laughed. "What's wrong?"

"I didn't know you needed such a big bed. I thought you would have built a smaller one for yourself."

He grabbed her hand and pulled her close. Looking around them as they stood at the bottom of the stairs, with the kitchen to one side and the bedroom behind them, he grinned. This was how he imagined his home would be. He only needed one more thing…

"I don't plan on living here alone."

"For sure you won't. Esther and Judith will be here with you."

"They won't live here forever. They'll get married and have their own homes before long."

"So who do you plan to share this house with?" She smiled, looking into his eyes.

"I think I know someone who would enjoy making this house into a home."

She lowered her gaze, suddenly shy.

"We've talked about it quite a bit, and you know we agree on so many things when it comes to having a family and running a household and farm."

Mary nodded.

"And I've seen the longing in your eyes."

She looked up. "Are you sure? After what happened…" She bit her lip and turned her head away.

Samuel put his hands on her shoulders. "What happened was in the past. Gone. Dead. Forgiven."

He swallowed. Forgiving the man who had attacked Mary was the hardest thing he had ever done. He smiled as she stepped closer, into his arms where she belonged.

"Mary," he whispered into her ear. "I love you so much. Will you be my wife? Will you help me make this house into our home? Will you trust me with our future?"

With her face buried in his chest, he felt her head nod, then she looked up at him.

"With all my heart."

Epilogue

"Isn't a fall wedding the best?" Judith tied Mary's white apron around her new blue dress. "I hope I can get married in the fall."

Esther tied her freshly cleaned shoe. "If you can find anyone who will marry you." She grinned at her sister.

Mary glanced at Ida Mae, fastening her own apron on the other side of the room. The four girls had decided to help each other get dressed for Mary and Samuel's wedding day in one of the upstairs bedrooms of the new house, but Mary had seen expressions flit across Ida Mae's face that made her think she would rather be alone. Her wedding had to make her sister relive the anticipation of her own planned wedding last year.

"Your dress is a beautiful shade of green, Ida Mae," she said. She was rewarded with a smile.

"*Denki*. And it goes well with your blue."

Esther patted her *kapp* to make sure it was in place. "Did you know that Thomas Weaver's favorite color is green?"

Ida Mae blushed bright pink. "I didn't know that."

Mary grinned as a smile turned up the corners of Ida Mae's mouth.

"Who are you going to visit first on your wedding trip?" Judith asked.

Mary ticked the planned visits off on her fingers. "First we'll stay with Bram and Ellie, and then Annie and Matthew." She looked at her audience. "We want to get those visits done before the new babies arrive." The girls grinned at each other. New nieces or nephews were such fun.

"And then you're going to Ohio, aren't you?" Ida Mae asked.

Mary nodded. *Mamm, Daed* and the rest of the family had arrived yesterday, and the reunion had been wonderful. But she was looking forward to traveling back to Ohio again. She couldn't imagine spending the first few weeks of her marriage among strangers, the way the *Englischers* did on their honeymoons. Visiting each other's family was the best way to form the family bonds that would last a lifetime. Her trip with Samuel would last for two months.

"We'll stay with the folks, and Aunt Susan and Uncle Henry. Then we'll go through Wayne County to visit the cousins there, and then back home before the winter weather comes."

Esther whispered something to Judith and the girls giggled.

"What is it?"

Judith giggled again. "We were just thinking how *wonderful-gut* it would be if you came home expecting a little one."

Mary felt her face heat. "Let us get married, first."

Even Ida Mae joined in the laughter that followed that remark.

Samuel had wanted to have the wedding at their new house, and Mary had agreed. The thought of starting their lives together in their own home was like the last piece of a quilt sewn in place. The church benches had been delivered yesterday, on Wednesday, and Samuel had reported that all was ready last night.

She and the girls, including Sadie, had spent the morning cooking the wedding dinner, along with most of the ladies from the church. Everyone had been in high spirits, and Mary could still hear Effie Hopplestadt's joyous voice above everyone else's. The aroma of the chicken and noodles in the oven wafted up the stairway.

"Mary, I think it's time to go downstairs." Judith stood at the window. "There is Preacher Jonas, and behind him is Bishop Kaufman's buggy." She pointed toward the road. "And look at the line of buggies that are coming! It's a good thing the day is fine, because some of the people are going to have to sit outside."

"You two go on down," Mary said. "I want to talk to Ida Mae for a minute."

Once the girls had left, Mary and Ida Mae looked at each other. It was a solemn moment. Mary was the first of their brothers and sisters to get married.

"So this is what it's like," Ida Mae said. "In an hour or so, you'll be Samuel's Mary for the rest of your life."

Mary blinked back tears. "I loved growing up with you. You're the best sister."

Ida Mae nodded, her own eyes wet and shiny. "You're right. I am the best sister."

At that, Mary giggled, then Ida Mae joined her, and soon they were holding each other and laughing, tears streaming down their faces. Mary grabbed her handkerchief from her waistband and dabbed her eyes.

"*Ach*, I needed a laugh like that." She grinned at Ida Mae and they started laughing all over again.

Mary jumped when Esther knocked on the door.

"Are you two coming, or not? We're almost ready to start."

Ida Mae reached for Mary and gave her a quick hug. "In case I don't get an opportunity to say it later, blessings on your marriage."

Mary followed Ida Mae and Esther down the stairs. The big front room, with the walls pushed back to form a large open area, was filled with people, but Mary only saw one face. Samuel sat on the front row on the men's side, next to Bram and the ministers, smiling as he watched her walk into the room.

Mary took her place on the front row of the women's side with Ida Mae beside her. She clung to Ida Mae's hand, almost fearful that her happiness would send her floating to the ceiling.

"You're going to be all right," Ida Mae whispered.

Mary glanced at her soon-to-be husband, who was still watching her as Bishop Kaufman began singing the opening hymn. He grinned and gave her a wink.

Her face heated into a blush and she grinned back. Life with this man promised to be *wonderful-gut*.

* * * * *

If you enjoyed this Amish romance,
be sure to pick up these other Amish
historical romances from Jan Drexler:
THE PRODIGAL SON RETURNS
A MOTHER FOR HIS CHILDREN

Available now from Love Inspired Historical!
Find more great reads at www.LoveInspired.com

WE HOPE YOU
ENJOYED THESE TWO
LOVE
INSPIRED®
BOOKS.

If you were **inspired** by these

uplifting, **heartwarming**

romances, be sure to look for

all six Love Inspired® books

every month.

Love Inspired®

www.LoveInspired.com

Save $1.00

on the purchase of any Love Inspired® or Love Inspired® Suspense book.

Available wherever books are sold, including most bookstores, supermarkets, drugstores and discount stores.

Save $1.00

on the purchase of any Love Inspired® or Love Inspired® Suspense book.

Coupon valid until September 30, 2018. Redeemable at participating retail outlets in the U.S. and Canada only. Limit one coupon per customer.

52615870

Canadian Retailers: Harlequin Enterprises Limited will pay the face value of this coupon plus 10.25¢ if submitted by customer for this product only. Any other use constitutes fraud. Coupon is nonassignable. Void if taxed, prohibited or restricted by law. Consumer must pay any government taxes. Void if copied. Inmar Promotional Services ("IPS") customers submit coupons and proof of sales to Harlequin Enterprises Limited, P.O. Box 31000, Scarborough, ON M1R 0E7, Canada. Non-IPS retailer—for reimbursement submit coupons and proof of sales directly to Harlequin Enterprises Limited, Retail Marketing Department, Bay Adelaide Centre, East Tower, 22 Adelaide Street West, 40th Floor, Toronto, Ontario M5H 4E3, Canada.

U.S. Retailers: Harlequin Enterprises Limited will pay the face value of this coupon plus 8¢ if submitted by customer for this product only. Any other use constitutes fraud. Coupon is nonassignable. Void if taxed, prohibited or restricted by law. Consumer must pay any government taxes. Void if copied. For reimbursement submit coupons and proof of sales directly to Harlequin Enterprises, Ltd 482, NCH Marketing Services, P.O. Box 880001, El Paso, TX 88588-0001, U.S.A. Cash value 1/100 cents.

5 65373 00076 2 **(8100)0 12377**

® and ™ are trademarks owned and used by the trademark owner and/or its licensee.

© 2018 Harlequin Enterprises Limited

LIINCICOUP0718

*When a former sweetheart reappears in this widow's
life, could it mean a second chance at love?*

Read on for a sneak preview of
A Widow's Hope,
the first book in the series Indiana Amish Brides.

He knocked, and stood there staring when a young, beautiful
woman opened the door. Chestnut-colored hair peeked out
from her *kapp*. It matched her warm brown eyes and the
sprinkling of freckles on her cheeks.

There was something familiar about her. He nearly
smacked himself on the forehead. Of course she looked
familiar, though it had been years since he'd seen her.

"Hannah? Hannah Beiler?"

"Hannah King." She quickly scanned him head to toe.
She frowned and said, "I'm Hannah King."

"But…isn't this the Beiler home?"

"*Ya.* Wait. Aren't you Jacob? Jacob Schrock?"

He nearly laughed.

"The same, and I'm looking for the Beiler place."

"*Ya,* this is my parents' home, but why are you here?"

"To work." He stared down at the work order as if he
could make sense of seeing the first girl he'd ever kissed
standing on the doorstep of the place he was supposed to
be working.

"I don't understand," he said.

"Neither do I. Who are you looking for?"

"Alton Beiler."

"But that's my father. Why—"

At that point Mr. Beiler joined them. "You're at the right house, Jacob. Please, come inside."

He'd never have guessed when he put on his suspenders that morning that he would be seeing Hannah Beiler before the sun was properly up. The same Hannah Beiler he had once kissed behind the playground.

Alton Beiler ushered Jacob into the kitchen.

"Claire, maybe you remember Jacob Schrock. Apparently he took our Hannah on a buggy ride once."

Jacob heard them, but his attention was on the young boy sitting at the table. He sat in a regular kitchen chair, which was slightly higher than the wheelchair parked behind him.

The boy cocked his head to the side, as if trying to puzzle through what he saw of Jacob. Then he said, *"Gudemariye."*

"And to you," Jacob replied.

"Who are you?" he asked.

"I'm Jacob. What's your name?"

"Matthew. This is Mamm, and that's Mammi and Daddi. We're a family now." Matthew grinned.

Hannah glanced at him and blushed.

"It's really nice to meet you, Matthew. I'm going to be working here for a few days."

"Working on what?"

Jacob glanced at Alton, who nodded once. "I'm going to build you a playhouse."

Don't miss
A Widow's Hope *by Vannetta Chapman,*
available August 2018 wherever
Love Inspired® *books and ebooks are sold.*

www.LoveInspired.com

Love Inspired®

**Inspirational Romance to
Warm Your Heart and Soul**

Join our social communities to connect
with other readers who share your love!

Sign up for the Love Inspired newsletter
at **www.LoveInspired.com** to be the
first to find out about upcoming titles,
special promotions and exclusive content.

CONNECT WITH US AT:

Harlequin.com/Community

 Facebook.com/LoveInspiredBooks

 Twitter.com/LoveInspiredBks

LISOCIAL2017

Looking for inspiration in tales
of hope, faith and heartfelt romance?

Check out **Love Inspired**® and
Love Inspired® **Suspense** books!

New books available every month!

CONNECT WITH US AT:

Harlequin.com/Community

Facebook.com/HarlequinBooks

Twitter.com/HarlequinBooks

Instagram.com/HarlequinBooks

Pinterest.com/HarlequinBooks

ReaderService.com

LIGENRE2018